REINCARNATION

Threads of Fate Book One

MICHAEL HEAD

CHAPTER ONE

Rise to the Top

It was nearing my 650th birthday, and I was finally ready to take the next step. The formation plates, a gift from my closest friend, were in their proper positions in concentric circles around me. Inside the rings of formation plates there were structured piles of elemental-affiliated cores, equal amounts of wood, earth, metal, water, wind, and fire. They were to help ensure I had an equal amount of energy from each element as I drew them into my cores. Balance was important when trying to break through to the highest levels of cultivation this part of the world has ever known. The alchemy pill bottles were in neat rows placed in front of my crossed knees, ready for me to take as needed. My preferred focusing stone was on a leather cord around my neck, helping to purify the energies of the universe that the formation plates were drawing towards me.

It was finally time. After centuries of preparation and planning, I had everything in place for my advancement to Emperor rank. I heard a knock on the door of my covered courtyard, and with a thought I waved away the knot of power holding the door closed.

"Enter," I growled, putting power into the word and causing

the walls to rumble with the annoyance of being interrupted. As one of the most powerful people within several thousand miles, it was very uncommon for someone to interrupt me when I was in seclusion.

In strode one of only a handful of people who had the power to approach my wards. My best friend, teacher, and leader, the emperor. He strode through the entrance, oozing power from his pores. He was a tall and distinguished-looking man, his thin mustache and beard hanging below his chin, with black hair going gray at the temples. He wore his customary purple robes with thread-of-gold embroidery, and the thin band of jade around his head that served as his crown kept his waist-long hair out of his face. Despite the gray in his hair, he still looked like a man who hadn't yet reached forty summers. He was closer to nine hundred years old, but being the highest-ranked cultivator in the Empire had its perks.

His powerful aura caused a few of my protection wards carved around the doorway to pop and crackle as they were disrupted. I sighed. I was going to have to fix those before I got started. This was only one of a few reasons why I always tried to visit him, and not the other way around. As the emperor, he never tried to hide his aura. This meant that unless a formation master spent days on a single ward, as soon as he walked past it was destroyed as if it had never been. It would take me hours to fix this.

The emperor smiled at me with a mischievous glint in his blue eyes. He knew exactly what he had done. He was a jerk, but he was still my friend.

"Jim, I am glad I caught you before you got started," he said, throwing his arms open in greeting as he walked over to me. Since it was just the two of us, I didn't bother with the bowing and scraping that the court normally demanded when in his presence.

"Ming," I said as I stood to embrace him, "while I am always glad to see you, what would cause you to interrupt me on a day as important as this?" I waved him over to a bench along the wall so we could sit.

"Jim, as you know, this process could take days, maybe even weeks, for you to restructure and solidify all three cores. I have two gifts for you, to help ease the process." He smiled as he held out his hands. Ming held a bright red crystal in one, and a pill the size of a thumbnail in the other.

"What are these?" I asked as I looked at them. The crystal sparkled in the light that came through the windows.

"The pill is a body stasis pill. It will ensure you do not feel hunger, or have the need to relieve yourself, for ten full days. It isn't useful for many things, but for extended cultivation like what you are going through, it is perfect."

I snatched it out of the air as he tossed it my way. "Thank you, my friend. A pill like this would be worth my weight in gold to most cultivators."

"Of course," Ming said with a smile, "when you become an Emperor like me, I can surely use the help. The eastern borders need a firmer hand to watch over them, and I think you are the man for the job." He pointedly looked towards my weapons rack hanging on the wall as we sat next to one another.

I couldn't stop the sigh that escaped my lips. This again. "We have talked about this at length, my friend. I do not wish to become one of your warlords, crushing peasants into submission. I understand, intellectually, why you take these tactics, but my heart is not in it. I would rather travel the northern mountain ranges, and test my new strength against the monsters that roam our borders."

Ming looked down, his cheeks slightly reddening in anger at my reply. "We will discuss this again after your rise. My other gift is an improvement over your focusing stone. It is paired with the formation plates I gave you, and will speed up the purification of energies as they move into your core."

I looked at the stone as he handed it to me. It was surprisingly warm to the touch.

The focusing stone I currently had was one I gained after

defeating a Sky Raven that destroyed a string of villages a few decades ago. I had grown attached to it, and I was well adjusted to the rate of absorption it could maintain. Using a new focusing stone, right as I was taking the biggest known step in cultivation, seemed like a very monstrous mistake.

Ming could clearly see the hesitation on my face. "Do you remember how I found you, Jim?"

I grimaced at the long-ago memory. Ming had found me wandering the rice fields of the southern provinces when I was nothing but a lost teenager. He recognized my potential when no one else did, and instantly accepted me into his group of students.

I was born with a malformed upper core, or brain core, and as a result my clan disowned me and cast me aside. Ming, having more knowledge about cultivation than most clan libraries ever held, had insight enough to realize that my core was a boon for later stages, and only a hindrance during the first few levels of cultivation. The emperor, quite literally, raised me from the dirt and into the glittering halls of the Imperial Palace.

I had spent over six centuries as his student, advisor, confidant, enforcer, and friend. I met him when I was still a Body cultivator, and he was a Sage. Since then, I had been slowly catching up to him. I was only days, maybe just hours, away from finally standing on the same level as my mentor, and the pride I had welling up inside was an emotion I was relatively unfamiliar with.

"I remember, Ming. I could never forget all that you have given me. I am your man, your *friend*, until the day I die," I said with as much conviction as I could convey.

"Good," he said with another smile, "then there should be no question that my intentions are for the greater good."

I gave him a defeated grin, and replaced my focusing stone with his inside my necklace. I felt another flash of heat from it, and lifted it away from my chest.

"Is it fire-aspect?" I asked with clear confusion in my voice. I was not unable to use fire, but I was not primarily a fire element user.

Ming leveled a flat stare in my direction. "It does have a strong fire affinity, but it should be well within your abilities to handle." He stood to go as I let the stone fall back against my chest.

"Sometimes," I started, shaking my head, "I think you over-estimate my abilities, my teacher."

Ming looked aside, and stood up to walk out the door. I watched him go, his long robe trailing on the polished marble floor as he looked over his shoulder to say goodbye.

"Jim, you know that I always do what is best for the greater good, right?"

I nodded, and Ming waved his hand to repair the wards he had damaged before he disappeared out the door. Uncharacter-istic of him to save me the trouble, but I appreciated it. His last statement was an interesting thing to say, but he and I had conversed at length about the minutiae of the greater good and the ethics of specific actions. I had long held the belief that while the greater good was always important, the ethics of your actions have to be weighed equally. We had disagreed on it for centuries, but as the student, I was honor-bound to follow my teacher's instructions.

I cleared my head and refocused on double-checking my wards. I couldn't have any further interruptions during my ascension. I looked over the formation plates again and ensured once more that everything was in place.

I sat down and crossed my legs, assuming my preferred cultivation method. I placed the sour-tasting pill under my tongue so it would dissolve slowly and extend the benefits for a longer period of time. I activated the formation plates, and they slowly began to concentrate the energy from around the palace complex. I funneled the energy into the focusing stone, and it began to glow with the massive amounts of energy being pumped into it. I reached out with an extension of my will and began to pull the power through my meridians.

The energy felt warm as it traveled through my body, centering on my lowest core. It began to swirl, and pushed against the walls as it funneled upwards into my heart core. The pill in my mouth was almost entirely dissolved by this point, and the rotation of my core pushed the effects throughout my body. I could feel strength suffuse into my body, just as the power from the stone hit my upper core.

I suddenly felt a stretching sensation through my meridians, and I knew that I was close. I had been on the cusp of Emperor for months, and the time for my rise was now.

I pulled all of my focus inward, and I watched as my meridians stretched to new widths. My three cores expanded to a new, massive limit. I had done it. I knew I was far from finished, but I had finally reached Emperor. Now I was in for most likely several days of strengthening my meridian and core walls, as well as pushing a more concentrated level of energy into my bones, organs, and muscles.

The problem was never expanding into the next level, it was maintaining the same level of energy long enough to keep your gains. If you didn't stabilize your meridians and cores, they would shrink back to their former size. The largest downside was if that happened to you, it would be twice as hard to get them to stretch into the next stage a second time. A third time was nearly impossible, even though I had heard tales of a few people accomplishing the task.

Time passed as I concentrated on strengthening everything. I didn't know if it was hours or days, because my entire concentration was completely internal.

As I switched my focus from my meridians to the muscles surrounding them, I started to run into a problem. When Ming told me that the pill put my body into stasis, he definitely understated how strong its affects were. I was having problems forcing my body to respond. I couldn't get the denser energy into my muscles, because the stasis pill was blocking me. I drew deeper from the stone around my neck and focused the energy into my lower core. I then spiraled the energy quickly up through my heart core to my upper core to help increase my concentration level, and I ran into problem number two.

The fire element seemed to condense in my upper core, and I was having problems controlling the heat. I couldn't use water element, because, well, steam being pumped into your brain pan was a bad idea. I needed metal aspect, but if I tapped into the metal cores I had in place, it would imbalance the formation. I tried to purify the energy in my middle core, but it was so intensely hot that I couldn't clear it of the fire aspect. The deepest part of my consciousness was starting to become concerned. The stress on my upper core was quickly becoming a serious issue. I really didn't want to melt my brain. I wasn't ready to panic just yet, but things weren't looking good. Suddenly, I felt a familiar presence.

"Ming! Thank the gods you are here. The stone and pill you gave me aren't working correctly." I risked losing my concentration to talk to him, but I needed him to adjust the fire qi around me. "The combination is making me cook from the inside out!"

Ming blew through my wards again, and walked to the edges of the energy building around the formations.

"Ming, I need your help. Please, shift some of the fire energy away from the formation so I can balance the temperature in my upper core."

He kept his eyes on the floor, apparently observing the formation plates. For some reason, I felt a spike of anxiety. Why wouldn't he look at me?

"Jim, I told you that I do everything for the greater good."

I was having trouble focusing on him and maintaining the energy levels throughout my cores.

He kept circling me, refusing to meet my eyes with his own. "I am the uncontested leader in this Empire. I am the only Emperor-ranked cultivator since my father passed, and I cannot allow a challenge from a student who doesn't follow my ideals."

I could feel the confused look upon my face.

Ming looked up for a moment before returning his focus on the formation plates. "Don't look at me like that, Jim. You and I both know it would only be a matter of time before you surpassed me, and your empathy would have led you to rebel against me."

I started to get a sinking feeling in my stomach. "Ming, I have never betrayed you. I would not turn on you, even if I did surpass you. You are my best friend. My brother. My own sense of loyalty wouldn't allow me to turn on you."

He continued to look at the formation, as if he were looking for something. "Jim, I know you feel that way now, but in the centuries of life ahead of us, you cannot guarantee me that your views would not one day override your sense of loyalty. No, it is better this way." He still wouldn't meet my eyes, just keeping up his slow walk around the circle.

The heat was building in my heart core now, working its way down my body from top to bottom. The qi spiral was out of my control. If I stopped cultivating, the stone on my chest would explode with the backlash. There was enough energy contained inside it that I had no doubt it would mean instant death.

Maybe it was time to panic.

I looked up at Ming just as he started to touch one of the corners of the jade formation plates. The plates *he* had gifted me, along with the focusing stone and pill. Despite the heat trying to melt me from the inside, I felt my blood run cold with realization. He had set me up.

"Ah, there it is. We can't have you leveling half of my palace, now can we?" Suddenly there was a clicking sound, and the entire array shifted into a shield formation. Instead of the shield facing outward, however, this one was set to contain whatever was inside the array. "If you only knew how many times I have had to use this trap array over the past two hundred years, you would be astounded at how well it has held up."

My eyes widened with disbelief. I had to pause to gather my thoughts before asking, "Do you mean you have done this before, Ming? How many of your students have you destroyed with your fear?"

"It isn't fear that drives this, my student." He looked at me with pity in his eyes, the first time he was able to meet my gaze for more than a second since walking into the room. "It is simple common sense. Do you mean to tell me that you haven't noticed how those who came before you were slowly disappearing? You honestly couldn't tell that they were burning out, one by one, as the years passed you by?"

"No, Ming," I said while shaking my head. "I actually believed you when you told me that they were off on special assignments. I had no reason to doubt you."

He turned to walk away from me. "Then you were a greater fool than I thought. You might have been a powerful cultivator, but you were far too naïve to make it in this world without my protection. I will see you in the afterlife, Jim."

He was already talking about me in the past tense. I felt a burning rage begin to build inside me. My best friend, my mentor, and the leader who held my undying loyalty, was about to throw me away like a piece of garbage. Ming may have been like an older brother to me, but he forgot one thing.

I was not some meek kitten, or powerless peasant. I was now, albeit temporarily, an Emperor-ranked cultivator. I was, quite literally, the second most powerful person in the entire Empire. I had over six centuries of knowledge and experience, and I would not be tossed into the midden heap that easily.

I gave up on trying to save myself, throwing away my fear, and began concentrating on destroying Ming. I spun out threads of qi as thin as spider silk in a cloud so dense it was visible to the naked eye. I cast them about me in an attempt to find a gap in the shield formation that had been activated around me. It took me but a single breath to find over a dozen tiny gaps in the formation plates. I shoved as many threads as I could into the gaps, widening them bit by bit, forcing the plates farther apart and allowing more of my energy to escape.

The shield cracked. I felt it happen just as the heat in my head caused blood to begin pouring out of my eyes, tinting the world around me red. That was fine, now the world looked more like how I felt. My rage was building at the injustice Ming had leveled in my direction. The greater good? My death would only serve Ming's good, and I would make him pay for it in blood. I forced the cracked shield wide open, and stood up.

I cast my qi threads as wide as they could reach in the confines of the room, and used them to latch on to all of the thousands of high-level cores placed around me. I knew I was dead, so there was no need to hold back now. I drained the cores. Every. Single. One.

The influx of power was like nothing I had ever experienced. Killing the Rock Wolf Horde sixty years ago was nothing compared to this. I became a pillar of qi, the energy flooding me, threatening to wash me away.

No, it was too dense for qi. The power became more than simple qi; it was concentrated enough that it had become the rarest form of energy. This was pure and unfiltered *mana*. I couldn't contain it.

However, I could direct it. I chose to point it in the direction of the main palace where I knew Ming would be walking towards, smug in his own victory. There was a cone of intensely white light that poured out of me like a wave, erasing everything it touched like it never existed. I could feel myself disappearing, the wave erasing me just like it did everything else. I only needed to hold on for a few seconds longer. The wave needed to reach the palace, to ensure Ming was caught up in the destruction, before I could let go.

I felt it then, a sense of resistance. Something was trying to push back against the wave, but it was like trying to hold back the ocean itself. This power would not be denied.

It wasn't Ming trying to hold the wave back, it was the wards placed along the inner wall of the palace complex. I felt them shatter like glass, and the walls were washed away. I began to rise into the air, buoyed up by the mass of energy that had been built around me. This was more than the cores could have possibly contained. I had no idea where this much mana could have come from. It was like I had broken open a floodgate on an invisible dam, and the floodwaters would never end.

I heard laughter. Was it me, laughing like that? It was me, but it was more than just my own voice. It was like a thousand voices were shouting out in maniacal cackles, their volume loud enough to shatter my ear drums, turning the sounds around me into a roar that shook what was left of my cooking brain matter. I was only alive now because of the force of will I had to see this done. I looked out across the plateau that held the seat of power in the Empire, and I was stunned as I saw the devastation.

Nothing remained. A massive city built around a towering castle, where millions of people lived, that had stood for millennia was just… gone. The towering castle pagodas were laying on their sides, shattered like toys kicked by an unruly child. Their size meant it took them longer to be erased. Miles away, I saw the edge of the city melt as if it was consumed by the lava from a volcano.

The wave of mana was washing over the far side of the plateau, dissipating as it fell down the steep sides of the flattened mountain top. As the mana was turning into a mist and washing away, there were… *things*… left behind. They were like nothing I had ever seen. They were similar to the demons found in the deep forests at the northern edges of the kingdom, but they weren't solid. They were like the mist given form. I felt a deep sense of dread as I watched them run into the distance.

Then, I saw him. Ming was standing at the edge of the former inner wall, a dazed look upon his face. He had a shield around him, diverting the mana around him like a rock in a stream. He looked up at me, his eyes wide in shock.

I felt the rage keeping me afloat begin to die. I had missed my chance. Instead of killing Ming, I had killed millions of innocent people. I fell, my heart going cold as my brain got hotter. This whole time, the stone around my neck had not stopped pumping fire energy through my meridian system, passing through my lower and heart core and dumping into my upper core, melting my brain with the heat. I was done. I fell into darkness, and I knew no more.

CHAPTER TWO

Wrath and Pride

———

I was floating, but this time it wasn't in the white light of pure mana. I was in darkness, and I couldn't see or sense anything around me.

I was dead. I knew it instinctively, like how you knew when a person was staring at you before you even saw them. I just *knew* I was dead. I tried to look around me, but all was darkness. I floated in a sea of black, and time passed.

I didn't know how much time had gone by, but it felt like years. It was torture. Imagine not being able to sleep, move, or do anything. For *years.* The sheer boredom would have driven me to suicide if I could have killed myself. Killed myself again, I suppose. I started to go a little crazy after a while. I relived my greatest hits; knowing lovers, fighting enemies, rehashing conversations with those I cared about, trying to reconcile the fact that I had killed more innocent men, women, and children in one instant than I could count, and generally screaming with impotence into the darkness for decades.

Finally, after what felt like millennia of nothingness, I saw a light. I wasn't sure if it was a side-effect of my prolonged state of insanity, but I hoped it wasn't. It was like a speck of dust, or a faint star far away in the night sky. It gradually floated towards me, growing brighter as it came. The light became so intense that I tried to close my eyes.

It was then that I discovered that I had no eyelids to close. I didn't even have eyes. I had spent what felt like over a thousand years in the darkness, and didn't even know that I was only a mote of black dust in an endless field of dark. I didn't have a body. I was only a ball of thoughts and memories, not a human being.

The light grew closer as I adjusted to it and I could see it was a woman. She seemed to float towards me until we were only a dozen feet away from one another.

I was looking at the most beautiful woman I had ever laid eyes on, and that wasn't just the over a thousand years of isolation talking. She was of middling height, and her hourglass shape was clearly visible through the thin white silk robe wrapped around her body. Her skin was like smooth marble, flawless and cold. Her legs were wrapped in strips of white leather and her feet were encased in sandals that exposed the tips of her toes. Her hair was as white as fresh snow blowing down from the mountains, and it fell past her shoulders to the small of her back in a smooth, wavy sheet.

Her eyes were where things started to take a turn for the weird. They were empty, yet I could tell she was looking at me. It was like staring into an abyss darker than the empty black that I had been surrounded by for at least the last thousand years. It was a darkness that was meant to consume, a vacuum that would see the end of everything. If I had a body, I had no doubt I would be shaking with fear. This woman was terrifying. She opened her mouth, and I heard a voice for the first time in over a thousand years.

"Jim Roh, you are the greatest fool this plane of existence has ever seen." Well, this was starting out well. "You fulfilled a prophecy that was so obscure, so impossible, that no one thought it could ever come true."

As you might imagine, I was a wee bit confused by this statement. "Milady, I do not know what you are talking about. I am dead. I have existed in this sea of black for longer than I was ever alive, and I do not know how I could have done anything." Did my voice always sound that shaky and high-pitched? No, I was just terrified. Maybe this was just a new level of crazy I had reached?

Wait, how did she know my name? I hadn't heard my true clan name since I was only in my mid-forties, and no one knew it outside the emperor and his court since I hit my first century mark.

"I know exactly who you are, Jim Roh. And no, you fool. I am as real as you. Some might say I am the most *real* person you have ever met."

That put things into perspective. I wasn't a fool, as much as she might claim I was one. I might have been the king of naïvety, but I wasn't stupid. I was most likely in the presence of a goddess, or some higher form of life that existed beyond the world I knew.

"Exactly right, Jim. I am what you might call the Goddess of Wrath. It is, or was, my job to watch over your world. Myself and a few others, of course, but it was my gateway that you shattered when you broke into the neighboring plane."

I had no idea what she was talking about, and I was definitely sure she could read my thoughts as if I was speaking aloud.

"Yes." She waved her hands around as if she was swatting an annoying fly. "You are practically shouting your thoughts at me. You are so loud that I would hear them if I was deaf. This is why I hate dealing with unrefined souls, they are worse than children."

"Goddess, if you hate dealing with me, why are you here?" I didn't want her to leave, of course, because I had been alone for what felt like forever. Still, I had a feeling that if I said or did the wrong thing here, I wasn't going to like it.

"Jim, when you destroyed my gateway, you unleashed a storm upon your world that will culminate in the end of all sentient life across seven different planes of existence." She sighed, looking off to the side. "This event was never supposed to happen. My fellow guardians and I emplaced several safeguards to ensure no one would ever be able to complete the Prophecy of Rage, but somehow, you slipped through."

"How?" I asked. I had never heard of any prophecy, let alone one that I could ever play a part in.

She closed her eyes and began to recite, almost singing a song,

"A brother betrayed, sacrificed for personal gain.

The brother betrayed rages against his fate.

A brother burned, in turn burns us all.

The reaping of souls are grains of wheat in a field.

The gate is opened, now all fates are sealed."

She opened her eyes, and looked at me with that blank, empty stare. It sent a chill down my nonexistent spine.

"You see, Jim, you have doomed us all. Even I will be consumed by your folly. If you had just died quietly, none of this would have come to pass. There are thousands of prophecies that spell doom for this universe we must guard against, but you had to go and find the most obscure way to spell our destruction by completing this one. You do not deserve to exist."

I looked on as she raised her hand, and I could sense a ball of the same emptiness that was in her eyes forming in her hand.

I knew this was the end. This was it for me. Honestly, I was a bit relieved. I didn't want to keep descending into madness, floating in the emptiness. I was ready for it all to just… end.

I could feel the emptiness moving towards me as she straightened out her arm. It was almost gentle, the way she was reaching out to me. Then, everything stopped. Something inside me snapped.

Did she actually tell me I was supposed to just die quietly? I was no lamb to be slaughtered at the whims of those who thought or claimed they were my betters. I should have just died? Accept the betrayal of the man who I thought was my best friend? My own brother?! It felt as if an invisible wall, one that I didn't even know existed, shattered. I could finally see the streams of energy passing around me. I reached out for them, and I *pulled*.

"You think to defy me as well?" Her black eyes widened in surprise as I pushed a wall of energy between us. "You who would be crowned the King of Fools?"

I ignored her as I formed a spear of darkness to her right and a wall to her left. I smashed the two together with as much force as I could bear. A shimmer of light appeared around her, and the spear skipped off. The wall, on the other hand, smacked into her like, well, a wall. She was flung a few paces away and her shield was showing some cracks. She eyed the cracks in her shield, and looked my way again. "So, you aren't the unrefined soul I thought you to be."

I cracked my imaginary knuckles and grinned. "I don't know what to tell you, lady, but I don't go down easy."

"Clearly," she snorted in brief amusement. "The last time your life ended, you wiped out a city filled with millions of innocents." I took a moment. That one hit a sore spot. "This time, your end will be much less dramatic."

Now I could see the energy she was drawing into her hand, and it was incredible. The amount of whatever this darkness was she could tap into was on a level that was increasing exponentially. She was concentrating it into a solid mass between her hands, and I knew instinctively that this wasn't something I would be able to handle.

Suddenly, a sound like thunder rumbled out and a man was standing next to the lady. He was the male version of the Goddess of Wrath, white hair, marble skin, you get the picture. The only real difference was his eyes. They were glowing a pale blue, and they were looking my direction.

"It looks like you found him first, huh Wrath?" She threw

the concentrated ball of darkness at the newcomer in a surprise attack, but the newcomer wasn't very surprised about it. The ball of darkness skipped off his palm, and shot into the darkness. "Temper, temper! Is that any way to greet your fellow guardian?"

"What are you doing here, Pride? It was my gate that was broken, and that means that I handle this problem my way."

He scoffed, and took a step away from her and towards me. "It might have been your gate that was broken, as it was this poor sap's rage that tapped into your mana well, but it was *caused* by the pride of another." He angled himself so he could see both of us at the same time. "That means I have just as much of a role to play in this as you do."

"You have no place in this, Pride. This soul shall be ended, as it deserves, and I will put the gate back to rights. Your place is only to guard your gate, and deal with your own sinners. If you want to help me put the *nox* back in their hole, I will welcome your assistance. Until then, it will be done my way!" She moved to shove him, but he wasn't there anymore. He had flashed behind her, and I could hear his quiet chuckle as she stumbled.

"Always so angry, Wrath. Sometimes I forget how much we resemble our namesakes. You and I both know it isn't as simple as closing the gate. The *nox* aren't going to just jump back in their hole, either. They have already spread across the entire planet, and their tentacles are deeply entrenched." He looked back at me. "There is only one way to fix this, and you know it."

She grimaced. "Pride, you would have us break an entirely different seal that was emplaced before even you and I took our posts. To send him back would allow the *nox* another pathway to invade this plane. And in the end, how do we know the same thing wouldn't happen all over again?" Wrath shook her head, and took a step towards me as she raised her hand once more.

"Hold on!" Pride jumped in front of me, holding his own hand up. "What if we didn't just send him back? We are talking about breaking the rules, why not break a few more?"

Wrath's face changed. It looked like she was finally listening to Pride. "What about the *nox* that will fall through the opening, Pride?" She was back to ignoring me, allowing her hand to drop. Phew.

"With the amount of time the door would be open, only a few dozen would fall through." Pride let a smug smile creep upwards on his face. "That is nothing compared to the hundreds of thousands we would have to deal with now."

Wrath slowly lowered her arm. "I see." She put a perfect finger on her marble chin. "We could easily handle a few *nox*, but with the smaller incursion, they will try to hide from us instead of fighting. They are intelligent enough to know they could never beat us. We might never find them all."

Pride nodded in agreement, and looked back over his shoulder at me. "As penance, we could have this one track them down. Since your attempts to end his existence awakened his soul, he would be able to fight them. It might take him a few hundred years to track them all down, but that isn't our problem."

Wrath smiled at that idea, and gave Pride a nod of acceptance.

Finally, I found my chance to speak up. "No offense to you both, but what in hell are you two talking about? What are these nocks you are talking about, and what are these gates and seals that keep getting broken?"

Pride flashed away from me, and he stood next to Wrath again, the two staring at me with their creepy eyes. "Ah, how rude of me. I never formally introduced myself." He gave a flourishing bow. "I am the God of Pride, and the Guardian of the First Gate. Wrath is the Guardian of the Seventh Gate. We are two of the seven Gatekeepers, and we protect your realm and others like it from the corruption of dark mana. We call the embodiment of this dark mana *nox*, because all it touches will slowly be turned to the darkness."

"You see, fool, when your rage spiked at the same moment you tapped into the power of *thousands* of energy cores, all perfectly balanced, you created a higher form of energy than you should have had access to within your realm." Wrath still looked angry, but not 'kill Jim just for existing' angry. "You changed qi into mana. While I am sure you have seen mana before, your realm can only contain tiny amounts of white mana in one location. You created so much white mana in one place that the scales of balance demanded an influx of dark mana. This influx of dark mana cracked open my gate, and allowed the *nox* to infiltrate your realm. This alone would not have been outside the scope of what we Gatekeepers are prepared to handle, but the near-instantaneous death of millions of innocents was a siren's song to any *nox* close to the gate when it opened. By the time I was able to close it, almost a million sentient beings of pure darkness were allowed to escape into your world." Uh oh. Mad face again. "Great job, fool."

If I had a body, I would have paled at the thought. If what these two were saying was true, I not only killed millions of innocents, but I doomed every living thing on my planet. That wasn't an easy burden to be saddled with.

"Don't feel too bad." Pride started to position himself to protect me again. Apparently, he saw the look on Wrath's face as well. "In your shoes, I would have done the same. Well, better, because I would have actually killed the cultivator that caused my death, but you get my point. The good news is, we have decided to give you an opportunity to fix your mistake. We are going to send you back. To before you opened the gate."

I wasn't going to lie, going back sounded pretty good to me. I could fix my mistake. I could refuse the focusing stone he gave me, rise to the rank of Emperor, and kill Ming before he could destroy me. I could literally save not just the Empire, but the world!

Pride started laughing, and Wrath covered her mouth as she smiled.

"Not so fast," Pride's eyes started to glow a little brighter as he tried to control his mirth, "it isn't going to be that easy. We can't send you back to 'right before you reached the Emperor rank. We have to send you back to the beginning."

Back to the beginning? "What do you mean? To the beginning of that day?" Pride was laughing so hard now he was holding his ribs. I was starting to get that sinking feeling again. I had a suspicion I wouldn't find any of this nearly as amusing.

"No, to the beginning of your cultivation." Wrath took over, since Pride was having trouble catching his breath. "You see, when you first open your lower core, there is an imprint of your soul that is recorded on the Wheel of Rebirth. We can use this imprint as an anchor to shove your soul back into your body. There is no other marker that we can use to send you back, besides the moment of your death."

"Wait," I started, "you want to send me back to when—"

"When you were a child, yes," Pride finished.

"How old were you when you started cultivating?" He had finally gotten himself back under control.

I had to take a moment to think. That was a *long* time ago. "I think I was nine, maybe ten years old. I barely remember that far back. I was 650 years old when I died!"

Pride lifted the corners of his lips in a cold smile. "I don't envy you." I had a feeling he was enjoying this. "The good news is, since we are putting you back instead of a natural reincarnation, you will remember everything from your first life! That should make cultivating the second time around much faster. Just remember, this time around you cannot come in contact with the emperor until you are prepared to kill him. If he does see you, he will undoubtedly snatch you up as a student again. Fate will be bound to repeat itself, and you will destroy your world all over again. This time, you must take a new path."

"Couldn't I still meet up with him, use him for his resources, and just kill him in his sleep or something?" I was definitely confused. Since I knew what Ming was up to, there was no way I would let history repeat itself.

"The risk is too great," Wrath answered as she shook her head. "He was a powerful cultivator, even when he first met you. Should he sense your ill intent, even for an instant, he would end you. And while that would also correct the gate opening, it would still leave dozens of *nox* slowly destroying your world."

Pride was nodding along in agreement. "That brings me to the second and most important point." His eyes were getting even brighter as he spoke, like he was building up to something. "While I would recommend you simply leave the empire you were born into, I know you will seek revenge on the man that caused your death. However, you won't just be working towards killing your corrupt emperor. You also have to hunt down any *nox* that you find. Think of them as invisible demons. Some will walk around freely, some will inhabit large plants or animals, and the strongest of them might hide in humans."

"They love finding corrupt humans, and turning their dark souls even blacker." He was making grasping motions with his hands, trying to emphasize how a creature formed from dark mana would latch on to someone. "Their ultimate goal will be corrupting enough lifeforms that they can open a new gate to their realm, and let more of them into your world. You have to stop them at all costs." He paused to look at Wrath, and I decided to speak.

"How will I find these monsters, and how do I even kill a creature made from dark mana?" I felt like a lot of information was going over my head.

"If you would let me finish," Pride sighed, shooting me a frustrated look, "I was getting to that. Now that you have channeled the energy that exists here in the space between realms, you will find that your affinities have changed. You are now beyond the elements you used to know. From now on, you can channel dark and light qi." He held up his hands, forming a swirling disk of pure shadow in one hand and pure light in the other.

"I'm sure you will spend several years experimenting with your new abilities, but you must remember to keep these two elements in balance within your cores." He let the display drop, the energy dissipating instantly. "If you use dark qi for ten minutes, you must use light qi for ten minutes. Keep it equal. If you allow them to go too far out of balance, you risk tainting your meridians. If that happens, you won't be able to channel any element except the one you have contaminated it with. You don't want to limit yourself like that. As for destroying the *nox*, you will have to fight each one to determine its weakness. Every *nox* has at least one element they are weak in, so you must use that to destroy them."

Wow. That was a lot to process. I was supposed to go back, find the resources to cultivate back to my former strength without the wealth of the single richest person in the Empire, avoid Ming and all of his recruiters spread across the land, and, finally, hunt down and destroy a bunch of invisible dark mana demons spread across the entire planet. Oh, and do all of that as a ten-year-old child. Great fun…

"No." Wrath was reading my mind again. "We don't care about you regaining your former strength, or killing your nemesis. We only care that you stay away from him, and find a way to kill the *nox*. You can figure out all of the rest on your own." She put her hand back on her chin to think. "The dark mana that will escape into your world won't be able to come through *all* over your planet. It will most likely be contained to your continent. You shouldn't have to travel the globe to find them all, just the empire you are familiar with, and the four others that share the continent."

While I felt a sense of relief, that was still an incredible amount of land to cover. The empire was huge. It took years to travel from one side to the other, and that was without stopping to look for monsters.

"Once you kill a few, they will most likely start hunting you." Pride frowned thoughtfully. "While rare, there are others who will be capable of killing some *nox* as well. I imagine you will only have to kill a little over half of what gets through. I think, as long as you don't allow yourself to be cornered by several of them at once, you should be fine."

Wrath was looking at me as if she was a stern parent correcting an unruly child. "If you fail in this, we will be forced to cut out the infection ourselves. You have four hundred years to kill them all. That is all the time we can give you. If there are any left after that, we will destroy the continent. It is better to sacrifice a single continent than an entire planet. Do not fail, King of Fools. Billions of lives depend on you now."

I would have gulped if I had the parts to do so. Well, no pressure or anything. While four hundred years sounded like a long time, it took almost ten years to travel by carriage from one edge of the Southern Empire to the other. In a straight line. And the Southern Empire was the smallest of the five empires on the continent. I had no idea how I was going to cover that much ground in only four centuries. I was going to need some help.

"There might be some side effects to this… transference, we can call it." Pride was sipping an amber liquid out of a clear glass that just popped out of nowhere as he talked. "I am sure you are aware, but this is not your first reincarnation. Your soul has been through dozens of lives. Forcing your 650-year life into the brain of a child might cause some bleed-over from your past lives. And just to let you know, your soul has done some interesting things. Be aware, your instincts might be thrown off, and you might have knowledge of things you have never done." He paused as his glass popped back into whatever place he had pulled it from. "Or I could be wrong, and you are going to be just fine."

"Prepare yourself, this is going to hurt." Wrath and Pride turned to face one another, and his eyes started glowing even brighter. Lights flashed across Wrath's empty orbs, her eyes seeming to somehow grow deeper, as if a whole field of stars was hidden inside. They both turned towards me, and I saw a bright flash of light. Once again, I knew no more.

CHAPTER THREE

Catching Up

Ouch. That was not fun. Have you ever tried to put ten cows into a five-cow pen? It was not what you might call a 'fun adventure.' My head felt like someone was using my skull as a gong. At a gong-only concert. And they were bad at it.

I tried to crack open my eyes, but the light was too intense. I could hear a lot of shouting, and it sounded like things were being knocked over and smashed. It was mostly muffled, because the ringing in my ears was trying to outperform the gong player pounding in my skull.

Bang *Bang* *Eeeeeeeeeeeee*.

I felt someone grab me and throw me over their shoulder as they started running. This, of course, made my head feel absolutely *fantastic.*

Everything was hazy as I passed in and out of consciousness for a few minutes, but as the person who was carrying me quit running, my head finally started to clear. I opened my eyes and I saw what looked like shooting stars flaming across the sky. But they were black. And it was daylight. Definitely weird.

As my head started to work again, I knew what it was. The *nox* were falling to the surface, and there was a whole bunch of them. There were definitely more than the few dozen the gods had talked about.

The person who was carrying me set me down on the ground, and promptly threw a bucket of water in my face. Well, that was unexpected. As I spluttered and blinked away the water, I finally started to look around. I was leaning against a well in the center of some shabby marketplace, and the person standing over me with a bucket was shouting in my face.

There were groups of people standing around the open market, pointing up at the sky and generally freaking out. I was pretty sure some were shouting about the 'end of times,' and others were on their knees, praying to whatever gods they worshipped. A few, mostly the older or more well-dressed people, were calmly watching the black stars fall, no emotion showing on their faces.

The loud ringing in my ears finally evened to a low hum where I could hear again, and I could finally understand the person shouting at me.

"Jim! I swear to all that is holy, if you don't say something to me, I am going to start dunking you in this well!"

I held up my hand to acknowledge I had heard them, and I was immediately struck by how small I was. Had I really been this much of a runt when I was ten? I refocused back on my savior-slash-attacker. "I think I am okay now. What happened?"

"You were in the testing pavilion, and just as you touched the testing stone, suddenly there was a bright light that flashed out of your body! We couldn't even look directly at you! Then, the light went away and you just collapsed. There was blood coming out of your eyes, ears, and nose, and you were completely unresponsive. Then, a few seconds later, there was a loud boom, like thunder. We looked up, and these black stars started streaking across the sky, dozens of them falling in all directions!" The speaker was very animated, flailing around in an attempt to reenact the events he was describing. "I grabbed you off the floor, and ran here to the well. I figured a bucket of water to the face might help bring you back, and clean up some of that blood."

I looked down at myself and I realized I was covered in streaks of blood and dirt. I felt like crap, I looked like crap, and I was pretty sure I smelled like crap. What a way to come back. On the bright side, I was pretty sure that either Wrath or Pride fixed the whole 'isolation for a really long time eventually drove me crazy' stuff. My thoughts were clear, and any confusion and thoughts of self-harm had faded away like fog at high noon. I finally focused on the face of my rescuer, and I was stunned.

"Donny, is that you? I haven't seen you in centuries! Gods, you look fantastic! How are you doing?" Donny, one of my cousins, and one of only a handful of people from my clan who didn't treat me like horse dung after my exile, was staring at me like I had grown a second nose from my forehead.

"Jim, I see you every single day. And what do you mean, centuries? What did the testing stone do to you?" Donny was exactly as I remembered. Dark hair, brown eyes, a little over six feet tall, and thickly muscled like his father. If I remembered correctly, he was only seven or eight years my senior. He crouched down in front of me, placing his hand on my forehead. "Gods, you are burning up! You have a nasty fever. I need to get you to the healer. Come on, if you can talk, you can walk."

He lifted me to my feet and started pulling me towards the main road running through the square. I immediately stumbled, and I would have fallen if he wasn't helping to support me. I was not used to having such short legs and tiny feet. This whole 'being young again' thing was not nearly as much fun as I remembered it the first time around.

It took a few minutes, but I quickly started getting the hang of walking again. I knew it was still going to take some getting used to having such short legs, compared to how tall I had been as an adult. After we had walked a few hundred yards, I was moving almost normally in my new body. Or, old body—not quite sure where to go with this one.

We rounded the corner and I finally saw a building I recognized. It was a two-story stone and wooden pagoda-style building with a flat roof, basic but well cared for. I remembered spending a fair amount of time in my youth here at the healer's house. After being falsely diagnosed as a useless cultivator, the kids in my clan were not kind to me while growing up. I recalled getting in several fights before I left to find my own path, and I distinctly remembered getting the crap kicked out of me in most of those childhood brawls. Donny knocked before pushing the door open, dragging me in behind him.

"Don, back again so soon? I just gave you an elixir a few days ago, I can't give you any more for several weeks." The speaker was standing behind a counter, leaning over a worn book laid out in front of him. He was an older man, with long gray hair pulled back in a thick braid behind his head. His weathered features were turned down in a frown, and his demeanor matched the dark gray robes he was wearing.

"Not for me, Hai Roh." Donny helped me stumble up to the counter before pointing at me. "It is Jim. He touched the testing stone, and a whole bunch of weird stuff started happening. Now he has a fever, and I am pretty sure he is delirious. Nothing he says makes sense, and he is staring at everything like it is his first time seeing it. If it weren't for him at least knowing my name, I would say he lost all his memories."

Hai finally looked at me, and concern flashed across his features. "He is practically covered in blood. Bring him around back so we can get him cleaned up and I can take a better look at him."

Donny pulled me around the counter, and we walked through a set of swinging doors into a room lined with shelves and rolled up mats stacked in the corners. In the back of the large room was what looked like a wooden rain barrel with the top third cut off.

"Jim, I need you to strip off that soiled clothing and jump in the tub. Wash yourself as best you can, and then put on a clean robe from the stack." Hai indicated a pile of worn looking robes sitting on a stool next to the tub. He glanced at Donny. "You and I can go back to the front and you can give me a more detailed account of what happened today. I heard some people shouting something about shooting stars?"

Their conversation faded as they walked back through the doors, leaving me to clean myself up. Normally, I would use some fire qi to warm up the tub, but my head was still too fuzzy to start messing with my channeling system. I had no idea what my cores and meridians looked like yet, and I didn't think that now was the time to start experimenting.

I took off my bloody robes and looked down at myself. Two words. Scrawny. Weak. My memory had apparently glossed over just how unassuming I had been at ten, and I didn't blame it. I had a *ton* of work to do.

I climbed into the barrel and started to scrub myself down with the brick of sandstone left on the rim. I was pretty sure this water was cold enough to get rid of my fever all by itself. I think this wasn't the fastest bath I had ever taken, but it was pretty close. I got dressed, the whole time trying to dredge up memories from this period of my life. I hadn't thought about it in a long time, but I was pretty certain that this was not going to be an easy start to my second life.

I had been exiled from my clan as soon as they could legally get rid of me. I was fifteen, and tossed out on my ear by the same people who called themselves my family. Only a few people—namely my mother, father, Donny, and Uncle Don, Donny's father—stood up for me at the council meeting that determined my fate.

You see, I was not a normal cultivator. I was not looking forward to facing the clan's testing again, because none of them were advanced enough to see that my malformed cores and meridians were actually a boon instead of a hindrance. The interruption at the testing stone that just happened meant I would be faced with even more inspections from the people in charge. Oh well, I needed to leave the clan soon anyway, otherwise I would not be able to find all of the *nox* spreading across the land before time was up.

I was too deep into my musings to realize that Hai had returned, so he surprised me when he laid his hand on my shoulder. He smirked at me as I jumped.

"I see you are still a little out of it. Let me take a look at you." He placed one hand on my forehead and the other on my solar plexus. I could feel his qi start to probe through my body. For a moment, I was taken aback at how clumsy he was with his qi. I remembered Hai Roh as an exalted master healer, one whom people would come from hundreds of miles around to heal their injuries and illnesses. Then I remembered that he probably wasn't much past a Meridian-level cultivator, a Brain cultivator at most, and I reevaluated just exactly where my skill level might land me in a short period of time. I had a feeling I was entirely too overpowered for the region.

"It isn't uncommon for the testing stone to cause problems, but your case appears to be more extreme than most." He was manipulating the energy down each limb, trying to get a better idea of what was wrong with me.

I remembered the Roh testing stone. It was a black obelisk that had been empowered by the first Roh to assist young cultivators in opening their first meridian, and activating their core. Every major clan and sect had some form of testing stone, even if they weren't required for a person to begin cultivating. It allowed children to start cultivating several years before their meridians would open naturally, giving the sect or clan an edge over those who didn't have one. Usually, the more powerful the testing stone, the earlier it could be used. Therefore, the more powerful the testing stone, the more powerful the clan or sect.

The earliest I had heard of one being used was the one held by the Imperial family, which could safely be used by a four-year-old. While it didn't seem like much, those early years of cultivation could show drastic gains later in life. Reinforcing qi in a young body would make it more stable as they aged, making the progression from one level of cultivation to the next much easier. Not only that, the more used to qi your body was, the more easily you could control it.

"Your whole body is feverish, and your brain is swelling." By this point, Hai had finished his fumbling search and looked at me with concerned eyes. "I have some herbs that will reduce the fever and inflammation, but I don't want you doing anything strenuous for the next few days." His lack of skill as a healer meant he didn't even look at my cultivation system, which I was thankful for. I hadn't even had a chance to look at it yet.

"Thank you, Hai." I nodded, and accepted the bundle of dried herbs he handed me. "I appreciate your help." He frowned at me, and I immediately realized my mistake. Hai was a senior member of my clan, and I should have addressed him as such. I was only an unproven ten-year-old boy, and did not warrant the familiarity of using only his first name. "I apologize, Master Hai Roh, I am still not thinking clearly. I think this fever is sapping more of me than just my strength." His eyebrows rose, and I could see the anger fade from his eyes.

"Yes, I understand, child. Just avoid any of your elders until your mind clears. Not everyone is as forgiving as I am, and I would hate to see you in here again for some lashes because you cannot guard your tongue. Have Donny take you straight home, and I want to see you again after the midday bell tomorrow." I nodded again, and started out the door. "Oh, and child," I looked back at Hai as he called out to me, "be sure you return the robe you are wearing when you see me. I know your mother would be angry if she had to pay for that old set of rags." I smiled and nodded as I walked out the door.

Donny was waiting for me outside the entrance and he led the way as we walked towards what I was assuming was my family complex. The Roh clan followed the normal standard for clans in the southern provinces, with a few deviations.

Families were clustered together in two-story square complexes, with only one main entrance to help ensure the security of each branch in the event of a rival sect or clan attack. They were practically miniature castles designed to protect the regular houses and structures in the city center.

Each family unit had their own set of six apartments, four upstairs and two downstairs. Inside, there were three bedrooms surrounding their private sitting room, with the fourth side of the square sitting room facing a shared common courtyard. The courtyards usually contained a covered outdoor kitchen, a cultivation garden, and a small well that could be used in the event of a siege. There was also a long table where meals were eaten as a group, and the back section of the bottom floor was a common bath and latrine.

Each small compound was its own miniature fort, with the compounds being close enough to one another that they could fire arrows or long-distance qi attacks from their rooftops onto any invaders assaulting the complexes around them. There were probably around fifty or fifty-five complexes arranged around the primary branch family facilities and marketplaces, if memory served correctly. It was honestly an ingenious system that ensured any attacking forces would have to massively divide their numbers in an attack, making it easy for the stronger members of each family branch to decimate their foes in coordinated attacks.

I had actually implemented similar styles of defense when I was a Captain of the Guard about three hundred years ago during some border skirmishes. With much success, I might add. Instead of standing directly against an enemy like an oak faces the wind, bend with the wind like a willow and break the enemy against your many branches. Wait. Three hundred years or so from now, there would be border skirmishes. I really needed to get my head on straight.

If I was recalling correctly, it was my mother and father, Donny's father, my grandparents on both sides, and my Uncle Hu that all shared my family compound. There was only one open family space left in my branch complex, and it was between Donny, my cousin Xiao, who was the son of my Uncle Hu, and myself to determine who would get the last set of rooms. The other two would have to either gather the funds to build a new complex, marry into another clan branch suitably distant to avoid childhood malformities, or leave the clan entirely.

While the Roh clan was militarily strong, it was far from a wealthy clan. It couldn't afford to provide housing for the weak.

Donny remained silent as we walked past a multitude of buildings, and I was surprised at how run-down the complexes looked. I remembered my clan as being powerful and mighty, but I was beginning to realize how much of that was childhood fantasy. My clan was clearly at the lower edge of average for the Empire, and I renewed my affirmation that I needed to leave quickly.

There was nothing for me here beyond seeing my family again, and I didn't have the luxury of time to waste. The fate of billions settled on my shoulders once again, and I straightened my back against the weight. I had failed once already, killing millions, and I had the opportunity to correct things. This weight was not more than I could bear, it was only what I deserved. I would not fail again.

Donny broke the silence as we approached a complex that seemed a little better kept than its neighbors. "Well, home sweet home, huh Jim? It would be best for you to go straight to bed. You don't want to deal with Xiao in your condition. He would love to pounce on you in a moment of weakness, and today you would make easy prey."

I nodded and thanked Donny as I walked towards the stairs leading to my family's portion of the complex. I had almost completely forgotten that my cousin Xiao had been a source of annoyance during my youth. During my long life, he was nothing more than the smallest of obstacles, but as a child he had been the bane of my existence. With the perspective of the world I had now, I was not overly concerned about Xiao.

My family lived in the upper back section, traditionally the worst place to live in the complexes. It was right above the latrine and bath, and the smells and moisture would frequently make them an unpleasant place to live. I think it was my Uncle Hu that subtly arranged for my father to get the section, but instead it turned out to be a boon for my family. My mother was primarily a wood element cultivator, and she used the humidity from the baths below to help grow dozens of pleasant-smelling plants and flowers all throughout our bedrooms and sitting area. It made our little set of rooms the best in the complex, and I couldn't help but chuckle at the memories of my Uncle Hu showing his frustration at my family turning his machinations into fortune.

As I walked into the sitting area, I could already sense my mother and father were absent. I was saddened, but not surprised. My mother spent most mornings gathering plants and herbs at the edge of the forest near our clan, and my father watched over her and hunted for game.

It was how they met, and it would be how they would die. When I was in my sixties, I remembered getting word that over half of the Roh clan had been wiped out by a wave of Spotted Snow Leopards that came from the forest my mother and father frequented. While large-scale beast attacks were rare in the southern provinces, they were not impossible. My parents had gone out the morning of the attack and were never seen again. I had led an expedition that had decimated the beasts in the area less than six months later, but there had been hardly any Spotted Snow Leopards remaining. It had been a source of pain for me for several years, but I eventually found peace and acceptance over the matter.

It wasn't necessarily a bad thing that they weren't here, however. This gave me the opportunity to explore my current cultivation levels in peace, and the wards emplaced around the sitting area would ensure that no others would easily detect my aura. Whatever aura I had at this point, anyway. I sat down in my preferred lotus position and finally took a look inside myself.

I was momentarily taken aback. I had next to nothing. I concentrated on my cores before letting loose a small sigh of defeat.

It was no wonder why Healer Hai's fumbling attempts at inspecting my body didn't raise any suspicion. The walls of my three cores seemed paper-thin, and my meridians were as tiny as I had feared. When I was kicked out of my clan, it was primarily for that reason alone. My clan had kicked me out for two specific issues.

My upper core, or brain core, was basically invisible. I was gifted with a larger-than-average lower and heart core, but my brain core was ridiculous. You see, most people have a brain core that forms around their cerebellum, helping them to improve reaction time, movement speed, and precision. I, on the other hand, had a brain core that encompassed my *entire* brain. Since no one in my clan had heard of anything like it before, they didn't know to check for it. It was far more common for people to not have all three cores, so they just assumed I didn't have one and marked me down as a waste of time and materials for development into a strong cultivator.

It was shortly thereafter, around fifteen, that I was exiled from the clan, Ming picked me up, and the rest was history. Having a full brain core had its ups and downs, like it took larger amounts of qi and focus to get the same effects as a regular brain core, but I could do more than just speed up my reaction time. I could speed up my rate of thought. While that might sound like a tiny benefit, in reality, it paired so well with my other abnormality that it made me very powerful. Once I had learned to use it, of course.

My other problem was my meridians. Most people, the exceedingly vast majority, had twelve meridians. Two in the hands, feet, elbows, and knees, three along the spine, and one at the top of the head. I had an extra one, right between my eyes. It was due to the oversized upper core, and it meant that I had a leg up on other people both in offense and defense, but most especially in endurance.

One more meridian didn't sound like much, but it meant that I could refill my cores with energy just a bit faster than anyone else. The downside? My meridians were extremely thin.

I eventually overcame this by the time I reached the Sage level of cultivation, but until that point, I had been forced to adapt my cultivation style to a more interesting path. More on that later.

I took a moment to think, and I actually smacked myself in frustration. Here I was, sad that my core and meridian walls were so thin, but I could actually *see* all of them. I had no blockages in any of my meridians, and all three cores were open.

I was, technically, a Brain cultivator. I literally skipped Body, Heart, and Meridian levels, and went straight to the fourth level of cultivation. My first time through, I was almost one hundred years old before clearing all of my meridians and opening my upper core.

This might make that 400-year deadline just a tiny bit more possible. Of course, I was probably the weakest Brain cultivator in history, but it meant that I could immediately use my preferred form of qi usage. I could also use all of the elements, meaning I wouldn't be limited to only one or two like most of my peers. Anyone wanting to mess with me was going to be in for a rather rude awakening. I was going to have to take it easy, naturally, and not rupture anything, but with what I currently knew and what I had access to, I had no doubt that it would take a Sage-level cultivator to bring me down. Even then, they would have to catch me.

I began cycling the energy around me and promptly started pumping qi into my skin, muscles, organs, bones, circulatory system, nervous system, and brain matter as densely as possible. I had a whole lot of catching up to do.

CHAPTER FOUR

What Worms Want

I woke up alone, in an unfamiliar bed, looking up at a black sky. I reached out with my senses, and didn't detect anyone. I sat up and took in my surroundings, shocked at what I saw. Even though I couldn't sense them, Wrath and Pride were seated in comfortable-looking armchairs facing my bed. I looked down at myself, and I was back in the body of 650-year-old me, not child me. I looked back at the two entities in front of me. "Did I die again?"

Pride shook his head. "No, Jim. We just wanted to reach out to you to let you know what happened. When we broke the seal and sent you back, there were a few more *nox* than we expected that slipped through. We haven't looked everywhere yet, but you are looking at about two hundred or so targets to work through."

I sighed, and nodded my acknowledgement.

Wrath picked up where Pride left off. "This shouldn't be insurmountable for you." She paused to visibly do some math on her fingers. "It means that you only have to kill one *nox* every two years to beat the deadline. The bad news is, you have to find them. We are only able to reach your dreams when you have a breakthrough in level. So, we won't be able to advise you for a long time. Your next level is the middle stage of Brain Cultivation, and you are bound to be stuck as a low-level Brain cultivator for quite a while."

I nodded once again, showing that I understood and agreed with her. After all, a cultivator could only collect and store a certain amount of qi at one time. Otherwise, they risked doing permanent damage to their cultivation system. Just like building up muscle. Go too fast, and you risked tearing something.

Pride leaned forward to make eye contact. "Jim, when we speak to you, your body will show a slight glow. Ensure you are alone when you go to rest after reaching a new level. Otherwise, you are going to have to answer some interesting questions. For now, the only advice I can give you is to travel into the forest nearest your current location. There is a single *nox* in the area, and I sense a few items you might find useful in your current situation. Look towards the center, near the ruins of a city that used to hold a people that forgot to respect the same laws of the forest they dwelled in. I am sure you won't make the same mistakes that they did, especially in your current situation."

"Someone comes," Wrath said, her eyes widening. "We must leave you or we risk your emperor hearing of your uniqueness."

I opened my mouth to ask about these ruins they mentioned, but I was already alone.

———

I sat up and heard a knock on my bedroom door. I shook my head like a dog shaking off water. The dream world had left me feeling woozy.

"Enter," I shouted, and Donny walked into my room. He was wearing full kit, hardened leather armor protecting his vital areas, with a spear on his shoulder and an axe on his belt.

"It is early, but I wanted to make sure you had enough time to clean the healer's robes before you met with him," he said, leaning against the doorway. "You should probably get ready. There is supposed to be some announcement soon."

"Thank you. I had honestly forgotten all about cleaning the robe." Donny grinned in a way that let me know he wasn't surprised at my statement. "I suppose I should bathe and get dressed, then go to see the healer." Donny nodded and left, leaving my door open on his way out.

My parents hadn't come home last night, and I was not afraid to admit that I was worried. It wasn't far outside the norm for them to venture too deep into the forest to return in one day, but I was worried after the warning from Wrath and Pride. If they didn't return soon, I was going to go looking for them.

I quickly gathered up my things and took the stairs back down to the bottom floor. I hadn't taken the herbs last night because I knew it would have been a waste. I needed cash, and those herbs were easily worth a silver or two. I had used my own qi to heal instead, strengthening my body as much as I could in the process.

The bathing area was empty, and taking advantage of my solitary state I took my time getting clean. I had pushed out a large number of impurities from my body last night, which left a thin film on my skin that was difficult to scrub off. Just as I was finishing, I heard the entry door slide open. I was standing naked in front of a polished piece of bronze, admiring my slightly improved physique, when I saw Xiao's reflection behind me.

He was smaller than my memories made him out to be, but the ugly scowl on his face was exactly as I remembered. He was close to the same age as Donny but not as tall. His features were pointed, and his thin lips and pale skin made him look sickly. He was thin, but not to the point of scrawny. He was wearing a dark red robe that made him look washed-out, and I could feel him circulating qi through his body in an attempt to push out an imposing aura. He was failing spectacularly, but I appreciated the extra effort.

"So, my youngest cousin has finally decided to improve his scrawny body?" Xiao sneered, stepping farther into the room. "About time you started taking your appearance to heart. You are a disgrace to this family, and you need to fix it."

I felt him pull in the water qi suffusing the area, preparing an invisible staff that he held at knee level. I knew exactly what he was going to try to do. The moment I started to turn around to face him, he was going to use that invisible stick to trip me and toss me back into the bath water. He would then be able to strike me wherever he wanted, and just blame any injuries I suffered on the fall. How in the world was I ever intimidated by this idiot?

I decided to just ignore him. He was expecting me to react violently, but I didn't think he could fathom me pretending like he didn't even exist. In fact, I had a feeling that it would cause far more pain and aggravation for a worm like him to be ignored, instead of being stepped on. Well, almost as much pain. I was fine drawing this whole thing out, though. Wiping the floor with him now would be too fast for the likes of him.

Instead of answering, I continued looking in the mirror. I had dark brown hair and a taller build that would eventually reach six feet, just like my father. I was probably about four and a half feet tall, which was pretty good for a ten-year-old. My eyes were a pale green like my mother, and my features were delicate enough that, as I aged, I knew that I wouldn't find issue with attracting the attention of the opposite sex. It would be difficult to put muscle on my frame, but with enough hard work and dedication, I would start to resemble my older self. Behind me, Xiao's face was turning an interesting shade of purple. I think I might have made him mad.

"You think to ignore your better? I will see you pay, ant!"

I finally turned to look at him as he was raising the invisible club to strike me. "Your Aunt? Do you confuse me as a woman, Xiao? I know that I am good looking, but for you to think of me as female is an entirely different issue." The club dissipated as his mouth started opening and closing like a fish out of water, and I was pretty sure he was so angry he had forgotten how to breathe.

I moved past him towards my things on the bench and began to get dressed. The robe I had been forced to borrow from the healer was basically dry, so I gathered it up in my arms to put it in my bag as I started for the door. Suddenly, Xiao was standing by the exit, hands held up in a fighting stance.

"After that insult, I don't even need to hide why I beat you senseless!" He lunged forward, left hand leading, holding his right hand low in preparation for an uppercut I could easily see coming.

I simply leaned backwards a bit, and his punch missed me by a hair. I stomped my heel onto his leading foot, and used my elbow to guide his face into the edge of the doorway. I heard the crunch of breaking bone before he crumpled to the ground. I stepped over his unconscious body, looking back to make sure he wouldn't drown in his own blood from his shattered nose, and headed out the door. I guess the worm really wanted to be squished after all.

CHAPTER FIVE

Gauging the Competition

I couldn't afford to be late to see the healer, because I clearly remembered what came next. It was my first class on cultivating since opening my core, and afterwards there would be the test that this time around would start me down the road to banishment from my clan. My first test was interrupted, so this would be when they saw my brain core, or to them the lack thereof, for the first time. I didn't want to miss my chance for an easy escape from the clan. Just up and leaving on my own wouldn't work. While my clan wouldn't tear down the heavens searching for me, they would certainly send out an expedition to bring me back. Family was always complicated like that.

The walk to the healer was fast, and he was waiting in a chair on his porch, watching people walk down the road in front of his building. I couldn't be sure, but I think he might have been watching the ladies with a bit more attention than the men. Dirty old men, you could find them everywhere.

He looked up as I approached, nodding as I set the robe on the porch railing. He looked tired. I couldn't help but wonder, what might keep him up at night?

"Glad you are up and about, Jim. You look to be feeling much improved today." He motioned for me to come closer, so I tromped my way up the stairs. I moved close enough that he could use his qi to inspect me. He placed his hands on my head and stomach. "I am going to examine you, but from your appearance, I would imagine you should be fine to attend the classes and competition this afternoon." I was once again glad that he wasn't skilled enough to actually notice that my cores and meridians were already open, otherwise this could get awkward.

"Competition, Master Hai? I don't remember hearing anything about a competition?" In my first timeline, there had only been a competition as a part of the annual New Year celebrations.

"Yes," Hai said with a sigh, "the rain of dark stars yesterday has the elders concerned. We were up all night long making plans. They wish for everyone to compete in a tournament to cement their clan standings in the event of a battle." He was moving his qi around me as he talked. "Don't worry, young Jim. You will only have to face fellow Body cultivators. Not much is expected of you, as your lower core was just opened yesterday when you touched the testing stone." He retracted his energy, and I could sense his shock. "Your body is in perfect shape, and if I didn't know better, I would say you were already reinforcing yourself with qi. Of course, there is no way you could know how to do that. You must be blessed with quite the amazing constitution!"

"I don't know anything about that, Master Hai," I said with a smile, "but I have felt much better after getting over the shock of my core being opened." The whole 'getting an old soul shoved into a young body' thing didn't feel great, but it was better than being dead. "Thank you, Master, I should get going." I turned to go, and the healer grabbed my arm.

"I would keep quiet about this, Jim. If you have any rivals, they might think it prudent to snuff out any competition, before their competition can snuff them out instead."

I nodded, taking his advice to heart. "Thank you, Master Hai. I will certainly keep that in mind."

He let go, and I started down the road again. I decided I should definitely take his warning seriously, and began subtly pulling in energy as each foot touched the ground. It was a technique I learned a long time ago, a simple way to surprise your enemies. Pulling energy through your meridians was normally an easily detectable process to other cultivators, but using small bursts through the soles of your feet as you walked made it difficult for others to discern. Unless they were paying very close attention, they would never know that the person they were targeting was constantly ready to defend themselves.

I walked down the road to the central pavilion and looked for the group of people waiting for the class on cultivation to begin. I found the place and took a seat towards the back. There was probably close to a hundred people in the courtyard, all of them at the Body cultivation level. Some of them were here to seek additional knowledge, and others were here to receive that knowledge for the first time.

I figured I might as well pay attention too. I had learned a long time ago that I didn't know everything, and knowledge could be the difference between life and death.

A few minutes later, a clan elder I vaguely remembered as being a pompous asshole walked into the courtyard from an interior door. He was short, middle-aged, with dark hair and crooked teeth to match his crooked disposition. He was wearing a set of leather armor over dark green robes with a red sash tied around his left bicep. Apparently, he was such a bad teacher that he was afraid of being attacked in the middle of his class. Everyone got to their feet as he walked towards the center of the stage area near the front.

"Take your seats, children. Some of you might have heard this speech before, but most have not."

I settled in to get comfortable, taking out my notebook and stylus from my bag. I looked around and noticed that no one else was doing the same. Had no one heard of taking notes?

Even if I had listened to the information a hundred times, you never knew when something might spark a moment of inspiration. The elder started speaking, and I started writing.

"In almost every person, there are three cores and twelve meridian channels. Meridian channels are like arteries that travel from the surface of the skin to the lower core. There is a central channel that connects the three cores together, and this allows energy to transfer between the three." He paused to eyeball the crowd before continuing. "There are multiple levels of cultivation, and we will discuss them in order. First, there are Body cultivators. They have opened at least one of the twelve meridian channels, and their lower core, located in their solar plexus. Body cultivators can use their lower core to strengthen their skin and muscles, which increases overall strength and durability." The elder stopped, giving people time to ponder what he had said so far.

"The second level is Heart cultivators. They have opened at least three meridian channels, and their middle core is located in the heart." He used his finger to point at his own chest. "The Heart core allows cultivators to strengthen their organs, reducing the possibility of internal injuries. It also allows them to purify the qi in their cores, opening the possibility of controlling more than one element."

"The third level is Meridian cultivators." He manipulated some metal qi to run across his skin, showing the approximate locations of the meridians found in the body. "Many spend a long time at this level, as a Meridian cultivator has to go from six open meridians to twelve. During this time, the expanded pathways of qi throughout the body allow them to reinforce their bones and circulatory system. This allows a cultivator to increase their stamina, strength, and durability even further." The elder demonstrated by widening the strands of metal, simulating the widening of the meridian channels that would eventually occur.

"The fourth level of cultivation is when you access the upper core, or Brain Core. Brain cultivators can strengthen their brain and nervous system, speeding up their reaction times. This stage is why it is vitally important for you to increase your strength and durability in the former stages. After infusing your brain and nerves with reinforcing qi, you will move incredibly fast." The elder flashed across the stage, the air crackling around him. "If you do not reinforce your body, every movement might break bones or tear muscles. It will almost certainly kill you if you rush the process. That is why most cultivators spend more than a decade, sometimes two, at the Meridian stage before moving up to brain cores." The audience clapped at his display. The elder strutted around, showing off a few more skills that the Body cultivators found amazing. I thought they were flashy and pointless.

While the class he gave wasn't necessarily wrong, he was leaving out a lot of information. Each stage of cultivation added time to your lifespan, about a century for each level. It depended on the cultivator, and how efficient they were at condensing qi into their body.

He was also leaving out the four stages in each level. Each level had low, middle, high, and peak stages, all referring to how condensed the qi was in their cores and bodies. At each increase in level, the core and meridian size would almost double. This reduced the density of qi in the body and cores, and the cultivator would have to basically start all over again. They would have to go from vapor, to fog, to liquid, and finally to a crystalized solid. It was more of a slurry-like consistency in the meridians, with a solid crystal in the cores. You needed the solid crystal to push on the walls of your core, eventually stretching the core to a new size.

He was also failing to mention the importance of thickening your meridian and core walls. It was extremely easy to puncture or burst a core or meridian if it wasn't sufficiently thickened and strengthened. Just like a muscle, you had to build it up by using it, and it also helped to force qi into the structure as well. Not only that, he was completely neglecting to mention the need to ensure you had a balance of all the elements of qi in your body and cores once you unlocked your upper core. By not doing so, you would create an imbalance in your body that got harder and harder to correct as you increased in level. Before unlocking the upper core, cultivators could usually use only one or two elemental forms of qi. If they didn't train in the use of all elements, they would never pass the level of Brain cultivation.

I was getting the feeling that my clan was leaving out a lot of information on purpose. The elders wanted to ensure they stayed at the top, and the people below them didn't rise up regularly enough to challenge them. It left a sour taste in my mouth. The elder stopped his strutting and went back into his teaching voice.

"The details of the later levels of cultivation are something you can worry about in more advanced classes, but they are Saint, Sage, Duke, King, and finally Emperor level." His tone indicated how unlikely he thought anyone would attain those, especially the latter.

"As I am sure you know, most clans require a cultivator to reach the Saint level before they can be considered an elder. A few people, like Healer Hai, or our alchemists and blacksmiths, can rise to the rank of elder based on their specialized skills. The level of most clan leaders is the Sage level. In a sect, the Sage level is frequently called the Teacher level of cultivation, because the elders are frequently Sages. The most powerful clans, like ours, have a Duke-level cultivator as their clan leaders." He swelled with pride at that statement. As if he had anything to do with it. And if he thought this clan was powerful, he clearly hadn't spent much time out in the wider world.

"Almost all sects have someone at the Duke level as their leader, and only the top five sects in the empire have King-level cultivators as their leaders or chief elders." He was right on that point. Most sects, especially those with a political presence in the Imperial City, were *much* more powerful than the average clan. "Most King-level cultivators serve the emperor as his enforcers, in the Elemental Guard, or as the kings in charge of a province. If you ever meet one of these kings, it would be best for you to do whatever they say. They could crush you with a thought. The only Emperor-level cultivator in the empire is the actual emperor, as it should be. Only the most powerful have the right to lead, and our Emperor Li most assuredly has that right."

Wait, what?

For a moment, I was taken aback. Ming was the emperor! It took me a bit, but then I remembered. Ming wouldn't be the emperor for another three hundred and fifty years. Emperor Li was actually a good ruler who wanted the best for his people. Unfortunately, he was an absolute dunderhead when it came to military matters. Ming would later be the polar opposite of his father. I sighed at the thought of just how long the road in front of me was, and I felt genuine fear at what this world might look like without someone like me in a position to help curb Ming's ambitions and violent reactions to civil unrest.

Another man walked out on stage and whispered in the elder's ear. Whatever he said, the elder was clearly put in a worse mood. I guess he didn't like someone interrupting his show.

"It appears we are out of time. The first rounds of the competition will be starting soon and we must test each of you to set up the brackets." He stepped back, giving center stage to the newcomer.

The other man began yelling orders for everyone who had not been tested yet to form four lines and approach the stage. As I rose, I saw three others come and stand next to the shouting man, and they walked to the edge of the stage together. Each of them pulled out a short bronze rod and I could feel them begin to pull in energy to activate the objects. They were simple testing devices, used to gauge the level of cultivators.

I didn't want them to know just how capable I actually was, so I began layering qi in all but the two meridians in my hands. I wanted to simulate blockages in order to trick the devices. I also stopped the flow of qi between my cores, and only kept the qi in my lower core circulating. It wasn't perfect, but I had no doubt it would fool the simple rods my clan was using. I finally made it to the front and the clan representative placed the rod on the top of my head.

"You might feel a slight pressure, but try not to move," the man said before pushing qi into the tester. He then sent out a wave of energy that traveled from my head to the soles of my feet, and lifted up the rod to read the results. He frowned and handed the device back to the elder.

"Two open meridians, low level Body cultivator, with at least two deformities. Put him in the lowest bracket, and mark him down for further review after the competition."

The man nodded at the elder, and motioned for me to move to the side of the stage that held the lowest level people that had been tested. I walked over to them and started gauging my competition.

CHAPTER SIX

So Far, So Good

The group mostly consisted of children around my age, their eyes downcast with the shame of being placed in the weakest group. I didn't recognize anyone, and no one approached me. While not huge, the Roh clan had enough people in it that I wasn't surprised I was surrounded by strangers.

I released the blockages in my meridians, and started circulating the qi in all three of my cores again. This competition did not happen in my past life, and I wanted to be ready for anything. I continued to pull qi in from only my feet, hiding in plain sight. It took the better part of an hour for them to finish with the testing, and the elder moved back to the front of the stage.

"Alright, everyone, you are now placed in your groups for the competition. We will move as a group to the battle arena for the tournament. As you all know, yesterday there was a mighty portent of change to this world, and the Roh clan must prepare itself for potential war. Your ranking in the tournament will give us a better idea of where you stand in comparison with your clanmates, and it will allow us to better plan for any upcoming battles." He waved his hands, and the doors to the exits opened. Flashy.

After looking around to see that the Body cultivators were suitably impressed, he walked towards the exit, motioning for us to follow. I held back and waited for the majority of the group to exit before me. The four testers brought up the rear, ensuring no one snuck off. I was concentrating on secretly building up my qi when I felt someone come up from behind me.

"Crazy stuff, huh? Man, I don't know how you can remain so calm with this last-minute competition coming up. I mean, they didn't even give us a day to prepare! No one was ready for this, and I imagine there will be quite a few ruffled feathers after this is all over." The speaker was a boy a few years older than my current body, probably fourteen or fifteen. He was only a few inches taller than me, but he was much wider. If he were to be diligent in his training, in a few years he would be able to hold much more muscle than my frame could support. His dark hair was long enough to frame his face, but I thought it looked odd with his square jaw line. He seemed like a nice enough fellow. "My name is Chu. Like a sneeze, but without the first half." He chuckled at his own joke, sticking his hand out in greeting.

"My name is Jim." I reached out to shake his hand. "It is nice to meet you, Chu."

He nodded, and released my hand. "Did I hear the elder correctly?" He was looking me over, as if looking for a deformity of some kind. "Do you truly have two things wrong with your body?"

"I just touched the testing stone yesterday. I don't know what they are talking about." I shrugged my shoulders, trying to convey a sense of nonchalance.

"How are you so calm, then?" Chu's eyebrows raised in surprise, and I could tell he was confused. "If I had just found out I had something wrong with me, I would be freaking out."

"First, they didn't say if my deformities were a good thing or a bad thing. Second, why worry about something outside my control? It isn't like I can fix it now, whatever it might be." I couldn't hold in the smile when I saw the flash of comprehension in his eyes.

"That makes sense. I guess I didn't think of it like that." He nodded to himself before looking back at me. "You know, someone with that level of maturity at your age is destined for great things. When all of this is over, be sure to look me up. My branch of the family is always looking for someone with a cool head."

I looked him over again, and this time I noticed how fancy his robe was compared to mine. It was the same color of light gray, but the fabric was of a much higher quality. There were also thin lines of embroidery at the wrist seams. They looked like miniature formation stitches, but I sensed no power from them. Just decoration, then. He was either from a trade, manufacturing, or mercantile branch of the family. While not the strongest in a fight, those portions of a clan were frequently the wealthiest. Besides the main family branch, of course. Chu noticed my inspection.

"My father is a trader. One day, I hope to expand our business into the neighboring provinces. The Roh families harvest some of the purest medicinal herbs in the region, but that is just the beginning! I want to turn the Roh clan into a name recognized by the entire empire!" His eyes had a faraway look in them, picturing his future trading network. "When I take over the business, even the Imperial Family will ask for our goods by name." He finished his tirade with true conviction in his voice, and I was genuinely impressed.

"I hope you find a way to make your dreams come true, Chu. I am sure that someone with your conviction will certainly go far." I knew for a fact that he would fail, because the only thing 'Roh' the emperor ever heard of—to my knowledge—was myself, but things were already changing. Maybe he would have a chance this time around.

"I mean it, Jim, stop by my family compound after the competition. Or our storefront, that would work too, I suppose.

We are located one street west of the main family compound, and our store is two buildings down from Healer Hai." His smile was genuine. It was easy to like this guy.

"I walk past your store almost every day." I waved my hand in the direction of the healing house. "In fact, my mother is one of the people who gathers the wild herbs that grow in the forest. She might already be doing business with your father."

Chu didn't have a chance to respond, because we had arrived at the arena. The elder stepped onto a raised platform next to the entrance and used wind qi to project his voice over the crowd.

"Clan members, your brackets have been decided. You need to move to the smallest set of arenas, near the far edge. The larger fields will be used by the more senior cultivators. You will receive further instructions once you reach your designated areas." The crowd started moving again, and I was separated from Chu. I had a feeling I would be seeing him again soon.

I had been formulating a plan since I had heard from Hai about the competition, but I couldn't finalize anything until I had more information. My first, and primary, plan was just to simply throw my first fight and walk away. While I could easily come first in my bracket, I didn't want to call attention to myself. I still had a lot to do before I was ready for a fight. I wanted to build up my physical strength, practice some of my preferred fighting styles in my new body, and better integrate my qi more thoroughly before risking injury.

I also hadn't even had the opportunity to find out more about the light and dark qi that Pride had mentioned. I had a sneaking suspicion that I was going to have to balance two extra elements into my body's foundation this time around, but I had yet to even tap into the new form of energy. It was hard enough the last time I went through this with six elements, and I wasn't exactly looking forward to doing it again with eight. Oh well, nothing was ever easy.

My second plan was to pretend to squeak by my first few fights, and finish somewhere in the middle of the pack. This was probably the best plan, because it meant that I wouldn't be putting a target on my back. I knew there was a penchant for the strongest to pick on the weakest, and finishing last would paint quite the target. My own cousin was a great example of this. He saw me as weak, and decided to bully me in an attempt to reinforce his place as the strongest of the new generation in our family branch.

The reason this was my second option and not my first was because I was afraid that I might tip my hand too early. To me, a simple technique that used the most minor of my skills might be seen by the people here as an amazing skill that someone might kill for. It wasn't unheard of for a cultivator with a new idea to go missing because he or she was kidnapped by someone stronger, and forced to reveal their secrets. I didn't want to have to worry about poison in my tea, or a knife in my back while I slept.

My third option was my least favorite, but one I might have to take if the prize for winning was irresistible. In which case I would have to win.

There were several things that I knew I needed. A storage device, meridian strengthening pills, formation-enhanced armor, and energy gathering formation plates were all high on the list. I could of course make my own, but the materials and time required to make them were something I didn't want to mess with right now. While I might know a fair amount about carving formations, alchemy, and blacksmithing, I was far from a Master level crafter. They could imbue complex qi matrices inside items that I hadn't bothered to spend years learning to form. I had finished the basic courses mandated by the Elemental Guard when I first joined them, but that had been a long time ago. I had specialized in fighting, not in crafting.

Of course, the basic courses the Elemental Guard received were more advanced than the average Expert level craftsman, but nowhere near the Master level. Grandmaster and Imperial level craftsmanship in any field was rare outside the Imperial City and the top sects throughout the Empire, but not unheard of. I wouldn't risk my invisibility for anything Journeyman-ranked, but it would be hard to turn down Expert-level and above.

As we reached the far side of the arena, a Meridian-level cultivator stepped forward with a large chalkboard that showed a bracket lined with numbers. Another Meridian cultivator was walking around with a canvas bag filled with numbers.

"Take a number from the bag, and find the arena with your number marked in the sand!" They were shouting instructions over the murmur of the crowd, trying to keep things organized. "The prizes will be announced once you find your positions and the judges take the stage!"

I snatched out a token as the man walked past, and saw that I was number ten. I looked at the bracket board, and saw that there was a total of 320 contestants. With that many, this was going to take forever.

Each arena was a sand-filled rectangle lined with stones. They were about fifty feet by thirty feet, and there were twenty of them surrounding a central pavilion that held a stage for the judges and the referees. A large section of seating ran down one of the long sides of the area, full of spectators.

Then, as I finally got close to the arenas, I saw it might not take as long as I thought. Each arena had eight numbers scratched into each side, for a total of sixteen contestants in each miniature battleground. That meant that everyone would be fighting. There would be no waiting for your turn, and checking out the competition. While the arenas were small enough that the fighting would be tightly spaced, it was still manageable. The random numbering system would also make it difficult for prearranged groups to gang up on weaker factions. While not perfect, it was smart. If there was a better method to get the competition for low-level cultivators done quickly, I couldn't think of it. I found my designated battlefield quickly, and eyed my teammates and competition. On my side, I immediately spotted a familiar face. I approached Chu, and shook his hand again.

"Good to see you again, my friend." Chu released my hand to point at someone across the arena. "Although I wish it was under better circumstances." I looked over my shoulder where he indicated, and saw a very large specimen.

There was a young man, probably close to eighteen, and he was huge. Well over six feet tall and probably over two hundred and sixty pounds, he was intimidation personified. I wasn't sure how much gargoyle was in his blood, but I was guessing it was a fair amount. He was preening under the fawning of his teammates, three of which were young women.

"I see what you mean." I moved to stand beside Chu. "He looks like trouble." Chu stopped looking across the arena and stared at me.

"Trouble?" I could hear him gulp. "He looks like he could defeat our entire team by himself!"

"We shouldn't beat ourselves with fear before we even fight him." I smiled, trying to reassure him. "With the right plan, we can at least ensure we don't embarrass ourselves."

"You are right, of course." Chu took a deep breath before straightening his back and nodding. "Thank you, Jim. We should try to make some sort of plan while we can." He then started gathering our teammates, most of which were just staring at the excessively large individual on the other team.

My team was evenly split, four females and four males. They all looked like they were close to Chu in age, somewhere between fourteen and sixteen. Chu was the largest, but not by much. The other two males looked like they could have been twins, and I could sense they were at the high stage of Body cultivation. They were thickly muscled for their age, but not ridiculously so.

The four females were all pretty, and all at the middle stage of Body cultivation. Those were the only two things they had in common. They were each clearly from different branches of the clan. The tallest, at about five feet and six inches, was in a snow-white robe, with her long hair a dark black that made a lovely contrast with her pale skin. The next tallest was in a brown robe, which matched her light-brown hair and eyes.

The last two females were probably within an inch of each other, both only a little over five feet tall. They were wearing the clan's traditional gray robes, and both were of a higher quality than my own. One must have been closely related with the main branch, because her eyes were a light blue and her hair was a pale white color. The last, and most timid, was most likely not originally a member of the Roh clan. She had red hair and green eyes, and I was momentarily taken aback by her porcelain beauty. If I were to venture a guess, I would say her mother was probably a trophy wife to one of the clan elders. We gathered at the back of our arena, and Chu spoke first.

"I'm Chu, and this is Jim. I am at the peak Body stage, and the strongest here. Jim is clearly the youngest and weakest, so I will designate myself to be his guardian during the match. He just touched the testing stone yesterday, so we really need to step our game up to cover for him."

The tallest of the four females looked at me with distaste and snorted. "We should just toss him at the monster over there and get it over with." An ugly sneer twisted her pretty features. "At the very least, he can distract him for a few moments while we prepare an attack."

I could tell the comment angered Chu, but I just smiled. I wasn't surprised. Cultivators were a pretty heartless group for the most part, and she was just staying true to form. I took a closer look at her and I realized she was suppressing her cultivation level. My many, *many* years of experience let me know the tiny fluctuations coming from her were clear signs of someone trying to hide their true power. She was most likely at the high stage of Body cultivation, maybe even peak. Hiding her level from her own team? Sneaky. It would be prudent to keep an eye on her.

"While I just opened up my lower core yesterday, I have spent the last few years studying battle strategy." I made sure to make eye contact with everyone, trying to show I wasn't afraid.

Which was pretty easy, since I really wasn't. "I already have a plan that could help, if you are willing to listen."

The two males looked at me with interested eyes. One of them spoke up. "I am willing to listen." The way he was looking at me didn't match his words. "Speak, boy, and prove your worth." Wow, blunt much?

"First, I need to know if any of you can project a wave of earth the distance of the arena. Ankle height would be fine, but the higher, the better." I looked around, waiting for an answer.

"I can do that," the female in the brown robe said, raising her hand. "It will pretty much empty my core, but I have a triple-wave attack meant to disrupt cavalry."

"Perfect," I said with a nod. "I can already tell, behemoth over there is going to go for a straight rush when this starts. If you can send the wave out as he takes his first step, he will already be committed. The others will simply follow him like the sheep they are, and be caught up in the same attack." I crouched, drawing what I was explaining in the sand at our feet. "The rest of you should be right behind the earth wave and strike while they are down." I finished drawing out my plan before standing back up. "If you allow him to stand up, this is going to be much more difficult." I knew we would win this round and I could see the acceptance of my plan in most of their faces. Of course, someone had to be difficult.

"That's it?" The tall girl had her hands on her hips as she looked down at me. "You have spent 'years' studying battle tactics, and that is the best you can do?" The honed edge of sarcasm in her voice was sharp enough to slice bread.

I might have been trying to hide here, but I was only willing to put up with a certain amount of personal animosity before I snapped. If she perceived me as being weak, this would only get worse.

"Look, Ice Queen." My tone conveyed my thoughts on her opinion. "You clearly have absolutely no idea what you are talking about. The more complicated the plan, the more likely it is to fail. If you don't like my plan, why don't you tell me your grand battle strategy?" She flushed bright red, either in anger or embarrassment. She opened her mouth to reply, but a gong rang out and silenced her.

We turned and looked up to the central stage. While we had been talking, we had missed the arrival of the judges and referees. There were twenty-five people, all of them in formal clothes. The referees were all in light blue robes, with a few wearing red sashes on their arms like the elder who had given the class earlier. There were even three people wearing ceremonial head coverings, their complex hats most likely covering up some embarrassing bald spots.

The elders weren't as structured, all of them wearing their own preferred fancy set of clothing. The twenty referees spread out to their assigned arenas, and the oldest of the five judges took a step forward. I felt a momentary thrill of excitement. I was finally going to find out what the prizes were, and if all of this was worth my time.

"Young members of the Roh clan, today is your opportunity to shine. You will all have the chance to fight, and those that distinguish themselves will receive the opportunity to select a prize from the clan vault!" The elder paused, as if waiting for some kind of reaction. A frown flashed across his face after not getting one, but he pasted a smile back on as he continued.

"Body cultivators that finish in the top five can access any item of their choice from the first level of the vault. The six through tenth place cultivators will receive a common core in the element of their choice, and the top half of all competitors will earn a diagram of a formation plate that they can trace in their family compound to increase the level of ambient energy for their entire branch. The lower half of all competitors will earn one gold, and the clan will offer free healing for any injuries." Now he got a reaction.

There was quite the outburst of excitement from the competitors, everyone excited to hear there were prizes no matter your place in the tournament. I, personally, was disappointed. I had no idea if the items in the clan vault were worth the effort, and everything else was practically a waste of time. I was sure I knew formation carvings that were far superior to anything they would hand out, and a common core in one element was only useful as a trade item. I was already developing a plan for earning some gold thanks to my new friend Chu, so I had no tangible reason to compete.

"Are you worried about not finishing in the top half?" Chu must have noticed my lack of excitement and had moved closer to me. "I think your plan is a good one, so you shouldn't worry too much."

"Do you have any idea what is in the vault?" I tried to make sure my question didn't betray my disappointment, but Chu was a perceptive person.

"Jim." Chu paused to take a breath. "I am beginning to think you are more than you appear. What kid your age isn't excited about prizes like that?"

I briefly smiled, and shook my head. "I am what I am, nothing more and nothing less." I needed to watch myself around Chu. I didn't want to give too much away. Something must have shown in my eyes, because he took a step back.

"Don't worry, Jim. Whether you are more than you seem, or just a very self-aware young man, no one will hear any gossip about you from me. As to your question, I have no idea what is in the vault. It hasn't been opened in my lifetime, and the elders are pretty quiet about it."

I sighed in disappointment with a tinge of relief. I might be able to trust Chu, but it looked like I would be aiming for the middle of the competition. Chu seemed to relax at my change in demeanor. The referees had moved off the stage while we had been talking and had taken their positions around the arena.

"Prepare yourselves," shouted our referee. As we lined up behind our numbers in the sand, the tall girl angled herself to pass close by.

"We aren't done, boy," she whispered angrily as she walked past me.

Oh my, I think I might have made a friend.

The team across from us was shouting taunts, and for some reason one of the females on the opposite team was pointing directly at me. I could see that they had simply selected one target each, in the most basic attack plan humanly possible. Our referee began shouting instructions.

"No deathblows will be allowed! You fight until surrender, or you are no longer able to continue! Ready? Fight!" That was rather sudden, but that was fine with me.

The female on my team wasn't ready. I could feel her begin to form her earth wave attack, but the other team was already a third of the way across the field. I spun qi through my brain core, and time seemed to slow down. I knew I couldn't move in this state, but it gave me time to think.

I measured the distance remaining, and how much qi I estimated the female would need to launch her attack. She would get it off with a few seconds to spare, but it wouldn't be tall enough to trip up the two people on the outside edges of their line of attack.

She opened her mouth, undoubtedly shouting out the name of her attack in an attempt to help focus her mind and move the qi into the form of construct she wanted to use. I personally thought it was incredibly stupid to yell out the names of your attacks when fighting, but a lot of people did it. Some thought it was a tool used to intimidate the people they were fighting, but when people did it to me, I used it to help formulate an effective counter.

Anyway, back to the matter at hand. I decided to risk a small expenditure of qi to assist the girl actively warning our enemies of our surprise attack. I couldn't sense anyone around me who would be able to tell what I was about to do, so I activated the method I was known and feared for across the entire empire. Used to be feared for. Would be feared for. Ah, stupid reincarnation shenanigans!

With my oversized brain core and extra meridian, it was hard for me to find cultivation techniques that worked. Instead of recreating the wheel, I had adapted a method that most people thought was relatively useless. The average cultivator could control five or six qi threads, but the concentration required to control each separate thread was extremely difficult. A single qi thread was useful for small tasks and fine detail work, but they were easily broken when used in attack and defense.

Most people would rather focus their time and energy on larger, more powerful attacks and defenses using a single qi construct. They were faster to master, and were obviously effective. If I wasn't forced during my early stages of cultivation to adapt to my unique upper core, I would probably be the same as everyone else.

I was unique, so instead of fighting it, I had decided to embrace it. I made my core deformity a way to drastically change the way I used qi. The ability to augment my brain made it easy for me to slow my perception of time, and increase my level of concentration. I could use far more than five or six qi threads. Instead, I could use *thousands*.

Currently, I didn't need to use nearly that many. I spun out four qi threads, and ran them from the meridians in my feet through the ground towards the two attackers on the outside edges. I prepared four more qi threads for defense, running them from the meridians in my hands and wrapping them around my forearms.

Everyone was still nearly frozen in time from my perspective, so I reduced the flow of qi in my upper core to speed things along a bit. Now it looked like they were moving under water, their qi flowing around them like waves of pure energy the color of their chosen elements.

The big guy was apparently a water cultivator, the dark blue energy flowing over his skin showing the proof of his preferred method. His danger factor went up a few notches in my eyes. Water cultivators could move very quickly, and their injuries could heal at a much faster rate. They couldn't move as fast as an air cultivator, or heal as fast as a wood cultivator, but at the Body cultivator level, the blending of the two advantages gave water cultivators an edge over their competition. I hoped my teammates were up to the challenge, because I really didn't want to step in.

Finally, the moment of impact came. I could see the big guy's eyes widen in surprise as the wave of sand rising up from the ground caught him mid-stride. They were less than ten feet away when the three small waves of dirt and sand turned their sure footing into an ankle-breaking mess.

I pushed the tips of my qi threads a few inches out of the ground and snatched at the leading feet of the attackers on either side of their line. They all fell on their faces with only a foot or two of separation from my team's line, which meant it was over quickly. Chu immediately landed a punch on the back of Mr. Gargoyle's head, and he was instantly knocked unconscious. The others landed their necessary kicks and punches, and I even handled the girl who was headed directly for me.

I waited for her to try to get to her feet before I returned time to normal. I didn't want to risk even *walking* at increased speeds without more reinforcement of my body, but slowed time wasn't necessary to beat her. I just reached down and grabbed the girl by the ear and twisted, pulling her back down to the ground.

"If you want to lose the ear, keep going." She winced as I twisted harder, trying to prove my point. "If not, submit. I don't know if the healers can reattach an ear correctly or not, but I will rip it off if you fight me." She didn't like the sound of that, and immediately raised her thumb and pinky in defeat.

It actually took me a second to figure out what she was doing, but apparently that was the Roh clan hand symbol for defeat. Good to know. I released her as I waited for the referee to announce the end of the fight, but when I looked over at him, he was clearly in a state of shock. I was worried he had seen me use my qi threads, but instead he was looking at the female who had used the ground attack.

"Uh, um, the fight is over! Numbers nine through sixteen are advanced to the next round!"

My team cheered, and the twins lifted the girl in the brown robe onto their shoulders. She was laughing in joy, and the rest of the team gathered around her in celebration. There was plenty of back slapping and hand shaking, with words of encouragement traded between them all. I only spared a moment on the group, instead looking outward at the other arenas. This was far from over, and I wanted to know as much about the others competing as possible.

We had finished so quickly that the other matches were still well underway. I only saw a few others that were at a clear advantage, and no single competitor who was at the same threat level as the giant who we had already beaten.

Looking around the arena, I happened to notice one of the judges was eyeballing my team with a fair bit of anger. He was the youngest of the elders on stage, without any gray in his hair. I saw the oldest judge tap his shoulder, and he handed a pouch over to him. Ah, a wager placed on the big guy turned sour for one of our 'impartial' judges.

I wondered briefly at how corrupt these elders might actually be, but decided it wasn't worth the effort to find out. Making side bets as a judge was certainly frowned upon, but this wasn't the Imperial City and I wasn't an Enforcer anymore. Or maybe I wasn't an Enforcer yet? This was entirely too complicated. I just hoped there weren't any other bets going on that would skew voting away from my team. Looking out at the crowd, I saw a lot more people with angry faces than I expected aimed in our direction. Apparently, the big guy had been a fan favorite of more than just the judge. A few minutes later, the final battles finished up and the head judge stepped forward once again.

"Our first round has concluded. Congratulations to our young clan members moving on to the second round of the competition!" He waited for the applause to die down before continuing. "There will be a thirty-minute break while the arenas are repaired, and you are certainly encouraged to cultivate to replace any qi you might have used in the last battle. For our next round, your teams will be divided into groups of four. If you cannot decide on your own how to divide your groups, your numbers will be redrawn into new teams. You have until the next round to decide. Don't be overly concerned, you won't have to face your teammates right away. Please move to the edge of the arenas so the earth cultivators can do their jobs." He waved his hands towards the entrance, dismissing the competitors.

Okay. I was moving on to the next round with no one noticing me. So far, so good.

CHAPTER SEVEN

Getting to the Semifinals

We moved as a group towards the entrance, and I could already see how our team would be broken up. Ice Queen had pulled the female earth cultivator to the side, and the twins had followed. That left Chu, the two short females, and myself as the members of the other team. I was fine with that. There was no way the earth cultivator could refill her core in the allotted thirty minutes, and Ice Queen and the twins clearly didn't appreciate my brilliance. I chuckled at the thought.

Chu heard me and shuffled closer. "I take it you aren't upset that the girl who wished to throw you away has chosen to leave your side?"

I looked in their direction as they further separated themselves from our group. "You hit it on the nose, Chu. Honestly, we got lucky with this team. While the earth cultivator was strong, there is no way she can gather enough qi in thirty minutes to be of any use, and the twins only listened to me because they couldn't think of a better plan than what I had proposed." I looked over at our team of four. "Our group is relatively fresh, and I have a sneaking suspicion they decided to come with us because they recognize why we actually won that fight." I eyed the two females, and they both smiled.

"We aren't dumb, Jim. It was clearly your idea that led to the quick victory," the girl with white hair spoke up, her friend almost hiding behind her. I smiled in return, and they took a step closer to Chu and I. "My name is Valerie, and this is Jamila. Before you ask, I am an air cultivator, and Jamila is a fire cultivator." My smile only grew wider. I really liked capable people, and she was clearly showing how capable she could be. I didn't even need to ask her what they could do, and she was already telling me.

"You know," I said as I looked at Chu, "I don't actually know what element you prefer. What is it?"

Chu blushed as both girls' attention was suddenly focused on him. "I can use wood and metal, but not both at the same time. I have more practice with wood, and I can use metal to defend myself. My father says when I unlock my middle core, I will be able to use both at once. I can't wait until I get there." His eyes got that faraway look again. "Can you imagine how amazing I will be? I will practically be invincible!" He danced around a bit, pretending to fight imaginary enemies. "A metal cultivator's defenses with a wood cultivator's regeneration will mean I can keep fighting long after everyone else on the battle-field falls."

I nodded in agreement. It was a great combination to have, all the way up through the Brain level. Past that, things started to balance out more. For example, it didn't matter how long you could keep fighting if you could never catch your opponent. An air and water combination would beat him senseless and he would never lay a hand on them.

"Well, I already have a plan, if you are willing to listen." All three of them jolted in surprise. What could I say? I worked fast.

"Already, Jim? Let's hear it." It was the first time I had heard Jamila speak, and her voice was as beautiful as the rest of her. I cleared my suddenly dry throat. Stupid hormones. Gods, I was going to have to deal with puberty *again*!

"I am sure you already know this, but an air cultivator can easily enhance the flames of a fire cultivator." They all nodded in agreement. "Instead of creating and directing the flames, all the fire cultivator has to do is produce a moderate-sized fireball. The air cultivator can increase the size, heat, and control the direction of the blast while using only a fraction of their power as well. So, the plan is a simple one." They all gathered closer, huddling up to keep anyone else from listening in. I knelt on the sand and waited for them to settle before continuing.

"We will stand in a diamond formation, with Chu in the front, Valerie and Jamila in the center, and I will be in the back." I drew an elongated diamond pattern out on the ground, pointing at their positions. "Chu will coat himself in metal qi, and Jamila will launch a fireball directly at his back as soon as the enemy team gets close. Valerie will launch two wind tunnels, one to either side of Chu, but passing through the fireball first. The wind will turn the simple fireball into two giant cones of flame in an instant, blasting our enemies away." I looked up to make sure they were following along, and Jamila used the opportunity to ask a question.

"Won't it hurt Chu to get blasted like that?" She was looking at him with concern, making Chu blush.

"His metal qi will protect him, and I have a plan for it. Don't forget, he can heal himself if necessary. Fire is weak to metal anyway." I motioned back to my drawing in the sand. "I will be free to provide support if there are any stragglers. Chu, your only job is to be the bait. They will hopefully pounce on you as a group, thinking you are confident and brash after defeating the giant we just beat. They won't suspect a thing. If any of them get through, don't drop your metal qi. Just stand there like a statue. It will take a moment for the temperature around you to drop, and I don't want you getting burned if we can help it. You won't even be able to breathe for the first minute of the attack. I know you can just heal yourself with wood qi if necessary, but I am trying to do this without using up all of our reserves. If this plan works, everyone should still have well over half of their qi left for the next round." Well, I think that was the most I have said all at once since my reincarnation.

My teammates were looking at me with a mixture of awe and fear. What had I said?

Chu was the first one to say something. "Gods, you are terrifying. Who thinks up things like this?" Chu hadn't stepped away from the huddle, but he was definitely leaning away from me.

Valerie answered for me. "A person who is determined to win, that's who. It sounds like a great plan to me." She turned to her friend. "Jamila?"

"I can't think of a better one." She blinked, then looked back down at the plan before turning to me. "And don't think I haven't noticed, Jim. This will be two fights in a row that you haven't had to use any qi at all. I have no doubt you have plenty of skills of your own. If this keeps going, I have no doubt who will be getting first in this tournament, level of cultivation be damned."

Wow. I think she might have made me blush. "I just unlocked my first core yesterday, Jamila. How could I have developed any techniques? Especially a technique that would allow me to take first place?" I did my best to convey a sense of innocence.

She frowned at the question. "I don't know how, but I just have a feeling. My intuition is seldom wrong." She just stared at me as I shrugged. Hard to argue that point.

Valerie came to my rescue once again. "Either way, we should all take the time we have left to cultivate as much as we can," she said, pointing at the rest of the competitors. They looked around and realized that we were the only ones not focused on replenishing their energy. We all sat, and I could feel the pull on the energy around us as they started funneling it into their bodies.

While I pulled in a small amount of qi through my hands, the only meridians I was supposed to have open according to the testing rods, I took the time to think. Jamila was definitely wrong about one thing. I most definitely wasn't going to be placing first. I only needed to place in the top five to get into the vault, and I was still on the fence about ranking even that high.

I could see how the setup for the matches was going, and I was still impressed with the efficiency. The first round had two teams of eight facing off against one another, ensuring all twenty arenas were used at once, and all 320 competitors would fight. This round used two teams of four in all twenty arenas, once again ensuring all 160 fought at the same time, with the same amount of break time between matches. I was pretty sure the next round would split us into teams of two, all eighty still fighting, and then the solo matches would begin. One round of one-on-one to determine the top twenty, and a final round featuring the last ten would determine the top five who would gain access to the vault.

That meant I would potentially have to fight two single matches, and I would be forced to show some of my capabilities. I guess it really depended on who my opponents were, how difficult it would be to defeat them, and whether I wanted to risk winning.

The time finally came, and we all quickly found our arena. We immediately fell into formation without any discussion, and I felt everyone begin cycling their cores. The referee caught us off guard last time, and we wouldn't let it happen again.

The elder made some speech about glory and victory, but I didn't bother listening. It was a pointless speech, less about morale and more about the elders getting a chance to hear themselves talk.

I was focused on our opponents instead. All four of them were males, around sixteen years old. Three were above average in size, but not nearly as large as the gargoyle-sized man we faced in our last match. The one leading them was whipcord thin, and I could tell he was the real threat. I was guessing he would rush Chu, engaging him while the other three came up to smash him. That is what I was hoping, anyway. I looked at the girls.

"Wait to launch your attack until the three bigger ones are in range. Chu can handle a few blows from the thin one." I could see the question in their eyes, but they both nodded and faced forward once again. Eventually, the elders got tired of talking, and the referee finally raised his arm.

"Same rules as the last match. Ready? Fight!" There was a much longer pause between the words ready and fight this time around. The surprised look on our last referee's face, coupled with the speed of the last team we faced and the anger of the younger-looking judge made me rethink the corruption level of this competition. How bent was this organization? Was it completely broken, or just close? I refocused, and I looked on as my team enacted the plan.

I had been correct in my assumption that the thin attacker would jump in the lead, but I was wrong about his target. He was coming straight for Jamila, and the other three were headed towards Chu. Luckily, Chu was up to the task. He jumped to the side, intercepting the lead attacker before he could get past him.

"Iron Soldier!" shouted Chu, forming a thin metal coating over his entire body before colliding with the thin cultivator trying to flank him. The other three kept to form, sprinting to the aid of their leader. Chu was trying to grapple with the thin guy, but he was getting the shit kicked out of him.

The girls weren't waiting any longer, and Jamila shouted out something like 'Phoenix Burn,' before launching a fireball, but I wasn't really listening. I was focusing on the distance from the three trailing behind, and I didn't like what I saw. They were going to be too far away for the fire and wind tunnels to do any real damage.

"Wind Blades!" shouted Valerie, shoving her hands out in front of her. I instantly relaxed. Valerie had seen the necessity to change the plan, and acted accordingly.

The arcs of wind collided with the slow-moving ball of fire, and the hell storm that followed would have been impressive for any Heart-level cultivator to pull off. I watched as the group of wind blades picked up the flame-aspect qi and turned into miniature comets of doom. Two of them slammed into the thin cultivator, and a cluster of eight hit the three buffoons closing with Chu. They were thrown off their feet, all of them crying out in pain. The referee instantly threw out a wave of water qi, quenching the flames before anyone was injured too severely. After ensuring there wasn't any immediate need for medical assistance, he turned and looked at us.

"Good job, cultivators, you all advance to the next round." His praise seemed genuine, making me think he wasn't a part of the illegal gambling ring. I rushed over to Chu, but he was getting to his feet as I approached.

"Are you okay? That definitely didn't go exactly as planned." I looked him over as I talked, looking for any obvious injuries.

"It went better than I expected," he said with a smile, brushing himself off. "He was really laying into me there, but my metal qi shell held up." He had some scrapes and bruises, but he wasn't nearly as bad off as I expected. I heard the girls come up behind me.

"Chu, are you okay? That guy was really laying into you." Jamila had grabbed him by the shoulder and commenced with poking and prodding him, looking for injuries.

"No, he barely scratched me." Chu was basking in the attention, practically striking a heroic pose. "I am tougher than I look. Honestly, the heat from that crazy fire storm you two unleashed hurt worse than what he did to me. I didn't get a chance to hold my breath, so it is definitely a good thing you didn't go with that fire wall thing we first talked about."

"He is right, you know." I looked at Valerie. "Your quick thinking is what really got us the win this round. If it wasn't for your wind blades, I don't think the other three would have been in range."

She blushed at the praise, staring at her feet in embarrassment. "I could tell a simple wind tunnel or two wouldn't do the job. I didn't know if the wind blades would meld with the fire or not, but I knew that they would at least buy us a few moments."

We all nodded to show our agreement. It had been a good idea.

"Sometimes, it is better to be lucky than to be sure. Either way, good win, everyone." I went to stand next to Chu. "Now, I would recommend when we split that you two continue to use the same technique, because no one else could have seen you use it. We are the first ones done again."

They were visibly confused. Chu spoke up first. "Wait, you know how the next rounds will go? Can you see the future?" It was like the girls were struck by lightning. Now all three of them were looking at me with suspicion.

"That would explain so much! I knew there was something different about you!" Valerie seemed triumphant, as if her declaration had solved the world's greatest mystery. What was with these people?

I couldn't help it, I burst out laughing. I don't know if I had heard a statement that was more completely correct and incorrect at the same time. See the future? I lived it!

"No, my friends," I said after catching my breath enough to answer. "I cannot see the future; I can just perform basic math and use deductive reasoning. There are twenty arenas, and they want to use them all at the same time. They also don't want anyone getting more of a break between fights than anyone else. That means they have to keep dividing the teams in half." I waved my hand between the four of us to indicate the teams I thought would work best. "So, like I said, you two should use some variation of the same attack in your next fight, and Chu and I will think of something for our round."

I could see the calculation go through their heads, and they eventually realized their mistake.

Chu had done the math the fastest, and was the first to give me a chagrined smile. "I see, I guess that makes more sense. You can't fool us though, Jim." He stuck his finger in my face.

"What ten-year-old uses words like 'deductive reasoning'? I am going to figure out how you can do all this eventually."

I decided silence was the better part of valor.

Suddenly, I felt a qi thread brush my shoulder. I tried not to react, but my reflexes caused me to make a slight turn before I caught myself. I looked out of the corner of my eye and saw a retreating air thread that led back to one of the judges. It was the one on the far left. I hadn't heard him speak yet. He appeared to be middle aged, which meant he could be anywhere from fifty to four hundred years old. Age was difficult to measure with cultivators.

He had black hair, with white at the temples. He had a thick beard that reached his chest, and his features seemed somewhat familiar. I could tell that he had seen me notice his qi, and the glint in his eye concerned me. The trick he just used was a thread of air qi that cultivators spun out to those far away in an attempt to eavesdrop. It was a common tactic used the world over, and I should have noticed it sooner.

I silently kicked myself as Jamila walked over.

"I see you noticed my father poking into our business. Somehow, I am not surprised you can detect an air qi thread thin enough that most Brain cultivators would miss it." She looked towards where her father was sitting. "It took me years to notice him listening in on my private conversations. I wouldn't worry too much about him though, he is harmless."

I thanked her, and we started our walk back towards the entrance area before anyone had to tell us. It was easy for her to say that, he was her father. I had a sneaking suspicion he wasn't as harmless as she made him out to be. A few minutes after we reached the waiting area, the other matches ended, and the oldest elder took center stage again.

"Congratulations, young warriors! The second round is over, and the top eighty contestants have been decided. At this time, your teams must be split again. Just like last time, if you cannot decide how to divide yourselves, we will hold a small drawing to decide for you. You have thirty minutes to cultivate while we fix the arenas. Remember, you have all come far, but the hardest part is yet to come. Your endurance will play a much larger role in the matches that follow." He waved to a team of earth cultivators along the far edge of the arena, and they got to work fixing the damaged battlegrounds.

The girls gave each of us a hug and we went our separate ways. Chu spent a long time watching them walk away.

"Do you think Jamila liked me? Stars, that girl is beautiful." Chu's eyes were glazed over again. He was definitely a daydreamer.

I replayed the afternoon over in my mind, and shook my head. "I have no idea. She was the first to run and check on you, but who knows the mind of a teenage girl? I think women of all ages are one of the great mysteries of the universe."

Chu chuckled at my comment, and nodded in agreement. "Well, Jim, just as I thought the moment we first teamed up. It is just you and me now, my friend." He hooked his arm around my shoulder and started to walk us a bit farther away from everyone else. "What glorious plan do you have for the two of us?"

I frowned in thought. "This is going to be much more difficult. It will all depend on who we are facing. As long as they don't have a water cultivator, we should be fine. You use your metal or wood qi to fight them, and I will attack as soon as I see an opening. I only have my hand meridians, but I can use them to strengthen my fists. A few blows in the right places, and we might make it."

Chu nodded in agreement and immediately sat on the ground to start cultivating to replace his spent qi.

I looked around at those who had come this far, and I was honestly surprised to see that the Ice Queen had made it through. I kept looking around and finally spotted the twins. It appeared as if they had been run roughshod over a washboard, and I quickly realized how she had made it through the round. It was pretty apparent she had charmed the twins with her good looks, and used them to take the brunt of the match. After it was over, she dumped them and kept the earth cultivator. Now it was her turn to rise a notch in my danger estimate. Someone that devious was most definitely a person I needed to keep an eye on.

Soon the thirty minutes were up, so Chu and I moved out in search of our designated arena. As we were walking, I felt her highness of ass-hats approach. I paused to let her pass. I didn't want her walking up behind me without having eyes on her. I saw her pull something back into the sleeve of her robe. I raised an eyebrow in return, letting her know I had seen her hide something. She didn't even have the common courtesy to look ashamed. Instead, she seemed angry that I had dared to interrupt her nefarious plans.

"I will end you this day, *insect*, and there is nothing you, or anyone else, can do about it."

Wow, what a winner this lady was in the personality contest. I hated bullies, and this girl was definitely the definition of one. I was getting tired of being called names, so I decided to show her that I was not a pushover. If I didn't stop this now, word would spread and I would be facing problems like her for the rest of the time I was in the Roh clan.

I raised my voice so everyone could hear. "I formally challenge you to a match to the death. No surrender, no second chances. Face me, you oversized pile of horse dung, and I will bury you under a manure pile where you belong."

Everyone froze. The look of sheer incredulity on her face was amazing. I don't think anyone had spoken like that to her before. Not only that, I could sense the fear in her. She had to know for me to say something so self-assured, I had something up my own sleeve that would end in her death. Either that, or I was completely insane. She knew she couldn't risk it. She took a step back, and opened her mouth to answer. Before she could retort, Jamila's father was suddenly standing between us. Definitely favored the air element for him to move that fast.

"No personal duels today, children, and no duels to the death until after you are adults. Both of you know this. Now, go to your separate battlefields before I disqualify you from the tournament entirely!"

He seemed mad. Oh well, Mr. Eavesdropper could piss off.

I silently turned away and walked towards my arena. I could hear the talking dung heap sputtering in response, but I just kept walking. The moment was over, time to move on. I would probably have to kill her later, but now I would have to do it quietly. If she died too soon, people would automatically assume I did it, and I had drawn enough attention as it was.

This time Chu and I were in an arena located in one of the far corners, farthest from the crowd of onlookers and judges. Maybe I could risk winning this one after all. I didn't really care about winning, but losing now would mean Chu would miss out on a chance to make the top ten. He genuinely was a good cultivator, and he deserved to go as far as possible. Besides, I was beginning to like the guy.

Our opponents arrived a few moments later, and I almost laughed. It was the twins. The thirty minutes weren't nearly long enough for them to recover from the beating they received in their last match, and I could tell they knew it too. They approached the middle of the field, and waved us over.

"We were idiots. Fooled by a pretty face." They were both looking down at their shoes, shame keeping them from meeting our eyes. "Now we realize who the real power was behind our first win."

We stood in silence for a minute, but then Chu decided to speak up. "I get it, guys. She is really pretty, even if she is just a pretty snake." They finally raised their heads. "How do you guys want to do this?"

The other twin finally said something. "We are going to give it our best shot, but we can both barely put together a single qi strand. Just promise us, if either of you comes up against that harpy, you make sure to beat her bloody. She didn't lift a hand to help us last round, just sat back and shouted insults at the other team." Anger flashed across his face. "Sometimes, at her own team. Be careful though, I think she has some form of weapon hidden in her right sleeve. She was messing with it between rounds."

We obviously agreed, and shook hands before returning to our own sides.

"How do you want to win this?" Chu was whispering, trying to keep the twins from hearing our plans. "If they are as worn out as they look, I can probably take them both by myself." I took a moment to gauge his qi levels, then I shook my head.

"You still haven't replaced all the qi you used in the last match. I will handle them. You focus on bringing your qi back to maximum for the next round." I took a long look at all the people still in the tournament. "I think you have a shot at making the top ten at least, but only if you are at full strength. In fact, if you want to just sit and cultivate the whole time, I wouldn't mind."

Chu just smiled, raising an eyebrow. "Okay, Jim, if that is how you want to play this. I won't even bother to mention how *interesting* it is that you, a person who just opened their core yesterday, know how much qi I have left. If it was anyone else, I would say they were crazy, but I have begun to learn that I shouldn't doubt you."

I smiled in return, and moved out to the center of the field.

"I'll figure you out eventually, Jim!" he called out to me as I walked away. Maybe he would, maybe he wouldn't. I waved him off as I faced my opponents.

The twins were clearly surprised when it was just me walking out to meet them, but they obviously weren't taking the move lightly. I saw them begin whispering furiously to one another, and they were clearly concerned.

Another referee, this one with a red arm band, finally came over. I could hear him snort. "Just you against those two? This should be the fastest defeat in the whole competition." The twins just looked at him, and returned their attention to me. The shock on his face at their reaction was obvious. He took a closer look at me, and he was definitely confused. He had no idea why the two larger boys weren't laughing at his joke, and were instead taking me seriously. "Whatever," he said, getting in position. "Get ready. The fight starts in a few minutes."

In reply, I spun out two fire qi threads, one from each hand, and pumped a small amount of energy into them, thickening them into qi strands. I had decided to use one of my most basic attacks, fire whips. They were simple enough that they wouldn't draw an undue amount of attention, but versatile enough to cover most eventualities these two could produce. The use of whips also made it easy to explain away any advanced skills. After all, I could have just used regular whips to train, and only used qi strands after I opened my core. It was also extremely easy to combine and harden the whips into a flame staff, but I didn't think it would be necessary.

The twins across from me crouched into sprinter's stances. They were clearly planning to just rush me and try to overpower me with their greater mass. I kind of felt bad for them.

The referee, a bored expression on his face, finally raised his arm. "Ready? Fight!"

The twins sprang forward, and I lifted both arms up, the whips trailing on the ground behind me. I waited for them to cross into my half of the arena, and snapped both arms forward. The whips launched towards the twins, aiming for their legs.

One tried to block, and the other tried to sidestep. The one who tried to block just got a whip wrapped around his forearm instead of his leg, and the other didn't dodge quite far enough. The very tip of the whip caught the inside edge of his heel as he was planting his foot for another jump forward. I pulled. The one with the whip around his arm was yanked forward, his arm popping out of socket at the shoulder.

The one who was practically standing on the whip was flipped into the air, his head almost instantaneously replacing his feet. He impacted with enough force on the sandy ground that I was worried I might have broken his neck, but the stirring of sand in front of his unconscious face indicated that he was still alive.

The first twin had vomited from the pain, whether from the fire whip scorching his forearm or the dislocated shoulder, I wasn't sure. I released my hold on the qi strands, and the fire instantly dissipated. I looked over at the judge, and his formerly bored expression was gone. Instead, he looked worried. That was new. What had he done before the match that made my winning worry him?

"Referee, isn't this over with?" I asked, raising my voice. "You should call the fight."

His look of worry was replaced with one of anger. "Know your place, contestant! This isn't over until I say it is! Besides, that one hasn't submitted yet. Until he does, this isn't finished."

Wow, this guy might have been the dumbest rock in the rock pile. I looked over at the twin still awake, and saw he was trying to get to his feet. I wasn't sure why, because there was no way he could win. And he had to know it too. I decided to end this quickly. He needed medical attention. I walked over to him, ready in case he was planning a surprise attack.

As I got close, I could see the light in his eyes was out. His body was only moving on instinct at this point, and he was one conk on the head away from nap-nap time. I walked over and smacked my hand against his ear, knocking him the rest of the way unconscious. I looked over at the referee, this time simply judging him with my eyes. He could see exactly what I thought of him, and he flushed with shame. Maybe anger. Probably both.

I turned away from him and started walking to the entrance, collecting Chu along the way. The referee simply waved over the stretcher teams, silently ending the fight. They rushed forward, clearly worried more about the twin I had flipped than the one with a dislocated and burned arm. I really hoped Healer Hai was capable enough to handle injuries like this.

I was quietly fuming the whole walk back, angry at the referee for drawing out the process. I did not enjoy hurting those two, and drawing out their suffering because of a lost bet or injured pride rankled my internal sense of justice. I was thinking about how far I was willing to go to root out the corruption in this clan when Chu interrupted my musings.

"Jim, that was incredible. Two simple strands of qi from a lower stage Body cultivator absolutely *destroyed* two cultivators at the high stage. No one will believe it. Stars, I was there and I hardly believe it!"

I raised a corner of my mouth in a smile. "You know, I was probably just lucky. They only had enough qi to augment their bodies, which gave me the distance advantage. I am good with a regular whip, so I figured I could use qi in the same way. If they had been able to project their qi out of their bodies, I think the fight would have gone much differently."

Chu nodded, but I could tell he wasn't convinced. I wasn't worried. I had a feeling I had won over my first follower in this new life.

"Either way, you taking those two down gave me a fair shot at winning the next round. Win or lose, I still owe you a debt. Now you *must* swing by my family's shop sometime, so I can make this right."

I wasn't going to argue with him. After all, ten-year-old me had pretty much nothing to my name. I needed to start gathering resources as soon as possible.

We reached the waiting area by the entrance and I was a little surprised to see we weren't the first ones to arrive. The competition was sifting out the weak, and the ones who were still here were either the strongest or the cleverest the youngest generation of the clan had to offer. Minus the gargoyle we took out in the first round, of course. Either way, we were now looking at the last few fights. It was time for the semifinals.

CHAPTER EIGHT

Need to Be Careful

The highest-ranking judge took center stage. Again. Didn't this guy get tired of hearing himself talk?

"The time to determine the strongest individuals has come. Before, you were tested on your ability to work as a member of a large group. Then, you were tested to see which of you could fight in a team. Your last match was a test to see how you could function with a single partner. Now, we will see how you handle a fight with only yourself to depend on. This has all been a test to see how you might function in our military. You might be expected to fight in the main army, serve on a special team, act as a sentry patrol, or sent out as a scout. Those who have shown they can succeed will be given the best positions in the event of an attack or outright war."

Well, color me impressed! The forethought and planning that went into this whole event was much more involved than I expected, especially for such a last-minute tournament. Someone higher up in the chain of command was a very capable individual.

"The matches will be determined by demonstrated

strength." The elder looked around the contestants, judging them with his eyes. "The judges will confer and post the brackets in thirty minutes. The strongest will rise to the top, and their rewards will be great!"

The crowd and competitors roared in approval. Everyone loved prizes, even me. This was most likely going to be my final match, even though my curiosity about the contents of the vault was killing me.

I decided to do some stretches. This new body wasn't constantly ready to fight like my old body was, and I needed to keep that in mind. I knew I had an audience so I figured it was time to start setting up some possible assumptions for others to make about my capabilities. Some basic katas from one of the martial art styles I knew would show those around me that I practiced physical fighting forms, and it would help provide an excuse for any advanced moves I might make in the future.

I started with some slow forward punches paired with long lunges, and transitioned into slow turns while executing high blocks by swinging my arms across my body and upwards above my head. Soon, I lost myself to the flowing motions taught to me centuries ago by a teacher who was long dead. Well, long dead to me.

As I was finishing my last set of proscribed motions, I took notice of those around me. The entire waiting area was silently staring at me. Chu was towards the back, clearly attempting to mimic what he could remember. As I wiped the sweat from my brow, it was like the other thirty-nine people in the roped-off area suddenly remembered how to breathe. They all looked away from me, mumbling to themselves and whispering to one another.

There were four notable exceptions. Chu was looking at me with clouded eyes, as if picturing something else while he watched. Probably imagining how to turn his newfound friend into some form of profit. I didn't mind at all, as long as his plans included cutting me in on a hefty percentage.

Valerie and Jamila were also openly staring, both of them wearing determined looks on their faces. I wasn't sure what they were so determined about, but I felt some butterflies in my stomach. They were both really pretty, after all. Oh, how I was dreading puberty.

The other watcher was the future corpse, the beautiful but cold Miss Ice Queen. The pure hatred in her eyes only cemented my plan to kill her. Some people just rubbed me the wrong way, and she knew how to push all my buttons. I was going to have to find a way to kill her. Sooner rather than later.

I could tell she was thinking the exact same thing about me, and this body had absolutely zero precautions built up for poison immunity. I was dreading that process as well. It had taken me the better part of a year the last time I went through poison therapy, and it had nearly killed me. Developing an immunity through gradual exposure to most poisons was a long and painful process, but I knew it would be a necessity. The path I had chosen to walk demanded no less. She might not use poison, but I had a feeling she was sneaky like that.

A gong sounded and we all headed towards the judges' pavilion. I saw the chalkboard, but there were no numbers marked on the brackets. What had we just waited around for thirty minutes for? Finally, the youngest of the elders stepped forward.

"Competitors, please assemble in the original teams you were assigned. As many members as remains, that is." We all shuffled around until we were back in our groups. Chu, Valerie, and Jamila situated themselves around me, so the Ice Queen and the earth cultivator couldn't approach me while we were standing close together. I appreciated the gesture, even if it wasn't necessary.

I was surprised to see that our group was the largest remaining. Everyone else was standing in groups of either four or two. The judges quickly jotted down numbers, and finally posted the brackets.

Ah, I saw what happened. They had decided to make sure

we never faced someone who we had been teamed up with. The judges wanted everyone to face an opponent that they had no prior knowledge of, to better represent the circumstances of a scout coming across an enemy on the battlefield. A scout would certainly have no knowledge of a single cultivator they might come across while on a mission, so they had to be prepared for anything.

Seriously, I was getting some major dichotomy from the Roh. There was a clear and deep-seated level of corruption, but the leadership decisions and planning for this competition were top-notch.

I was beginning to wonder if the people making military plans were normally outside the decision-making process of the day-to-day operations in the clan. That would actually explain a lot. If someone were to remove the corrupted elements and empower the capable members of the hierarchy, this clan could actually be quite formidable.

It reminded me of the politicians and members of the nobility in the Imperial City, and the military leadership of the Elemental Guard and Royal Army. When things actually got rough, the politicians and nobles were self-aware enough to shut up and let the real leaders take charge. But, as soon as things calmed down, they decided to take the rudder and steer the ship where it best served themselves. No matter the size of the group, the same problems always existed.

Ah well, nothing I could do about it now. I saw my first match was once again in a far corner, this time on the opposite side near the entrance but closest to the crowd. I would have to be careful; I had no idea who might be watching.

I moved into position and waited for my opposite to show. The referee was already in place. It was the same man from the first match. Great, another thing to worry about. If he had a bet placed against me, there was no telling what he might do to skew the match. He was still wearing a red arm band. What was it about people wearing red today?

My opponent finally walked up just as the match was about

to start. I see. He didn't want to give me any time to size him up before the match to ensure I couldn't formulate a plan to take him down. Clearly, someone had warned him about me.

Unfortunately for him, no one here really knew what I could do. I simply spun the qi in my brain core a bit faster and moved my perception of time to a crawl.

He was a fire cultivator, and at the high Body level. I could see the heat shimmer from his fire qi building along his forearms in a technique I was unfamiliar with. Fire gauntlets, maybe? Or perhaps he was forming fire blades along the outsides of his forearms in an attempt to slice and burn me to pieces?

That was actually a cool idea; I needed to remember that one. You could easily turn an arm block into an offensive strike, thereby using your enemy's own momentum to drive their kicks or punches onto your arm blades. Metal qi might work better, but if they were wearing armor, fire could heat the metal enough to burn them. Definitely a neat trick.

I also found it curious that I found a strong fire cultivator as my opponent. I mean, the chances were one in six, but I wasn't facing my first fire cultivator until after I had shown I could use fire. It would be harder for me to take down a fire cultivator with fire whips. Not impossible, just more difficult.

I supposed I could just use metal, as that would be what a fire cultivator was weakest against, or earth, as it was also a strong choice, but I didn't want to give away too many of my secrets. If everyone thought I could only use fire, they would plan any future attacks against me using that as the foundation for their ambushes.

Unfortunately for them, fire was actually my weakest affinity. I decided to stick with the fire whips, and if I couldn't defeat him within three minutes, I would throw the match. If I couldn't beat this poor sap in three minutes, I deserved to lose anyway.

With a plan finally in place, I allowed my perception of time to return to normal. I spun out my fire whips for the second time today, this time making sure to create them just a tad bit smaller. It would appear that I was slowly running out of qi in my core, but in reality, I was just condensing the energy into a hotter fire.

Once again, I kind of felt bad for the guy I was about to face. I threw my arms out to either side and with a roll of my wrists I positioned the whips behind me and to the sides. I probably looked like a giant V shape from above, the tip of my body the point and the wings the whips of flames.

The boy across from me was probably seventeen, with pale hair, light eyes, and a medium build, wearing a red robe that looked like silk. He could pass for Valerie's older brother. Actually, he might be Valerie's older brother. How was I supposed to know?

The boy jumped forward, crossing the centerline in front of the referee just as he yelled fight. Not even a ready this time. It was like they weren't even trying to hide their cheating any more, and right in front of the crowd!

I snapped my left-hand whip straight at his face, forcing him to backpedal to his own side of the arena. I rolled my wrist back sharply, getting the whip back in position.

"Quick, I'll give you that. Too bad though, little boy! I need to save my energy for the next round, so I will finish this now!" My opponent struck what he must have imagined to be a manly stance. I thought he looked dumb.

Ugh, stupid posturing. What was with cultivators? I wouldn't be shocked if he was going to shout out some stupidly pretentious name for an attack that was underwhelming at best.

"Dragon's Fire Strike!"

Yep, called it.

I felt him force fire qi out of a meridian in his right hand and bend it to his will. His fancy fireball was barely larger than a rain barrel, so I simply slid to my right and snapped my left whip at his attack, laying my qi strand along the side of his construct. I forced a little willpower through my qi whip at the moment of impact, and deflected it straight at the referee. Heh. Surprise, jerk.

I swung my right arm forward, snapping my whip straight at my opponents face again. He tried to just lean backwards to avoid the strike, but I simply lengthened the qi strand an extra inch and popped him right across the mouth with the very tip of my whip.

The fireball I had deflected at the referee exploded just as the sensory input from my whip impacting my opponent's face reached his brain. I honestly couldn't tell who was screaming louder. Apparently, the referee wasn't doing his job, and he had absolutely no defensive shields in place. The fireball splashed flames all over his fancy robes and nice hat, and he was dancing around as the flames were starting to burn into his skin.

My opponent dropped to his knees; his mouth neatly split vertically in half. He kind of looked like he had four lips now, and he was spraying out blood and bits of teeth in a rather impressive arc several feet in front of him. I deactivated my whips, and looked back at the guy wreathed in flames.

For a moment, I was torn. Clearly no one was expecting this outcome. I was afraid I was going to have to step in and put the referee out, otherwise he was going to go up like a piece of dry kindling.

However, I didn't want to expose my ability to control water qi, and the amount of energy it would take to put out those qi flames would be beyond the ability of someone at the lower stage of Body cultivation. I would be giving away far more than just one of my secrets.

On the other hand, this guy was a corrupt piece of trash that deserved everything he got. Not only was he corrupt, the fact he was on fire showed he was incompetent.

Luckily, a spectator stepped in. An older gentleman with blond and gray hair and beard vaulted out of the stands and immediately started soaking the human candle in a mixture of water and wood qi. He was wearing leather armor studded with bronze plates, and I could see each small plate had tiny formation runes carved into them. I guessed they were miniature formation plates designed to enhance the wearer, or deflect projectiles and hostile qi. I was impressed by his use of water and wood. The mixture would not only put out the fire, but start the healing process.

He then cast a strand of wood qi towards my opponent. By this point, he had fallen on his side, hands holding his face together and tears streaming down his cheeks. It was hard to understand him, but I was pretty sure he was sobbing at the loss of his pretty face. I didn't think he was good looking enough to cry about his busted features, but what did I know? The shock of the foreign wood qi knocked the poor boy unconscious, and I could see the bleeding from his face already starting to slow.

"Healers!" the man shouted over his shoulder at the stretcher-bearers standing by the entrance. "Get over here, it is obvious this match is over." He then angled himself to speak towards the audience. "This boy literally just won this match on accident. Elder Eso's boy launched a lazy attack, and the boy here easily deflected it. Then, the incredibly stupid referee allowed it to hit him!" He looked at the charred figure getting rolled onto a stretcher. "The idiot didn't even have a shield in place. I can't believe how awful this whole incident makes the Roh clan look. Oh well, looks like good luck can beat strength! Congratulations on your victory, boy." The armored man winked at me, and jumped back into the stands.

Great. Now that guy thought I owed him a favor. He jumped in, saved the dying guy, called the match in my favor, and even narrated a version of events that shifted all of the blame off of my shoulders and solidly onto those of the referee and my opponent. I could already hear the crowd in the stands murmuring in agreement, and a few people were even shouting in anger at how poorly the referee had handled the match.

I could have done all of that myself, but now Mr. Hero thought he was my savior. Worse still, his wink told me he knew exactly what I had done. Or at least he thought he knew. There was no way he could actually know if I intended the fireball to blast the referee, the only thing he could be sure of was that I extended the length of the whip just enough to knock the other kid in the mouth. It showed him I had exceptional qi control, but that was all. I needed to be careful with any future dealings I might have with him.

CHAPTER NINE

Keeping a Low Profile

I started walking back towards the entrance, and saw that once again I was one of the last fighters to finish. My fight was probably the first one done, but all the commotion made it end later than it should have. I looked for Chu, and I was relieved to see he was still here. Ice Queen, Valerie, and Jamila were all here as well. I didn't see the earth cultivator.

Just as I reached the roped-off area, the gong rang. I was confused. Weren't we supposed to get thirty minutes?

I trailed behind the others as they moved towards the stage, walking slowly and using the meridians in my feet to secretly refill my cores. I was starting to get a bad feeling about this.

The youngest elder stepped forward to speak. "Congratulations, champions! You twenty are the cream that has risen to the top!" He waited for the applause to die down a bit before continuing. "Unfortunately, time grows short, and we must finish this competition with all haste. Just like on the real battlefield, things don't always go as planned, so you must adapt and overcome! Instead of the structured battles we had planned to use to determine the top ten and top five contestants, we will be simulating a real battle! A grand melee, every cultivator for themselves!" There were more than a few shouts from the crowd, but he raised his hands and talked over them.

"The fight will continue until only one person remains. As before, no death blows, and you keep fighting until submission or unconsciousness. The judges and referees will keep track of who falls in which order. Your ranking will be determined by the order in which you fall. Outlast your foes, and be the last man, or woman, standing!"

Yep, there it goes. I knew I had a bad feeling about this.

"You all have five minutes to prepare. Good luck!" It might have been my imagination, but I was pretty sure he was looking right at me as he said that.

I started walking to the far side of the arena, opposite the crowd. I wanted to be as far away from prying eyes as possible. I glanced behind me and saw Chu following close behind. Tailing him were Valerie and Jamila, and I was genuinely surprised to see the grand snake herself, Ice Queen, following behind them. I turned around to face them as I reached the edge and sat down to cultivate as they approached. I was already back up to my pre-fight levels of qi, but they didn't know that.

"Hi Jim," Chu said as he approached confidently. "I figured you wouldn't mind if I happened to stand next to you while this madness was going on." I smiled, and indicated with my chin that he should sit at my right. The next two arrived, Valerie leading Jamila by the hand.

"Gentlemen, I didn't know if you noticed, but the lovely elder who came up with this plan forgot to say anything about temporary alliances." Valerie was smiling as she talked, while Jamila was quietly watching Chu. "In fact, we could simply stick together right up until the very end, and determine who gets first place by drawing straws."

"I did in fact notice that lapse in the rules, Valerie." I smiled in return. "You two are more than welcome to join us." I pointed to my left, and the two girls sat next to me, Valerie right beside me and Jamila next to her.

Finally, the serpent arrived. She held up her hand in a stopping motion, and I waited for her to speak.

"I was wrong, I admit it. I was so obsessed with your weak cultivation level that I failed to see what you are truly capable of." She was staring at the sand in front of me, refusing to meet my gaze. "I saw how you managed the first fight, and I tried to replicate it in the second. Saving all of my strength, while others fought in my stead. It didn't go smoothly." She finally raised her head to look me in the eyes. "My anger at my own failings made me lash out at you, and instead of folding under the pressure of my threat, you threw it right back in my face. I was convinced you would never make it this far, and you once again proved me wrong. I only wish to fight by your side, and prove myself to be more than what you have seen. Please, give me another chance."

Wow. Not quite what I was expecting, but I bet her end goal was still the same. Stick with us for as long as possible, and stab us in the back as soon as she got the chance. Even if everything she said was the truth, and I had completely misjudged her, she was still hiding her true cultivation level. I couldn't trust her, no matter what she said.

"What is your name?"

She looked taken aback at my question. I guess in her mind every random stranger should know who she was.

"You don't even know my name?" From the look on her face, it seemed to me as if she seldom required an introduction. "It is Xie, daughter of the retired General Quwe."

I nodded. I supposed she actually didn't need to tell people who she was very often. Having a prestigious father had probably inflated her ego from a very young age.

"Okay, Xie, here is the deal. I can't trust you. You are too far outside my circle of trust for me to allow you to fight beside us." Her face fell. Instead of the anger I was expecting to see, I saw disappointment. Either she was a very good actress, or she genuinely was sorry. Had I really misjudged her? "However, I do have a plan that might see you through the fight." Hope shone in her eyes, and I almost felt bad for what I was about to do to her.

"Whatever plan you have, I am willing to follow." She looked back down at her feet. "Failure is not an option for me."

"What element do you use, Xie?"

She looked back up at me. Were those tears in the corners of her eyes?

"I can use water and air. I am an ice user. That is why when you called me an ice queen, it actually hurt my feelings."

I sighed. Maybe I was being too harsh. These were only kids, after all. I mean, was I actually planning on killing a fifteen-year-old girl? What was wrong with me? This whole reincarnation thing was throwing me off my game. I would have never thought about taking the life of a child before. But why were my instincts still telling me something was wrong? I needed to pay close attention to this girl before making any decisions.

"That is actually perfect, Xie. What I want to do is set up a trap of sorts. You are going to run around the arena and draw people towards us." I looked to my left.

"Valerie, Jamila, you two keep doing what you have been with enhancing each other. You will take point this time. I will stand to the right, and Chu will stand to the left." I looked to my right.

"Chu, you pump as much wood qi as possible into Xie as she runs past you. The little bit of healing it will provide should keep her on her feet for a good bit of time, and you only step in to defend Valerie and Jamila as needed. I will flank anyone who tries to get around the fire attacks with my whips." I looked forward.

"Xie, as soon as you have someone on your tail, you run straight at us. Make sure you pass between the girls and Chu each time you swing around so he can heal you." Simple, but it kept her away from me and within reach of my qi whips. "Don't stop to help us fight. Keep moving. Head straight back out into the center to catch the attention of anyone you can. If you start to run low on qi, skirt the edges of the arena and try to circle back to us. It should drag anyone trying to stay out of the general melee in the center right into our trap. They won't be able to resist taking down a cultivator who is low on qi." I met each of their eyes, trying to convey my confidence in them. "Any questions?"

There wasn't time for any, because the gong sounded just as I finished. I looked over at the judges' pavilion, and saw that it was Jamila's father holding the mallet that sounded the start. I saw the smile on his face, and my internal clock told me he had given us a full minute more than the five that was announced by the other elder. Just enough time for me to finish laying out my plan. I think I liked the guy.

It took me a moment, but I finally saw the thread of air qi that he had been using to listen in on our conversation retracting along the ground. I might be starting to like the guy, but I needed to remember that he was sneaky.

Xie took off like a shot while the rest of us got to our feet. The earth cultivators hadn't had time to fix up the arenas, and we crouched in a line of craters that ran along the back wall of the battlefield. It wasn't as good as a bunker or series of slit trenches, but it would do.

It only took a few minutes until our first 'customer' was quickly approaching. I saw a male and female following Xie. She was throwing ice crystals the size of her thumb behind her, and each one would explode on impact with the ground. It left patches of spiky ground behind her, slowing the two down but leaving a clear trail for them to follow.

She didn't see us at first, but Chu popped his head up long enough for her to notice him. Xie corrected course and ran right between him and Jamila. He followed the plan and shot a condensed ball of wood qi straight at her chest. It perked her up, so she stopped throwing ice and shot off around the edge of the arena and back towards the center. I saw her duck between the rock dividers to hide from the two following her trail and she disappeared from my sight. While each of the smaller arena's dividers were still in place, we were using all twenty of them to fight in for the general melee.

Valerie and Jamila stood up as soon as the two others got in range and blasted them. It was over in less than five seconds. A referee jumped down and scooped up the cultivators, one under each arm, and bounded away towards the entrance. That female was going to be mad as all of her hair was burned off.

It took a few more minutes before Xie finally showed back up. This time, she was sprinting for all she was worth. She looked a little battered, but I figured she would be fine. I soon saw why she was sprinting. A very strong air cultivator was only a few paces behind her and he was throwing spears of air with every other step. Very wasteful. Why throw spears when an arrow or dart would do?

Xie dove between the girls and Chu, and I could see him reach a hand out to touch her leg in order to push more wood qi into her than he had last time. The girls were already launching a barrage of fire comets at the guy, but he threw up a wall of air that diverted all of them to either side. I guessed it was my turn.

I sprang out of my crater, a little behind and to the right of him. Well, my right, his left, I supposed. I already had both whips flying at him, one at neck level and one at his knees. He jumped, taking the whip intended for his neck around his waist. It wrapped around his torso, trapping his right arm against his side.

The air cultivator used his free left hand to thrust a hastily formed air spear at my chest. Well, we couldn't have that, now could we? I yanked hard on the whip before his feet touched the ground, and it threw him into a spin. It also broke his concentration, so his spear was just a refreshing breeze by the time it reached me.

The girls used the distraction to blast the guy off his feet, and another referee was there in an instant. I dissipated my whips again, and got back in my crater.

"Congratulations are in order once again, warriors! We are

down to our last ten fighters. Who will come out on top?" The announcement blasted everyone's eardrums. What a jerk. I poked my head up to see who had done it, and saw the smiling face of the young elder looking directly at me. That couldn't be good.

I ran over to Chu and motioned for him to heal our ears. If that guy wanted us deaf, I didn't want to be. I was tempted to shoot out some qi feelers under the sand to see if I could feel someone sneaking up on us, but I held back. Too many eyes were on us at this point, and I didn't want to risk exposing myself. Chu quickly complied and within seconds all of us could hear once again. I quickly scanned our group and I didn't like what I saw. Chu looked like he was almost completely out of qi, and the girls didn't seem much better.

"Chu, why are you so low on qi?" It didn't make sense; he hadn't been doing anything but healing.

"When I touched Xie to heal her, somehow she completely drained me." The anger in his voice was palpable. "I was barely able to hold anything back. I tried to call out to you, but all three of you were busy fighting the other guy. By the time you were done, she was gone."

I knew it! I knew my instincts couldn't be that far off. The memory of her hiding something up her sleeve flashed through my brain.

"Xie must have a very strong qi collection rod hidden on her somewhere. As soon as you touched her, she must have used it to drain you. The good news is, she can't actually use that energy herself until she transfers it into a core. The bad news is, I have a feeling we are about to be attacked." They all nodded, and I could see the determination in their faces.

"If Xie is working with them, we need to move. They know exactly where we are, and we don't know where they are coming from. Chu, did you see what direction she ran towards?" He nodded, and pointed off towards the left. "Okay, we are going to head towards the right. Try to keep the edge of the arena to your back, and keep moving until we are between the audience and the judges' pavilion. It will make it a lot harder for them to do something untoward if there are witnesses." They agreed, and we started moving.

I led the way, keeping low and moving from cover to cover as best as I could. When we were rounding the final corner of the arena we needed to reach before crossing directly in front of the audience, I heard a loud explosion and looked back at our former location. There was an actual pillar of fire that shot dozens of feet into the air where we had been. I couldn't be sure, but I think it was directly over the crater I had been hiding in.

"She must have broken the rod and thrown it into the crater. Who knows how much qi she allowed to build up in that thing?" The looks on my friends' faces showed their own disbelief. Now, I was pissed.

That would have most definitely killed my friends, and probably severely injured me. They weren't even trying to hide the fact that they were breaking the rules to the audience now. There was no way they couldn't see that pillar of flame, and any cultivator with a bit of sense could tell that a Body cultivator would have died. If they wanted to act like a very large collection of donkeys, I could certainly help them look like it.

I stood up and immediately started walking towards the audience. My teammates followed quickly behind. I walked right up to the raised wall, and started shouting up into the crowd.

"Ladies and gentlemen! Fellow clan members! Did you all see that?!" I could see they were surprised that a contestant was speaking to them. It wasn't necessarily against the rules, but it wasn't normally done. "I am only ten years old. A child! I touched the testing stone yesterday, and I am at the lowest level of cultivation humanly possible. But even I, the lowest of the low, can see how corrupt and broken this competition is. Has the Roh clan sunk so low, that the death of children is to be plotted out, and a blind eye turned to the nefarious deeds of those who carry it out?!" Now they were quiet, and I could see more than one person with a frown on their face.

"This was supposed to be a competition to help train the next generation of Roh warriors, and gauge any shortcomings they might need to correct before reaching adulthood. Instead, a group of judges and referees has placed bets on these contests, and they would rather allow children to die than miss out on an opportunity to earn some extra coin!" I took a breath, and waited a moment for the murmurs to start building.

"Yes! That explosion was caused by a broken qi collecting rod carried by one of the competitors. Everyone knows such an item is not allowed in a competition such as this, and to destroy an expensive item that could be used by the clan in this, our time of need, is a waste so extreme it should be considered criminal!" Now, they were all mad. "That's right! A genuine resource, a valuable tool of war that could help our entire clan, was destroyed so that a small group of people could make a profit. How many of your own wagers were skewed by this item? How many times was it used to ensure the proper contestant won, and the loser only determined by which way a fickle judge decided to place their bet?" There were plenty of people upset about that.

I lowered my voice to barely above a whisper. "I am but a child, but I was raised to expect more from my clan. My family. How am I supposed to trust my elders now, when the very people who hold my life in their hands value a few silvers more than they do my life? How can I be expected to hold my head high, and say my clan name with pride? I don't know. I just… don't know."

I turned away, and began walking towards the center of the arena. The crowd could no longer see my face, but my friends could see my smile as the angry roar of the audience began to rise behind me.

In less than a minute, the outraged cries of the onlookers were literally shaking the arena. I could see the judges in the pavilion start to stand up in confusion. They set their wine glasses down and finally looked at what was happening. They would pay for ignoring what was going on in the arena they were supposed to be watching over. The only one still in their seat was Jamila's father, and I was pretty sure I saw him wink at me.

I looked back to see a very thin line of referees trying to hold back a *very* large number of angry clan members. I was more than sure there were scores of parents who were a 'tiny' bit angry at the thought of an elder or two risking their child's life on a bet. I was almost halfway to the central pavilion when a group of six teenagers stood up from behind a dividing wall. I was wondering when they would show up.

"You may have avoided that explosion, but it doesn't matter. Now my friends and I are going to beat you to death, Jim. Your lovely distraction has all the attention elsewhere, so no one will stop us."

Xie was looking pretty smug, but I could see the light of crazy in her eyes. Earlier I asked myself what I was thinking when I was planning to kill a fifteen-year-old girl. Now I was wondering what girl, at fifteen, planned on killing a ten-year-old boy? This girl was broken on the inside. No matter her age, she was full-blown rabid, and she needed to be put down.

The five others in her group jumped forward, but my three friends were there to help. They just copied the first plan we used as a team of four, and this time it worked without a hitch.

Chu jumped in swinging, his metal qi protecting him from his five attackers. Jamila launched a fireball at his back, and Valerie blasted out a cone of air from each hand. They slammed into the fireball headed towards Chu and engulfed all six of them in flames. I actually had to take a step back from the intensity of the heat. The fire died out quickly, and I looked at what was left.

Chu was down on one knee, with all five of the attackers laid out on the ground around him. The flames died out too quickly to turn them into charcoal, but they weren't looking very good. Chu stumbled away and passed out on a clear patch of sand. He was either suffering from qi exhaustion or lack of oxygen, I wasn't sure which.

I looked back and Jamila was holding on to Valerie. She was definitely suffering from qi exhaustion, and Jamila wasn't far behind. She raised her hand in the sign of defeat and they collapsed. I glanced at a very angry-looking Xie.

"It looks like it's just you and me now, Xie. Are you sure you want to go through with this? I don't want to end you, but I won't hold back if you try to kill me." I figured I would give her one more opportunity to back out, but I didn't think she would take it.

"Look around, Jim," she said as she waved her hands around. "There aren't any referees anymore. The elders aren't even paying attention. They are fighting amongst themselves. It really is just you and me now, and I am going to kill you!"

I was looking around as she was talking, and she was absolutely correct. Even Jamila's father was busy fighting the oldest elder, and I couldn't tell who was winning. The other two elders were fighting the youngest one, and it looked like all the referees were dealing with the crowd I had riled up. Oh well, happy accident I suppose.

I finally refocused on Xie. She had formed a qi construct in the shape of a longsword with a jagged edge that was designed to rip people apart. Her eyes shone with excitement at the thought of my death. Xie really did intend to kill me. Stars, I didn't want to do this, but she had left no doubt that she was no better than a rabid animal.

As she was lunging forward, she must have seen her end in my eyes. She tried to stop herself, but I rushed forward to meet her. Her eyes were wide, and I could see her begin to understand that she was only rushing towards her own death. It had taken her a bit, but she had finally realized that she had bitten off a bigger piece than she could swallow. Now, it was time to choke on it.

Ever since her group had shown up, I had been preparing. The fire qi thread I spun out of my left palm was so thin, it was practically invisible. I caught her trailing heel with it and flipped her nearly horizontal. The twelve threads of earth qi I had spun out of my right foot and through the ground had finally found what they were looking for.

A thin stone, like the end of a paring knife, popped out of the ground right where the back of her head was landing. The rock was incredibly sharp, and it punctured the base of her skull like it was made of soft butter. Her body stiffened for a second, and then went limp. Soon, the smell of urine and voided bowels joined the scents of blood and burned flesh.

It was quiet for a few minutes. I stood over the body of a dead girl who was born without that something inside her that made her fully human. I had seen it before, of course. As an Enforcer, I had presided over the executions of murderers, rapists, and a few serial killers. All of them were missing a part of them that separated humans from animals.

Maybe it was a piece of their soul that was ground off on the crushing wheel of reincarnation. Probably not, but I knew I would most likely never really understand what made people like Xie think it was okay to simply kill anyone they didn't like. There were a few people who were better at hiding it than others, and I was pretty sure that Ming might be the champion of hiding that lack of innate humanity. Some people might think I was no better than Xie, or Ming, but I would like to think that they were wrong.

The streaks of tears on my cheeks, running clean spots through the dirt on my face, were entirely genuine when the crowd of onlookers and three remaining elders finally converged on me. It wasn't until then that I realized something.

I was really bad at keeping a low profile.

CHAPTER TEN

Warnings and Advice

It was several hours later, and many probing questions, before I was reunited with my friends. The elders had even used a truth token on me, and I hadn't seen one of those in two hundred years! It must have had several uses left, but still, those things were incredibly rare. They probably didn't fully realize how much it was worth, otherwise it would be locked up in the deepest levels of the clan vault.

They had me hold the coin in my hand and an elder watched as I ran my qi through it. If I had told even the slightest white lie, it would have cut off the flow of qi running through it, and the elder would have probably trussed me up and slapped a murder charge on me. Luckily, and technically, I hadn't killed Xie. The fall onto a sharp stone had.

The questions were pretty standard. And I had plenty of experience answering things in a way that conveyed the meaning I preferred. Yes, we were fighting. Yes, we were the last two contestants still conscious. Yes, she admitted to trying to kill me. Yes, the other five with her were willing participants. No, my friends were not involved. Yes, I tripped her. No, I didn't see the sharp stone poking out of the ground before we started fighting. (It only appeared right before she landed.) Yes, I only touched the testing stone yesterday. No, I was not secretly trying to incite a riot when I spoke to the crowd. (I did that entirely on purpose.) Yes, I was honestly surprised when the referee was hit by the fireball. (I was expecting him to block it.) No, I did not permanently scar an elder's son on purpose. (His scars would all disappear when he reached Sage level and his body was re-forged by his qi.) You get the point.

My friends were very happy to see me when I was escorted back to the arena, even though we were all a little ragged looking. They had not given us a chance to get cleaned up before moving us back to the roped-off staging area.

Looking around, I noticed the crowd was much smaller this time. It was probably just the parents and direct family members of the contestants, all of which would be receiving some sort of prize.

The bottom half were all in a separate group closer to the stage. The top half were in another group, and the top ten were in a small cluster, farthest from the pavilion. The five who had been with Xie weren't here. Instead, the others who had been knocked out early had moved up in position. I winced when I saw the girl who had lost her hair. Someone had grabbed a wig for her, but it was not a good one. I had a feeling she was not a fan of our little team.

I thought about trying to talk to the wind cultivator who used the air spear attack, but he was very determined to separate himself from us.

Chu bent closer to whisper into my ear. "Are you sure you're okay? This has been one hell of a day for you. I can't imagine going through all of this only a day after I had opened my core. And at only ten years old! I know you aren't the average kid, but still…"

"I didn't want Xie to die, but what happened can't be changed now," I said, looking at my feet. "All I can do is move forward." We put action to my words, moving forward as the bottom half of the competitors walked across the stage, receiving their prizes from the three remaining elders.

While the group of first round winners was filing through, Jamila tapped Valerie on the shoulder. She nodded, and I saw her form an odd air qi construct that formed tubes from each of our ears to a central round chamber hiding between us. Then another tube formed in front of Jamila's mouth, and it connected to the chamber. It was probably the most rudimentary form of secret communication I had ever seen, but it did allow each of us to hear what was said without anyone else listening in.

"Jim, my father wanted me to thank you." Jamila laid her hand on my shoulder as she was talking. "He knew what was going on, but he couldn't move against them by himself. The two elders, and six of the referees, were all using the competition to expand their illegal gambling operation. No one knows how long this has all gone on, but my father thinks it goes much higher than a few of the weaker clan elders. There has to be at least one council member in on it, because the eight who were caught have already been released back to their family compounds. They are only under house arrest, instead of facing a trial and banishment from the clan." She took a few furtive looks around us. "You are going to have to be careful. We all are. My father thinks we made a powerful enemy today." Valerie took the qi tube from Jamila and moved it up to her face.

"My grandfather sits on the council. I will ask him what he thinks about all of this after we visit the vault. You should all join me. At the very least, being seen going into a clan council member's compound should give them pause." Now it was her turn to look around. "They will have to see how connected you all are before they try anything else. There probably wasn't a lot of money changing hands over this minor tournament, but the rest of the clan is very upset about the destruction of the rod. It could have been used to power some serious defensive formations, and I can't imagine the loss sits well with the military leadership." Despite the qi device that was supposed to keep eavesdroppers from hearing us, she started whispering. "Whoever it is we made angry by exposing the gambling ring, they are going to be much more upset about the possibility of being caught dipping into the clan armory. That, and the obvious hit their pride must have taken."

I could swear I heard faint laughter. Was Pride keeping an eye on me? I wouldn't be surprised. I grabbed the speaking tube.

"I think going to see your grandfather is a very good idea. We should make sure we aren't separated. While I doubt anyone will try something today, we shouldn't risk it." I took a few seconds to scan each of them. "Chu, do you have the energy to give us all a quick heal? We want to be as ready as possible if something happens."

Chu took the tube. "I can do a little bit. I haven't had a chance to cultivate much since they took us for questioning. I imagine we should all expect at least one or two more rounds of questioning tomorrow, once they start to get a better picture of the whole series of events." A grimace crossed his features. "Talking to Valerie's grandfather before returning to our homes should definitely help make sure the investigators stick to questions, and not beatings."

I was a little surprised at how cynical Chu was being, but I completely understood. I was only ten, but the three older teens would face much harsher questions.

In fact, whoever this mystery ringleader was probably wouldn't believe that I had much to do with anything. Chu, almost being a Heart cultivator, would certainly receive the most scrutiny. I would have to keep an eye out for him, if I could.

Valerie let the qi construct dissipate, and started loudly chatting with Jamila about what prizes we might see in the vault as Chu pushed some wood qi into each of us. She was clearly trying to cover for the long silence anyone around us must have heard. It didn't seem like anyone was attempting to listen in, but it would be foolish to assume otherwise.

I simply looked towards the stage, trying to plan around this new obstacle. I didn't even know what the average cultivation strength was for the councilmembers in the clan, or how many there were. I hated not having an intelligence network. After having access to one for such a long time, I had begun to take it for granted.

That had actually been one of my duties for Ming, right after rising to the level of Duke. Looking back, I think it might have been him trying to slow down my rate of cultivation. Running a massive intelligence network meant long hours behind a desk, and less time cultivating and training. For someone who couldn't slow down time, that was. It turned out I was able to dedicate even more time to cultivation after being given the position. I got through almost all of the reports in less than an hour every morning, and I was able to give out orders to all of my agents in even less time.

I thought the emperor had realized how effective my larger brain core made me for the position, but now I was sure he was just underestimating me. I served in the position for almost five years before he promoted one of my best analysts to my position, and he sent me out to inspect the conditions of our northern border forts.

I only now realized that the move came at the same time I reached the middle stage of Duke. Five years was incredibly short for an increase to that level. Ming must have realized his mistake and sent me away to come up with another way to slow me down. How had I been so blind?

We finally reached the edge of the stage as the sun was starting to touch the horizon. We were lined up in two rows of five, the air cultivator and my group in the back. The person designating where we all were supposed to stand had put me at the end of the back row. Jamila was next to me, then Valerie, Chu, and the air cultivator at the other end.

Wait a minute. This was the order they fell unconscious. Oh

no. I had really stepped in it this time. I couldn't believe I just now realized that I had taken first place. I had been so concerned about the exposure of the corrupt elders and having to kill Xie that I had completely forgotten admitting I was the last person standing during the questioning.

The temporary fame of winning might keep me from being targeted by the mystery councilman, but being in the public eye would mean I needed to be even more careful. Stars, this was a long day.

"Members of the Roh clan, your champions stand before you!" The audience cheered, and Jamila's father started walking down the line, handing cores to everyone in the front row. He took a minute to describe the feats of each person, and they shook his hand before walking off the stage. Finally, he came to our row. "These five cultivators are the absolute best of the new generation of Roh cultivators. We can all expect great things from them in the future!" The crowd shouted in approval, and he waited until the applause died down before continuing.

"In front of you, they will all receive a purse of ten gold, a qi concentration formation plate, and a common-ranked core. After the ceremony has ended, we will escort them directly to the vault where they will be able to select one item of their choice!" The applause was almost twice as loud this time, and I saw my friends were all wearing wide smiles as they received their prizes. They all stepped off stage, and it was only the elders and I on stage.

"Finally, we have a very special prize for first place. You see, clanmates, Jim here is just ten years old. He only touched the testing stone *yesterday*." The collective gasp was audible all the way to the pavilion stage. "Jim Roh, for being the youngest champion to take first place in fifty years, you will receive fifty gold coins. For being the only person to remain conscious until the end, you will be awarded a common core of every element. And finally, for being the weakest person to ever win a tournament such as this, you will be allowed to select two items from the first level of the vault, and one from the second level!"

The audience went nuts. They might have been louder than when I started the riot. Many of them had no idea that I was the youngest and weakest person in the competition, and the revelation must have been earth shattering to most of them. For someone like me to do what I did was unthinkable.

I hoped that they all took away a little insight from this. It wasn't always the strongest who won, but the smartest. Of course, I was also the strongest, but they didn't need to know that.

Jamila's father handed me a heavy coin purse and a thin case that probably contained the elemental cores. We walked off the stage and started towards the exit. I guess when he said we were going straight to the vault, he meant it. My friends' family members were all waiting for them as we left the arena, and we split up so they could enjoy the congratulations from their loved ones.

I didn't have anyone waiting for me, and I was getting really worried about my parents. As we reached the intersection for the road that headed towards the vault, I saw a familiar face waiting by the guard post. It was Donny, and he looked worried. I stepped off the road to speak with him and my friends stopped to wait for me. The air cultivator continued on with his family and the two elders I didn't know, and I felt a tension I didn't realize was there leave my shoulders. Apparently, I was subconsciously worried about that guy. Or maybe one of the elders. I reached Donny and he immediately wrapped me up in a hug.

"First, I just wanted to say how proud the family is going to be when they find out that you won." He released me, dropping me back to my feet. "I only placed seventh in the Heart level tournament, and Xiao placed tenth. Uncle Hu was furious, and he was blaming you for his son placing lower than me. He is claiming you assaulted him in the bath house, and Xiao's injuries kept him from giving his best." The look on Donny's face told me he thought it was as ridiculous as it sounded. "Uncle Hu is demanding you give him one of the prizes you get from the vault as recompense for your actions."

I snorted. "That isn't going to happen," I said, shaking my head. "Xiao tried to attack me, and I was only defending myself. If he wants some of my winnings to soothe his feelings over having a worthless piece of garbage for a son, he can try to take it."

Donny took a step back in surprise. "I have no doubt that Xiao started it, but Uncle Hu is a very powerful Brain-level cultivator. If you try to fight him, he might take all of your winnings." He bent down to place his hands on my shoulders. "Your parents still aren't home yet, and you know they won't go against him anyway. The clan holds him in a much higher standing than they do your parents. They only hunt for herbs and meat, but Uncle Hu is an alchemist." He stood back up, allowing his arms to fall back to his sides. "If you pick something from the vault that will help him make his concoctions, he will be so happy that he will forget all about this whole incident."

I smiled. "Thanks for the warning, Donny, and for the advice. I will think on it." I turned and rejoined my friends, and we continued on our way.

CHAPTER ELEVEN

Good Choices

We left the various family members at the guard post at the start of the path, and only Jamila's father continued on with us. The trail led into a park to the side of the clan leader's pagoda-like palace.

The entrance to the vault was a hidden door in the side of a small hill located in the center of the tiny yet heavily forested park. It would be difficult for an enemy to find it, and the lack of any exterior guards would make it even harder for them to spot the entrance. I liked it.

Once again, I was reminded that somewhere in this clan there was a person who actually knew what they were doing. If I could find them and convince them that the *nox* existed, I might be able to leave this region to whoever was capable and move on. While I had been distracted, Jamila's father moved to the front of the group.

"Okay, listen up. You three will each get two bronze tokens, one to open the door to the first level, and one to select your item. There will be a slot at the base of each display. Place the token in the slot to deactivate the defensive wards around the item. You can see a short description of each item near the base of each pedestal, but many of the items have more abilities than what is shown. Good luck." He handed each of my friends their tokens, and ruffled Jamila's hair as she walked past him into the vault. Then it was my turn.

"Hello Jim, it is good to finally talk to you. My name is Elder Tou. You really impressed me today, and I have no doubt you have a future as a military genius."

I smiled, trying my best to look like an innocent child. "Thank you, Elder Tou. I do hope to one day be a great general." I already had been one, but I needed to do it all over again. Gods, the mountain of tasks in front of me was so high, I couldn't see the peak.

"You will get three bronze tokens and two silver tokens," Tou continued, holding up a small pouch. "Don't accidentally use a silver token instead of a bronze in the first area. In fact, I would recommend that you walk straight past the items on the first level and go to the second level immediately. That way, you can use your silver tokens first, and you don't get something in the first level that has a higher quality in the second." He leaned down a bit so he could look me in the eye. "I know it is easy for a young boy like you to get a little excited about all the prizes in there, but take your time. You probably won't get another chance like this for a long while."

I nodded in agreement. "Thank you, Elder. I will take your advice to heart." Did this guy think I was an idiot? No, I was just overestimating what he knew about me. Earlier I had been afraid he might have figured out I was a fox in the hen house, but he must think I was just a very lucky kid with a head for tactics. I was relieved. That was one fear that turned out to be nothing. Now, I only had to worry about that guy who saved the referee. I had a suspicion he might have caught on to more than Elder Tou had.

He handed me the leather pouch of thick coins, and I hung it on my belt next to the purse that held my winnings. Carrying around the box of cores was getting annoying. I really hoped there was some form of storage device in the vault.

I walked through the door, and saw the entrance was actually a small apartment. There was a tiny kitchen, a small sitting area, and a door that most likely led to a bedroom or two. There was a man cooking at the small stove, and a woman sitting in front of a desk going over papers.

Of course! The secret door meant that guard shifts must be spread out over weeks, not hours or days. Otherwise, any spies might notice a group of people disappearing into the woods every few hours and guess there was something hiding in the small copse of trees. Anyone guarding the entrance would need to remain here for a long time, and keeping your guards comfortable was always a smart move. Especially when they were both Saint-level cultivators.

"Stars, and I thought the first four were young!" the woman at the desk exclaimed when she finally looked up and noticed me. "Well, boy, don't just stand there. The door is past the kitchen. You should see the slot for the entrance where the floor meets the wall." She pointed at a blank spot on the wall roughly the size of a doorway. "Drop in your token, and the door will open for exactly five seconds. Make sure you get all the way through; the door closes hard enough that it can sever limbs." She looked back down at her papers, and I headed for the second secret door.

It took me a moment, but I found the tiny slot hidden where she said it would be. Unless you knew where to look, it would be almost invisible. Very clever. I shoved a bronze token in the slot, and the door silently slid into the floor. I jumped through, not wanting to risk the five second delay being a second or two off. The secret door flew back into position, and I looked around.

I was standing on a balcony that looked out onto rows upon rows of white marble pedestals that stood about three feet high. On top of them were weapons, armor pieces, rare herbs and flowers, crafting materials, and various bits and bobs of jewelry.

I took a moment to count, and there were over a thousand items to choose from. I could see my friends had reached the midway point of the pillars, and the air cultivator who had come before us was standing near the center of the back row. I descended the spiral staircase at the edge of the balcony and started my search.

First, I needed to prioritize my needs. A storage device was at the top of the list. I could use the six common cores and a piece of cheap jewelry to make a basic storage device, but with the energy of only common cores, I would be lucky to make one that had twenty square feet of storage space. That wasn't nearly big enough for my needs.

Second, I needed armor. I was hoping for some armor that I could conceal under a regular robe, or maybe a set that could expand from a simple bracelet or necklace when pumped full of qi. They were rare outside the northern and central provinces of the Empire, but I was sorely missing my old set issued by the Elemental Guard. As an Enforcer, I had rated a full set of concealable armor, and I could cover my whole body in qi-enhanced dark steel plate with nothing but a thought. This weak body needed protection. It would take me months of concentrated effort to get to the level of just an average Brain core cultivator, maybe even years. This time around, I didn't have the assistance of Ming buying me alchemy pills.

Third, I needed a suitable weapon. By the time I reached the King level, I only carried a weapon during ceremonies because I no longer needed one. I could form whatever weapon I wanted out of qi, and maintain it with almost zero effort. Now, my internal qi stores were reduced to the point that a protracted fight would certainly drain me. If I had a decent weapon, I could save my qi for other things.

I started walking down the rows of items but I was not liking what I saw. The descriptions were incredibly brief, and nothing I had seen so far was higher than the Expert level of craftsmanship. Most items were Journeyman level, and I could produce better versions myself. I started walking faster, only skimming over the descriptions.

As I passed the halfway point, things started looking up. The

Expert level items were starting to outnumber the Journeyman level junk, and I came across something I liked.

It was a leather vest so festooned with throwing knives that they were practically an extra layer of armor. I read the description. *Qi-infused leather vest. Contains throwing knives.* Wow, thanks for the detailed information. Jerks. The knives ran horizontally over the front and back and vertically along the sides.

They were simple sheets of metal, thick rectangles with the tips shaped into a sharp V. The knives on the chest, back, and abdomen were probably five inches long, one inch wide, and nearly a quarter of an inch thick, with a small hole drilled in the end opposite the point. The knives running along the sides were longer, more like twelve-inch daggers, and they had thin leather wrappings around the lower third which formed crude grips. There were twelve in the front and back, and one along each side. If you didn't need to use them, they would serve as armor thicker than some plate mail, and if you did need to use them, there were more than enough to fight a large group of people. If you used up all of the throwing knives, you still had the two fighting daggers to attack with. The best part? No one would even know I was wearing it if I kept my robe closed.

I was picturing using threads of qi to hurl knives at imaginary foes when I heard the scuff of a boot behind me. I turned around, and the air cultivator was only a few steps away. He stopped, and I could tell he was surprised at being caught while sneaking up on me.

"If you give me one of your tokens, I won't hurt you." Really? I hadn't even picked anything yet, and someone was trying to rob me.

"Here's an idea. How about you turn around and head out the door, or I kick the crap out of you—again—and take what I want off of your bleeding, unconscious body?"

He laughed at me, clearly not taking my threat seriously. "I was only going to take one of your tokens, but now I am taking all of them! You may have beaten me last time with the help of your friends, but now I have this!" A spear made entirely of wood sprang into his hands. The tip was just a sharpened point, but I could feel the qi running through his hands, and the spear was soaking it up. He thrust the tip forward, but he was clearly out of range. That was, until the spear suddenly grew six feet longer in a single heartbeat.

Color me shocked, but I wasn't expecting a cultivator at the Body level to be able to use a piece of spirit wood. Spirit wood wasn't exactly rare, but a piece old enough to have developed an affinity for qi strong enough for someone to use it like he just had was *incredibly* rare.

This guy might have just found the single best item in the first level of the vault. I decided I wanted it.

I didn't even need to dodge to miss his first attack. He wasn't expecting the weight increase that an extra six feet of wood added to the spear, causing it to drop and skip off the marble floor to my right. Since he was using all of his qi on the spear, he didn't have the speed advantage a normal air cultivator could use.

I sprang forward, trying to close the distance. He had probably planned to use the spear to keep me at a distance, so I decided to ruin whatever plan he had concocted and got right in his face. The spear shrank back to its former size and he tried to position it to intercept me.

The problem with only a pointy tip instead of a regular spearhead was it had no cutting edge for him to swing at me with. I simply slapped the tip to the side, and kicked him between the legs as hard as I could. I could kick pretty hard. I might have heard a sound like a grape popping, but it was probably just in my head. His breath left him in a rush, and he dropped to his knees.

"That… isn't… fair…" he managed to wheeze out. I smacked the loosely held spear out of his hand, and grabbed him by the hair on top of his head.

"Fair? You just tried to rob me of my winnings, after I *fairly* earned them. Do you know how ridiculous you are being? Look, I don't even know your name. I don't even care to know, because you are not a threat to me. Even after you obtained an item from the vault, you couldn't beat me." I shook his head a bit to prove my point.

"You thought I was an easy mark, and you were going to bully me into giving you what I rightfully earned. Instead of being happy with what you got, you tried to steal even more. You need to take a long look at yourself and decide the type of person you want to be. Now, I am going to take your stick over here, and you aren't going to tell anyone about it. If you do, I will explain to them how you just tried to take my tokens after you attempted to sneak up behind me and stab me in the back like a coward." I made sure to pull his hair a little harder to drive the point home. "Not only were you afraid of a weak ten-year-old little boy, but you lost to him. Twice. If I were you, I wouldn't want anyone to find out about that. No one will respect you again. Ever." I released him, and he curled up in a ball on the floor. I think he might have been crying. He was a bad apple, but nothing on the order of Xie. He might even change his ways after this. Probably not, but one could hope.

I reached down and picked up the spirit wood spear, inspecting it with my qi. It was definitely ancient, probably over two thousand years old. I poked my finger with the tip and drew a bead of blood. I used a thread of wood qi to force the blood into the spear, expecting to feel some resistance. Instead, the blood fused immediately, and it bound itself to its new owner.

The air cultivator hadn't even forged a bond with it before he tried to use it on me. What an idiot! Now that it was bound to me, it wouldn't accept anyone else's qi. I could also sense its presence when it was close to me.

I sent it a mental command and it shrunk down into a ring that fit around my first finger. I sent it another command, and it formed a set of knuckle dusters, with four sharp wooden spikes jutting out almost an inch from my fist. I tried to get it to form a crude punching dagger, but it didn't accept the command. Whoever made this thing had engrained a few set forms into its internal qi matrix. I would have to experiment to figure out what they all were.

I stopped sending qi into it, and it formed back into the single ring around my finger. If I got the knife vest, I would have two different options for concealed weapons. Man, I sure was glad that guy attacked me.

I heard running footsteps and I looked over to see my friends approaching.

Chu was in front. "Jim, are you okay? We heard shouting."

I pointed with my thumb behind me, indicating the air cultivator still curled up on the ground. "This guy just tried to take my tokens. We talked about it, and he changed his mind." The girls standing behind Chu started laughing, and Chu just shook his head.

"What a jerk. Want us to report him to the guards?"

I waved the idea away. "Him and I have reached an agreement. I won't say anything, and he won't mention it again. I would appreciate it if you three would keep it to yourselves as well. Unless he attacks me again. Then, we can tell the whole clan what he did." He whimpered behind me. "Did you guys find anything good?"

"I found a bracelet that can carry fresh herbs and produce without killing them, or spoiling," Chu said with a smile, holding up a thin silver band. "With this, I can carry expensive and rare items from our region and deliver them to other cities far away from here. The price difference between dried foods and herbs, compared to fresh ones, is well worth the investment. Once I get my caravan running, I am going to be rich!" He was right. While it wasn't the type of storage device I was looking for, it was definitely a good fit for him.

Jamila spoke up next. "I found a bracer that can launch wind blades." She already had it on, and demonstrated by sending out a weak blast of air. "It accepts any form of qi, and turns it into an air attack. Now, I can do the same attack Valerie and I were using by myself. Or, I can store a pretty good amount of qi inside it, and blast someone without even needing to activate my core. It is the perfect surprise attack! They won't even feel it coming."

I could see why she chose it. For a fire qi user, it could definitely come in handy.

Valerie finally spoke up. "I found a necklace that can heal people. It constantly soaks up the ambient qi around it, and the description said it can hold three charges. It takes a whole day to replace a single use, but I can use cores to recharge it as well." She pulled it out from under her shirt, spinning around a green gemstone that sparkled in the light. "I think it might come in handy."

I nodded. "Having another way to heal someone's injuries will definitely take the strain off of the medic in a group. And when you are by yourself, it might literally mean the difference between life and death. Good choices, everyone." I looked around at the rows of pedestals. "I need to start figuring out what I am going to pick." Chu nodded and walked around me to grab the young man still lying on the floor.

"We will be waiting for you up top. I can drag this piece of dung out of here on our way out."

I waved my thanks as they left, dragging the air cultivator behind them.

CHAPTER TWELVE

Successful Trip to the Vault

I waited until I heard the door close behind them. Finally, I was alone. I looked around, making sure there were no hidden recesses where someone could hide or spy on me. It was taking entirely too long to search the first level. I needed a quicker way.

I activated all three of my cores and spun out one thousand incredibly thin individual qi threads. This was towards the upper edge of what I could manage right now, but it would be enough for this. I cast them in a net that covered the whole room, looking for anything that was putting off an elevated amount of qi. There were six pings, and I memorized their locations. I was only looking for things that stood out. I didn't bother inspecting every item closely, as most of them weren't worth my time. I walked quickly to the first item that stood out to my senses.

It was a ring that allowed the wearer to fly over short distances. I almost bought it immediately, but after closer inspection, I saw that it wasn't worth it. The internal qi storage matrix was miniscule. This was more like a long jump ring than a flying ring. It couldn't hold enough qi to provide true flight.

Next up was a sword that looked like it was made of green-tinted glass. The description said it could help the wielder tame wild beasts, and it could cut through almost any material that wasn't enhanced by qi. Interesting, but not what I was looking for right now.

The third item was actually the same vest of knives I had already looked at. I inspected it with my qi this time, and I sensed that the leather was as tough as chainmail. It could also be blood bonded, which meant there was some form of internal qi matrix. I wouldn't know what it could truly do unless I bonded with it.

The fourth item was a pill making cauldron. It was cast iron, but the lid was cracked. The description said it kept all residues the owner wished, and sloughed off the ones they didn't. That could be extremely useful. The ability to keep the residue from a sleeping powder meant that anything else created would also have that effect. If you were to make a healing pill, it would also help the person fall asleep, speeding the healing process. Or, if you wanted to poison someone, there were all sorts of interesting combinations you could use.

The fifth item was a traveling forge. It condensed down to the size of a brick, but when expanded, it had all the basic tools, forge, and anvil necessary to make spot repairs on armor or weapons when in the field. It also contained a fair amount of steel and iron ingots. I could picture myself using this within the privacy of my family courtyard to produce high-quality goods that I would sell for a hefty profit, without anyone knowing where the new and very skilled blacksmith came from. Then, I thought about my uncle and cousin. Maybe I would have to find a clearing in the woods.

The sixth and final item of interest was a set of clothes. I took a moment to read the description because I had no idea why my qi net pinged on something like this. *Masterwork cloth used to make linen shirt. Does not stain or smell, and sheds all dirt and blood on contact. Pants are leather from Brown Three-Clawed Bear. Same effects as shirt. Both items inscribed to self-repair when infused with qi.* Okay, now I saw why these stood out. After the day I had today, I could really see the use for something like this. My robes were looking pretty rough.

I couldn't decide what I wanted, so I went to the back wall to see the next section of the vault. I dropped a silver token in the slot and rushed through the gate. On this door, the timer was extremely short. It neatly snipped off the trailing inch or so of the back of my already frayed robes.

There was no balcony overlooking the area this time, but it wasn't necessary. There were only twenty pedestals in this room. It was really more like a hallway, with ten pedestals on each side. I walked quickly to the end and started looking at the items on my way back.

I wanted all of them. There were twelve full sets of formation-inscribed lamellar armor, sized for an adult. Most likely they were obtained when the clan defeated the honor guard of some sect elder, or maybe a minor noble.

A katana that was midnight black, clearly the weapon of an assassin, sat across from a golden cauldron and alchemy set.

A set of jewelry made for a woman that stored enough earth qi inside it to rival a Saint was clearly meant to be paired with the staff on the pedestal on the opposite side of the hallway. I wasn't sure, but I thought the staff was a giant focusing rod. The pair combined would allow a cultivator to launch a blast of earth qi hundreds of yards away, with enough power to knock down the wall of a fort. Or make one.

The next to last set of pedestals held a silver war hammer that looked like it weighed a ton, and a silver helm that was probably intended to fit on the head of a giant. I had no idea when the clan had killed a giant, but I was most certainly impressed.

The last set of items was clearly meant to be the lowest quality, which was why they were closest to the entrance. A worn and battered looking belt sat across from a leather-bound book. I tried to read the title, but it was too faded. The description said it contained a secret cultivation style that allowed a cultivator at the Saint level and higher to master an attack that could call down a meteor onto their enemies. It was more likely they just formed a large rock using earth and fire qi, and launched it at someone, but cultivators liked to make things sound more impressive than they really were.

The belt was a storage device. Finally! I looked closely at it, but the wards in this section were too thick to give it a close inspection without disturbing them. I didn't know what would happen, and I wasn't sure it was worth the risk to find out.

As much as I wanted everything else in the room, I had to have that storage device. In my last life, I had hundreds of storage devices contained in a bracelet designed to hold other storage devices. If you tried to store a storage space ring inside another regular storage space device, the qi interaction usually led to a catastrophic failure of the internal qi matrix of one or both of the devices. Basically, they blew up.

The description on the belt said it could hold three hundred square feet of items in three separate areas. I had a feeling it was the copper studs running along the center of the belt that actually held the storage spaces, not the whole belt itself. The question was, which three studs were the spaces? There were a dozen coin-sized studs spaced evenly along the belt, and I couldn't tell which ones were important and which were decoration. If the three studs out of the twelve used for storage were located closely together, I might be able to cut the belt down and turn it into a bracelet. If not, I would have to wear the ugly thing as it was.

I dropped my token into the slot on the pedestal, and watched closely as the ward around it dissipated. Huh. I just got an idea. Too bad I had already used both of my silver tokens before I thought of it. There was no reason I couldn't look at the qi matrix inside the coins and copy it into a temporary qi construct. I could totally rob the Roh clan blind.

Remembering the guards outside, I thought maybe taking everything out of the vault was a bad idea. If they searched me, which they would probably do once they saw the storage device, I would get in some serious trouble.

I picked up the belt and finally inspected it with my qi. I was right. The tarnished copper studs made up the storage devices. Only three of the twelve were meant to actually hold items, but they were too far apart to turn it into a bracelet. They were located at the left, right, and center. When wearing it, you would be able to access things from the belt from either hand and the small of your back. I ran a few qi threads over the whole thing, looking for the spot to place a drop of blood for the bond. Instead, I felt a very faint echo of energy when my qi passed over the buckle itself. I spun out more threads, and gave the thing a closer look.

At first, I wasn't feeling anything, but I knew something was off. I tried running qi threads of each element over the buckle, but nothing happened.

It wasn't until I heard the echo of faint laughter again that I remembered something very important. I now had access to two more elements! I spun up my brain core to full capacity, and started to inspect the ambient energy around me. I was underground, and the only light was coming from fire constructs on the ceiling. There should probably be plenty of dark qi in this place.

It took what felt like hours, but I finally picked up some faint traces of what looked like liquid shadow between the pedestals and the wall. I pulled on the energy with my lower core, and a tiny amount made it through the meridians on my feet. I immediately spun out a thread of this new energy and instantly searched the belt with it. This time, the buckle reacted, and I saw where to place a drop of blood. I did so immediately, and the belt demanded all the dark qi I had gathered into my core to integrate the bond.

Once it was formed, I finally had access to the full belt. It wasn't just the three copper studs that were storage devices. They were *all* storage devices, and the buckle itself was a huge storage space. The best part was, all but the three obvious studs still had stuff inside them. I couldn't access the two studs closest to the buckle on either end. I suspected it would take light qi to tap into them. I was still using slowed time, so I decided to look over and organize what was in the belt.

The vast majority of the items were for crafting. There were bolts of cloth, sheets of leather, ingots of various metals, and a lot of herbs that could be used in alchemy. One stud held a basic but high-quality alchemy set and cauldron, along with a number of tools and camping supplies. Another stud held an impressive array of trail food and dried meats and vegetables, with a wide assortment of cooking spices along with a nice cookpot and tripod to hold it over a fire. There were several purses filled with coins from all over the empire, and even some from the empires surrounding this one. Most of them showed the face of Emperor Li's grandfather. Whoever had this belt last had died a long time ago.

There were also enough sets of basic arms and armor to outfit a small army. They were in an older style, but they were definitely still usable. The best find was a silver-inlaid longbow that I knew I would have to bind to me as well, if I chose to keep it. There were dozens of filled quivers, ready for use. Based on what I was seeing, the original owner of this belt was probably a traveling trader who met their end either at the hands of the Roh, or somewhere nearby their city.

With the discovery of this belt, my prospects were looking way up. I now had well over three thousand square feet of storage space, and I hadn't even accessed the light qi studs. Best of all, there was absolutely no added weight from all the stuff it carried inside the dark qi storage areas. I had never heard of such a thing. It must have been some side-effect of using dark qi instead of the more commonly known forms of qi.

The dark qi aspect needed to detect the storage spaces also meant I might be able to sneak a few things past the guards. The fact that no one in the Roh clan had noticed the stuff hidden inside the belt meant that there wasn't anyone here capable of using dark qi.

I returned my perception of time back to normal. Then, I put the belt on and pulled the lever that let me walk back into the first area of the vault. I pulled out one of my bronze tokens, and it only took a moment of concentration to copy the design of the qi matrix hidden inside it.

I used the actual tokens to get the vest and the clothes. I would be seen wearing them, and I didn't want them to be marked down as stolen while walking around with them on. I placed both items in the right-hand stud of the belt, that way it would make it easy for the guards to find them when they inspected me. I noticed a tiny weight gain when placing items inside the regular storage spaces. I guess the belt wasn't perfect, but I couldn't complain.

I then made a qi construct mimicking the tokens and placed it in the slot for the traveling forge. It was too useful to pass up. The trick worked like a charm, and I shoved it into one of the 'hidden' studs.

Next up was the cauldron. I had a fun plan for this, but I would have to wait and see if it worked. I worked my way over to the green sword and ring, and snatched them up too. I decided to put the spirit wood ring in a dark qi stud as well, just to be safe.

After grabbing the items, I dissipated the qi constructs and the wards sprang back in place. No one would notice anything was missing unless they physically looked at each pedestal. I didn't imagine that happened very often. Nothing else was worth the effort, so I headed for the stairs.

Upon exiting the vault, the female guard checked me over and cleared me to go. I walked out the front door and made my way back up the path to my waiting friends. This had been quite a successful trip to the vault. I was feeling much better about everything, and I was ready to visit Valerie's grandfather before getting some rest. It had been a very long day.

CHAPTER THIRTEEN

Cauldron Plans

My friends were talking in a huddle, Elder Tou standing off to the side. Donny had joined them at some point, and he was marveling at Valerie's new necklace.

I quickly put my new vest on over my undershirt so I had something to show off when they asked. I formed a blood bond with it as well, but I didn't have time to explore what it could do. I wasn't going to put on my new clothes until I had washed off the grime of the day. It would also look odd to have a traveler's shirt and pants on under the traditional clan robes. I would need to find some sturdy boots as well. These slippers wouldn't perform well in the woods, and I was going there as soon as I could. I missed my parents.

"Jim!" Chu was the first to notice me. "What did you end up getting?"

I smiled, and took a few minutes to show off my belt and vest. Valerie yawned, and I was reminded that it was getting close to midnight.

"We should meet with Valerie's grandfather." I indicated the yawning girl to prove my point. "It is getting late, and we have all had an exhausting day." Everyone agreed, and Valerie started leading the way towards the center of the city.

The councilmember compounds surrounded the city center complex of buildings, ensuring the most important parts of the city were protected by the strongest members of the clan. Valerie stopped in front of the compound directly across from the entrance to the main branch family pagoda. Apparently, Valerie's grandfather was either the most important council member, or the strongest.

Elder Tou stood behind us, looking out at the plaza surrounding the central pagoda. There were several groups of people out despite the late hour, and more than a few of them were watching us.

Valerie knocked on the gate and the door swung open. A tall, thin, gray-haired man with a long white beard wearing spotless white robes was waiting for us in the entry parlor that was also painted white. Apparently, he liked the color white. The room was lined with benches, most likely in place for people who needed to wait for an audience with the old man.

"Come in, young warriors. I am glad you chose to visit me before returning to your own families." We shuffled into the room, and he indicated we should sit. "Elder Tou, your daughter does your family proud. If she continues as she has, I have no doubt she will succeed your seat on the lower council."

Elder Tou looked proud, but then I saw the confusion hit. He couldn't decide if he was being threatened or complimented.

The old man chuckled. "It will be necessary, because a man with your attention to detail belongs next to me in the upper council."

Now Elder Tou was beaming. His joy over not only his daughter, but his own exploits being noticed, was clear.

The old man turned to Donny. "Your own intentions towards my granddaughter are clear. I expect you to act like a proper suitor, and ensure you conduct yourself like a gentleman at all times. Your mother and father should come and speak to me tomorrow." Both Donny and Valerie turned bright red. Wow, even I hadn't picked up on that dynamic. It must have happened while I was still inside the vault.

Donny cleared his throat. "Of course, Chief Elder. I only met Valerie this evening, but she has already stolen my heart. I know my family doesn't have the prestige that would normally allow me to pursue her hand, but I will climb any mountain to be with her." Valerie was so red now she was practically purple, and I think her grandfather was enjoying her discomfort.

"After the showing that you and your cousin gave today in the tournaments, I think your family is on the rise." Valerie's grandfather took a moment to look Donny and I over. "I am willing to accept your petition for her hand, but her father and I will speak on the matter before any decisions are made." Donny nodded in agreement, and scooted closer to Valerie on the bench. Chu cleared his throat, but the old man held up his hand to stop him from speaking.

"You will have to speak with Elder Tou about petitioning for Jamila's hand, but your family is wealthy enough I would think everyone would approve of you two joining families. Of course, both of you would have to wait another year or two to be considered adults. As for any preferential treatment you might seek in future business ventures, I would have to see a full proposal before making any decisions." Chu visibly gulped. Whether it was from the talk of marriage or business, I couldn't tell. "While you provided a great deal of assistance to my granddaughter today, and showed your character in the process, I don't know enough about your business acumen to make a decision about finances." Elder Tou didn't seem surprised at what the chief elder said, but I was personally shocked at how perceptive this old man was. Now it was Jamila and Chu's turn to flush red, and they both just looked at their feet.

Finally, it was my turn. The old man just stared at me for a minute, trying to gauge me with his eyes. I looked back impassively, trying my best not to give anything away.

"Jim, I have heard a lot about you, but I don't think the reports I read do you justice."

I nodded before answering. "Thank you, Chief Elder. The reason we came here with Valerie tonight is because we believe there might be a member of the council that will seek revenge for what happened this afternoon. We were hoping that you could offer insight into this belief, and give us a modicum of your protection."

The old man smiled. "I sometimes forget the bluntness of youth. I have my suspicions, but I lack proof of any wrongdoing by a member of the upper council. The two members of the lower council have already been removed from their positions, and a deeper investigation will be taking place in the next couple of days." He glanced at Elder Tou before looking back at me. "Until I have had time to look into everything, I would suggest you all avoid traveling alone and avoid any dark alleys. I think it would be wise for you all to plan on meeting with me again in three days. We should know more by that point, and I will tell you all what I have found." With that, he dismissed us and we headed our separate ways. Valerie waved at us from the gate as we walked away.

Elder Tou and Jamila only lived a few compounds deeper into the city, so Donny, Chu, and I were the only three headed towards the outskirts. Chu's parents were waiting for him next to their own compound and we dropped him off after saying our farewells. Once it was just the two of us, Donny picked up the pace. My shorter legs were having trouble keeping up, but he seemed lost in his own thoughts, so he didn't notice.

"So, you and Valerie, huh?" I asked him as we rounded the last corner onto our street.

He paused in the middle of the road before answering. "I have never felt this way about anyone before, Jim. You have introduced me to the love of my life, and I will forever be grateful. I just hope that my parents give a good impression at the meeting with the chief elder." He turned around and continued walking, this time keeping it to a pace more comfortable for me. Soon enough, our destination was in sight.

I only noticed him as we neared the gate to our complex, but there was no missing my Uncle Hu. His belly was straining his robes, and his extra chins were quivering in anger. The bald patch on top of his head was gleaming like a polished jewel, while the hair on the sides of his head stuck out like a wiry bush, blending into the mutton chops running along his jowls. He was a short man with the attitude of a Green Forest Wasp. Not a friendly creature, believe me. Before Donny or I could say anything, he started shouting at us.

"What have you done to anger the chief elder, boy? Haven't you done enough damage to our family for one day?" What in the stars was this idiot talking about? "Not only did you two shame our family by starting a riot and cheating your way into a higher position than my own son in the tournaments, but you have brought the attention of the second most powerful person in our clan down on our heads?!" He was working himself up, and shouting loud enough that heads were poking out of windows around us. Ah, I see. He wanted witnesses.

"Uncle, it isn't like that. The chief elder wishes to speak to my parents about his granddaughter's hand in marriage." Donny was showing some backbone. Good. I guess love brought out the inner strength inside everyone.

Uncle Hu's eyes widened, and his shouting got louder. "You *what*?! I can't believe a piece of trash like you thinks they have any chance at marrying someone as important as the chief elder's granddaughter. More likely, your parents will be whipped in the public stacks for raising such an impetuous son!" He rounded on me. "And you! You attack my son in the bathhouse, when he is unprepared and vulnerable, right before a competition that determines his clan ranking? I should beat you myself, since your own worthless parents are never around to do it!"

Okay, now he was crossing a line. If he said one more word, I was going to remove his lungs so he couldn't insult my parents again. I think he saw it in my eyes, because he swallowed whatever he was going to say next. I stormed past him, and headed towards my room.

"And what of the payment for you damaging my son?" he shouted after me. "If you don't give me one of your prizes from the vault, I will do everything in my power to make your miserable little life even worse!" I could barely hold in my grin as I turned back around. I pulled the cauldron with the cracked lid I had stolen out of my belt, and set it on the table in the courtyard.

"I will give you nothing, but if you choose to steal this, any consequences are on your head. Stealing does seem to be in your nature." I turned and walked away.

"Consequences? From you? Ha! I will take what is my due, and there is nothing you can do about it." He stomped over and snatched the cauldron off of the table before heading back to his apartments. The greed shining in his eyes was visible from across the courtyard. It was hard to keep my grin from stretching across my face.

That fun little plan went better than I could have imagined. I didn't know how long it was going to take, but eventually his loud mouth would brag to someone about his shiny new cauldron. It would only be a matter of time until someone connected the dots, and he would be up to his fat neck in trouble with the clan for owning a cauldron that was stolen goods. If he said to a truth tester that he got it as a gift from me, it would show him as a liar because he stole it from me. I didn't know if he had the pull to get out of it, but he would certainly come out of it worse than if he had just left me alone.

The best part was that I failed to mention the ability the cauldron had. Unless he was smart enough to figure it out, all of his alchemy concoctions would be tainted by whatever effect was currently stored by the item. I couldn't wait to see the aftermath.

I went into my room and put absolutely everything I owned inside my belt. I didn't know if I would have to leave in a hurry, and I didn't want to leave anything behind. I headed down to the bathing chamber and took a long soak. I made sure to keep my belt next to me the whole time. I hadn't seen Xiao yet, and apparently his favorite time to ambush people was when they were naked. I wonder what that said about his personality?

By the time I climbed out of the bath, it was probably close to two hours after midnight, and I needed some rest. My body wasn't anywhere near the level where it could go without sleep for several nights and getting it there wasn't going to be easy. I had almost forgotten how much time was lost in a day to sleep. It was a little frustrating. There was a lot I needed to get done in a very short period of time.

I got out of the bath and quickly headed up to my room to rest. I had already put my bedframe and mattress into my belt, so I just pulled out a sleeping mat and laid down to get some sleep.

CHAPTER FOURTEEN

Another Dream

I knew I was dreaming, but it felt odd. I was standing in front of the chief elder's compound, and a small beam of light was casting a line across the dark square in front of his gate. I walked closer and noticed it was because his gate was cracked open, the light escaping from the inside. I could hear two voices. It sounded like the chief elder, and the other voice was familiar.

"Where is he now?"

"Sleeping. I have two men watching his compound right now. We can't afford to let anything happen to him until we know more."

"I agree. Have you had any progress on tracking down the person who started all of this?"

"No. They know how to cover their tracks. Either way, we can't let them get to the boy. If you could have seen how he handled that fireball thrown at him, you would know this kid is going to be a force to be reckoned with when he grows up."

"I don't doubt it. I didn't sense a bit of fear when he looked at me, and even Saint-level cultivators look at me with a bit of fear in their eyes. Whatever happened to him, he is the future of this clan. As long as we can keep jealous people from killing him first, of course."

"Did you see the note that said the testing rod detected two deformities? We will need to find out what they are before we can call him the future of the clan."

"I can't imagine they will keep him from a bright future, but you are right. We will see."

"If not, the other three with him have promise as well. I know we aren't the only ones who noticed. We need to be careful here, or the clan could end up going even farther down the road to ruin than it already has. I didn't like the way those dark falling stars made me feel yesterday. We need to be careful."

"What if you were to take him away from the clan for a few days? His parents still haven't come back from their mission in the forest yet. Take him and a few others on a search. As long as he is with you, he should be safe. You can even give him some scout training along the way."

"That is a good idea. That rotten Hu might try something otherwise. I saw him yelling at the kid when he got back to his compound."

"Yes, Alchemist Hu is a vindictive man. I wish his father was still strong enough to keep him in line. I have a feeling he won't be a problem for much longer. If our new young friend is as capable as I think he is, Hu and his son will wish they had just left him alone. Take the others with him when you go. It will be good for them to get out of the city for a bit. Try to be back in seven days, and don't pass the lake at the center of the forest. Come back sooner if you find his parents, but not for at least three days."

"We will leave before the tenth bell. I have a few men who can be spared to babysit."

"Just be careful, and watch your back. We don't know how daring the enemy might be."

The door opened, and out walked the man who had

jumped in to save the referee. I knew that voice was familiar. He walked towards me, and I raised my head to speak to him. Instead, he walked right through me. It was weird. I didn't feel anything. I turned to look back at the gate, but it had already closed.

Then, a dark figure I hadn't noticed before darted away from the corner of the building. They had clearly been listening in on the conversation as well. I tried following him, but as I rounded the corner of the complex, a bright light flashed in my face.

CHAPTER FIFTEEN

Shopping Trip

"Time to wake up! You have a visitor waiting by the gate." It was Donny, and he had thrown open the shutters covering my window. He looked around the room. "What happened to all of your stuff? Was it Uncle Hu? That bastard, I am going to tell my father about this. He has gone too far!"

I rubbed my eyes as I sat up. "No, I did this. I don't want any of my things out for someone to tamper with. The belt I got yesterday has more than enough room for all of my things. Tell our guest that I will be down as soon as I am dressed."

Donny nodded, and headed downstairs to entertain our visitor.

I got dressed in my new clothes and put on my vest and belt. I still needed to look at the qi matrix inside of the vest to figure out what it could do, but one of the things had to be the ability to resize itself. I pushed in some qi through the point where I created the blood bond, and it adjusted to my body. It fit like a glove, the knives moving into perfect position. I slipped the spirit wood ring back on my finger, and did my best to straighten my hair. I put the ring that helped with flight on my opposite hand. I rolled up the sleeping mat and put it in my belt.

I would have to swing by a cobbler on the way out of town, because I didn't have any boots fit for walking and fighting in the woods. I had a good guess that my guest was the man from my dream, and we would be leaving in a few hours. I wasn't sure of what to make of my new dreaming ability, but I wasn't one to turn down any advantage. Maybe it was a side-effect of the way I was reincarnated?

I walked down the stairs and took a seat at the long table in our courtyard across from our guest. Donny placed a plate of rice and strips of meat in front of me, and I started eating as our guest looked on.

"You aren't surprised to see me, Jim. Interesting. Do you know who I am, and why I am here?"

I shook my head. "I don't know your name, but I would guess you are here about the tournament yesterday." I didn't want him to know how much I knew about why he was here, but I had to give him a reason for not acting surprised.

"My name is Kory, and I am the leader of the Roh Clan Scouting Force. I am here about your parents. They have been gone for longer than their mission demanded, so I was wondering if you and your friends wanted to join me in a search for them?" Kory was wearing the same armor as yesterday, and I took the opportunity to take a longer look at him. He was a small man that appeared to be in his thirties, but from the level of his cultivation I guessed he was closer to one hundred than thirty. He had tan skin, darkened by time in the sun. I could see smile lines around his blue eyes and a hint of gray in his sun-bleached hair. I was still wary, but I was starting to warm up to him. I didn't feel anything negative in his aura.

I nodded to show I was interested. "What was their mission?"

He looked down at his own plate of food before answering. "They were supposed to track down a den of Red Spring Wolves, and either kill them or come back to report their location." Kory looked up from the table. "Your parents are powerful enough that it should have been an easy mission for them, but I think we should go take a look. If they are stranded or injured, they might need some help. Your friends are welcome to come along."

I stood up from the table, ignoring the rest of my breakfast. We needed to hurry.

"I have to grab some things from town before we leave. Donny, are you willing to join in the search?" He stood as well.

"Yes. Just let me grab my pack and some food and I will be ready to go."

I slapped my hand on his back. "Thanks. Would you be willing to gather up Valerie and Jamila? I will swing by Chu's family shop and ask him to come."

Kory stood up as well, having quickly shoveled the rest of his food in his mouth. "I will meet you all by the start of the western road. Make sure you all come prepared, every person will be expected to bring their own supplies and weapons. I would recommend a bow and a spear at the minimum." A spear appeared in his hands out of nowhere. "If we have to fight off anything with claws or teeth, you are going to want to keep it away from your skin." He turned and walked out the door. I didn't see any storage rings on his fingers, so he must have some form of storage device hidden somewhere on his person.

Donny ran towards his room and I headed out after Kory. I wanted to give Chu plenty of time to get ready, and he might even have something in his store that I liked. I also needed to get a regular bow and spear, because I didn't want to show off my spirit wood weapon or the bow I found inside the belt.

As I left, I noticed someone was tailing me. Probably one of Kory's people sent to keep an eye on me, but I decided to lose them just in case. I picked up my pace, darting between groups of people as they walked down the street. I slowed as a crossing street was coming up and quickly turned at the last second. I then ducked in close to a family as they walked right back out onto the main thoroughfare. I blended right in with their other kids as two men ran past, heading down the side street. That was easy. I picked up the pace again and left them behind.

Up ahead there was a wagon blocking the road to Chu's family shop, so I went to walk around. A pair of adults in red robes were shouting at each other, blocking the small space I could have used to get past. I turned back to take a side street around the roadblock, but paused for a moment. The side street was narrower than most, and the shadow cast by the buildings made it too dark to see deeper into the alley. My instincts screamed ambush. I cast some threads of qi out of my feet, keeping them under the cobblestones to stay out of sight. I sent them to inspect the alley and I wasn't surprised to sense four cultivators at the Meridian level.

I could easily take care of them but I didn't want my enemies to know just how strong I was. Instead, I crouched down and crawled under the wagon to the other side. Did these idiots forget I was a kid? I continued up the road, and when I looked back the two arguing had magically stopped fighting and had cleared the way. One of the men in the red robes was looking my way with an angry look on his face, so I waved at him and kept walking.

I entered the store Chu had told me belonged to his family and I was surprised at the quality of the goods it contained. There were shelves filled with jars of medicines, bins containing herbs that helped with cultivation, and rows of canned goods. I walked towards the back and saw a glass display case that held inscribed items. There was also a rack on the wall behind the counter that held a random assortment of weapons. I grabbed a basket and got started.

I picked up enough medicines, poultices, and bandages to cover most eventualities. I also grabbed several vials of anti-venom, and all of the healing pills they had. I dropped off the full basket at the counter, and went back for more. I got a wide assortment of food and grabbed a qi stone that got hot enough to cook on from the display case. It would allow me to have a warm meal if it was raining, or I was worried about starting a fire.

I approached the sales clerk and asked if there were any boots in stock. They had a suitable pair of brown leather and canvas boots, with the soles made from some exotic form of reptile skin. It was rough enough to grip the ground, but soft enough to make my steps quiet. I was also pretty sure the skin would keep sharp rocks from puncturing through and stabbing the bottoms of my feet.

Finally, I asked if I could see all of the bows and spears currently in stock. By this time, the clerk was eyeing my selections and looking at me with a doubtful expression on his face.

"Are you sure you have the money for all of this, kid? I haven't counted everything up yet, but you are looking at spending over seven or eight gold."

I pulled out the purse I had won from the competition, and showed him a handful of gold coins. "I took first place in the competition yesterday with Chu. Is he around?"

The clerk immediately apologized, and yelled back behind the curtain at the rear of the store. He was laying out an assortment of weapons as Chu came out from behind the curtains.

"Jim, glad you came! Chan, this is the boy I was telling you about last night."

Chan apologized again, and headed behind the curtain to find some more bows. Now that I was looking, I could easily see the family resemblance between the two.

"Chu, would you be willing to join me on a search for my parents in the forest? They have gone missing, and I am worried about them. It might take a week, but we have the clan scout leader coming with us so we won't get lost."

He frowned. "I am supposed to meet with Jamila's father today, but this is more important. Let me tell my parents where I am going, and grab some supplies."

I smiled, reaching up to pat his shoulder. "Jamila will be coming with us, so I don't think the meeting would be taking place anyway."

Chu sighed in relief, and headed back behind the curtain to grab his things.

His brother walked back out and I selected eight decent spears and six bows from the pile. I also grabbed twelve full quivers of arrows. I wanted to be able to outfit my friends and still have a few spares. Chan totaled up my purchases, and I handed over ten gold. He gave me back a few silvers and coppers in change, and I took a moment to situate everything in my belt how I wanted it. I asked Chan to tell Chu that I would meet him at the western road, and he agreed.

I walked out the door and headed for the next shop. I didn't really need anything else, but I thought it would be a good idea to see what was available. The streets were crowded with people, so I slipped between a pair of carts into the store across the street.

There were several other people walking along the aisles, all of them looking at what was on the shelves. They were filled with formation plates about the size of the palm of my hand, most of them made of iron or stone. I started shuffling down the rows, looking at what was carved onto them. There were a lot of defensive wards, alarm wards, and a few were meant to help concentrate the qi in an area. Most of them were weaker versions of formations than what I could make myself, but I grabbed a few of each anyway. I then found a set of carving tools, and I grabbed them along with several stacks of blank copper disks. I could use their versions until I found the time to carve my own. I paid the two gold and left the store.

I was going to head down to the next shop, but someone grabbed the back of my belt and threw me into the bed of a familiar-looking wagon waiting outside the shop. I almost destroyed everything in a twenty-foot circle around me in a storm of earth, steel, and fire whips, but I held myself back at the last second. Whoever had grabbed me was clearly not afraid of doing so in public. They must have a very powerful backer.

I had absolutely zero intelligence on my enemy, so I decided to let this play out a bit. Someone threw a bag over my head and snapped some shackles over my wrists, and I felt the wagon move quickly down the road. I could tell it turned into an alleyway after only a few minutes, and I was tossed out the back into a pile of empty canvas sacks. I was right back in the alley I had avoided less than an hour ago. I heard a voice.

"Take the bag off of his head. I want to see the look on his face!" The bag was yanked off, and I finally got a look at who I was dealing with.

It was the referee who had been burned. Behind him were a few of the other referees, and a person I hadn't seen before. He was medium height, and stick thin. He was shaved bald, and he had a dark, pencil-thin mustache. All of them were in red robes.

"He doesn't look afraid at all. Maybe we should show him why he should fear us!" The burned guy was screaming in my face, but the thin man pulled him back before turning to look at me.

"We just want you to pass on a message. Tell your friends on the council to back off, or they won't like what happens next." The thin man waved his hand, and the burned guy and his friends stepped forward, all of them holding short clubs. I couldn't hold in the sigh that escaped from my lips.

"I see. You guys are all tough and strong, so you tie up a child and beat him? Were you all born as spineless cowards, or did you choose to be like this?" They paused. "Well, are we doing this, or are you going to let me go?"

Ever since they had grabbed me, I had been carefully spooling out several threads of air qi from only my lower core, using the three meridians along my spine to hide them under my shirt and vest.

With my kidnappers being in such close proximity, I didn't want them to sense that I could use anything but my lower core. I was also hoping that they weren't using their own cores, because if they weren't, my threads of air qi would be invisible to them. My guess was they were planning on using simple physical strength to beat me, because using a qi attack would be overkill for half a dozen men to use on a kid. Well, any other kid.

I could see them decide through unspoken agreement to wallop the sense out of me, so I let loose the twenty threads I had prepared through the sleeves of my shirt. Three went to each of my attackers, and two went to snap off my shackles. I wrapped one thread around each of their necks and covered their mouths, one to hold their legs together, and the last to snatch the clubs out of their hands.

A few of them tried to activate their own cores, so I just squeezed tighter around their necks. That did the trick. Unless you trained for it, most people found it next to impossible to use their qi if they were unable to control their breathing. It was a bad habit the majority of the population picked up early. When gathering in energy, it helped to meditate when you were first learning to cultivate. During meditation, you used controlled breathing. Therefore, people subconsciously used their breathing techniques to help use their qi.

It had taken me almost a year of actual torture from Ming's instructors in the Elemental Guard to break the habit. These jerks clearly hadn't practiced it at all.

I pulled the bald man around so he was in front of the others. I knew he was the least likely of them to talk, so I decided to make an example out of him. I let them all get a good look at him, and then commenced beating him bloody with their own clubs. I took my time, making sure to really work over his joints. He tried being tough at first, but after I moved to his ribs, we could all hear his muffled cries. I also made sure to break all the little bones in his hands and feet. I stayed silent the entire time, remaining clinically methodical. The other five were definitely freaking out, their eyes all wide with fear. After I was sure he wasn't a threat anymore, I tossed him into the back of the wagon. I brought the next guy forward, and finally spoke to them.

"If you answer my questions, I only knock you out. If you don't answer my questions, you get what he did. Understood?"

I uncovered the mouth of the one in front. "You are crazy! Who are you?! What are you?!"

I covered his mouth again. "You clearly didn't understand. Maybe the next one will." He tried shaking his head, but I did the same to him as the first guy. He passed out after the first few minutes, but I didn't let up until he was in the same shape as his boss. The next one I pulled forward was the referee who had been burned. "How about you? Do you understand how this works?" He nodded his head vigorously. "Who is the person behind all of this?" I uncovered his mouth so he could answer.

"We work for Councilman Yisi! He sent us, but he told us not to kill you, just bruise you up some. We just wanted a little payback after everything that happened, that's all!"

I nodded my head. "And what else is this Yisi planning?"

He looked genuinely confused by the question. "Planning? He isn't planning anything. What else would he be up to? All we tried to do was fix a few fights!" From what Kory and Valerie's grandfather were saying, this Yisi was doing more than just fixing a few fights. These idiots just didn't know anything else.

Well, time to finish this. These six had seen too much, and I had learned a long time ago that only an idiot left enemies alive. Someone you beat now would only come up with a better plan and try again later. Never give your foe a second chance to kill you.

I snapped their necks, killing the four in front of me instantly. No sense in making them suffer. I wasn't a monster.

Then, I pulled out the other two from the wagon and did the same to them. I stripped them of anything valuable, finding a decent amount of coins on each and a storage ring on the bald one. I put the ring in the small coin purse hanging off of my belt, not sure if it would react poorly if put in the belt storage. I would check inside it later.

Next, I sent out some earth and wood threads to dig a pit right there in the alleyway. I threw in the bodies and covered them up. Then I made sure the spot blended in with the rest of the dirt around it. I didn't want to make it easy for someone to find them.

I looked in the back of the wagon. It had a few crates I didn't bother opening and several burlap sacks stuffed with root vegetables. More loot. I would take a closer look at what was inside everything later. The wagon itself was plain, no distinguishing marks on it. I found a set of hoops and a tarp under the seat that could be used to turn it into a covered wagon. I didn't know if something this big would go into the belt, but I figured it was worth a shot.

I disconnected the horse that had been pulling it and I leaned against the wagon, making sure I was touching a copper stud that was completely empty against the wood. I sent the command to pull it into the storage space, and promptly fell over. The wagon had fit! I think the belt might have gotten a few ounces heavier, but I barely noticed it. Man, I loved this belt.

I looked the horse over, not seeing anything wrong with it. It was getting close to the time I would need to meet up with everyone, so I started in that direction. I guess my shopping trip was over.

CHAPTER SIXTEEN

More New Friends

I found a stable near the edge of town and sold the horse for a few silvers. I didn't have any equipment for caring for a horse, and I didn't have the time to track some down. I also had a feeling there weren't many saddles readily available that would be sized appropriately, and I didn't want to bother putting in an order for one. I had occasionally used horses when serving Ming, but I preferred to either walk or ride in a carriage or wagon. I might revisit the issue later, but I didn't have the time to worry about it now.

I eventually found Kory and my friends waiting for me a few hundred yards outside the city limits, waiting on the road running between the fields of rice and grain that fed the city. I apologized for being the last to arrive, even though it was still before the designated meeting time.

"It's fine, we are still waiting on a few of my people to arrive. While we are in the forest, how would you all like to receive some instruction on scout training? Since you finished in the top ten of your respective tournaments, you would be assigned to my scouting units in the event of an attack anyway."

We all agreed, and he took a few minutes to explain the most common assignments we might receive.

Most of it was common sense stuff, like gauging any enemy numbers, composition, and troop movements, but some of it was actually interesting. In all my years, I had never thought to use scouts as a way to wage economic warfare. One of the Roh clan policies was to send scouts into enemy towns and villages and buy up as much food and supplies as they could, and then set up some shops to sell cheap and inferior goods at a much lower price than the normal products found in the region. It was pretty smart. An army on the march would suddenly hear word of financial problems back home, and it would lower morale while making their own supply lines difficult to maintain. Chu was especially impressed by the idea.

Around noon, three men and a woman finally showed up. By that point we had been sitting around for almost three hours, so I was starting to feel impatient. They were wearing cloaks meant to serve as camouflage while in the forest, and they kept their hoods up, hiding their features from the rest of us. The woman approached Kory and saluted with her fist to her heart.

"Captain, we were followed as we attempted to leave the compound. It took more time than expected to lose them, but the spies are currently following a trail leading down the southern path. By the time they realize their mistake, we should be deep into the forest."

Kory sighed. "It is starting already. Could you see how many there were?"

She shook her head. "At least seven, but there could have been more. What do you want us to do, Captain?"

He pulled out a small notebook, and flipped through it for a few minutes. "There is a patrol only a few miles deep into the southern woods. Two of you find them and tell them to keep an eye on the people searching for us. Once they get an actual count, have them report back to me."

They nodded and two of them took off, using qi to enhance their speed. The other two split up, one in front of our group, one behind. We started for the wall of trees in the distance and Donny started singing to lighten the mood. He had a nice voice, and soon the girls joined in. The news of someone trying to follow us had brought everyone down, but the songs, bright sunlight, and pleasant breeze helped reduce the invisible weight on our shoulders.

Wait a minute. Bright sunlight should make finding light qi easier, just like looking in deep shadow made finding dark qi possible. I fell towards the back of the group and waited until no one was looking in my direction. I ramped up the qi in my upper core to my maximum, my perception of time slowing until everything practically stopped. I had to make this fast; I didn't want anyone with me to notice I could use my upper core.

I looked at the energy flowing around me and I was surprised at how easy it was to see the dark qi in every shadow now. Apparently, since I had used it once, finding it again was a lot easier. I concentrated on where the sunlight was bouncing off the ground at my feet but I didn't see anything. I started looking everywhere.

It only took what felt like an hour or so to notice a white shimmer around the outline of every shadow. I felt like an idiot. Obviously, it was easiest to see the qi where contrast existed. I reached out to the shimmer and pulled it towards me. I was trying to use the same meridians I had channeled the shadow qi with, remembering Pride's warning to try to balance the two inside my body.

It was hard work, like trying to catch a beam of light with your hands. Not only that, but since time slowed down for me but not for the rest of the world, qi always moved like cold molasses from my perspective. After what felt like a few more hours of concentrating, and long enough that even the nearly frozen people in front of me had taken a full step forward, I finally caught a wisp of light qi and directed it towards my lower core.

It felt like I got punched in the gut. The faint traces of dark qi still in my system did not appreciate being contained next to the light qi. Which was odd, since they went hand-in-hand in nature. I decided to use the light qi immediately, to reduce the already small amount in my system. The obvious decision was to access the last two studs on the belt I was wearing. Just like before, they drained me, but I finally had access to all of my belt's secrets.

It was incredible. These studs weren't intended to store items. They were for storing qi! Even the emperor himself only had a single qi battery, and it was one of his most prized possessions. The benefits of having an actual qi battery were uncountable.

It wasn't like an elemental core, or a qi collecting rod. You could use those, but only to charge a formation, or after cycling the energy through your own body first. It was even better than the jewelry that was inside the Roh vaults. Instead of just one element, it could hold them all.

A qi battery was like having an extra, *external* core. As long as it was your qi that was stored in the battery, you could use it immediately. No spinning up the energy in your core first, no directing it through your meridians, you could just order it to do what you wanted directly from the battery itself. That meant you could attack or defend yourself without anyone sensing you were about to use qi. If you were unable to concentrate enough to use your own cores, like what happened to my ambushers in the alleyway, you could just use the qi battery directly.

In all of my years, I had never owned such a treasure. I don't think I had even *heard* of such a treasure. One battery, yes, but two? On the same object? Ming would have leveled cities to get his hands on it.

I was suddenly very suspicious. What were the odds of such an item ending up collecting dust in the vaults of a relatively minor clan like the Roh, and then for me happening into the circumstances that would allow me to obtain it? I heard the faint laughter again. Ah, I see. Somehow, either Pride or Wrath had orchestrated this.

I felt a chill run down my back. If they could orchestrate something like this, what else could they do? More importantly, what else did they have planned? I also remembered that Pride said there was something I needed inside the forest, but he hadn't said a word about this belt. If the belt wasn't something big enough for him to mention, what was waiting for me in this forest? I didn't know if it was going to be amazing or terrible, but I had a sneaking suspicion whatever it was would be a challenge.

I started to drain the qi currently stored in the batteries into my body and cycled it back into the batteries. If I was going to be able to use them to their full potential, I would need to make the qi stored inside them my own. Even though the energy I was draining wasn't mine, it felt odd, like it was more pure and complete than my own qi had ever been.

I took a closer look at it, and I realized that there was an equal representation of all eight types of qi in the energy. I also saw how the person before me was able to contain the dark and light qi without them interacting poorly with one another. The light qi was surrounded by wood qi, and the dark qi was contained by metal qi. I guess it made sense. Wood was the qi of life, and metal was the qi of death. There was some type of symbiosis going on here, but I would have to ponder more about it later.

After circulating the strange qi mixture through all three cores, I also used some to reinforce my body, core walls, and meridian channels. It was like my body was a desert, and this new qi was the water it had been waiting for. It was soaking it up faster than I could supply, so I slowed the flow going back into the batteries and focused more on my body.

By the time I had circulated everything the batteries held, there was less than a quarter of what I started with inside each of them. That was still a whole lot of power, but I couldn't help feeling shocked at how much my body absorbed.

It was difficult to tell what changes it had wrought on me without a mirror, but internally I could see my core walls and meridian channels were already at the point I could easily compare them to a Heart cultivator. I had just done six- or seven-years' worth of cultivation strengthening in less than a second of actual time. Now, I just needed to finish refilling the two batteries, and I could do it all over again.

However, by this point, I was mentally exhausted. I relaxed my upper core, and time returned to normal speeds. I stumbled at my first step, my balance and perception thrown off. I think I might have grown an inch or two. I looked down at my pants, trying to gauge if they looked shorter or not. Nope. Magic pants. They automatically resized to the perfect fit.

At least the others might not notice the changes, because my clothes hadn't changed. The vest felt a little tight, so I fed it some qi to give it the energy to resize itself as well. Just as I finished up, there was a commotion in front of the group.

As I had fallen to the back and I was still the shortest, I couldn't see anything. I swung out to the right, trying to see what the problem was.

Standing at the edge of the tree line a hundred yards away from us was the young elder from the tournament. He had two dozen friends with him. Once again, they were all wearing red robes. Methinks there might have been a pattern with their attire…

Kneeling at his feet were the two scouts Kory had sent off to find the patrol, and the hooded female scout who had been leading our group.

"We have been waiting for you," said the young elder, "and personally, I have been looking forward to this."

Great. More new friends.

CHAPTER SEVENTEEN

Sobering Thoughts

My group started spreading out, giving each other room. Kory took a few steps closer, moving in front of us while keeping his hands out and away from his body.

"I don't know what you are thinking, Conrad, but we are all clanmates here. That means we are all on the same side. Why don't you release those three, and we can talk about this like the adults we all are?" The young elder, apparently named Conrad, didn't take that comment as it was intended.

"Are you trying to say that I am not an adult? I might be the youngest elder the Roh clan has seen in a few centuries, but I am not a child!" I couldn't help it. I let out a tiny laugh. Apparently, this guy had a complex. "Do you think this is funny, boy?! You and I are going to have a very long talk about respecting your betters! If you survive that talk, you can go back to your masters and tell them that their plan to remove my friends and I from power is futile. The Roh clan will follow our lead, and there is nothing you can do to change that."

While Conrad was yelling at me, Kory had been subtly giving hand signals to the scouts that were tied up. I saw the female nod her head, and all three of them crouched down as low as they could. Kory took another step closer.

"Conrad, all I was trying to say is that there is another way we should be going about this. We are all family here. That boy you are threatening shares the same ancestors as you do. That means you should be protecting him, not threatening him. Let my people go, and we can sit down over some tea. I am open to talking with you."

I had been spinning out earth qi threads underground during the threats and talking, and they were close enough to them that I could gauge their strength. It was a mix of Meridian and Brain cultivators, with the elder being at the middle stage of the Saint level.

So, he was the only real threat. I could probably take care of them all on my own, but I wasn't sure I could keep a few from escaping. I decided it would be best to let Kory handle what he could, and I would step in only if things were looking bad.

Conrad finally spoke up again. "This is what is going to happen. You are all going to surrender yourselves to me. Then, we are going to talk about what plans the chief elder has shared with you. After that, you are all going to spend some time in the comforts of a location some friends and I have set up deep in the woods." They all let out a sinister chuckle. "You can choose to come quietly, or you can be carried. You decide, but I know which way I prefer."

His group of friends all laughed and grinned at his comment. Stars, I hated sycophants. Conrad's joke wasn't even funny! Well, not funny enough to warrant them laughing out loud. I *really* wanted to kill these people.

The scout Kory had trailing behind us finally caught up to the group, and that must have been the signal.

"Tiger's Sweeping Claws!" Kory shouted out, sweeping his hands in front of him. The three that were tied up rolled forward, dodging under the wave of metal and fire qi that launched from Kory's outstretched hands and running back to us. I used my hidden earth qi threads to trap Conrad and his friends' feet in place, forcing them to take the brunt of his attack instead of dodging it.

Some of them were able to put up some form of shield, but most of them were looking a little rough after the attack. I released them from my qi threads and a few fell to their knees in pain. I had tried to time it so that they thought my qi threads were actually just an aspect of Kory's attack. I hoped it worked.

The scout who wasn't tied up freed the others as they reached our group. They looked like Conrad and his friends had worked them over a bit, but they were all still on their feet. I glanced at Conrad, and he did not look like a happy individual.

"You think this makes a difference?! We will crush you all, and I will personally make sure that none of you walk away from this!" I felt him spin up all three of his cores, and I was mildly impressed by how much power he could call upon. Apparently, he actually earned his ranking as a clan elder. He must have been a very gifted cultivator. Too bad I was going to have to kill him.

I had noticed something about Conrad while he was shouting. Even though an attack had just come from underground, he hadn't adjusted his qi shield to cover the bottoms of his feet. Clearly, he hadn't been in many serious battles.

He opened his mouth to shout something else, but I speared up an earth qi thread into his right foot. His eyes widened from the pain. I shoved it up several inches into his calf before he managed to block it with a wall of his own qi. I looped the thread around the bones in his leg, an inch or two before they reached his foot. I pulled down sharply, bringing my qi thread back underground. The thread was thin and strong enough that it passed through bone and flesh with ease.

From the outside, I imagined it looked like a faint line of blood appeared on the back of his leg and heel. I knew that on the inside his bones were severed at an angle, and as the leg collapsed under his weight, they were like miniature knives inside his body. The bones of his calf slid backwards, shoving through the skin and all the way into the ground. The bones above his foot shoved forwards, poking out of the skin of his shin. Whatever it was he was going to say turned into screams of agony.

And that, kids, was why you spent the extra time at the Brain level to strengthen your body and bones with *all* the elements of qi. If he had used an equal amount of all types of qi to strengthen his bones, none of this would have worked.

No one had any idea what had happened. Fortunately, Kory was experienced enough to take advantage of the circumstances. He and his scouts sprang forward, my friends a heartbeat behind them. I brought up the rear, my shorter legs making me slower than the rest of them. The enemy group tried to form a wall in front of the downed Conrad, but they were no match for the professional scouts.

Chu was battling a pair of Meridian cultivators and the girls were moving to support him. Donny was flanking to the left. I crouched down in the high grass along the edge of the trail, moving to a position where I could see Conrad again. It took a few seconds, but I finally saw him limping away between the trees at the edge of the forest. He had two of his people helping him escape.

We couldn't let him get away. I had some questions about who else might be at this location they had in the woods. If he had my parents, I needed to know.

I looked back at how my group was faring against the red robes and it looked like we had the edge. They might have more people, but there was a huge difference in skill. Professional fighters would always beat village toughs.

After being sure they would come out on top, I headed towards Conrad. They weren't moving very quickly as they stumbled through the woods, which was good for me. I could move incredibly fast if I used qi, but like always, that would give too much away. I pumped my cursedly short legs for all they were worth and caught up to the three as they stumbled into a clearing. Finally. No witnesses. None that mattered, anyway.

"Elder, what happened back there? You should be able to easily handle Captain Kory. He just made it to Saint last year!" One of the red robed idiots was pulling out a canteen as he was talking.

"I don't know what happened. The dirty trick they used on me was far more vicious than anything I have ever seen. I didn't even know someone could make a qi construct that thin!" He collapsed to the ground between the other two, trying to inspect the damage to his leg as he talked. "The control needed for that would take decades of training and practice. How did Kory manage something like that?"

Well, I was smart enough to recognize a great entrance when I heard one.

"It wasn't Kory," I made sure to speak loudly as I stepped into the clearing, "it was me." The looks on their faces were classic, mouths making perfect 'o' shapes. "And it doesn't take decades to learn the techniques I use. It takes centuries."

With that, I speared two metal qi threads through the throats of the red robes on either side of Conrad. I pulled the threads free as they dropped, and I felt Conrad try to spin up his cores. I used the qi threads to give him some new and very fashionable ear piercings, which broke his concentration.

"We can't have that now, can we, dearest Conrad?" He hissed in pain as I manipulated the threads to force his face up to look at me.

"Who are you? How are you doing this?"

I smiled at his discomfort. Something in my face must have scared him, because he started trembling as I got closer.

"First, I have some questions for you. Where is this place in the woods you were talking about?" He tried to pull away, so I moved closer, placing my foot on his severed bones. "I didn't ask you a hard question, so only you can make these hard answers. Where. Is. The. Hidden. Location?"

He swallowed in fear. "Two miles east of the lake, at the center of the woods. There are some ruins. We restored a few buildings."

I took my foot off his wounded leg. "Are there any prisoners there already?"

He shook his head, wincing in pain as his new ear piercings pulled. "I don't know! This was going to be my first trip there. All I know is to keep a lookout for traps. I have the qi pattern to disarm them memorized."

I nodded. I believed him. I released the metal qi strands that were shoved through his ears.

"Who is your boss? Who is the ringleader for all of this?"

His eyes widened, and he scooted a few feet away from me. "You don't understand! I can't answer. If you force me to answer, the blood oath I swore would kill me before the words passed my lips!"

I frowned. Blood oaths were nasty things. They were reinforced by your own internal qi, and until released by the holder, you were forced to do their bidding. I hadn't even sworn a blood oath to Ming when I joined the Elemental Guard, and later became one of his Enforcers.

Something like that could limit your cultivation potential, holding you back from making a breakthrough to the next level. Councilman Yisi, if he was the true man in charge of all of this, was a nasty customer.

I raised my right hand, the one currently carrying the spirit wood ring. I still hadn't had the time to inspect it further, but I knew one form that could be useful. Conrad was already trying to inch away from me.

"Wait! You need me to get past the traps! There is no way you can get past them without me. Besides, we're family. You don't want to kill members of your family, do you?"

I scowled at him. "You were going to beat me, abuse me, and most likely kill me. You knew I was a member of your family, but it did nothing to stop you. Why would I let something like family stop me?" I activated the ring and shoved the spear through his eye and into his brain.

I quickly dug another pit and tossed the bodies inside. After searching them, I found another storage ring on the elder. The other two only had a few silvers, and one had a map with no reference marks on it.

I buried them without ceremony, using the life energy of wood qi to make the grass grow evenly over the area to hide the makeshift grave. I moved back towards my friends, making sure I erased any trails that led to the clearing. It took longer than I expected, but by the time I reached the edge of the forest, the fighting was finished.

The four scouts were standing around a group of people that were tied up. Kory was standing by another group, but no one had bothered to tie them up. They were dead. I rushed over, afraid that my friends were among their number.

The thought that I might have miscalculated and one of them had died as a result of my own hubris was a sobering thought.

CHAPTER EIGHTEEN

Revealing Some Secrets

Once I reached Kory, my fears were proven false. All four were okay, just laid out on the side of the road, suffering from qi exhaustion. Kory walked over to me, looking me over for injuries.

"I was worried about you. I didn't see you after the fighting started. When I noticed that Conrad was missing as well, I was afraid they had somehow taken you."

I shook my head. "No, I saw them running away, and tried to follow them. Unfortunately, I couldn't keep up and they got away. Two of the red robes were carrying the elder, so we should only be missing three. Unless more got away during the fighting here."

Kory looked off into the trees. "I don't think any got away. There might have been a lot of them, but they weren't really fighters. Once we took the momentum, we had the fight won. Did you see what direction they were going towards?"

I sat down, feigning exhaustion. "Before they noticed me and sped away, I heard them mentioning a hideout a few miles from the lake at the center of the forest. We should take a look.

Maybe whoever is there saw my parents in the area, and captured them."

He grunted, and moved over to the bodies.

I quickly joined him, and pretended to find the map I had found on a different person. "Kory, I found a map."

He rushed over, and brought it to his scout team. While they were looking things over, I finished searching the last few bodies. Nothing was as exciting as the storage ring or the map, so I moved over to check on my friends.

Donny was the only one awake. The others were still knocked out, and Chu was snoring loud enough to scare the smaller creatures along the edge of the forest away. Donny was still pretty out of it, but his eyes cleared a bit as he saw me come close.

"Jim, thank the Stars you are okay! You disappeared, and I was afraid someone had kidnapped you! I don't know what I would have told your parents if I had lost you."

I sat on the ground next to him. "I appreciate the concern, Donny, but I am doing okay. I was trying to track down the elder as he escaped, but I couldn't keep up with them. How about you? What happened here while I was gone?"

He glanced over at Kory, who was now questioning the prisoners. "You should have seen the captain in action. It was like he was everywhere at once, blocking their attacks, knocking someone clear across the field the next, and all the while coordinating his four scouts into the best places to be effective. Kory has clearly been fighting for a very long time." I nodded along, showing that I was paying attention. "Kory even made sure that the rest of us were never overwhelmed by someone who was too powerful for us to handle. It was almost like he was funneling the weaker enemies to the four of us, and the stronger ones to his people. I have never seen someone command a battle like that in my life."

I see. I was beginning to suspect that Kory was part of the faction inside the Roh clan that knew what they were doing.

"I am glad that everything went okay." I inspected my

unconscious friends with a few qi threads. "Do any of you need healing?"

Donny shook his head. "No, Chu was able to patch us all up before he passed out. Do you think we will still be able to search for your parents?"

I frowned. I hadn't thought of that. Kory probably wanted to head back with the prisoners first.

"I don't care what the others want to do, I am still going to look for them. I don't know what has kept them away for so long, but I am not willing to abandon the search before even trying."

Donny nodded in agreement. "I will go with you. It wouldn't be right to leave you in the woods by yourself."

While it would be easier for me to just do all of this by myself, I was actually happy that Donny was concerned about me. My childhood memories about him were all proving to be correct. Donny had always been protective of me, and I remembered him being a good person. If I could, I would like to take him with me when I left the clan.

The other three would be nice to bring as well, but I wasn't sure if I wanted a party that big traveling the countryside with me. The more people there were, the more careful I would have to be. I would decide how things would go when the time came.

I told Donny to get some rest, and I went back to check on Kory and the scouts. They were all looking pretty beaten up, but the prisoners looked worse. Kory stopped whatever he was saying as I got close.

"Captain Kory, it is already getting close to evening. Would you like me to try to find a campsite near the edge of the forest?"

He looked towards the tree line; his face pensive. "We need to get these prisoners back to the clan before sunset. There are thirteen of them, which is too many to keep an eye on in the dark. We need to ensure their safety, and our own. We should head back to the city and try this again tomorrow."

I frowned. Not the answer I wanted, but it was the one I

expected. "There is nothing saying this wouldn't happen again tomorrow, and there is no way I am going back. Whoever these people in red robes are, they clearly have enough chaff in their ranks that they don't mind throwing some away." I looked back towards the city in the distance. "It would be better for you five to return, get some healing and rest, and catch up to us tomorrow. We should be fine spending just one night in the woods. As long as we don't go deep into the forest, we should be able to handle anything that thinks we are food." I could tell he didn't like the plan, but he couldn't afford to force me back to the city and keep tabs on all of his prisoners.

"I don't like it, but since you won't return, I can't think of anything better. Just make sure you leave an obvious enough trail that we can follow it, and don't go past the second river before we meet up with you. There are some nasty creatures in that water, and I don't want you kids risking it by yourselves." I agreed, and they rounded up the prisoners and started moving out.

I had a sneaking suspicion that the captured red robes would be back on the streets before Kory even made it back out of the city, but I didn't think it prudent to kill them all with so many witnesses. It went against my own rule of leaving enemies around, but I didn't have a choice.

Instead of walking directly over to my friends, I decided to take a look at what was in the two storage rings I had captured. The first was from the man in the alley and it was a relatively small space, around a hundred square feet. It contained a small chest filled with silver coins, about two hundred of them. It was probably the pay for the other men in the alley. I was happy to have it. I needed smaller denominations besides the gold I had, and it had the current emperor's face printed on it.

I would certainly be able to spend the older denominations I had found in the belt, but I wanted to wait until I was in a bigger town first. There were also a few sets of clothes, a cheap sword, and several accounting books. I would have to take a closer look at those later. I emptied the contents into the various studs on my belt and pulled out the elder's ring.

This time, things were looking much better. The ring could hold close to five hundred square feet, and it was crammed full with all kinds of goodies. There were three pouches of coins; copper, silver, and gold. Combined, the value was probably worth over seventy gold.

I also found over a dozen sets of red robes and a few sets of dyed leather armor that matched. There were three full weapon racks, one of short swords, one of spears, and one of halberds. The rest of the space was filled with pill and elixir bottles. There was medicine for healing, pills for cultivation, poisons, antidotes, and qi refinement pills. I took a moment to catalogue them all, and I moved some things around to make room for everything in my belt. Now, I could give the rings to my friends as gifts. I thought about keeping them for myself, but I really didn't want to walk around with a ton of rings on all of my fingers. One on each hand was my normal limit.

I walked over to Donny and handed him the smaller of the two. He looked at me with surprise.

"Is this what I think it is? How did you get this? Why are you just giving it to me? You do realize this ring is worth a small fortune, right?"

I laughed at him. "Donny, you need something to give you an edge. Walking around with that heavy pack on isn't doing anyone any favors. Just take it. I wanted a way to say thank you for standing beside me, anyway." He tried to protest some more, so I just walked away.

The next ring was for Chu. I woke him up and handed him the ring without saying anything. He was still a bit groggy, so he accepted it with a simple thank you. I gave him the larger ring because he would be able to use it to help him carry more goods for his future business. I woke the girls, and after some water and a basic plan was roughed out, we headed into the forest.

We traveled silently along a small game trail, single file because of the narrow gaps between the trees. I was in the lead, then Chu, the girls behind him, and Donny bringing up the rear. I had my underground feelers out, but I wasn't detecting anything bigger than a rabbit within a few hundred yards. I had decided to follow the game trail because it had a high probability of leading us to water. If possible, I wanted to reach the first river Kory had mentioned. We would stop for the night on the far side, and wait for the scout captain on the banks of the second river tomorrow. Donny was using a spear to leave marks on the occasional tree we passed, making it easy for the scouts to find us.

Our group reached the river without incident, but we hit our first snag trying to cross it. The water was too deep, and traveling too swiftly to pass through safely. We decided to follow it downstream for a while, trying to find a safe place to cross.

It was almost dark before we found a place narrow enough that we felt like we could jump across. Once we made it to the other side, I couldn't find another game trail to follow. We had to walk back upstream to the trail we had used before. It was now fully dark, and I knew that my friends were getting close to exhaustion.

We had all been through quite a day, and I knew they needed rest as well. We only followed the trail a few hundred feet into the forest before finding a spot that would work as a campsite.

The girls set a fire and Chu pulled out the ingredients for a stew. I helped Donny set up two tents, one for the girls and one for the boys. By the time we had the bedrolls stretched out, the smell of the food was wafting in our direction.

We sat in a circle around the fire, quietly watching Chu stir the pot. I was shocked when I saw tears glistening on a few faces. Then I realized how detached I was being. They had just killed people for the first time. Everyone they had killed was obviously an enemy and I had no doubt that they had no other choice. Still, it wasn't a good feeling to take another life, and processing it for the first time wasn't easy. I tapped Donny on the shoulder, and motioned him to go sit with Valerie. I did the same to Jamila, and she moved to sit with Chu.

"I know you are all going through a lot right now, and it isn't fair that you were put in a position to have to take another's life in self-defense. Unfortunately, the life of a cultivator is never easy, and you walk a long road that will be filled with death. You each have to decide for yourself if it is worth the journey." I left them to ponder that nugget of wisdom, and pulled out some blank copper disks to carve a few protection-formation wards. Eight should be enough to set up a strong barrier to keep predators away and allow us all a full night of sleep.

Chu dished up the stew as I set the wards, and I took mine as I sat down next to the fire again.

Jamila cleared her throat. "I think it is time we all had a talk, Jim." The lack of surprise on the other's faces told me they had been talking while I was away from the fire. "You are like no child I have ever met. You offer sage insights, advanced battleplans, know how to move through the forest, fight like a demon, and can carve powerful formation plates from memory. There are moments when I feel like I should be bowing to you, and others when you are so awkward around Valerie and I that I think I imagined the whole thing. Who are you, really?"

Everyone stared at me, even Donny. He frowned before talking, looking at me as if searching for something. "Ever since you touched the testing stone, you have changed. You are still Jim, but not the same Jim I know."

Chu took his turn next. "I have never met a ten-year-old that would simply hand over a storage ring fit for a clan elder. A treasure like that could change their life, but you just handed one to me like it was nothing. I appreciate it, but I don't understand it."

Instead of talking, Valerie just nodded her agreement.

Okay, so I was apparently *very* bad at hiding.

I took a deep breath and thought about what to say before answering. "I can't explain everything to you right now. Just know, when I touched the testing stone, it changed me more than anyone could guess." I looked around, and saw on their faces that it wasn't enough to convince them. "I was given a mission by the gods. That storm of darkness that happened when I touched the stone was an invasion. Our world has been infested with a new type of demon, and it is my job to stop them. I was given the insights and abilities needed to stop them, and if I fail, everyone dies. There is one of them here, in these woods." They had all gotten really still, as if afraid that making any kind of movement would keep them from hearing me. "I need to find my parents, but I also have to find and stop the demon. If you join me, you will see that I am telling you the truth." They were all stunned into silence. Then, I realized they weren't looking at me anymore. They were looking behind me.

I spun in place, throwing out a fire qi whip from my left hand and ordering the spirit wood ring into a spear in my right. At the edge of the firelight stood Kory.

"Now I understand what is different about you. You are a Chosen One, given a mission by the gods themselves." He took a knee. "I will fight by your side for as long as you would have me, and assist you in your endeavors."

I had to admit, I was more than a little shocked. I hadn't felt him approach my wards, and I was sure a Saint-level cultivator wouldn't have been able to get past without triggering them.

"How long have you been there?"

He stayed kneeling, but looked up to answer me. "I caught up shortly after you made camp. I thought it prudent to wait a bit, to see if there was anything I could learn. Now, I know how foolish I was being. If you had announced to everyone what happened as soon as you spoke to the gods, the full might of the Roh clan would stand behind you."

I had to smirk at that one. Things were *never* that easy, not even in the tales told to children.

"Get up, Captain Kory. Have some stew, and take a seat by the fire." I was surprised at how easily he complied. As he settled himself and got a bowl of food, I continued. "Tell me truly, Captain. If some random child were to approach you and say that the gods had spoken to them, right after touching the testing stone, would you take them seriously?" He pondered the question while eating his stew, then silently shook his head. "As for you fighting by my side, let's take care of the demon within these woods first. We need to secure our own backyard before moving towards bigger projects." Everyone nodded at that idea.

We quietly finished our food, everyone lost in their own thoughts. Kory eventually got up and collected the bowls, using some water and fire qi to clean them before handing them back to Chu. Donny helped him set up his own small tent, between the two already erected, before everyone stumbled into their sleeping rolls. I had a few things I wanted to do before going to bed myself.

I took a longer look at the spirit wood ring I was wearing and finally got a better idea at what forms it could take. A thin round shield, a short dagger-like stake, the knuckle dusters, the spear, a thick walking stick, and curiously, a spoon, were all the forms it would accept. I could probably add a few more if I wanted, but I didn't think it would be worth the effort. It would eventually need a wood-aspect elemental core or two to increase and reinforce the internal power matrix, but it was fine for now.

Next, I took a longer look at my vest. The qi matrix inside it was much more robust, but it appeared to have been done in layers. The leather could be expanded to cover the neck and arms, but not lengthened to cover any lower than the waist.

The best find was the lowest pair of sheaths on the abdomen. If I was seeing things correctly, all I would have to do was feed the vest metal qi and it could form more blades. That meant if I lost a knife, I could easily replace it. The system was slow, so it would take a few hours of concentrated effort to replace one, but I wouldn't need to worry about retrieving every knife thrown.

I had seen qi matrixes like it before, but they were usually placed directly on weapons, not on hard leather sheaths. If it was used on a weapon such as a sword, it would repair any chips or cracks the weapon might suffer from. I really liked this vest, and the ideas it was giving me were numerous.

Finally, I pulled out the silver-inlaid bow. It would be considered a short bow by most, but to me it was definitely a longbow. I took my time inspecting it, trying to make sure I didn't miss anything. From what I could tell, it could imbue the power of whatever qi you infused it with into the arrows it fired. There was no limiter in place, so the only limit to how much qi the arrow held was up to the strength of the arrow.

I could already see the upside for someone who was hunting a creature that was weak to only one element. It would be easy to just try out each element on the *nox* I was fighting until I found the one that hurt it.

The downside was, it would take some practice. Too much fire qi would make the arrow burn up before it reached the target, and I was sure that pumping in too much metal or earth qi would make the arrow too heavy to reach a target that was far away. I also couldn't help but wonder what wood qi would do to a *nox*. Unless it was an undead creature, wood would just heal it. Unfortunately, I didn't know enough about my enemy to come up with any real plan.

I thought for a bit about how much I had told everyone. I didn't think I had given too much away, but I had no idea how this would play out. I needed to make the intelligent faction inside the Roh clan aware of what was going on with the *nox*, but I couldn't have them following me around. I wanted them to stop any *nox* that came into their area, but beyond that they would only become a burden.

A small group of seemingly weak people could easily pass between regions, but a large group of powerful people would draw too much attention. Like Pride and Wrath had warned, I didn't want any of the emperor's spies or recruiters to notice me. All it would take was one false move, and I would either be killed or captured, destined to repeat the folly of my first life.

What I really needed to do was make the leader of the entire southern province aware of the *nox*, without him noticing

I was the one who warned him about it. I actually knew the man from my first life, but I had no idea how to approach him in this timeline.

Either way, I had a plan for my next few steps. Find my parents, kill the *nox* hidden in the woods, stop the leader of the red robes, get the Roh clan to let me go while keeping an eye out for any other demons in the region, and gain entrance to the capitol building of the Southern Province. It sounded like a lot, but I had to keep moving forward. The lives of billions were depending on it. With that sobering thought, I finally went to my own bed roll for some rest.

CHAPTER NINETEEN

Bend the Knee

I was back in Roh City. This time, I was standing outside what looked like the city guardhouse near the western road. I was dream walking again. This time, I knew I needed to take advantage of the opportunity. Someone was trying to show me something, and I didn't want to miss my chance.

I approached the wall of windows in front of me, seeing torchlight flickering through the closed shutters. I heard voices.

"How did they capture you?"

"I don't know what happened, but Elder Conrad just collapsed! Him and a few others managed to get away, but that bastard Kory was able to keep the rest of us from escaping."

"I see. We will have to be careful. Were you able to kill the boy?"

"No, sir. He disappeared when the fighting started. He didn't seem all that powerful."

"I would hope not, but that is two groups I have sent against him that have failed. The first one has vanished and the second was overpowered and captured. I don't like unexpected surprises, and this boy is surrounded by them."

"What do you want us to do now, sir?"

"I want you and the others to head towards the base in the ruins. You can send out search parties from there. Try not to come into contact with Kory, but kill the kids if you have the chance. If they run into any of our traps, our problems might be over with anyway. Either way, I want their heads on my desk as proof. I have come too far to let mere children keep me from my goals."

"I will do as you command, sir. Will we have anyone to help, in case Kory spots us?"

"Find Conrad. I don't have any Saint-level cultivators to spare for something like this. He should be more than enough to handle the scout captain."

"Of course, Councilman. I will make it happen."

"Good, now gather your friends and get out of my sight!"

I heard the shuffling of several pairs of feet, and then a gate opened in the distance. There were more than the thirteen prisoners I remembered being captured that were heading down the path. I would have to warn my friends somehow, without giving away how I knew.

A few seconds after the last man cleared the gate, a tall man in blood-red robes stood in the entrance. He had long white hair, and a thin goatee that matched. His face was twisted into a permanent scowl. Not from scars or anything, just from what appeared to be a generally negative disposition on life. His dark eyes were squinting into the night, watching his men walking down the trail. I think I was getting my first look at Councilman Yisi. Another man dressed in the armor of the city guards walked up behind him.

"Is there anything else you need, Councilman?"

Yisi handed over a large pouch to the man and shook his head. "That will be all. Make sure you leave this out of the report, will you?" He nodded, taking a look inside the pouch as he answered.

"Yes, Uncle, of course. Is everything still proceeding as planned?"

It was Yisi's turn to nod. "By this time next month, control of the clan will fall to me. We will finally get back what was taken from us, and any who stand against us will either bend the knee or be removed."

I felt someone grab my shoulder, and I was pulled back into a bright light.

CHAPTER TWENTY

Scorpions

"Time to wake up, Jim. I swear, you sleep like the dead." It was Donny, shaking me awake. I saw sunlight coming through the tent opening.

"What time is it? Is everyone else awake?"

Donny nodded, still getting his gear on as he talked. "They are packing up camp now and Jamila is making breakfast. Kory already slipped the wards, and is checking around camp. Come on, help me pack up." I helped take down the tents, and put away the bed rolls.

Apparently, Donny was now carrying everything we needed to camp in his storage ring. Chu seemed to have taken all the cooking materials and food. It made sense, I supposed, dividing up the tasks and speeding up the process for when we stopped to make camp. As long as we weren't separated, of course. I needed to find some more storage rings for Valerie and Jamila. I didn't want them to feel left out.

Kory returned as we were starting to dish up breakfast. It was some type of fried sausage next to a steaming bowl of honeyed porridge. He spoke while we ate.

"There weren't any signs of predators nearby, and I think

this trail will lead us straight to the second river. Once we cross over, things will start getting more dangerous. The deep forest is seldom patrolled, and the beasts within are not nearly as afraid of humans as I would like. We should wait for my team to arrive before we move too far past the riverbanks. I can't ensure the safety of all of you by myself."

I nodded in agreement. "What about the enemies you captured? By now, word has to have reached whoever wants us dead. There are probably people already hunting after us. We can't afford to wait too long."

Kory took a few minutes to eat his food and think it over. "I agree, even though I don't like it. My team will catch up as soon as they can. We should probably stop marking our trail. The scouts are trained well enough to find us without them. We shouldn't make it easier for our enemies to find us."

We all agreed, and finished packing everything away. Kory gave the campsite a once-over, making sure we weren't leaving behind any signs of our passage.

Today, everyone was wearing armor, their weapons out and ready. The girls were wearing a mixture of chainmail and leather, while Donny and Chu were wearing full breastplates with greaves and vambraces to protect their lower legs and forearms.

This time Kory led the way, and I brought up the rear. My friends didn't treat me any different after what I had told them last night, and I appreciated it. I had never enjoyed people fawning over me, or fearing me, in my past life. I had never seen the appeal. That they treated me the same was a gift they didn't even know they had given me. Even Kory, after he had sworn his service to me, had fallen back into his old habit of taking charge. I didn't mind. I had a feeling I would better serve as the force behind the scenes for a long time to come.

I spent our time walking subtly erasing the majority of our tracks as we traveled. I half-suspected the scouts following us wouldn't make it past the group of red robes trying to track us, but in case they did I wanted to leave them an opportunity to find our group.

It took until midday, but we finally reached the second river. This one was much wider, and we could cross as long as we watched our footing. The water was swift, but only knee deep for the taller members of our party across the majority of its width. Kory waded across first, the very center of the river reaching his hips. After reaching the opposite shore, Kory yelled back some instructions.

"Watch out for the deeper section in the center! It almost pulled me off my feet!" We waved to show we heard him, and Jamila went across next. The water was up to her chest as she reached the middle, and the cold took her breath away. She was struggling across when I heard her try to scream. Something yanked her under the water and started pulling her downstream.

Kory and I reacted instantly, the others a half-step behind. He was on one side, I was on the other, both of us sprinting along the banks. I looked up ahead and saw a fallen tree sticking out into the water. It was large enough that it would slow me down trying to climb over it. I didn't have time for this.

I jumped in the water, using the current to help pull me along. As soon as I reached the deepest section, I dove under, trying to see any sign of Jamila amid the swirling debris that was stirred up by all the commotion. I couldn't see anything.

I threw out some threads of water qi, trying to feel anything. I thought I felt something a few yards past the branches of the tree, but I couldn't be sure. I was still over a hundred feet away but the current was dragging me closer by the second. I pushed my qi threads farther downstream, trying to keep up with whatever I had nudged.

As I cleared the tree, I popped up to the surface, looking back for my friends. Kory had run into a problem. Somehow, all the activity had drawn the attention of a group of some *huge* scorpions. Valerie and Donny were trying to cross the stream to help, and Chu was trying to climb over the tree to continue the search for Jamila.

I hated scorpions. I hated them with a passion unbridled. It might have something to do with the time period in my life when I was building up an immunity to venom and poisons, but if I could have one wish, it would be for all scorpions to die a painful death filled with fire and agony.

I refocused. I hadn't felt anything from my qi threads in a while, and I was growing more concerned about Jamila. She was a fire cultivator and she was entirely out of her element. I hadn't seen her surface in a long time. She probably had less than a minute or two to get a breath, or she was going to drown.

I flattened out some of the qi threads I had in the water, using them like an underwater sail to propel me faster down the river. There. A qi thread felt like it brushed up against some hair, floating in a deep pit towards the side of the main channel. I covered the area with threads, trying to hone in on her.

I felt her outline, and the outline of what was most likely some form of serpent or eel. It was wrapped around her, holding her down in some sort of pit on the other side of a large rock. I needed to get her some air.

I spun out two massive strands of earth qi from my hands and buried them at the base of the pit. I pumped over half of the qi in my system into raising up the riverbed, trying to form a type of plateau that would bring her and the creature up to the surface. I felt my meridians straining, but I dared not stop.

It took longer than I would have liked but an oval pillar of earth and stone eventually shot up out of the river. I had floated past them by this point, so I could barely see what was going on. Luckily, the large rock at the edge of the pit blocked enough of the current that it didn't wash Jamila away as they rose above the churning water.

Chu finally caught up, and I swear he actually ran on the surface of the river to get to her. The creature wrapped around her was some form of water snake, and he had a spear through its head faster than I could blink. Stars, he really liked that girl.

I finally made it over to them, having to swim against the current for a bit. Raising the riverbed had really taken it out of me. It was a blatant reminder for me to focus on getting stronger.

Upon reaching them, I saw that her lips were blue and she wasn't breathing. Chu was shouting nonsense, and pumping enough wood qi into her system that he was lucky she wasn't sprouting extra limbs. Life energy was tricky, and if used improperly, it could do more harm than good.

I grabbed him, and turned him towards me. "Chu! Snap out of it! She needs air, focus on clearing the water out of her lungs!" He was nodding, but I was afraid he wasn't really hearing what I was saying. I pushed him out of the way and knelt over her. I rolled her onto her side and pounded on her chest. Then, I spooled out a strand of air qi and shoved it down her airway. Her lungs were completely filled with water.

I forced a stream of air in, and her diaphragm spasmed. She pushed out a massive stream of water and she started coughing. Thank the gods, she was going to make it.

Now it was Chu's turn to shove me out of the way. He held her against him, trying to help her as she vomited up more water. This time, he was applying a gentler stream of wood qi, trying to help repair any damage her lungs might have. Now that she was okay, I needed to get back to the fight. I shuddered, thinking of having to face those monstrous scorpions.

"I need to help the others. Are you okay here?"

Chu nodded, waving me back towards our friends. "I have her, you get going. We will catch up as soon as we can." I turned around and launched myself towards the opposite bank.

I wasn't running at top speed, but I was close. I was trying to cycle as much qi back into my system as possible before I reached my friends. I could already hear shouting on the other side of a thick cluster of trees, and it didn't sound like things were going well. I had already almost lost one friend today. It was time to stop hiding and use my full skill set.

I spun a wood qi thread from the meridians in each knee and launched them into the thick branches of the trees above me. I became a human slingshot, shooting myself into the sky above the fight between ten scorpions the size of dogs and my three friends. I spun qi into my brain core, slowing time and seeing what I had missed.

It looked like the scorpions were resistant to qi attacks. Otherwise, Kory would have killed at least a few of them by now. Instead, he was trying to keep up a qi shield to stop them from reaching Donny and Valerie. Both of them were down. I couldn't see what had happened to them, but they were both extremely pale.

That was the moment I saw a creature straight from my nightmares. A scorpion the size of a bull was slowly poking its head out of the tree line. For it to be moving that fast with time slowed down, this scorpion was incredibly quick. If these guys were resistant to qi, I would have to use something else. Time for my vest to shine.

I was running low on qi, so I had to allow time to speed up a bit to form the number of threads necessary to pull out all of my throwing knives. I held on to the knives running along my sides, but every other knife was being manipulated by threads of air qi. I lined up my shots and flung them forward with as much momentum as I could impart.

As I released the knives, I allowed time to return to normal. I fell behind Kory's shield, rolling to reduce the impact with the ground. The knives hit the scorpions before I touched down, cracking into the hardened carapaces with a sound like a tree snapping in half.

Most impacted where I wanted, piercing them through the center of their bodies. I knew nothing of scorpion anatomy, besides the fact that they were absolutely disgusting creatures birthed from the nightmares of a madman, but I figured there must be something important in the middle of all that nasty.

I looked towards the tree line, trying to see if momma scorpion was down. I had thrown five knives at the big one, just to make sure it was stopped. It walked into the clearing, my knives poking out of its shell in a line down its middle. Apparently, bigger body meant thicker shell. This was the opposite of good. I looked toward my friends to see Kory was staring at me wide-eyed.

"Well, I have to admit, that was quite the entrance. Unfortunately, I think you just made the big one mad."

I looked back towards the scorpions. "Have you fought these things before?"

Kory shook his head, pulling in more qi before answering. "No, first time, but everything we tried on them just bounced off. Donny and Valerie got stung. If you can distract this thing long enough, I can use that medallion Valerie has to get them back on their feet."

I moved up against the edge of his qi shield and got ready to take on the giant scorpion nightmare.

I pulled out one of the spears in my belt and formed the spirit wood ring into its shield form. I was really low on qi, so I needed to do as much of this as I could manage by hand. While I was getting ready, the big one rushed at us.

A stinger the size of a human head smashed into Kory's qi shield and it instantly shattered. I hadn't even seen it move. I was in trouble. I still couldn't make large movements when I used my brain core, because my body would literally rip itself apart. I needed to speed up my reaction times to stay alive, but I had to find a way to strike back with only tiny movements.

To make things worse, it looked like two of the 'little' ones were getting back up. If I had to, I would use the qi batteries in the belt, but I never got far by giving up. Every challenge was a stepping stone along the path of cultivation. The greatest breakthroughs were made during battle, and certainly not the ones you give up on.

I slowed down time at the slightest flicker of movement, and I was barely able to deflect the stinger over my right shoulder with my shield. Time stuttered back to normal speed as the stinger rolled away from me. I shoved the spear forward, trying to push the monster back. It used its front claws to snap the spear right out of my hand. Okay, definitely not working. I started to spool out a single thread of wood qi from the base of my spine.

"Kory, you need to hurry! Get those two out of here!" I didn't have the time to check how he was doing, because the gigantic stinger slammed into my shield head-on and blasted me backwards off my feet. I slowed time again and threw the wood qi towards the tree line opposite my friends. I felt it catch something, so I pulled myself towards it as time slipped back to normal. I ended up dangling from a thick tree branch and pulled myself on top of it.

The move was fast enough that the scorpion had trouble following me, so it turned in a circle, trying to find me. I had to hurry, before it retargeted Kory and the others. I pulled the fancy silver bow out of my belt, nocking an arrow and dumping air qi into it to try to make it travel faster. I could only pull the bow back three quarters of the way without enhancing myself, but I figured it was good enough. I aimed for the head, and released.

The arrow missed, slamming into the ground a foot away from the scorpion's face. Ugh, I hadn't missed a shot like that in decades! This smaller body was completely throwing off my perception.

I nocked another arrow as the scorpion began moving in my direction. Apparently, it was smart enough to figure out where I was from the single arrow I had fired. It was getting close, so I used metal qi this time. I tried to impart my intent for it to have a long, pointy tip, but I fired before checking too closely. The arrow missed the cluster of eyes I was aiming for but it hit a little lower, right in the mouth. Mandibles? Chelicerae? Stupid brain, now is the time to worry about this?

The scorpion wasn't happy about its new decorative mouth piercing. For the first time, I had really hurt it. I tried to get another arrow on the bowstring, but the monster blurred forward, slamming into the tree. Time to move.

I jumped to the next tree over, using the flying ring to make it easier, while finally getting my next arrow nocked. I dumped earth qi in this time, trying to make the arrow as heavy as possible. Getting a closer view of the scorpion had given me an idea. I slowed time, making sure my movements were smooth and measured as I lined up my shot, trying to calculate the angle of impact carefully. I released, and let my time perception go.

The arrow impacted exactly on target. I had aimed for one of the throwing knives still embedded in its carapace. The hit drove the knife into the scorpion's back, causing it to arch back in pain.

I used the distraction to see how Kory was doing. He was fighting the other two scorpions I hadn't managed to take out, holding them to a standstill. I didn't see Donny or Valerie at first, but then I looked farther out into the river. Chu and Jamila had made it back, and they were trying to hold on to the other two as they floated them downstream. Not the best option, in my opinion, but I supposed it would do for now.

Taking my eyes off the monster I was fighting turned out to be a bad idea. In retrospect, that should have been obvious, but as I was getting lower on qi, I was finding it harder to concentrate. It slammed its stinger directly into the tree and I fell.

I still had the thread of wood qi, so I used it to ensure I landed on my feet. Unfortunately, I landed less than a foot from the right claw of the scorpion. I had just enough time to expand the spirit wood shield and position it in front of me before the scorpion backhanded me hard enough to knock me all the way across the clearing to the river.

I was pretty sure it had broken my arm, but I was mad enough that I didn't feel it. This thing was really pissing me off. I stood slowly, trying to absorb as much of the ambient qi around me as possible. The wood qi thread was absorbed back into my body, slowly healing the numerous minor injuries I hadn't even noticed getting, and painfully shifting the bones in my arm back into place.

I used a dozen threads of earth qi from each foot, forcing them underground towards the scorpion. Somehow, it could sense them coming, and started backing towards the tree line. I don't think so, bug. No getting away from me.

I doubled the speed of the threads and they sprang out of the ground in a circle around the giant scorpion. It may be able to shrug off qi attacks, but I was hoping I could use qi to hold it in place. I wrapped two threads around each of its eight legs, two around each claw, and three around that damnable stinger. That left me one extra thread, and I balled up the end of it like a hammer. I still had four more throwing knives to pound through its carapace, so I got to work.

The scorpion was trying to get away, so I just adjusted the lengths of the threads to compensate for the direction it was straining. I started towards the back, hammering each throwing knife through the shell. It shuddered in pain and made a terrible hissing sound as I slammed the last one through. It was leaking blue-colored blood onto the ground, making a disgusting pool of mud around it. I tightened the qi threads, and the slippery footing finally brought it to the ground.

I looked over at Kory, who was staring wide-eyed at me. Apparently, he had finished up with the two smaller scorpions and had been watching me for a bit.

"How can you control so many qi constructs at once? And how many elements can you use?" I shook my head. Now was not the time.

"The mission from the gods requires me to use an array of abilities beyond the norm. We can talk about that later. We need to finish off this monster, before I run out of qi."

Kory swallowed and nodded. "If you can hold it in place, I can finish this." He pulled a spear out from his hidden storage device and approached the scorpion.

I adjusted the qi thread I had used like a hammer to help

hold it down as he approached. Kory then commenced stabbing the life out of the terrifying creature.

It took a few minutes, but the monster finally died. I sighed in relief, and relaxed my hold on the qi threads. I sat on the muddy riverbank and immediately started cultivating. I used all thirteen meridians to draw in as much energy as possible, deciding that Kory had seen enough of my secrets that hiding the number of open meridians I had from him was pointless.

I was suffering some pain in my meridians, the strain of the day taking its toll. My body wasn't ready for the kind of action it had been going through. Risking a tear in a meridian wall was not something I wanted to do, but I was running low on options.

It was almost half an hour before my friends finally joined us, their weapons out and ready. I was nearly back to full strength, besides feeling sore and tired. While I had been cultivating, Kory had been looting the dead creatures and cleaning up the battlefield.

I was surprised to see a number of glass jars sitting next to the pile of weapons and various scorpion parts he had been amassing. I stood up and walked over, wanting to make sure everyone was doing well. Kory was the first to speak.

"Is everyone injury-free? That was a much nastier fight than I was expecting this early in our journey. You don't normally see this number of monsters close to the patrolled region." He stared deeper into the woods with a concerned look on his face. "Something must be pushing them out of their homes deeper in the forest."

Chu nodded. "We are all okay. I was able to patch everyone up and then we got here as soon as we could. The river swept us farther downstream than we intended, but we didn't run into anything else on our way here. I am glad you two were able to finish off these creatures."

Kory shook his head and looked back at everyone. "I barely did anything. Jim did most of the work." Everyone looked at me, most with little to no surprise on their faces.

I just shook my head. "We need to hurry," I said in an exasperated voice. "There are people looking for us, and all this commotion will clue them in to our location. Let's gather up our things and get out of here." I walked over to my share of the spoils and got a look at what I had gained. All of my knives were in acceptable condition, so I sheathed them in their proper locations.

I also had several pounds of unblemished scorpion chitin, which would make for some pretty effective armor. I had more than enough to make several complete sets, if I ever found the time to assemble it.

Lastly, there were seven glass jars. Four of the jars were certainly the venom from the stingers, two were the blue blood I had seen, and one contained an elemental core. It was most likely the core from the big scorpion. I was surprised to see it, but I didn't bother inspecting it further. We needed to get moving.

I popped everything into the belt and took a few seconds to make sure I was washed clean by walking back out into the river. Everyone else thought it was a good idea and did the same. Especially Kory. He was covered in scorpion guts from doing all of the butchering. Everyone else was just sweaty.

After getting as clean as possible, we headed deeper into the woods. I walked in the front next to Kory, sending out my qi senses to help look out for any beasts or monsters. I was hoping for a more peaceful walk through the woods for a bit.

CHAPTER TWENTY-ONE

Turning in for the Night

After a few hours of steady and silent walking, the terrain started to shift into tree-covered hills. This slowed us down and I could tell everyone was struggling. We needed to find a place to hole up for the night, but I hadn't seen anything promising our entire walk. Kory seemed to know where he was going, however, so I just kept following him.

I decided to take advantage of the slower walk and took the time to draw in qi to try to completely refill the batteries in my belt. Pushing qi into the belt wasn't taxing, it just took time. I was pulling in energy from the meridians in my feet, circulating it through my lower core and into my heart core, purifying it, and pushing it back out through the meridians in my hands which were hooked into my belt. The entire process was practically invisible to the outside world. After I refilled the belt, I figured I would start to focus on my body, meridian, and core reinforcement again. It was going to take some time until I resembled a true Brain-level cultivator.

After the battle with the water snake, it had become clear to me that I needed a source of energy that didn't strain my meridians when I needed to form a large qi working. Having the qi batteries meant I could also use large amounts of energy while my perception of time was sped up.

I couldn't cultivate quickly while slowing time, because the act of pulling in qi from the outside world barely moved faster than everything else around me did. I could use the qi batteries to refill my own energy stores, as well as using it directly for attack and defense. I was not a fan of how reliant on this belt I was becoming, but until I could improve my own body, I didn't have much of a choice. After all, Wrath or Pride must have made sure I got this belt for a reason.

The sun was touching the horizon before Kory took a moment to stop and look around. Each of the batteries were nearly recharged by this point. It would have gone faster, but I was still having difficulty ensuring there was enough dark and light qi in the mix to keep everything balanced. Kory looked back at our group before turning to speak quietly to me.

"My scout team should have reached us by this point. I am starting to get worried about them." I nodded in agreement, and he pointed in a direction slightly off the trail. "There is a small cave cut into one of the hills near here. If they got ahead of us somehow, that is where they would be waiting. Either way, it is the best spot in the area to camp for the night." I looked off where he indicated, studying the area before answering.

"It sounds good to me. I will fall to the rear and cover our tracks. You lead the way." Kory turned off the trail at a slight angle, and silently moved through the undergrowth. I waited for everyone to pass me by and fell in at the rear. I used a few strands of earth and wood qi to ensure any traces of our movements were invisible.

It was fully dark by the time we reached the hillside that had the cave. It was more like something had taken a scoop out of the side of the hill, but it was deep enough that building a fire wouldn't create a beacon of light for something to see for miles around. They would have to be extremely close to notice anything.

I was looking forward to a hot meal, and the worn faces of

my friends told me they felt the same way. I signaled to the group that I was going to do a walkaround of the area before I joined them and Kory waved me on.

I was looking for any signs of predators, both animals and human. I also took the time to place a few formation plates around the area. I spaced them out in a rough square shape around the cave, and connected them using qi threads. Now, if anything broke the makeshift qi tripwires, I would know about it. They were knee high off the ground, giving enough room for the smaller forest creatures to avoid them. It wasn't the greatest, but it would work for one night. I finished as quickly as possible and moved in to help set up camp.

Chu was already stirring a pot of something over a fire, and everyone else was erecting tents. I thought about pulling out the stone that could convert qi to heat but decided the fire could stay. There was something soothing about gathering around a fire, and our group deserved a chance to relax. The qi heating stone would only give off a faint glow and it wouldn't warm up the whole cave like the fire did.

I stepped closer to the flames, taking advantage of the light to pull out the elemental core Kory had left for me. It still had some scorpion goop on it, so I rolled it into the edge of the fire to burn it clean. Regular fire wouldn't damage it, so I left it and sat next to Chu.

"How are you doing after everything that happened today, Chu?"

He took a deep breath, and let it out slowly before answering. "I didn't handle that very well. Jamila getting taken, I mean. I should have stayed to help Donny and Valerie fight alongside Kory. Instead, I rushed off to help you. If I had been there to help, I could have healed Donny and Valerie as soon as they were injured. I put everyone at risk."

It was clear that this was weighing on him. If I had been paying closer attention, I might have noticed him beating himself up about it sooner. I shook my head.

"No, Chu, you did what any person in your position would

have done. If you had stayed with the others, Kory would have been defending three people instead of two. Those scorpions were incredibly fast, and I can't imagine you would have been able to heal everyone and protect yourself at the same time." I glanced over to where Jamila was arranging her bedroll. "Also, you clearly have very powerful feelings for Jamila. I can't blame you for wanting to protect her." He silently stirred the pot, thinking on what I said. I was about to continue, when Kory walked over and sat on the other side of Chu.

"He is right, you know," Kory said, poking at the fire with a stick. "You did the best thing possible in the situation. Even as talented as Jim is, him going off to fight an unknown enemy that had already captured a member of our party by himself was a recipe for disaster. No one knew what had grabbed Jamila, and two fighters are always better than one in a situation like that."

Chu nodded, and I could see him straighten up a bit. "I didn't think about it like that. Thank you. Both of you. I guess I wasn't as stupid as I thought I was."

Kory nodded, looking at Chu's face to make sure his message had sunk in. "Exactly. Now, pay attention to what you are cooking. The stew is going to burn if you don't move the pot from the center of the fire."

Chagrined, Chu repositioned the pot as the rest of the group joined us. I moved over to give room for Jamila to sit next to Chu and found myself sitting next to Valerie. She reached out to put my hand between hers.

"Jim, I want you to know that I appreciate everything you have done for me. First, you helped me bring honor to my family branch in the tournament, then you introduced me to Donny, and now you have saved my life. From now until the day I die, I will always do whatever I can to help you."

I gently pulled my hand free from hers. "Valerie, you don't owe me anything. Honestly, I am the one who owes you. All of you were only put in danger because you are here to help me find my parents. I would rather you see me as your friend, and not as someone who trades favors."

She immediately looked affronted. "Jim, of course I see you as a friend! And I wasn't saying I owed you anything, or that you owed me. I was simply stating that I recognized everything you have done for me, and I appreciate it. For being someone who has been touched by the gods, you sure don't understand people."

Donny let out a short bark of laughter. "It isn't that he doesn't understand people, Valerie, he just doesn't understand women!" That brought chuckles from everyone around the campfire.

I felt my cheeks redden in embarrassment. I was blushing? What was wrong with me? I cleared my throat. "You are right, and I apologize. I guess I didn't understand what you were trying to say. I just want all of you to know that I don't think you owe me something. If anything, I owe all of you for helping me find my parents." Everyone looked at me, and I felt my cheeks turn from warm to hot. Seriously, what was going on with me?

Kory was the first to speak up. "Jim, we are all glad to help. You might be more powerful than any ten-year-old in the history of the Roh clan, but you are still just a boy looking for his parents." They all nodded at that statement. I felt my eyes trying to water, but I was saved from having any more emotional outbursts by Chu announcing the food was ready.

We ate in silence, everyone once again lost in their own thoughts. A close brush with death could make a person take a long look at their life and maybe rethink their own priorities. Kory was the first finished and he leaned forward to speak to us.

"My scouts should have caught up to us by now. I am afraid they have been either captured, or killed. That means we need to be extra careful tomorrow. There are enemies out here." He leaned forward to draw a rough map of the area in the dirt with his stick. "We are still a full day of travel from the lake at the center of the territory the Roh clan claims. The need to travel swiftly is paramount. We need to reach the lake, set up camp, and search for Jim's parents, all while avoiding the people searching for us. From now on, if we get separated, this is our rendezvous location." He indicated our position on his map.

"Get back to here and stay safe if you find yourself alone. We don't want to have to send out a search party for the search party." There were a few dry chuckles as he paused. "Now, we all need to get some rest. I will set up some more formations inside Jim's, so we have a layered alarm. With two separate systems in place, we should all be able to sleep soundly tonight." With that, they all turned in for the night.

I watched them go before I pulled the core out of the coals left by the fire and inspected it. It looked like a basic earth core; the lowest quality possible. I put it with the cores I had won at the tournament. With what I had on hand, I could make an impressive set of armor with the chitin from the scorpion, and empower some formations on it with the extra earth core. It would take several hours to shape, combine, and carve everything. Something to work on later.

I crawled into my tent, then I spent almost an hour cultivating inside my bed roll, trying to calm my mind and be productive at the same time. I used all the qi I gathered to reinforce my body. I needed to get to the point that I could at least move a little bit while slowing my perception of time. The fight with the scorpions would have been much shorter if that had been the case.

CHAPTER TWENTY-TWO

First Look at the Nox

I was standing on top of a deserted and crumbling stone tower. I looked around me, and saw dozens of old foundations around the column of stone. There was what looked to be a temple in the distance that appeared as if it was still whole. Several buildings around it had signs of recent construction, but it looked as if the building projects had been abandoned midway through completion.

I guessed I had dream walked into the ruins near the lake. I must have fallen asleep while cultivating. If things stayed true to form, I needed to find whatever clues the dream walking was trying to show me. I looked around, but couldn't see anyone nearby. I crouched to jump down from the tower, and that was when I saw it.

If I thought the giant scorpion was a creature from my nightmares, I simply didn't understand the difference between a mildly bad dream, and a horror engineered for death and destruction. It had to be the *nox*. I wasn't sure if it was because I was seeing its true form through the lens of dream walking, or if it actually had tentacles emerging along its spine, but it was an abomination I immediately wanted to wipe from existence.

I think it used to be a Spotted Snow Leopard, but it was three times the size it should be. It was larger than a wagon, but somehow it could move silently. In my original timeline, this must have been the beast that led a horde to destroy a large portion of the Roh clan and kill my parents.

The tentacles of what I guessed were dark mana growing from it seemed to have a mind of their own, whipping about and silently killing any insect or rodent that ventured within range. I wasn't sure, but I think it might have been absorbing them. Then it hit me. A normal predator would scare off any small rodents, but these seemed to be ignoring its presence. Somehow, it was blending into the environment perfectly.

I would get no mundane warnings if it was near. I made a promise to myself to do a better job of maintaining my situational awareness from now on. I couldn't let this thing sneak up on me.

The *nox* was silently moving towards the temple in the distance. I dropped down from the tower, gravity apparently still working on my dream self like it did in the regular world. I kept my distance from the *nox*, trying to make sure it couldn't sense me. I didn't think it could hurt me, but I knew next to nothing about my enemy.

Once it got closer to the temple, I saw the deformed leopard drop into a crouch, the tentacles layered flat along its body to reduce its profile. There was a sentry walking along the far side of the courtyard in front of the temple.

I could see light flickering from the empty windows on the second and third stories of the massive building. It had obviously been abandoned for a long time, but there were some people who had made an attempt to repair the worst of the damage time and neglect had wrought. It was a giant rectangle that appeared to have four stories above ground, but I had no doubt there were a few underground levels as well.

There were always underground levels inside creepy abandoned temples. I was pretty sure that was one of the secret rules of the universe, even though no one ever wanted to talk about it.

I lost sight of the *nox* as it rounded the far side of the building, but its target was clear. The sentry was not long for this world if he didn't notice something soon. I tried to swing around the opposite side of the courtyard to get a better angle on the *nox*, but I wasn't fast enough. The leopard pounced from the corner of the courtyard, flying almost fifty yards in a perfect arc before smashing into the sentry. An alarm formation immediately shot three large balls of orange fire into the sky, lighting up the courtyard and casting the edges into stark lines of shadow and light. The leopard bolted.

Apparently, it didn't like fire. Definitely something important to remember. The sentry was in a crumpled mess, moaning in a broken and bleeding heap. Seven men and three women ran out of the front of the temple, weapons at the ready and shouting at one another. They were wearing red robes with red leather armor. These people really liked red.

"Did you see it? Where did it go?!"

"Somebody check on the prisoners, we don't want them escaping!"

"Was it the same creature?"

"Get the wards back up! It could be anywhere!"

Two of the men ran back inside while another knelt next to the sentry. One of the women walked to the edge of the courtyard, trying to stare into the darkness and reset the wards at the same time. Apparently, the *nox* had been terrorizing them for at least a few nights. They also had prisoners. I had a sinking feeling two of those prisoners were my parents.

I needed to get to these ruins as fast as possible. If they were here, they were in danger from both their kidnappers and the *nox*. I couldn't believe I was thinking this, but I hoped the group coming from Roh City got to the ruins soon. If the people here were feeling overwhelmed, they might kill the prisoners to reduce the number of things they needed to worry about. The larger numbers would give the *nox* more targets, and me more time.

I went to move closer to the temple in the hopes of finding the location of the prisoners but I couldn't cross the threshold. It was like there was an invisible wall blocking me. I looked for any carvings that would give away the location of any formations or wards, but there was only weathered stone. Was there some form of divine protection on the temple? Was that keeping the *nox* out as well? The elder I had killed said they had a base with multiple buildings here in the ruins, but I only saw people staying here in the temple. It felt like every time I had one of these dreams, I was ending up with as many questions as I had answers.

I decided I was going to try to find a window to look through, when I was once again yanked into a bright light.

CHAPTER TWENTY-THREE

A New Medallion

"Jim, we need to move." This time, it was Kory shaking me
awake. "The sun is breaching the horizon." I shook myself
awake. This dream walking stuff was great for the intel, but not
so great for getting actual rest. Kory backed out of the tent, not
waiting for me to talk.

I got my always-clean clothes and vest back on, and moved
my spirit wood ring to my left hand and the flight ring to my
right. I dumped a fair bit of qi into the ring, making sure it was
ready to go. I preferred to use a shield with my left side and I
wanted to be prepared if that *nox* monster snuck up on me. I
involuntarily shuddered, remembering how disgusting it was.

Then, I pumped qi into the vest to expand the sleeves and
neck covering. I wanted to make sure I was as armored as possible, even if that meant I was going to be uncomfortably warm. I
pulled my boots on last, using some earth qi on them to remove
the dirt and grime stuck to the soles.

I was the last person ready to go, but not by much. It took a
few minutes to get the tents and bedrolls packed away, and we
sat around a smaller version of last night's campfire. Chu was

frying up some sausages and flat bread while Valerie added a few chunks of hard cheese to melt on top.

I tried to think of a way to warn everyone about what I had seen without explaining my weird dream abilities. While I trusted everyone here, I knew that the best secrets were the ones no one heard. Chu was passing out the food when Kory spoke up.

"I see you are more armored today than yesterday. Did the gods give you forewarning of some danger?"

Well, that works, I supposed. I swallowed my bite of food before answering. "More like a feeling than an actual warning, but I think we should be extra careful today. Your scouts are still missing, and there are at least two groups of enemies out there, maybe more. And don't forget, there is a dark mana creature hiding somewhere." I shuddered, remembering how awful it was to look at. "We have no idea what it is capable of, so we need to be prepared for attacks and ambushes." There, I couldn't think of a better way to warn them without outright admitting I had seen the stars-damned thing in my dreams.

Everyone agreed to be more diligent, and I saw each of them take a few extra minutes to make sure their armor was in place. We finished eating before cleaning up the campsite and heading out. I left my formation plates in place since I knew we would be returning to the area. It would also let me know if anything came to explore the cave while we were away. It could easily be a large animal that set off the tripwires, but I would still want to know.

Kory was in the lead again, with the girls close behind. Donny and Chu were about fifty yards back, leaving room to react in case we were attacked. I trailed another fifty yards from the boys, giving me time to make sure our trail was hidden. I was pulling in qi from every meridian besides my hands and feet, making sure my cores were completely full in case of an attack.

I was using my hand meridians to finish topping off the

batteries in my belt, and the meridians in my feet to level out our footprints and straighten any bent branches. The only way something would be able to track our passing was by scent, and I hadn't seen any tracking animals with the groups trying to find us. The *nox* was my only real concern.

We moved from a hilly region to flatter ground and our pace picked up. Kory had us spread out a little more, making my job covering our trail a little more difficult. By the time the sun was directly overhead, I was thoroughly miserable.

I felt like I was cooking inside the thick leather armor, and for some reason the lack of hills meant more insects that enjoyed biting me. On the positive side, I finally finished refilling the qi batteries. With those, I was pretty sure I would be able to defeat a low stage Sage-level cultivator if I could surprise them. I wouldn't be able to have a drawn-out battle, but I figured a Sage would most assuredly underestimate me, allowing me an opportunity to 'whip-up' an attack that could take one down. I was chuckling at my little pun when all hell broke loose.

With no warning, Kory was blown backwards off his feet. His head hit a protruding rock with a hollow knock, and I knew he wasn't getting back up right away. I just hoped he was still alive.

I sensed the girls activate their cores as they backed up to stand next to our fallen party member. The guys rushed forward, Donny pulling out a spear and Chu drawing wood qi into his hands. I dove into the bushes on the left side of the narrow trail and tried to move up silently along the flank of whatever had attacked us.

Jamila was shouting something, and Valerie was spinning a large disk of air like a flat shield in front of everyone. I was glad none of them had looked back for me. No sense giving away I was nearby.

I finally got close enough to see what was going on. There were six people standing in a cluster in front of my friends, with a seventh hiding behind a thick tree on the opposite side of the trail from me. They were all wearing red robes under matching cheap leather armor. It looked like they hadn't seen a bath for several days, and their robes were encrusted with dirt and sweat. I could just barely see the edge of a shoulder sticking out from the man trying to hide. From the amount of energy they were putting off, the six in front were all Heart cultivators. The one hiding was a weak Brain cultivator, but his cores were almost empty. He must have been the one who ambushed Kory, which meant he was probably hiding in an attempt to recharge his qi. We couldn't allow that, now could we?

I pushed closer to their group, making sure I stayed low. I guessed, if I had to admit it, at least having this smaller body made it easier to hide. I kept moving forward until I could finally make out what everyone was saying.

"My grandfather won't stand for this! If you know what is good for you, just back down and let us pass!" Jamila was still shouting, but I think she was running out of things to say.

The guy standing in front cut in. "You can't win, and your grandfather isn't here, girl. If you give up without a fight, we won't hurt you. Not too much, anyway…" The others chuckled, the leering smiles hinting at the direction of their thoughts. Okay, now I knew how to handle this.

Threatening a young lady like that? Only one way to fix their thought process. Kill them all, with as much pain as possible. Now, how to manage that without showing my friends how strong I really was?

I pulled out my bow and started to dump as much metal qi into the arrow as it could handle. I aimed for where I imagined the head of the guy behind the tree to be and let go of the bowstring as soon as I had the shot lined up. The arrow blasted into the edge of the tree, blowing wood chips everywhere. The figure behind the tree didn't move, but I felt the pull of qi stop immediately.

I didn't have time to worry about him anymore, because the other six were already tossing qi constructs in my direction. I took a diving leap right towards them, the various fireballs, wind blades, and what I think was a shuriken made from ice, all flying over my head. I was lucky they were aiming where the chest of a full-grown adult would be, because they clearly hadn't actually seen who their attacker was yet.

I pulled out the two longer blades that ran along my sides as I came rolling out of my dive at the edge of their little group. They seemed surprised at my size, and none of them made a move to attack. Their mistake.

I ran straight at them and sliced a dagger along the outside edge of the knees of the two attackers closest to me. They dropped to the ground screaming, their blood coating the edges of my blades. The remaining four stopped standing around, finally getting in on the action. I jumped sideways to dodge their attacks. I ignored their qi constructs as they flew past me, doing my best to get close enough for melee combat.

A spear came flying in from the side, slamming into the armpit of the man farthest from me. Thanks, Donny. It caused the other three to look over at my friends for a second, so I whipped my arms forward, throwing the heavy daggers into the chests of the two attackers closest to me. The last man standing took a step back as they dropped, but he was instantly immolated by a tornado of fire. I guess that was an indication as to how disgruntled Jamila and Valerie were feeling about their earlier treatment from the ambushers.

I was about to run towards the man hiding behind the tree when I felt a stabbing pain in my foot. Literally.

One of the pair I had dropped at the start of the fight had pierced my foot with his belt knife, stabbing all the way through my foot and into the ground. While I was pretty good at ignoring pain, getting stabbed in the foot was not a fun experience. In fact, it made me quite angry.

I made a downward chopping motion with my hand, extending an extremely thin blade of air qi from my fingertips. It removed my attacker's head, and accidentally cut into the side of the other man I had taken out at the knees. He had been trying to get close as well, but he was slower than his friend. I had wanted to leave those two alive long enough to answer some questions, but I guess my anger got the best of me.

I bent down to pull the knife out of my foot and saw Donny running over to see what I had shot my arrow at when the fight started.

I was going to shout a warning to him, but I found myself flat on my face instead. Apparently, pulling a knife out of your foot can cause you to momentarily black out. Good to know. I made a mental note to double down on my body reinforcement. My old self wouldn't have even been scratched by the knife of a Heart cultivator.

I went to roll over, but a hand held me down. I tensed up, ready to throw out a spike of metal qi from my lower back, but Chu must have sensed it.

"Easy, Jim. It's just me. I am almost done fixing up your foot, and then you can get up. I don't know what you are going to do about your boot, though. I don't think this one is good anymore." I looked around, finally remembering to breathe.

"Where is Donny? There was a Brain cultivator hiding behind that tree, and I saw him running that direction."

I was pointing at the tree, and Donny himself answered my question as he came into view from behind it. "I'm okay, Jim. You are probably going to want to see this. Let's just say, he didn't get away."

Chu helped pull me to my feet and we went over to see what was going on.

I walked around the tree to see what Donny was talking about. I had definitely hit the Brain cultivator. The arrow had pierced the tree, but hadn't penetrated all the way through. My aim had been a little low. The cultivator had been leaning against the tree, and the arrowhead had come through the tree and hit dead center in the back of his neck. The arrowhead poking through his throat was all that was holding him up.

It was pretty gruesome, even for me. It sounded like Chu was losing the contents of his stomach, but I didn't look back to check. Instead, I helped Donny pull the man off the arrowhead and carry him over to the edge of the trail. Jamila and Valerie were searching the bodies of the other red robes while Kory was lining them up in the brush. I was glad to see him on his feet.

I walked over to see how they were doing and to see what they had found. They were following in the footsteps of Kory from our last battle, piling everything in one place for easy sorting. It was looking like some decent spoils of war.

Instead of interrupting them, I went back to the Brain cultivator. I looked through his pockets, pulled off his armor, and cut free two pouches from his belt. I checked for storage devices, but he apparently wasn't important enough to rate a magical ring. I was about to walk away, but the sunlight glinted off of something around his neck.

It was gory, but I started poking at the mess around his throat. I found a small medallion on a thin bronze chain. I didn't recognize what it could be, so I inspected it with qi. It had an internal qi matrix embedded, but it was faint enough that I was having trouble figuring out what it was meant to do. I took it, and the other items, and dropped them in the growing pile of assorted stuff the girls were making.

Then I took a moment to try to fix my boot. I had to take it off and then tried to rinse as much of the blood out as possible. I ran a needle and thread I took from a tent repair kit through the cut portion on top, but there wasn't much I could do about the half-inch cut through the sole. I would just have to be careful where I stepped.

After doing what I could with the boot, I decided it was time to add another item to my gear. I was lacking a focusing stone, which helped collect and purify ambient qi in the area. They allowed a cultivator to quickly draw in vast amounts of qi, helping them to refill their cores faster. They usually had some elemental aspect, like the fire stone that Ming had used to kill me. I didn't have a high-level core or elemental stone to make one, but I could form a simple version that would help me if I was injured again.

If Chu hadn't been around, there was no telling how long it

would have taken me to wake up from that stab wound. I needed some form of token to help wood qi, or life energy, collect and filter into my body if I was ever knocked unconscious again.

I went back to the tree I had shot with the arrow and pushed some wood qi into it. I was looking for a smooth knot of wood about the size of a coin or medallion I could pull free. I found one higher up the tree after searching for a few minutes. I used wood qi to push it out and then formed it into a smooth disk. I then used my carving tool to design a qi matrix across the surface, ensuring the energy flow was smooth and uninterrupted. Then, I had to dump a third of the qi from one of my batteries into the wood itself, activating the qi matrix and tying it to my specific energy signature.

It was crude, and the qi it gathered was only a trickle of energy, but it would help keep me from bleeding to death if I was injured.

I then cut a hole in the waistband of my pants, slipping the wooden coin inside. I pushed some qi into the pants and the self-repair function sealed the hole right back up. Now, I would have to be stripped naked to be without it.

Something was beginning to bother me. How did these people find us? These woods were huge, and only Kory and his scouts should know the area well enough to track us down. Not just track us down, but set up an actual ambush. Were they just really lucky, or was it something more? I was starting to think that either the chief elder or Kory had someone on their staff who was leaking information to the red robes.

Oh well, nothing I could do about it right now. Just keep my eyes and ears open.

Everyone was done searching the bodies a few minutes later and Kory started sorting our loot while the rest of us talked about the fight. There was a fair bit of back-slapping and congratulations on our various performances during the short battle, but we all stopped when Kory let out a shout of surprise.

"We need to get moving. This is a listening device, and

whoever is on the other end has been listening to us this whole time!"

Well, on the bright side, I guess I now knew a new way to design the qi matrix for a subtle listening device. Downside? I had no way of knowing how much the people on the other side heard, or how close they might be.

CHAPTER TWENTY-FOUR

Having a Lot of Fun

I just snatched everything up and put it in my storage belt, and we left the medallion next to the seven bodies lining the trail. We were moving out again in less than five minutes. Kory took us off trail, trying to make it harder for our pursuers to find us. We were traveling single file, Kory leading and me bringing up the rear.

He set a punishing pace and it took most of my concentration just to keep up and erase our trail. Stupid, short, ten-year-old legs! I could only occasionally look back to check for someone following our trail, which was probably why the group behind us was able to get so close without me noticing.

I saw them as we came up a slight rise, their red robes poor camouflage for the environment. I didn't think they had seen us yet, but if I could see them, it was possible they could spot us. I crouched low, making a hissing noise to get everyone's attention. They looked back, and it only took a moment for them to see the movement below us. They crouched low as well, trying to make sure we wouldn't be silhouetted against the sky. I stopped the qi from spinning through my cores. I didn't want them to feel any qi fluctuations in the area. Kory started moving for a thicker cluster of trees, almost doubled over in an attempt to stay hidden.

We kept moving but now I couldn't cover the footprints we were leaving in the soft forest floor. I knew it was only a matter of time until our enemies would be hot on our trail. I needed to take control of the situation, and flip the dynamic.

I waited until we were on the far side of the rise before pushing up next to Kory. I signaled for everyone to gather close and I pulled out several blank formation plates.

"Okay everyone, it is time to adjust how the people trying to catch us are viewing the situation." They looked at me with various states of confusion mixed with determination. "I am going to set some traps, and then lead them on a chase through the forest. Kory, where did you say that den of Red Spring Wolves was supposed to be?" Kory's eyes showed a bit of a predatory gleam. I guess he could figure out some of the more fun aspects of my plan.

"The den is supposed to be closer to the lake than we are, about a mile or so south and west from the edge of the lake."

I nodded, pulling out my carving tools while he talked. "That's perfect. The ruins they are using as a base are about two miles east of the lake. Don't ask how I know, I just do. I need you to get there, and get those prisoners out. There are traps all over the area, and I think the *nox* might be nearby, so be careful. I will get over there as quick as I can."

Everyone nodded, but Donny spoke up. "I don't think you should do this by yourself." He put his hand on my shoulder. "You may have been given many gifts from the gods, but you are still only a child. It isn't right."

I smiled and shrugged off his hand. "Donny, I appreciate where you are coming from, and you would be correct if I actually intended to fight them. I am just going to lead them away, set some traps, and guide them right into the teeth of an *actual* den of wolves. Trust me, this will be hilarious." I could see he still had some doubts. "If I get captured, they will just take me straight to the ruins, which is where you will be. Just set an ambush and rescue me. Either way, we get out of this situation."

He frowned. "I still don't like it, but I guess it is the best option."

I nodded again and made a shooing motion with my hands. "Good, now get moving. It is only going to take me a few minutes to finish these traps, and then things are going to get pretty interesting around here." They all wished me luck, and took off.

Finally. Now I could really let loose. I had been holding back in our last fight, trying to make sure my friends didn't think I was some kind of murdering death monster in the body of a child.

I had three full cores, two almost-full qi batteries, and a whole lot of frustration to work through. I hadn't had a single easy day since I came back, and these red robes were the reason for that. Time to let them know I didn't appreciate their actions.

I carved a few different formations into a dozen copper disks, trying to make sure I had a wide variety of surprises for anyone dumb enough to chase me. I took a few minutes to hide the trail my group of friends left behind, and then spun up my cores.

I left my upper core alone for the most part, speeding up my perception of time just enough that it would give me a slight edge in combat. I spun out a single thick thread of metal qi from each hand and started walking back towards the jerks following us.

I whipped my arm across my body, slicing through the base of a large tree in my path. It crashed into the ground, making quite the racket. Then I spun up a qi formation I hadn't used in a while. It did a fantastic job of enhancing sounds over a large area. Great for making announcements, leading troops into battle, or luring exceedingly stupid people into traps. I was using it for the latter.

"Hey, you idiots in those ridiculous red robes! Yeah, you! I can see you! Your camouflage is only useful inside a tastelessly decorated brothel, not the woods, you brainless jerks! I guess you are just used to visiting your mothers at their place of employment!" I was pretty sure that caught their collective attention.

I started running in the direction I hoped led to the den of wolves, whipping my metal qi strands around me as I went. I was creating a trail that not even these dunderheads could miss, and kept moving at a pace they would find difficult to match since they would have to climb over or around the trees I was knocking down.

I knew from my dream walking experience at the Roh City jail that the highest-level people in the group chasing me were Brain cultivators, so I wasn't too worried if they caught up. That being said, I didn't want to run the risk of an actual fight against a whole bunch of people that could have weapons or abilities I knew nothing about. The belt knife through my foot had been a great reminder that I was not well-prepared for a drawn-out physical confrontation with a large group of enemies.

I was running for a good ten minutes or so before I dropped my first trap. I engineered a curve in the trail, and then I felled another large tree, angling it across the path I was cutting in order to funnel my pursuers into a group. I couldn't see them yet, but their shouts were getting close. I chose a formation plate trap that would inject a massive amount of wood qi into the tree laying on its side. In theory, it would force a massive growth spurt from the tree, turning its branches into makeshift spears at best, and tangling everyone up at worst.

Just to keep things interesting, I threw down another trap right behind the wood trap. It would project a wave of fire at hip-height for about twenty feet in a cone shape pointed directly at the gap in the trail. I hoped it would catch the freshly-grown branches on fire, but at the very least it would make the idiots following me a bit more cautious. It should hopefully slow the group of red robes down enough that I would be able to find the wolves and arrange a meeting for them. I didn't relish the thought of getting caught between the two groups.

The voices were close enough now that I could actually understand what they were saying. Most of it wasn't very nice. Okay, all of it wasn't very nice.

"…going to kill that kid!"

"…don't care what our orders are, he is dead meat…"

"…make sure you save some for me…"

"…talk about my mother like that, I'm going to…"

Stuff like that. I guess I had hurt some feelings. I decided it was time to get moving before they had a chance to see me. I spun out my metal whips again and got back to clearing a path. After a few dozen yards, I curved back in the direction I wanted to go. It made an almost perfect half circle in what was basically a straight line, but I was betting my opponents weren't smart enough to just push through the forest and skip the pointless curve.

I wanted to see how the trap worked out, so I pushed forward another hundred yards or so before turning back around.

I followed the curve until I could barely see the ambush location and I crouched down. It only took a few seconds for the first of the red robes to round the corner into my view. They weren't looking for any traps, or even keeping scouts pushed forward. They were just walking in one big angry group, not as tightly packed as I could have hoped, but closer together than they should be.

Didn't any of these people stop to think for a second? They were walking down a trail carved through the forest by someone who had the power to continuously use enough qi to clear-cut the trees for well over fifteen minutes by this point. The stupidity of large groups of people was always a bit surprising to witness in action. I didn't have a solid count, but I could see almost forty people so far.

I held my breath as the lead group hit the invisible line that would trigger the traps, but I was disappointed by the initial results. The formation plate activated flawlessly, but the tree didn't react like I had imagined. Instead of sending thick spears of new growth into my enemies, the branches grew equally along the full circumference of the tree, while simultaneously growing a new set of roots out behind. The branches pointed towards the ground lifted the tree off the trail at a forty-five-degree angle, which caused most of the other branches pointed towards the red robes to shoot out over their heads. It knocked two people over, not doing any damage. It did, however, manage to slow them down as they bunched up nice and close to watch the tree grow in amazement.

Then, the person in the front set off the fire trap. That one worked as intended.

The cone of flame blasted out directly into the center of the group, throwing people off their feet. At least ten people were lit on fire, their screams echoing through the forest. The vast majority of them were running around like idiots, throwing qi attacks into the trees around them. Had none of them seen a trap before?

It would probably take a few minutes for them to realize they weren't under attack by a person, and by then the people on fire would either be dead or too injured to continue their pursuit. I wasn't sure how many I had actually taken out of the fight, but I needed to capitalize on the time this had given me.

I took off, slowly narrowing the trail I was cutting. I would only be able to catch one or two people with my traps now, but I was guessing they would push out scouts after the last trap. If I couldn't catch more of them, I might as well slow them down even more.

The trail went from being well over a dozen yards across to only wide enough for two or three people to stand side-by-side. The narrower trail allowed me to pick up my pace, and I began randomly placing trap formation plates.

I started about six hundred yards from the site of the first attack. One I set to go off when the third person passed by. It was a wind blade trap, basic but effective. A hundred paces later

I placed a second wind blade trap in the branches of a tree that arched over the trail, pointed down, and set to go off when the first person walked past. Less than fifteen steps from that, I placed a plate on the left side of the trail that would send out three metal spears in an arc at waist height. I went over a mile before placing a trap that would cause the earth to shoot spikes three feet up out of the ground for a six-foot circle in all directions. That left me with six copper disks, so I stopped worrying about traps and started moving faster. I needed to find the wolf den.

It was late into the evening before I found them. I had stopped making the clear-cut trail through the woods about three miles back. The total length of the trail was well over fifteen miles long, and I would have to start from the den and work my way back to where I had ended.

I hadn't heard my pursuers for quite some time, and I hoped that the random spacing of the traps had caused them to slow down and carefully search the trail as they moved forward. I moved less than a hundred yards from the small cave opening, watching as five wolves sunbathed in the small clearing in front of their den. Probably trying to catch the last bit of sunlight before night hit.

I was sure there were more of them inside, but I didn't have the time to sit around and watch to get a solid count. Instead, I spun out my metal whips and made a new clearing. I was sure they heard all the noise I was making, but I hoped it was enough noise that they were cautious about rushing toward the sounds.

As soon as I judged the clearing to be big enough to serve as my impromptu battleground, I ran to connect the space with the trail I had made. It was almost perfectly flat ground, so I didn't slow as I whipped the metal qi through the underbrush and trees in my path. It took almost half an hour to connect the two trails, which was longer than I wanted, but my shorter stature was doing the best it could.

The sun was almost past the horizon, causing long shadows

from the trees to be cast across the ground. The connecting of the two parts of my trail caused a slight angle to be formed, and I placed another trap where the two met. It was a quicksand trap, one that used water qi to soften the ground into a giant soupy mess for two minutes before a pulse of earth qi hardened the ground into stone. It wouldn't be impossible to get free, but I was hoping it would trap a few of them for a bit of time. Ideally, it would split their group up some, making sure the wolves wouldn't get overrun too quickly.

I walked back up the path, taking the time to refill my cores. It had been a long day, and I was starting to run low on both qi and stamina.

I was close enough to hear shouting in the distance a few minutes later. I guess they found the trap. I kept walking, figuring it would take them a few minutes before they caught up. I saw my man-made clearing in the distance, and used a thread of wood qi from the meridian in the small of my back to pull me up into the trees. I used air qi and my flying ring to help me run across the tree limbs, keeping off of the ground in case the wolves had come out of their den to inspect the area.

Soon I reached the edge of the clearing and then used some more threads of air qi to emplace my last five surprises around the open space. I set these to go off manually. I would wait until the opportune moment to spring the last phase of my attack.

It was well after the sun had gone down before the first group reached the clearing, holding torches high above their heads to illuminate the area. I looked in the direction of the Red Spring Wolves den, and I saw the glint of light from the torches reflecting off of their eyes. Perfect.

The red robes were moving silently, spreading out into the clearing. I counted seventeen, and I couldn't help but wonder how many were left after all of my traps. Were there still some trapped past their knees in the stone a few miles back? Or were these the sacrificial lambs sent out by the others, a larger force waiting to see what happened? It was also possible this was all that remained. I never had a solid count of how many I was facing, and all of my traps were capable of causing death.

Finally, I heard a deep growl come from the far side of the clearing. The red robes heard it too. They bunched up in the center of the clearing, forming a circle to make sure they could keep an eye on every direction. It was the smartest thing I had seen them do yet, and I realized something.

If this was all that was left, I was looking at the smartest and strongest of the group that had been following me. It would be a good idea to remember that.

One of the men threw his torch into the trees, and the wolves pounced at the provocation. There were at least thirty of them, and they were all angry. Or hungry. Maybe both, I didn't know. They were kind of hard to read.

The thing that made Red Spring Wolves so dangerous was their ability to absorb metal qi, and their bodies used it to armor themselves. The wolves would form layers of iron over their fur, and after some time the iron would rust, giving it a red color. Heavy spring rains would speed up the rusting process, making them more red-looking during the spring. Hence the name Red Spring Wolves. The iron armor also made killing them very difficult, as the people in the clearing could attest to.

After a few minutes of fierce fighting, there were only ten red robes still standing, and around twenty wolves were up and circling them. The other seven had been pretty much torn apart, pack tactics being what they were.

Suddenly, a storm of fire qi came in from the side of the clearing where the path was, and five more cultivators attacked the wolves from the rear. I guessed the people in the earth trap finally got free.

There was a lot of shouting between the groups, and they quickly pushed through to the center of the clearing. There were only eighteen wolves now, and they were backing towards the edge of the light cast by the flames that the fire storm had started. All fifteen of the cultivators were watching them, slowly walking towards the retreating wolf pack. It seemed like the appropriate time to set off my traps.

I had saved these last five for a moment just like this. They were all the same kind of trap, just using different elements. The formation used looked like a five-pointed star, and a qi thread the thickness of my pinky finger formed from each point. They were all basically just smaller versions of my qi whips, each flailing around in a circle ten feet from the disks they came from. I had two of each from what I thought of as the more offensive elements, fire and metal, and one of air. The poor bastards didn't know what hit them.

The whips sliced through all of them, and even caught the tail edge of the wolves as they ran. It was a gore-fest. There were limbs flying through the air in fountains of blood, human and beast parts mixing together in a layer of meat across the ground. The gurgled screams of the red robes and howls of pain from the wolves didn't last long.

My parents wouldn't have to worry about coming back out to take care of the wolves, because there weren't enough left to still be a threat. I guess I could check off two of the things on my to-do list.

I waited a few minutes for the traps to run out of energy and hopped down from the tree I was hiding in to search what was left of the bodies. It was not fun. The ground was muddy from all of the blood spilled, and I felt it seeping up into my boot from the gash in the bottom of it.

It took the better part of an hour, but I collected everything useful I could find. There were three basic cores from the wolves, a few coin purses, and even a decent sword I found under a pile of body parts. Once again, no magical storage devices or something similar, but I did find two more of the listening medallions. I destroyed them immediately.

I was also able to recover my traps, which was nice. I took a moment to recharge them and reset the matrix for automatic activation. I wanted to be able to just throw them where I wanted and not worry about manually setting them off. I put everything into my storage belt and took a moment to cultivate to refill my cores. The moon was high in the sky before I finally stood up from my rather disgusting task, and I turned to head towards the ruins. It was time to find my parents.

I decided to backtrack on the trail I had already cut for a few miles to save on time, but as I stepped out of the clearing, I heard a twig snap in the woods to my right.

When I turned to look, something smashed into the back of my head, and I fell to my knees. The world was spinning. I tried to bring my cores to life. I was having trouble, and I couldn't seem to get my body to respond. I heard a voice from the trees where the twig had broken.

"Tie him up, and get his gear off of him. We need to hurry up and get back to the base before that creature shows up again." I tried to stand, but someone hit me on the head again, and I fell on my face. Turning my head to the side a bit I saw a pair of black boots move in front of me.

I was starting to lift my head to look when someone grabbed me by the hair, tilting my head back and lifting me so that I was close enough to his face to smell his rotting teeth. He looked at me with his face twisted into a sneer, making him look even uglier. I was not impressed and sneered right back at him, only making his face twitch with anger.

"We are going to have a lot of fun, boy." He had an oily voice to match his unwashed body. "Time to show you the ruins." He raised his fist, and I knew no more.

CHAPTER TWENTY-FIVE

The Altar

I came to slowly, trying to figure out where I was. I did my best not to show anyone who might be watching that I was awake, keeping my breathing even and eyes closed. I didn't hear anyone—or anything—breathing nearby, so I took a risk and cracked my eyes open enough to see what was around me.

I was tied to a chair in a dark room, the only light in the room coming through the crack under the door in front of me. I was just wearing my pants; everything else had been stripped from me. I had no idea how long I had been out but I was pretty sure it was natural daylight coming in under the doorway. That made it the first night since I had been reincarnated that I hadn't dream walked. Apparently, all I needed to do to get uninterrupted sleep was knock myself out.

I could see the outline of a table next to me, and it looked like there were tools of some sort on top of it. Great. Torture chamber. I couldn't keep in the sigh that escaped.

This was all my fault anyway. I let a bunch of idiots capture me, all because I got overconfident. I never had a solid count of the people following me, but I acted like I had killed them all. I just hoped they hadn't messed up my stuff. The blood seals

216

should keep them from actually stealing everything, but they could still destroy them. I couldn't feel any of my items nearby through my connection, so they must have been somewhere else.

I did my best to try to diagnose any injuries I might have from the hit to the head, but I felt fine. The blood caked into my hair was a clear indication that I had been badly injured, but I couldn't feel any ill effects.

I was about to try the ropes, to see if I could break free, when I saw shadows move under the door. There were the outlines of two sets of legs, and as they drew closer, I could hear their muffled voices through the door.

"Did you get it?"

"No, he had me put it with the other stuff in the basement."

"What did he say about it?"

"We won't divide up anything until after we finish up here. He said to think of it as an extra reward for a job well done."

"Too bad. I saw that vest when I was a kid, when it was just collecting dust down in the vaults. I used to mess around down there when my parents were pulling guard. How do you think this kid got his hands on it?"

"Who cares? Did you see when they brought him in? Half his skull was staved in. There is no way he survives that. After he dies, the blood connection dies with him. We can get his stuff after he quits breathing. Remember, you get the vest, but I get the belt. That thing has three different storage spots!"

"You don't think one of the higher-ups will take it?"

"Nah, it looks too beat up. They are all about their image."

"When are they coming back to talk to the kid?"

"Probably after the midday meal. According to them, this kid wiped out over three-fourths of Elder Conrad's crew. That's probably why the guy is still missing. He doesn't want to face the punishment for losing so many people."

"That kid? How could some little boy take out that many people?"

"Exactly why they didn't kill him right away. They want to

know how he did it. Those formation plate traps he had on him were like nothing anyone has seen before, and Councilman Yisi wants to know where he got them. We don't need any surprises this late in the plan."

"Definitely. But how are they going to find out anything if his skull is caved in?"

"Not my problem. Shazi is the one who got carried away, let him deal with it."

"They are going to kill the kid anyway, I guess it doesn't matter if they heal him some first. You want to go with me to check on the others? I have two gold pieces on if that spear wielder survived the night."

Their voices faded as they walked away. Well, that answered a few questions. My stuff was somewhere in the basement, and I had some time to engineer an escape.

I was trying to figure out how getting my skull crushed didn't kill me when I remembered the wooden disk I was using as an impromptu focusing stone. It was hidden in my waistband, so they hadn't removed it when everything was taken. I was definitely lucky. That silly little disk just saved my life.

I tried to wiggle free of the ropes tying me down, but they were extremely tight. I started to spin up my cores to cut myself free but I was met with some resistance. What was going on? I tried harder, forcing the pool of energy in my lower core to start spinning. I pushed the qi through my meridians, trying to form a metal qi thread from my hands. It was like something was keeping any energy in the area from moving, and making it impossible to actually form the qi thread.

I hadn't experienced anything like this before. Was it something inside the temple doing this? I couldn't pass through the doors when I was dream walking. There must be some ancient power source controlling the qi in here somewhere. I had no idea what it could be, but I definitely wanted to check it out. If there was some way to freeze the qi in a large area, I could set up a very diabolical trap for a powerful cultivator. Someone like this Councilman Yisi. Or better yet, someone like Ming…

Since I couldn't use my qi in here, I was going to have to figure something else out. I tried rocking the chair back and forth, but it was bolted to the floor. I tried straining against the ropes, but all I did was rub my skin raw on the rough hemp material. It wasn't a big deal, because the wooden disk healed me right back to normal within a few minutes.

I knew I was running out of time, but I was starting to draw a blank. Hold on. How was the disk still healing me, when the qi in the area was frozen?

I took a closer look at what was going on with the energy around me. The wood-aspect disk was designed to draw in all types of qi, and convert it to life energy. What qi was it drawing in when everything was stagnant? It took me a few minutes of focus, but I finally picked up on what was going on. Whatever was locking down the qi in this area was limiting the flow of the six traditional forms of qi, but it wasn't having any effect on dark and light qi.

Since I had used the qi battery in my belt to set up and power the formation matrix in the disk, I had inadvertently included dark and light qi in with the collection commands. The disk was pulling in what qi it could to heal me, but in this nearly lightless room, that meant it was primarily bringing in dark qi.

Fortunately, I could also use dark and light qi, even if I wasn't very proficient at it yet. It took a bit of concentration but I managed to pull a good amount of dark qi into my lower core. I formed it into a dark qi thread and used it to slice through the ropes holding me. It turned out dark qi was extremely similar to metal qi. There was definitely some kind of relationship between the two, because I had used metal qi to contain the dark qi that was in the batteries and my cores.

I walked over to the table, trying to see if there was anything useful. There wasn't much, but I snatched a thin-bladed dagger off the table. It was well over six inches long, but it was thin enough that I decided it was likely a stiletto. I had never really used such a thin blade in my past life, but I didn't have the luxury of choice right now.

I also found my shirt crumpled in the corner next to the door. It apparently had enough qi to do what it was intended for, because the shirt was spotlessly clean. I was exceedingly happy I had picked these clothes when I was in the vault.

I moved to the door and I was surprised to find it unlocked. I listened for any noises, but I didn't hear anything. I moved out into a long hallway, one side lined with doors and the other had to be an exterior wall because it was lined with high windows missing their glass. They were well above head height, but the light was coming straight in. That meant it was almost time for my interrogators to show. I needed to move fast.

My room was in the middle of the hallway, so I started by checking the rooms to my right. All I found were a bunch of empty rooms and disappointment. I tried the other direction, and it was more of the same. I moved to the end of the hallway in the same direction the guards had gone, and came into a large room filled with supplies.

There were building materials, crates of packaged food, bundled bales of clothing, and a row of empty armor and weapon stands. I guessed my enemies were already dressed for battle. Not so good for me, but good for them I supposed.

There were three doors at the opposite side of the room and my bare feet silently moved across the room to inspect them. The central door was massive, but I could tell by the fresh-looking scrapes on the stone floor it had been used recently. The other two doors were smaller, and one had some crates piled up against it.

The doors were all made of stone, with some banded iron running around the hinges. I checked the door without crates first. It opened up to a narrow stairwell that was headed up. I could hear voices coming from above, and silently closed the door. I wanted to avoid any confrontations until I had a better idea of what was going on. The ability to use only light and dark qi drastically limited my fighting abilities, and I had no idea if my captors were facing the same limitations.

I had moved the crates far enough away from the next door that I could get to it when I heard thumping footsteps coming down the stairway I had just inspected. It looked like it was time for some people to ask me some questions.

I tried to open the door, but there was no way to open it from my side. There was only a design on the edges—some type of scrollwork I had never seen before—and three grooves dug into the center of the door in a circle. I spun out some dark qi to try to run under the edge of the door to open it from the other side, but there was no gap at the bottom. The door completely and perfectly filled the entryway. Instead, the scrollwork reacted to the dark qi and the door cracked open.

A cloud of dust escaped with a puff, and then there was a rush of wind as the space on the other side sucked in air. Strange, it seemed like I had broken some sort of seal. Apparently, the current occupants of the temple hadn't figured out how to open this door yet. The door leading to the stairwell started to open and I rushed inside, silently pulling the door closed behind me.

It was pitch black inside, so I leaned back against the door, waiting to see if my eyes would adjust. The stone door had sealed again behind me but it was thin enough that I could faintly hear the people on the other side. I couldn't actually make out words, it was more like murmuring as it faded away into the distance.

My eyes finally started to pick out some details and I realized that I was standing at the top of a stairwell heading down.

It was a spiral staircase, the curve limiting me from seeing beyond a few feet in front of me. The air smelled dusty and stale. Clearly, the air I let in earlier wasn't nearly enough to freshen up the place. I realized I was able to see because there was a faint green light emanating from below. It was barely enough to navigate by, but I slowly walked down the spiral steps.

I made sure to test each step before putting my full weight

on it, ensuring they were stable. As I kept my hand on the outside wall, I could feel carvings and the occasional recess in the stone. The recesses were all empty, and I was sure that at one time they were intended to hold candles or lamps of some sort.

It was too dark to see what was on the walls, but they felt like images of people. Probably depicting some form of battle scenes, or maybe a god-like figure doing god-like things. If you have seen one temple, you have seen them all. Pretty much the same thing the world over.

It took the better part of ten minutes to reach the bottom of the stairs. I must have been pretty deep underground. I was sure I had to be well below the level of the basements the red robes were using. It was quite the feat of engineering, and I couldn't help but wonder when this was all built.

There were ruins of ancient cities all across the empire, and I had spent my fair share of time exploring them for the emperor when I was younger. This land had seen plenty of kingdoms rise and fall for thousands of years, before an invasion by the empire over the Northern Mountain Range three thousand years ago united all the various kingdoms and warbands under one banner.

It was a war that lasted almost a century, until the invaders were pushed back over the mountains. The hundred years of fighting as a united group made it easy for the leaders of the time to design five kingdoms, and they appointed their strongest member as the emperor to rule over all of them. Our Empire was formed, and the infighting stopped for the most part, allowing the people to prosper in a way that no one in the region had ever seen before.

People eventually resettled along the trade routes established by the emperor and his kings, leaving entire cities to be reclaimed by the wilderness. These later became great places for bandits or some of the more intelligent beasts to live and operate out of. That meant people like me had to come in and clean them out from time to time. This, however, was definitely something new.

The light had been getting brighter the lower I went, and as I reached the bottom I finally saw where it was coming from. There was an arched entryway into a giant room lined with thick columns. Inside the room there were hanging braziers heaped with stones that glowed with an intense green light.

I tried extending my senses to figure out what they were, but the suppression was so strong I couldn't even extend my will an inch outside my body. At the far side of the room there was some kind of raised stone forming an altar. Probably a sacrificial altar. Honestly? Not surprised one bit. What else would be down in the bottom of some creepy temple that was glowing a weird green color? Fluffy bunnies? Nope. I was probably lucky it wasn't some gateway to a dark dimension.

As I walked into the underground cathedral the green stones flashed bright enough to hurt my eyes before dimming to a more muted glow. Fantastic. Either I tripped some ward, or a creepy monster of some kind was going to jump out at me. This whole reincarnation thing was really starting to suck.

Instead of moving down the central aisle, I decided to see what was on the outside of the rows of columns. I chose the left side first and took it slow. I didn't want to get snatched by something with how weak I currently was.

There were stone shelves recessed into the walls directly across from each column. The walls were completely covered by intricate carvings. The amount of detail involved had to be equal to thousands of hours of work, and I felt a pang of sympathy for the people who made this place. The carvings depicted a wide array of animals and beasts slaughtering humans, and one another. The most recurring image was some kind of giant cockroach-looking thing. From the carvings, they must have been the size of an adult human. And my favorite part? They liked to fight in swarms. I couldn't help the shudder that passed through me. These things looked nasty.

I checked the shelves and saw they all held desiccated

corpses. I poked one in the head with my stiletto, just to be sure they weren't going to reanimate and kill me. Thankfully, down here, the dead stayed dead.

I thought about searching the bodies, but I didn't think desecrating some graves was currently the best use of my time. I finished searching both sides, which were the same, before finally approaching the altar. The pressure coming off of it made the qi inside my cores feel like solid lead. I knew a few formations that could limit the flow of qi in a small area, but nothing like this. This was actually affecting the qi *inside* my body, and I didn't even know that was possible without directly contacting another person.

On top of the altar there were five metal objects. On each corner there were small cubes, each side with swirling designs in a style I had never seen before. In the center there was some kind of scepter that was about eighteen inches long, with each end shaped into a three-pointed claw. I wasn't sure, but it looked like the claw could be used to hold the cubes. I reached out to touch a cube but as my hand got closer the pressure grew more intense.

I backed off and the pressure on my cores and body went back to normal. I tried reaching for the scepter, and this time I actually felt the pressure lessen. Somehow, it seemed this weird altar was making this entire building a qi stagnation zone.

I picked up the scepter with the intent of manipulating the cubes, but as soon as I lifted it off of the altar I was struck by a streak of black lighting, and I was thrown backwards into unconsciousness.

CHAPTER TWENTY-SIX

The Sacrifice

When my eyes opened, I was standing in the middle of the underground cathedral. There were some big differences in the temple this time around. It was filled with black-robed people kneeling in supplication, and the room was spotless. Everything looked newer somehow, as if it had just been completed by the eighty-odd people on their knees. They were all facing forwards, and as I watched, a man dressed in a bright green robe came out from a hidden door behind the altar.

He stood behind the altar and looked out at his congregation. In front of him on the stone the four metal cubes were stacked on top of one another in the center instead of being at each corner as I remembered them. I tried to take a step forward, but something was holding me in place. This felt like when I was dream walking, except I had no control. It was like I was viewing a scene from the past as an outside observer.

Everyone was skeletally thin, as if they hadn't eaten anything sustaining during their entire lives. They were so emaciated, I had absolutely no idea how they were all alive.

The man behind the altar was even worse. I was nearly convinced he was an actual skeleton, except I could see him making subtle hand movements inside the sleeves of his voluminous robes. His lips were so thin they practically disappeared into his face, the hair on his head was patchy and thin, and his eyes were so sunken into his skull that they were only pools of shadow.

He opened his mouth, and unnatural hissing sounds came out. I had no idea how a human could make the noises he was making. Maybe I wasn't even looking at humans.

After a few seconds, I could understand what he was saying. It was like another voice was speaking for him inside my head, as if some sort of creepy talking snake was serving as a translator.

"We know what we do this day makes us more. We know why our lives have mattered. We know where we go forever. We know who we serve transforms us. We know how we must serve."

His congregation answered as one. They sounded like a pit of hissing snakes.

"We know. We know. We know. We know. We know."

I get it, you know, no need to repeat yourself! If I was able, I would have snickered at my own joke. Then I sighed. That would have killed in some circles.

My humor died rather suddenly when the entire congregation formed daggers of dark qi in their left hands and, as one, cut their own throats. Well, that escalated quickly.

I was disgusted and confused, but upon closer inspection, I realized their blood wasn't normal. It was more like the flammable black sludge that came up from the ground in the deserts of the Eastern Province. I was pretty sure it wasn't just the green light causing it, either. I was beginning to think that these were either very corrupted humans, or definitely not humans at all.

After the congregation stopped moving, the man behind the altar raised his hands straight above his head, humming something while holding the scepter horizontally over the altar. The scepter started to glow at each end, as if the empty claws on either side were holding small white glow stones.

I could tell whatever the man was doing, it was causing him pain. His whole body was trembling, and it looked like there was smoke coming from where his hands were touching the scepter. Then things got *really* creepy.

The blood covering the floor started moving. It all started running together in the central gap between the pillars, forming a thick stream that traveled to the altar. Upon reaching the altar the blood crawled up the sides and was sucked in by the stack of cubes. As the blood was absorbed, the light globes on either end of the scepter grew larger.

Instead of them both getting brighter as they increased in size, on one side the light seemed to diminish, as if being seen through a darkened piece of glass. The opposite end acted like normal, growing brighter as the other side dimmed in equal measure. I was not sure how much time passed, but eventually all the blood was absorbed into the cubes. The man holding the scepter stumbled, and I think he would have fallen over if he didn't have the altar to lean against.

By this point, the scepter had formed a globe on either end large enough to fit inside its sculpted claws. One globe was pure white, the other solid black. It looked like the scepter was a device intended to capture light and dark qi, but this was the most demented form of creating a qi battery I had ever seen. They were substituting elemental cores with the blood of their people, and the cubes seemed to be some form of blocking mechanism that ensured the only qi that was absorbed was dark and light. I suddenly felt the urge to demolish this entire complex, starting with everything in this room.

The man finally stood and tried to take a step. Instead, he collapsed, dropping the scepter onto the altar into the same place I had seen it when I came in. It knocked the stack of cubes over, and they were each drawn to a corner as if by a magnet. Now, it looked exactly as it had when I walked in. Except for all the bodies, of course.

He started crawling away from the altar, I assumed to get to the exit of the room. He only made it a few feet before collapsing. Then, he looked up, and it seemed like he was staring directly at me. He said something, and the snake voices in my head translated again.

"You have borne witness to our sacrifice. Finish this so that we may rise again, and only then will you reap your reward."

He then slumped over, dead on the floor. The globes of dark and light qi on the ends of the scepter began to pulse, as if they were beating hearts. They started to collapse inwards upon themselves before winking out. My vision dimmed to black.

CHAPTER TWENTY-SEVEN

Jailbreak

I woke up on the floor, no evidence of being struck by the black lightning anywhere on my body. Besides a slight headache, I appeared to be fine, and even my clothing was in perfect condition. The scepter was laying on the ground next to me. I was on my back near the center of the room, in the same place that I had been standing during my vision.

Whatever that madness was, there was absolutely no way I was going to finish any stupid ritual. Rising again? Reaping a reward? Did these people think I was born yesterday? Actually, considering my situation, that hit a little closer to the mark than I wished, but either way there was absolutely no way I was going to complete any form of a ritual blood sacrifice of any kind.

My reward would either be corruption, death, or joining those people in some form of undeath. The total lack of subtlety was honestly a little insulting.

I gingerly picked up the scepter and walked back over to the altar. I used it to knock one of the cubes off the altar, but it snapped right back in position as if it was pulled there by an invisible string. I had no idea how to manipulate these things, but I knew for sure that I didn't want to push qi through the scepter without a long look at its internal matrix.

The metal looked like steel, but it had some kind of oily sheen that felt slick to the touch. There were swirling designs running up and down its length that matched the cubes, and it was thin enough that I could easily wrap my hand all the way around it. It felt heavier than it should, and the oily feeling made my skin crawl. When I moved it to my other hand, there was no residue left behind. It was definitely unnatural. I would have to inspect it better once I got out of this place.

I gave up on trying to manipulate the cubes and started to look for the hidden door behind the altar I had seen the man use in the weird vision thing. Even though I knew it was there, I couldn't find the stupid thing. I tucked the scepter into my waistband next to the pilfered stiletto and I grabbed a few of the green glow stones out of a hanging brazier. I brought them over so I could get a better look at the area, since it was pretty dark behind the altar.

Finally, I found the seam of the door. I felt along the edges for a button or switch of some kind and I eventually discovered a part of the carving on the wall that could be pushed in. Of course, it happened to be one of those disgusting roach creatures. Stars, I hated this place.

The door swung inwards and I was assaulted by a blast of dust. How long had it been since the mass suicide I had seen? And who had moved all of the bodies? I held up my handful of glow stones to light up the narrow hallway, and I got my answer. This place wasn't a temple, it was a gods-be-damned tomb.

The area wasn't originally a narrow hallway. In fact, at one point it was probably pretty wide open, practically another room. Now, bodies were stacked like logs along the sides of the hall, from the floor to well over head height. There was barely room to walk along the path to an open doorway on the other side. The corpses were all tightly wrapped in their black robes, and they had all been mummified by the dry air. They were practically skin and bones before they had died, and now that was pretty much all that was left. I did my best to walk past without disturbing them. I didn't want an avalanche of mummies falling on me.

I made it past the mummy hallway without incident, and entered the next room. There I found the answer for how the bodies got moved.

A green-robed mummy was laid out on a rudimentary cot in the far corner. From the looks of things, the head priest guy must have had some kind of assistant who survived the insanity of the past. I could tell it wasn't the actual head priest, because this one was much smaller. Either a child, or possibly a female.

The room looked like it was meant to be some kind of study, with a desk and wardrobe on one side and a set of shelves covered with books and artifacts on the other. An arched doorway led to another set of stairs in the center of the back wall. Curiosity demanded I go look at the shelves first, but compassion drove me to inspect the small desiccated figure on the cot.

It was a child. I didn't bother to check if it was male or female, but I could see that they were probably close to my physical age. I tried to imagine what it must have been like for them to be sealed up in this tomb, struggling to stack the bodies of the people who they might have considered to be family.

Then, after suffering that torture, to slowly die of dehydration, starvation, or asphyxiation. I took a moment to better cover the body, trying to show it the respect in death that it didn't receive in life. I had no idea what god or creature these people worshipped, but I instinctively hated it with every fiber of my soul. If there was a way to make them pay, I swore to myself that I would take my pound of flesh in retribution. And another pound or two for this poor soul.

After a few minutes of silent reflection, I moved to the desk. There was a fair amount of paper and writing materials but I didn't understand the text. The language was different from the swirling designs on the walls, altar, cubes, and scepter, leading me to believe that the designs were actually a form of formation writing that I had never seen before. I would have taken everything if I had my storage belt, but I left it all where it was. I might come back for it, if I had the time.

The bookshelves were more of the same. Books filled with unfamiliar writing, artifacts, jewelry, and unidentifiable bits that I couldn't give a thorough inspection without my qi. There were a few things I was pretty sure I would be able to sell for a good bit of coin, but it wasn't worth the trouble at the moment.

I was also pretty sure there were a few magical items included in the mix, so if I got back down here, I would have to make sure I didn't put anything in my belt before identifying what it could do. Putting a storage device inside another storage device in an area where I couldn't access the full spectrum of qi was an incredibly bad idea.

With all the books available, I could probably work out a translation for the language if given enough time. It might give me insights into the knowledge these people had about dark and light qi, which I desperately needed. I knew enough about the six normal types of qi that I could fill a small library, but so little about dark and light that I could barely write a single page. Coming back down here just moved up on the list of things to do.

Since I knew I had to return for the potential knowledge I could gain, I took the time to sort everything into piles. Books and papers went into one, jewelry and knickknacks into another, and items giving off magical vibes into a much smaller pile. I used a green robe from the wardrobe to make a sack for the magical pile. After a few minutes of thought, I even moved all of the furniture into its own stack. At the very least, you never knew when some spare firewood could come in handy. I decided everything was ready for a quick retrieval and I headed up the stairway.

It was a much shorter climb, helped along by the glow stones I was holding. I wasn't sure, but it seemed as if this stairway ended lower than the first. It probably ended on one of the basement levels instead of ground level. The door was exactly the same as the one leading to the last set of stairs, with the scrollwork border along the edges and the circle of grooves in the middle. I had a hunch, and pulled out the scepter.

The three claws on the end fit perfectly into the grooves, so I pushed it inwards and heard a faint click. Huh. It was a master key for the temple. I guess it was more useful than I thought. The door actually swung inwards, so I had to back up a step for it to open.

The room I walked into was large, likely the bedroom for the head priest when the temple still had one. It was empty now, except for the ridiculous amounts of dust. I moved across the room to the only door I could see, and used the scepter to open it.

This time I was a bit more careful, making sure my glow stones were covered and the door only opened wide enough for me to look out. The door led to a long hallway and I was at the end of it. There were six doors lining each side, and I could see light coming from a torch at the opposite end. I could hear voices, but they were muffled.

I quietly snuck into the hallway, closing the door behind me before checking each of the doors that I passed. Most required me to use the scepter to open, and they were filled with dusty furniture and piles of junk. I guessed the red robes occupying the temple didn't know how to open these doors either, so they were exactly as the former tenants had left them a long time ago. The muffled voices were getting louder, so I made sure to take my time opening the last few doors. It was the last four rooms without locking mechanisms where I found something interesting.

They were the jail cells the red robes were using for anyone they had captured. In the first room I found all four of Kory's scouts. As I opened the door, all of them looked up with fear in their eyes, but upon seeing me it was quickly replaced with confusion. I held my finger against my lips to signal them to remain silent, and closed the door until it was almost latched again behind me.

As I got closer to them, I saw that they were in pretty rough shape. They had clearly been beaten more than once, but I didn't see any obvious broken bones or serious injuries. I spoke to the female scout.

"Can you move? We need to get you out of here before they return."

She nodded, scooting forward to get a better look at me in the dim lighting. "We can all move. I don't know how well we would do in a fight, though. Somehow, they have cut off our qi, and we can't use any of our abilities." She paused to try to look behind me. "Where is Kory? Did he send you down here? How many others do we have that can fight?"

I held my hand up to stop her. "I don't know where Kory is. I was captured, and managed to escape. We are going to have to do this on our own. The good news is, it isn't just you that has their qi cut off. It is this temple we are in. It has cut off everyone from their qi. That means our captors are just as limited as we are. If we can find some weapons, we will at least be able to fight them using basic martial arts. I bet they aren't nearly as trained as you are."

She nodded at that, and I used my stiletto to cut off the ropes binding them. They whispered amongst one another, gave me a nod, and snuck out the door. Thinking of Kory, I hoped he and the others were okay.

They clearly saw me as just a child who got lucky and snuck out. I was perfectly okay with letting them take charge, as long as I could get my stuff back and look for my parents. One of the scouts was headed back the direction I came from, and the other three were checking the doors I hadn't opened yet.

There were more prisoners in each, and it didn't look like Kory or the others had gotten captured, but it was the last two who stumbled out that I cared about. It was my mother and father. I hadn't seen them in centuries, and it was impossible to stop the tears from leaking out of the corners of my eyes.

They were younger than I remembered. My mother was as beautiful as I recalled, her short stature not diminishing her fine features. The single streak of gray in her long black hair only helped to accentuate her face.

My father was more rugged-looking, with a tall and heavily muscled frame. He had more gray in his short brown hair, but it was less than when I had last seen him. They looked tired, but I didn't see any serious injuries. They were both wearing their forest clothing, but our captors had stripped them of the customary armor I was used to seeing them in.

I rushed to them, grabbing them around their waists. There were muffled shouts of surprise, and it must have taken them a moment to realize that the kid holding on to them was their own.

I didn't blame them. I was pretty sure I was the last person they were expecting to see. After all, the last time they had seen me, I hadn't even opened my lower core yet. Now, I was their rescuer.

My father was the first to speak. "Jim! What in the stars are you doing here? This is no place for a child. Did these bastards capture you? I swear, I am going to gut every one of these motherless dogs!"

My mom was quick to follow. "Are you hurt? Where did all of this blood in your hair come from? Did these people rescue you? Why aren't you at home where you belong?"

Before I could answer, the female scout butted in. "This is your boy? You should be proud. He is the one who rescued us, not the other way around." The entire group looked at me in surprise at her announcement. "Now, I understand you just had a rather interesting family reunion, but we need to get organized, find some weapons, and get out of this place. We can't use our qi, so we will need to fight hand-to-hand until we get out of here."

My father nodded, and my mother pushed me to the back of the group as they pushed forwards. I hadn't even had a chance to get a word in. Not exactly how I pictured our reunion going.

The scout that had gone back to check the other rooms came forward and handed out some broken-off table legs as clubs to the few who looked like they could fight. There were twenty of us now, if you counted me in the mix. About half looked like they could barely stand, so we only had ten people who could swing a club.

We moved into the room at the end of the hall and the injured people rested on the floor while the fighters huddled up in the center of the room to make a plan. The room had two doors not counting the one we had come through, and I went to check the one farthest from the huddle. It was just more dust and disappointment. I turned around to walk back to the huddle to listen in on the conversation when the other door slammed open.

A woman in spotless red robes, black hair, and arched eyebrows had come down another set of stairs, a spear in one hand and a shield in the other. Her eyes popped open wide in surprise at the scene in front of her, and she turned back to shout something up the stairs.

Before she could say anything, my father threw his club at her, and it spun through the air in a perfect arc that ended when the club slammed point first into the side of her head. She crumpled to the ground like a puppet who had its strings cut. Unfortunately, the clatter of her falling onto the room's floor and dropping her spear and shield must have alerted whoever was at the top, because we all heard someone shout a question down the stairs. A shadow fell across the opening.

"I think she fell! Get over here and help me, and you, go get a healing elixir!"

There were two sets of boots thumping on the steps, so we all rushed into the shadowed corners of the room, trying to hide until they came through the doorway.

I readied my stiletto, and as soon as the second man entered the room, I whipped it through the air and straight into his neck. He gurgled as he fell to his knees, and the other man shouted in surprise as he was overwhelmed by the former prisoners wielding clubs. I walked over to pull my thin knife free when a shadow fell across me from above. We were caught.

I looked up into the wide eyes of another guard just in time to hear him shout behind him at the top of his lungs.

"Jailbreak!"

CHAPTER TWENTY-EIGHT

Things Are Looking Up

One of the scouts had already picked up a fallen spear, and he thrust it up the stairs into the chest of the guard before he could look back at us. He fell down the stairs to join his compatriots at the bottom.

The female scout was up the stairs before I had finished standing from retrieving my knife, her three friends close behind. I heard more shouting from above as the rest of the fighters ran up the stairs, my parents bringing up the rear. I rushed to keep up, not wanting to risk them getting injured right after I had been reunited with them.

As I reached the top of the stairs, I saw the scouts finishing off two more guards. The others were leaning against three doors, one on each wall. There were pounding sounds coming from all of them. I guessed the red robes were trying to push in from all directions.

We didn't have nearly enough people to fight them all, and there was no telling how long the weakened people holding the doors could keep them out. The room was nearly empty, with only a few crates stacked on the wall next to a table and chairs. I rushed over to see if there was anything useful inside.

My mother had the same idea. She and I quickly pried the crates open to see what was inside. It was mostly armor and a few weapons, with several hiking packs mixed in. It wasn't until I opened the last crate that I found what I was hoping for.

My vest was laying on top, with my boots and belt under it. The spirit wood ring and flying ring were in the very bottom, hiding under the copper disks I had used to make all my traps. Apparently, they had collected the other formation plates I had used on the trail. How nice of them.

I used some pieces of the broken crates to wedge under the doors. It wouldn't hold forever, but it could give the people trying to hold them closed a break.

I got my gear situated as my mother was passing out the other items to our fellow former prisoners. Even the people who could barely walk seemed to perk up some after getting their stolen items back. I took a moment to pull out some of the healing poultices, herbs, and bandages I had bought back in Roh City. One of the more lightly injured people started distributing them as needed.

I took a moment to test if I could use the qi inside the batteries on my belt. It took far more concentration than it should have, but I was able to form a single thread of air qi from the meridian in my hand. Finally, I had access to the type of elements I knew how to fight with! Just as things were finally starting to look up, one of the doors started to splinter. Apparently, one of the red robes got tired of banging their shoulder on the door and started to use an axe.

I was waiting for someone to step up, but even the scouts and my parents seemed to be at a loss as to what we should do next. I ran back to the steps leading down and turned to look at everyone.

"We have to go back this way. I can take us through the way I came. It is a little creepy, but I don't see any other option."

One of the scouts stepped forward, shaking his head. "There is no way out. I checked. We must make a stand here, or we face being captured and tortured again."

I pulled free the scepter, waving it about like a talisman. "How do you think I got up here? Trust me, I have a key that can get us through the door at the end of the hallway. We just need to find a way to slow them down."

My father walked over to me. "My son wouldn't steer us wrong. We need to hurry. I have a shield formation that will stop them from coming down the stairs, but with the qi in this place being frozen, it won't last long."

That seemed to galvanize everyone but two of the scouts. I didn't have time to fight it out with them, so I just turned to head down the stairs. If they wanted to stay and die a pointless death, that was on their own heads, not mine.

I waited at the bottom of the steps for my parents. My father was helping get everyone back downstairs so he could set his shield formation on the top step. I could hear the wood splintering from the door and sounds of fighting. From what I could tell, one of the scouts who was staying behind seemed to be stabbing a spear through the hole in the door at the red robes on the other side. It was only a matter of time until they got an archer to take him down. We needed more time to move the injured.

I fought against the flow of people coming down and reached the upper room again. I pulled out two of the throwing knives that were over my abdomen. I probably wouldn't get these back, so I would need to reform them in the lower sheaths anyway. Walking behind the scout who was thrusting through the door with a spear let me see the crowd of red robes standing on the other side. It was too narrow of an opening to be sure, but there were at least ten people waiting for the door to fall.

I waited for the scout to pull his spear back before throwing a knife through the ragged hole in the door. A scream of pain from the other side let me know that it had hit someone, so I followed up with another. This time I didn't hear anything. Either I had missed, someone had blocked it, or it had killed someone instantly. I was hoping for the latter, but it would have been sheer luck if that was the case.

Finally, everyone who was going with us got down the stairs and my father was able to set up the shield. I walked past him as he lined up the formation carvings on the row of three plates. It activated just in time, an arrow smacking against the wall of energy just as my father turned to walk down the steps. I pushed my way through the crowd of people, pulling the scepter back out as I made it to the door.

It sprang open the moment I got it in the slots and I opened it all the way before moving on to the doorway to the stairs. The next door popped inwards and I pushed it open to allow everyone to follow me down.

I looked back at the female scout who had positioned herself to serve as the rear guard. "Make sure you close the doors as soon as everyone is inside. They will have to get a pickaxe or something to get through the stone."

She nodded in agreement, and I led the way into the dark stairwell.

As I ran down the stairs, I took the time to put the stiletto, glow stones, and scepter into my storage belt. I needed both hands to get everything in the head priest's study put in my belt before the others behind me saw how much stuff it could hold.

Now that I had access to the qi batteries in my belt, I could inspect the magical items as well. It would only take a moment to scan them all and pull out any storage devices that might be in the pile.

I was moving so fast that I practically slid into the room. I put the furniture and books into the largest storage space in the belt buckle, and scanned everything else in less than a minute.

There were four storage items in the pile, so I pulled them out and put everything else in the storage disk that held the old coins. I didn't hear anyone coming down the steps yet, so I took a moment to inspect my new storage devices. My eyes widened a bit, and I felt a smile stretch across my face.

They were all filled to the brim with jewels, precious metals, and ingots of the oily metal the cubes and scepter were made from. I quickly transferred everything shiny into the stud I was beginning to think of as my personal bank, alongside the old coins and other fancy items. The metals went into the stud with the chitin and traveling forge.

Each of the four storage devices were close to seven hundred square feet of storage. That was practically the size of the room I was standing in! Not as exciting as the belt, obviously, but still a nice find.

The storage devices themselves were a bit odd. Instead of something you could wear, they were all miniature statues depicting some form of bird. It was too dark to tell, but I was pretty sure they were all a stylized crow or raven in various poses. They were small enough to fit in a coin pouch, so I just emptied one of the bags I had gained from the former Elder Conrad and hung them on my belt.

I had just finished up when the first of the escaped prisoners stumbled into the room. I helped them to sit down against the wall that used to hold the bookshelf and walked back to assist the next one in line.

It wasn't until nearly everyone was seated that I realized what I had done. I was the only person with a light source. I had left everyone following behind me lost in a stairwell of darkness, with only the faintest of light coming from below. Oops. Oh well, no one said I was perfect. It left me plenty of time to finish up down here anyway.

My parents and the female scout finally stumbled into the room. I could clearly see they were exhausted. There was no telling when the last time they had eaten was, and I couldn't even imagine when they had last gotten some sleep. For high-level cultivators, it was easy to go for extended periods without food or sleep, but without access to qi they were the same as someone born without a core. I led them to an open spot on the floor and they practically collapsed.

My father was the first person to come to his senses enough to take a look around. The room didn't hold much now, just the cot with the desiccated corpse and a few scraps of paper I missed in my rush to collect everything. His eyes finally settled on me.

"Jim, what are you doing here? Of course, I am glad to see you, but you shouldn't be in this place. None of us should."

I took a breath, and sat down in front of him. It took the better part of an hour to recount what I had been through in the past five or six days. I didn't know how long I had been unconscious, but I figured it couldn't have been too long. After a while, the two remaining scouts started to chime in, filling in details and recounting their own version of events.

I downplayed my own role in most of the adventures and left out the whole reincarnation and talking to the gods stuff. The scouts hadn't been around for much of it anyway, so our versions matched pretty well.

My parents were definitely surprised to hear that I had won first place in the tournament. They were happy, but I could see the confusion in their eyes. They would know first-hand that I hadn't extensively trained in fighting before I opened my core, and they had both seen me perfectly throw a knife into the neck of a guard from several steps away.

My mother was the first to bring it up. "Jim, your story is leaving a few things out. None of this explains how you were able to do everything you have done, and I can't understand why the chief elder and Captain Kory thought it was a good idea to bring you out here, no matter how well you performed in the tournament."

I opened my mouth to answer, but my father cut me off. "It isn't important right now. We all need to eat some food, get some rest, and come up with a plan for getting out of here. Figuring out what Jim has been up to can wait until we get back to Roh City and inform the council what has been going on out here. Our own clanmates are trying to kill us, and we still don't know why."

Thanks for the save, Dad.

With that, the questions ended. I pulled out a case of trail rations and we all passed them around. One of the other cases had several waterskins and wineskins that got shared about as well. Once we had all eaten our fill, people began to stretch out on the ground in an attempt to get some sleep. I laid down between my parents. Both of them had fallen asleep within moments.

I thought about pulling out some bedrolls, but almost everyone was already unconscious. The male scout had gone back up the stairs to listen for anyone trying to break through the door above, and the female scout was sitting at the foot of the stairwell in case he shouted down a warning. I had no idea if it was night time outside, but I was tired enough that it didn't matter. The black lightning and subsequent vision had apparently sapped my energy.

I closed my eyes and quickly nodded off.

CHAPTER TWENTY-NINE

Many Paths to Power

I opened my eyes to darkness. I was lying in a bed again, back in my old body. I looked over and saw Pride standing in front of a fireplace that had familiar green flames flickering inside it. The fireplace was the only thing besides the bed, Pride, and myself in a field of black.

"I thought you could only speak to me when I increased my cultivation?"

Pride turned to face me. "Normally, that is true. You also shouldn't give off any light while we talk, since your body isn't going through any changes in structure. The temple you are in has allowed me to reach your mind for a few minutes, so pay close attention and don't interrupt."

I opened my mouth to ask a question, but the frown on his face stopped me.

"Good. You can learn. What I am about to tell you must stay between us. If anyone else were to know what I am telling you, they would hunt you down and end your existence just for a glimpse at the knowledge you are about to receive." I swallowed. Was that why Wrath wasn't here? "I am the oldest remaining of my brethren. I have seen more threats to this portion of reality than any other, and only I know of the danger you have stumbled across."

He turned back to look at the fire before continuing. "The people who built the temple you are in were a cult that happened upon a path to power that should never be followed. You saw how it ended for them. They were only steps away from reaching into a place that even the creatures in the dark mana dimensions fear to tread. The gates to the outer realms hold many secrets, and some of those secrets can lead to great power. Others lead to places filled with things that do nothing but devour. They consume everything in their need to feed, until nothing is left." His voice dropped an octave. "Not even the *nox* wish for an end to all things. They only wish for everything to be twisted into a reflection of their own darkness. The scepter and cubes you found can be used to force open a gateway to a realm filled with the *vorare*."

He looked back at me. "You can keep the scepter, but the cubes must be destroyed. Use one of the ravens you found to collect the cubes. Putting all four of them into one raven will cause the containment matrix to overload. The resulting explosion should be powerful enough to destroy them, keeping that gateway sealed forever. After you have gained whatever knowledge there is in those books you found, make sure to destroy those as well. We don't want someone to reconstruct their rituals and practices."

He paused long enough to turn back to the fireplace, so I used the opportunity to ask a question. "Are there any other random gateways or evil cults you need me to stop? In case you hadn't noticed, my hands are already full with the whole *nox* assignment you saddled me with."

Pride sighed before answering. "The *nox* were released due to your own mistakes, not mine. As for the cult, that was just a happy accident. Your world is filled with people searching for easy ways to power. Even I don't know how many places are hiding with things like the temple your clanmates stumbled upon. You are far from the only weapon I have on the surface of your planet, but you were the closest one I had available at the moment. If I have need of you to stop a possible incursion of extra-dimensional monsters from destroying your planet, I will position you to end the threat. Or the threat will end you. Either way, I have one less problem to deal with. I am beginning to like you, Jim, but that won't stop me from using you. Never forget your place in all of this."

Pride waved his hand, and the fireplace was replaced with a window. On the other side, I could see the sleeping chambers of the head priest inside the temple. The red robes had already busted through the main door, and they were using hammers to pound on the door leading to the stairwell.

"Our time draws to a close, and you are about to have company. Time to wake up." He turned back to look at me, and his glowing solid blue eyes flashed.

____

CHAPTER THIRTY

____

Escape

I jerked awake, the people around me still sound asleep. I looked over to the stairs, and I saw the female scout slumped over against the wall. I was about to stand up when the male scout stepped into the room. He was holding a short sword, blood dripping down its edge. The female wasn't sleeping. A second glance showed me she was dead.

I wasn't one to jump to conclusions, but it appeared as if we had a traitor in our midst. The fact that the red robes had so easily found us time and again was starting to make more sense. The man turned to the next closest person, raising his sword above his head. I jumped to my feet, and immediately tripped over my father's pack. He must have repositioned it while I was dreaming. Thanks, Dad, hugs and kisses.

The commotion caused the scout to pause his attempted murder, trying to see in the dim light where the noise had come from. I decided to use the extra time he had given me to enact some poetic justice.

I used the qi from one of my batteries to spin out an invisible thread of air and run it across the ground to the dead female. I grabbed the dagger out of her belt and stabbed it straight into the traitor's groin. He started screaming in a higher pitch than was most likely normal for him, and I quietly rejoiced. Take that, you evil scum.

His screams served as an excellent alarm, and everyone was soon on their feet. It didn't take long for the others to realize what he had done, and his screaming ended soon after.

The silence that fell after he stopped his racket let us all hear the sounds of hammers striking the stone door at the top of the stairs.

With the female scout dead, my father took charge. "They will be down here in moments. Jim, tell me there is another way out of this place."

I pointed towards the hall of mummies. "Through there. The room is filled with stacks of dead people, so try not to disturb them. We don't want to have to climb over piles of bones to get out of here. On the other side of the altar room, there is a stairway that leads up to ground level. It is our only chance."

My father nodded, and took a few minutes to assign people to help the more wounded of our party.

It was going to be speed that saved us now, and no one wanted to leave someone behind. I took a moment to grab a necklace from the female scout so I could give it to Kory when I next saw him.

I led the group through the narrow pathway into the creepy underground chapel. I waved them towards the back as I stepped up to the altar.

Pride hadn't given me a timeframe for how long it would take one of the raven storage statues to explode, so I pulled out all four of them. I would store one cube in each until we were clear of the building. After that, I would combine them all and throw it back inside this tomb. Hopefully, the explosion would bring this whole place down. I just wanted to make sure we were all clear before that happened.

My father brought up the rear as the group made it through. He closed the door behind him. The secret door was thinner than the ones at the top of the stairs, but it would still buy us some time. I waved my father over as I positioned one statue over each of the cubes.

"What I am about to do will release the hold on the qi in the area. I don't know if it will be instantaneous, or take a little bit, but everyone will be able to use their cores very soon. That means our enemies will as well, but they hopefully won't realize it right away. We might have one chance to surprise them with an attack."

My father seemed surprised that I knew so much, but he was a practical man at heart. Instead of taking the time to question me, he ran off towards the others, shouting plans for an ambush.

I took a deep breath and I activated the ravens all at once, pulling the cubes into storage at the same moment. I didn't know if there was going to be some form of catastrophic qi overload or not, but I had a gut feeling it would be better to store them all at once instead of one at a time.

My fears were thankfully unfounded. There was no massive qi explosion, so I gathered up the statues into their pouch and headed for the stairs. I could feel waves of power leaking through the storage devices, but now wasn't the time to worry about it.

My father had positioned six people for the ambush, one behind each of the pillars nearest the exit. My mother was helping the more injured people get up the stairs. They had each grabbed some of the green glow stones to help light the way. That gave me another idea. I rushed back into the cathedral and started knocking over the braziers that held all the glow stones. I then started shoving the piles of stones towards the altar, turning the area near the secret doorway into a bright patch in an otherwise black room. The long shadows cast by all the pillars would make it much harder for the people coming through to see their ambushers.

I also took the opportunity to store a few braziers of the glow stones in my belt. While I was beginning to hate this specific color of green, they did put out plenty of light. You never knew when you might need a few extra light sources. Or a few hundred extra light sources.

The light from the people working their way upstairs was almost gone before we heard the first thumps of a hammer against the secret doorway. They knew to wait at the top of the stairs for the rest of us. Not that they had a choice. I was the only person who could open the door.

The banging sounds were getting louder, and it would only be a few seconds before they broke through. I tried spinning up my cores and, for the first time in at least a whole day, my qi responded like it should. It was still sluggish, but I was able to push out dozens of earth threads from the soles of my feet.

I used the rest of my meridians to start pulling in as much qi as possible. No one was paying any attention to me, so I wasn't bothering to limit myself. I wanted to have as much qi as possible before this kicked off. I could sense the other people in my group pulling in qi as well. Their backs slowly straightened as their strength returned. These red robed idiots were in for a nasty surprise.

The door finally shattered, and two people wielding large steel hammers stepped into the room. I could see the narrow path in the room behind them was packed with people. It made me wish I had dropped some of my traps in the room before we closed the door. One or two of my whip traps would have decimated those idiots.

As a few more people walked into the cathedral, my group started to spread out a bit. The red robes had their night vision ruined by the large pile of glow stones, so we were practically invisible.

The idiots were staring around in wonder at the chamber, keeping the people behind them from pushing further into the room. The person closest to our enemies raised their arm before dropping it quickly to their side. That must be the signal.

I could feel each of the people on my half of the room ramp up their cores. The energy they were putting off meant that all of them were at least low-level Brain cultivators. That meant they could use all six elements, making the coordination of their attack easier. From the sudden increase in temperature inside the room, I guessed they had picked fire.

The wave of flames the six cultivators on my side unleashed was hot enough that it made my skin redden from halfway across the room. It rolled over our pursuers fast enough that the ones in front couldn't even shout.

I used the commotion as an opportunity to run my threads of earth qi under their feet and wove a net of stone across the doorway on the other side of the room filled with corpses. It trapped everyone inside the small room, and the dried bones and clothing of the bodies went up like kindling. It turned the space into an impromptu oven, baking everyone inside the room. The screams died off quickly.

Anyone trying to run through the flames into the cathedral was blasted back by the force of the inferno. I could sense others trying to break through the stone net I had made from inside the study, but there was no way they could get through in time to save their friends. The mummies burning in the room would ensure no one would be getting through that doorway for at least a little while, unless they felt like getting burnt.

It took less than two minutes before our side had to stop. A well-executed ambush was like that sometimes. As soon as you sprang the trap, the fight was over.

After looking at how my side was doing, it was a good thing it only took a few minutes. They weren't in any shape to keep fighting. Most of them looked like they were going to throw up. I didn't know if it was because of the savagery of the fight, or them having to use so much qi after their cores sat stagnant for so long. Probably a mixture of both.

My father got everyone collected as I released my hold on the stone net. My qi levels still weren't back to normal, and now that I was surrounded by people I didn't know, I couldn't use all my meridians to help refill my cores. The qi batteries were getting lower than I was comfortable with as well. I would need to be careful.

We all headed for the stairs, my parents bringing up the rear. I pushed towards the front so I could open the door at the top. I would have dropped some of my trap plates along the way, but I didn't want to take the time to set them up. While I wasn't exactly impressed by the intelligence of the red robes, it wouldn't be long until they figured out there had to be another way back to the surface. We would be lucky if they weren't already waiting when I opened the door.

I was able to squeeze past the people waiting at the top of the stairs after the long climb and stood with my ear against the door. I was pretty sure it was clear, but it was hard to hear anything with so many people standing around. Time to roll the dice, I suppose.

I pulled out the scepter and went to push it into the grooves. Instead, someone grabbed my shoulder and pulled me back. I looked over my shoulder to see who it was, but it was too dark to see their features. All I could tell was that it was an older gentleman.

"I think it would be best if you let a few of our stronger people go through that doorway first. We don't want our rescuer getting injured in an ambush."

I nodded, but realized he wouldn't be able to see me. I didn't mind stronger people leading the way, and the guy talking was much stronger than I was currently. "Yes sir, I understand. I will set the key in place, but I won't push it in far enough to trigger the door mechanism."

I felt him pat me on the top of my head. "Good lad. Now move back a bit, and let the adults handle this." I put the scepter back in the door slot and moved a few steps back.

It took a few hushed whispers and some shuffling in the order of people, but after a few minutes, they were ready to go. They slammed the door open, four people springing into the room. I was expecting to hear shouting and violence, but everything was quiet.

I waited for everyone to shuffle forward up the stairs and reclaimed the scepter while standing off to the side. I was looking for my parents. After the last person walked past me, I was starting to get concerned. I moved deeper into the storage room to look for them, leaving the door open in case they were still downstairs.

Our party had split into four groups, one at each of the three other doors leading into the room, and a few people sorting through the various boxes piled around the room. The largest group was standing by the main gate. I sighed with relief, seeing my mother looking through boxes and my father standing by the gate. I needed to put a bell or something on those two!

They must have been in the group that rushed into the room to spring any ambushes. While I wasn't happy that they were willing to put themselves in harm's way like that, I understood why they did it. I walked back to the stone door leading down to the underground cathedral to close it, but I was stopped by something slamming against the main gate. I scooted over to see what the commotion was about.

As I got closer to the gate, I could hear screams coming from the other side. I looked over at the adults and I saw more than a few pale faces. Apparently, they had been hearing the screams for several minutes.

I stepped closer to my father. "Has anyone been able to figure out what is going on? It sounds like a serious battle is going on outside."

My father shook his head. "We were waiting until the fighting moved away a bit, but it only seems to be getting worse. Someone said there is a massive chamber on the other side of this door. They were dragged through the room on the way to being questioned in the cells down the hallway."

I nodded. "That hallway is where I was held. There isn't an exit down there, so we will need to either go through the gate into whatever is going on, or go up the flight of stairs to the second story. I think it is where the red robes were setting up camp earlier, but for now they seem to be preoccupied."

He looked around at our ragtag group of people. "I wish we knew how many people they have here. I would like to think they are starting to run out of fighters, but there could be dozens more running around these woods. We can probably fight our way clear of the ruins, but there are several people who will not make it all the way to Roh City without a long rest and some healing." He turned back to the others to continue their discussion, dismissing me for the moment.

I looked around at the rest of the people in the room. If anything, he was understating the problem. Even the people in fighting shape looked like they could be taken out by an angry gust of wind.

I turned back to my father and got his attention again. "We should head up the stairs. We might find a more defensible location farther up in the building where people can heal and rest. After we find a place, a few of our strongest people can come back and see what is going on."

The group around my father looked at me with surprise and confusion on their faces. A man I vaguely remembered as a family friend, his torn and dirty robes making it hard to place him, was the first to speak up. "Since when did you become so good at organizing a group? And how do we know that it won't be worse up those stairs? I don't think taking the advice of a child is in anyone's best interest."

I shook my head in anger. Who cared where a good idea came from, as long as it was still a good idea? "None of that matters! We need to move. There are too many entrances to this room to make it defensible. If anyone doesn't want to listen to me, I would like you to remember how that worked out in the basement. People who didn't need to die pointlessly sacrificed themselves due to their own stubbornness! Just because you don't like the source of a good idea doesn't mean you should ignore it."

He looked down at his feet in embarrassment. "Okay. I see your point. We need to move," he said.

I felt my mother's hand fall on my shoulder. "Help me organize these supplies. We will need some of these if we are stuck here for a long time." I turned away from the adults and began sorting through the crates and piles of goods.

I left the scouting of the floors above to the adults. I was apparently overstepping my bounds too much. At first, I was angry, but after thinking about it for a bit I realized that I would probably act the same way in their situation. It was definitely outside the norm for a child to lead a group of adults. I was a little surprised at how well they had all been following my lead up to this point. It was probably due to the suddenness of the situation.

Now that they had some time to gather themselves, the group would fall into the more regular pattern of cultivators the world over: the strong led while the weaker followed. That thought process had been a problem for a long time. The strongest people were not always the best leaders, but leadership capability wasn't the primary measurement for those in power. I didn't like it, but I couldn't think of a way to tackle something like that right now.

A few minutes after my outburst, a group of five rushed up the stairs to see what they could find. I took the opportunity to stuff as much as I could into my storage belt.

It was still far from full, and most of the crates in the room could be used as either trade goods or supplies for when we got out of here. The various building materials might be useless for now, but it didn't feel right to leave them to the red robes.

Who knew? I might end up needing to build something after I left the clan. That thought made me pause. I didn't want to leave my parents right after seeing them again. However, I knew it wouldn't be long until I would be moving on, no matter what my feelings on the matter happened to be.

It was less than ten minutes later when two of the people checking upstairs came back down. There were some hushed whispers between the impromptu leadership and the two who had returned before they turned to address the larger group.

"We think there is a good place to hide and recover for a bit. Everyone, grab what you can and get up the stairs. Make sure you stay low when you cross the balcony section. You will know what I mean when you get past the first room. Don't get distracted by what is going on down below, just keep moving. We don't want to draw attention to where we have gone."

There were nods all around and people started shuffling towards the stairs leading up. I stayed towards the back and finished loading everything I could get my hands on into my belt, which still hadn't increased in weight by much.

If anyone took the time to look back, they would certainly be shocked at how empty the room appeared to be now. Luckily for me, it seemed like everyone was more concerned with getting to a place to rest than checking on what the kid was doing behind them. Mother and Father were herding the most heavily injured up the stairs, leaving me to bring up the rear.

I closed the door behind me. Instead of the sounds of battle getting quieter, they were getting louder as I climbed the stairs. I began to spin the qi faster in my cores, getting ready for a fight.

Instead of finding a battle at the top, I saw the tail end of our group heading through a door to the right. Directly across from the stairs was a thick stone railing overlooking what must have been the above-ground cathedral that was on the other side of the gate in the last room. I could see vaulted arches and fluted columns that mimicked what was belowground. I walked closer, trying to see what was going on.

When I finally got a good look, the pieces to everything that had been happening fell into place in my mind. Pride had set up the perfect situation. I knew what I needed to do. I had figured it out.

Below me a battle between close to fifty red robes and a single creature was raging in full force. There were over a dozen red robes already out of the fight, with what had to be another dozen in pieces thrown around the area. The sheer number of people in the uniform of my enemies was shocking.

Just how large was this faction? With what I had seen underground, how many I had killed, and the numbers I was looking at, this had to be a much larger group than I initially thought. Counselor Yisi must have been putting this together for a very long time. I could only hope that the people here were the majority of his forces, otherwise we were in for a heap of trouble when we returned to Roh City.

The creature the red robes were fighting was the *nox*. When I broke the hold over the qi in the area the cubes were enforcing, it must have finally been able to enter the temple.

The *nox* was moving so quickly it was leaving after-images behind, flickering around the room like a wasp loaded up on coca plant. It was throwing people around with ease, their reaction times not nearly fast enough to keep up with the infected Spotted Snow Leopard.

They were tossing around qi attacks with abandon, making the room crackle with all the power that was being expended in such a small area. Nothing came close to the malformed big cat, its speed making it invulnerable to the relatively low-level cultivators. It was toying with them, just like a house cat playing with a mouse before it went in for the kill. Made sense, I supposed.

The cubes must have been what was drawing the *nox* to the area, their power like a lodestone to its senses. The red robes must have been using the building as a prison at first, but were forced inside the temple after the *nox* showed up. The abandoned construction projects I had seen when dream walking made perfect sense now.

I wonder how many died before they were forced into their own prison? Karma was poetic like that sometimes. It wouldn't be long until the *nox* got tired of playing and started looking for the source of the power it was searching for. The power hanging from a pouch on my belt. Seriously, could a guy catch a break sometime?

I stayed crouched as I worked towards the doorway my group had disappeared through. The next room was completely enclosed instead of looking over the larger room. Once again, I closed the door behind me, trying to keep as many obstacles between me and the *nox* as possible.

My parents were standing on the right side of the room, staring out a set of empty windows that overlooked the ruins. The sun was nearly down, the last rays of light casting long shadows over the former city. They were the only other people in the room. A door opposite the one I came through showed me the group must have kept moving. As I approached my parents, they both turned back to look at me. I saw them share a look with one another before my mother broke the silence, her voice barely above a whisper.

"Jim, we need to know what is going on." I opened my mouth to answer, but she cut me off. "Not about the situation we are in. We need to know what is going on with *you*. No lies this time. I can tell you are my child, but you are not the same child we last saw when we left Roh City." My father standing beside her nodded in agreement.

I took a deep breath, ready to tell them the version of events I had told my friends and Kory. Being given a mission by the gods was the truth, and it would assuage their fears until I could come up with something else. Instead, I saw shadows moving around in the ruins outside. I rushed to the window, my parents turning to look at what had distracted me.

"Jim," my mother started to say, "there isn't anything—"

"Look!" I interrupted, pointing to the figures moving down an alleyway between two partially built buildings. "I think our way out of here just got easier," I said, waving an arm out the window.

It was Kory and the others. They didn't see me until I threw a rock near their position, but after a few minutes of signaling I was pretty sure they understood what I wanted. I was the only person here who had a chance fighting the *nox*, and my plan required getting everyone else out of the building.

I pulled a long length of rope out of my belt, tying one end around the stone divider between the two windows. I used a spear out of my stockpile to tie the other end around, and had my father throw it to my friends. His many years of hunting and strong build made the long toss easy for him, and my friends found a place to tie off the other end of the rope. I now had a zipline the injured could use to easily get clear of the building. While my father and I had been arranging everything, my mother had rushed off to bring everyone back into the room.

It took less than a minute to explain everything before the first person was wrapping a belt around the rope and sliding down to safety. I pulled my father off to the side.

"Tell Captain Kory that I will catch up to everyone at the cave in the hillside. I haven't sensed anything breaking the warding I left in place, so it should still be safe. With the extra help, even the injured should have no problem making it to the campsite. Rest there until I show up. Don't let anyone come back for me. I move faster alone." He opened his mouth to argue, but it was my turn to cut him off. "Kory can explain what happened when I touched the testing stone. He knows everything, and he trusts my judgement."

Father placed his hand on my shoulder. "I will tell him, but I can't promise that I won't come looking for you if you take too long. I saw that monster they were fighting. I don't know how you expect to deal with all of this, but I can't ignore everything you have done so far."

Mother moved over. "I don't like this. You should just come with us, and we can come back with the military to handle that beast. And our captors."

I shook my head before answering. "We can't afford to let that thing escape. Can you imagine the damage it could do inside Roh City? Besides, I have a feeling our military will be preoccupied with other matters upon our return. Whatever you do, don't trust Councilman Yisi. I can't prove it yet, but he is the leader of the red robes."

Both my parents gasped at the revelation.

"Are you sure?" my father asked, "Because an accusation like that could land our entire family branch in prison."

I nodded, looking him in the eyes to let him see how serious I was. "I am sure. He is planning to overthrow the clan leader and take control of Roh City. We can't afford to let this creature divide our forces even further." I looked over at the window. "There are only a few people left. You both need to go, and I need to kill a monster."

While we had been talking, the sounds of fighting had finally started to die down. There couldn't be many red robes left, and every moment that monster was distracted was a moment I could use to bring it down.

"I will see you soon. Make sure you leave the rope in place. I might need a quick escape route. Now go." I turned away from my parents, pushing through the door I hadn't been through to move farther into the building.

I looked back just in time to see my mother sliding down. My father raced her, balancing on top of the rope as he ran down it. Showoff.

Now that everyone was clear, I could enact my plan.

CHAPTER THIRTY-ONE

Teaching a Cat a Lesson

I pushed myself to run as fast as possible. I needed to find the way into the basement levels before the *nox* caught up with me. If I could feel the power the cubes contained in the birds hanging from my belt were giving off, I had no doubt the *nox* could sense them as well.

I didn't want to use the doorway I already knew about, because that was my exit strategy. Trying to escape a massive explosion while running through unfamiliar hallways was a recipe for disaster. Not only that, but I wanted to be able to close the door to the underground cathedral behind me. If there was an angry *nox* chasing me, the doors that had already been busted down by the red robes wouldn't serve as much of an obstacle. Trying to plan all this out was exhausting!

It took me longer than I wanted, but I eventually found a stairway leading down. It was in the second to last room on the second floor. In my rush, I had missed it the first time, but back-tracking a bit led me back down to the first floor. I came down the stairs into an empty room off the side of the main cathedral. There was only one other door, which of course led straight to the last place I wanted to be.

Peeking out the door let me see that there weren't any red robes still fighting. The *nox* was near the front of the room, less than fifty feet from the door I was hiding behind. I couldn't see what he was hunched over, but from the sound of things, he was taking part in the buffet-style meal laid out around him.

The bodies, or parts of bodies, were thrown around the room in splashes of blood and gore. The smell of exposed organs, coppery blood, and voided bowels nearly made me vomit. I had been a part of thousands of battles, but the sheer savagery of this massacre was pretty close to the top of my list of worst things I had ever seen. I took my time looking around the room, trying to find a way to sneak around the monster while it was distracted.

It took a minute or two, but I finally saw what I was looking for. A blood trail led to a doorway almost directly across from mine. It looked like there was a set of stairs leading down on the other side of the door. The blood trail appeared to be from someone dragging themselves towards an escape from the fight.

I couldn't blame them for trying to get away. This thing was awful. I pulled the door open farther, trying to time my sprint across the open area with the sounds of crunching bones the *nox* was making. I took a deep breath, checked to make sure it was still bent over its meal, and ran at top speed for the opening.

The *nox* had either been aware of me and waiting for my move, or its reflexes were incredible. Whichever it was, the end result was the same. I was a bit more than halfway across the room when it slapped me so hard, I was pretty sure my future children would still be feeling it.

I hadn't been using qi because I was attempting to hide my presence, which in retrospect was pretty pointless. The only good news was, its paws were nearly the size of my whole body. That meant instead of me getting hit hard enough that my limbs were blown off, the force of the blow was evenly spread across my torso and limbs, accelerating me to the opposite side of the room and straight into a pile of rubble in one piece. Small victories.

It hurt. My ears were ringing, my whole body felt like one massive bruise, and I was pretty sure some ribs were broken. And an ankle. And probably my right arm. I couldn't hold in the groan that escaped. This body was definitely not in my preferred fighting shape.

I looked towards the *nox*, but it had already lost interest in me. The pouch holding the birds had fallen free during my sudden flight, and the *nox* was trying to gently get it open with one of its massive paws. I was having trouble drawing in a breath, the broken ribs pushing against my lungs. I used some of the qi in my batteries to dump power into the medallion hidden in my waistband. The influx of wood qi that pushed into my body popped the broken bones back into position while simultaneously clearing up the head injury I hadn't realized I had. That explained the ringing in my ears. After giving it a few seconds, I stood up. Time for round two.

If a *nox* inhabiting an animal could communicate, I was pretty sure it would have said something along the lines of, "Huh?" It cocked its head to the side as I stood, as if trying to figure out how I was still alive. Honestly, I understood where it was coming from.

"Okay, no more taking it easy on you," I said.

The *nox* took a moment to stare at me some more before it began making a weird chuffing noise. Was it laughing at me? Wait, could it understand human speech? Oh my. This just got much, much harder.

I used its moment of humor to spin up my cores to maximum. Time slowed to a stop, and I took over half of all the qi remaining inside my batteries to form an earth construct in the shape of a spiked maul the size of a cow. I positioned it directly in front of the cat, and swung it straight down for the center of its back. I loosened my perception of time by half, accelerating the hammer with pointy bits with as much power as I could. Let's see who is laughing now, jackass.

I could feel my own mouth drop open in surprise when the cat started to dodge the attack. Damn, this thing was fast. By the time the maul reached the *nox*, I barely clipped its side. The impact was still enough to send the monster flying off to the side, the spikes on the hammer ripping open a wound along its ribs. It crashed through the door I had tried to run out of, wedging its massive frame in the narrow doorway. Now was my chance.

I returned my perception of time back to normal before sprinting for the bag. No need to rip my body apart with the increased reaction times.

I snatched the bag off the ground and ran for the stairs, practically running along the walls as they spiraled down. There was light coming from below, but this time it was normal torch-light. I skidded to a halt once I reached the bottom, trying to reorient myself before I ran into a room with no escape route.

The light was from a torch hanging on a wall to my left, next to a door that had a body hanging halfway through the door jamb. Well, most of a body. I could see where a leg had been ripped off at the knee, and the blood trail I had seen earlier ended there. I pushed the door open, trying to see deeper into the room. As I stepped over the body, it reached out and grabbed my leg.

"Don't leave me! That *thing* is going to be here any moment!"

I thought my adrenaline was already pretty high, but when a person you thought was dead reaches out and grabs you, there are entirely different levels of adrenaline you can tap into. I didn't even need to use qi to pull myself free from his grasp. I looked back at the man. I recognized him as the one who had hit me over the head and captured me back in the woods.

"While I might rescue someone in your situation under more normal circumstances, I feel like I might be interrupting karma if I interfered with what is about to happen." The crashing sounds coming from above only accentuated my point.

I turned and ran, leaving the screaming man to his fate. Sorry, not sorry. That jerk nearly killed me, and had I not escaped, he would have tortured me to death. Like I said, karma could be pretty poetic sometimes. I blasted through the next two rooms, looking for the one that led to where we made our escape and two of Kory's scouts had made their last stand.

The noises coming from where I had been let me know that the *nox* had made it down the stairs. The screams from my former captor were cut off abruptly, providing me with more motivation to hurry. I ran into a room that had three doors, one of which had been hacked to bits. I moved into it, searching for the stairway leading down.

Inside the room, the remains of the two scouts were tossed into a corner, the bloodstains telling the tale of their last stand. As pointless as it might have been, I could see they died standing alongside one another, trying to hold the stairs for as long as possible.

I walked over and grabbed what I could off of their bodies. At least their families could have a few things to remember them by. The only things of note were a broken sword and a pair of bloodstained daggers. These two had definitely gone down fighting.

The crashing sound of the *nox* plowing its way through the narrow doorways behind me snapped me out of my moment of reflection. Time to move. I ran down the stairs, this time dropping some of my trap formation plates behind me.

It probably wouldn't do much, but every second counted at this point. I wasn't even paying attention to the order I was dropping them in, just throwing them down and activating them as fast as I could as I moved down the hallway that led to the sleeping chambers.

The mighty stone door at the entrance to the former religious leader's rooms was shattered. This wouldn't slow down the *nox* for one second. I took a moment to throw up a wall of earth qi strands, using the rubble from the broken door to help form the net of stone faster. It took less than a minute to get everything in place, but the speed of forcing out that much qi from my meridians let me know I was straining my body.

After everything I had put my body through the past few

days, I wasn't surprised that things were starting to catch up to me. Speaking of catching up to me, there was a blast of fire from one of my traps that came from the room that held the bodies of the scouts. The *nox* was getting closer.

I turned and ran for the stairs, not bothering to repeat the impromptu repairs on the much thinner door at the entrance to the stairway. I could feel myself slowing down as I tried to go as fast as I could down the pitch-black spiral of steps. I was running low on energy, and my poor body was letting me know.

I dropped another trap plate as I reached the bottom, placing it off to the side so the giant cat couldn't see it until the last moment. I was panting and out of breath when I reached the room that we had turned into a furnace. There was little more than ash remaining, and the heat was still intense. At least the light spilling in from the cathedral lent enough light to see by. I spread some metal qi around me in an attempt to shield my skin, but I could do little about the hot air burning my lungs.

I moved through as quickly as possible, nearly diving through the opening into the underground cathedral. I nearly knocked myself out on the edge of the altar, slamming my head on the corner as I stumbled through the door. If I hadn't been shielding myself with metal qi, I might have cracked my skull on the blackened stone. Or worse, been knocked unconscious and made an easy meal for the *nox* to stumble across.

I took a moment to catch my breath, leaning on the edge of the altar. Looking down, I saw one of the large hammers the red robes had used to smash through the stone door still clutched in the burnt bones of its former owner. I stashed it in my belt. No need to let a good weapon go to waste.

Suddenly, I heard a yowl of pain behind me. The *nox* had triggered the trap I had left at the foot of the stairs. I was out of time.

I put the four birds at each corner of the altar and quickly ejected the cubes from their storage. They snapped into position, and the qi circulating in my cores slammed to a halt. I collapsed, my body being unprepared for the qi reinforcing my injuries to stop working all at once. Apparently, the wood qi hadn't finished healing my broken bones. Oh, how I loved this whole reincarnation stuff. Definitely my favorite life experience up to this point.

I crawled to the edge of the stone altar, trying to see where the *nox* was, and to see how the cubes had affected it. When I rounded the edge, I was looking right into the eyes of the monster.

After my heart rate went from hummingbird-wing speed to something a bit more regular, I pulled myself up the side of the altar to get a better look at the monster. Its head was sticking through the door leading into the room, the rest of it still inside the makeshift furnace. The fact that I wasn't dead yet told me that something the cubes did had locked it in place somehow.

I limped closer to the beast, trying to get a better look at it in the dim lighting. The *nox* was staring at me the whole time, its anger a physical force I could feel through its eyes. The narrow opening had held it back, giving me enough time to get the cubes in place. I could see the black tentacle-like things squirming along its back, and smoke was starting to rise as a result of the heat in the room.

It brought back the memory of the *nox* running from the fire-flares in my dream. This one didn't like fire. I kicked myself for making my first major attack out of earth qi. If I had used fire, I might not have found myself in this conundrum.

I needed to place all of the cubes into a single storage device to overload it and destroy them, but the moment I did the *nox* would pounce. I had no chance of getting free before it killed me.

I took a moment to rest and gather my thoughts. With enough time and planning, I could do anything. I looked around and realized that I was in nearly the exact same position of the head priest I had seen in my vision when he tasked me with completing his mission. It made my skin crawl.

I stood back up, shifting so I could lean on the altar and

keep an eye on the *nox*. Think, Jim, *think*. There had to be a way. I replayed the events of the past few days, trying to come up with a plan that left me alive at the end of it. While I was standing, I could feel my wooden medallion doing its best to heal me with the small amount of dark mana it could draw in.

I took stock of what I had to use. My belt was loaded with items, but unfortunately, none of them were useful in this situation. I had four trap plates available, yet the qi lockdown made them almost pointless. The qi remaining in my batteries was enough for one more big hit, except then I would be tapped dry.

My own cores still had a fair amount of qi, though most of my meridians were dangerously overused. I still had some use in the meridian on the top of my head and the one between my eyes, but their placement made them rather difficult to use in battle. Everything else had been heavily used over the past few days and I risked rupturing them if I forced too much qi through them. I was stumped.

That was the perfect time for the *nox* to shift its body. I nearly jumped high enough to hit my head on the ceiling. My heart was going to explode before this day was over, I swear. The *nox* was trying to lean into the broken door frame.

Either the effects of the cubes were weakening, or the *nox* was figuring out a way to move while under their influence. If only there was a way to hold it in place for a few minutes, I would be able to get enough of a head start that I should be able to get away!

Wait. Hold it in place. I had a trap that could do that. It wouldn't work when the *nox* could move at its normal speed, but it wasn't moving fast now, was it?

I hurriedly shuffled through the few plates I had remaining, hoping that I hadn't used it already. In my rush, I dropped them on top of the altar, one of them rolling off the edge. The three on top were all whip attacks. I shuffled over to the other side, closer to the *nox* straining against the forces holding it in place. I leaned forwards, getting a look at what was carved on the surface.

Yes! The plate was the one I used to separate the red robes right before they had reached the ambush with the wolves, the trap that imitated quicksand. I immediately activated it using the qi in my batteries, using as much as I could to power the formation.

The *nox* sank into the ground up to its shoulders, barely keeping its head out of the muck. I was running dangerously low on qi, so that would have to be deep enough. I cut the flow, and dense stone formed around the *nox*. It would hopefully take it several minutes to pry itself free. I then placed two of the three remaining whip plates on either side of the altar. As soon as the *nox* passed into range, they would give it a beating.

I knew it wouldn't do too much since it had already made it past some of the traps already, but it should help buy me a few more valuable seconds. I saved the last whip trap, making a few adjustments to the formation carved on its face before putting it back in my belt. It was one of the fire traps, and I wanted to save it in case of an emergency.

Finally, I was ready. I picked up three of the storage ravens, putting them back in the pouch and hanging it off my belt again. The last one I positioned over the cube farthest away from me. Time to move quickly.

I tapped the raven on each cube, shoving them inside the storage device as quickly as possible. The *nox* reacted instantly, straining against the stone holding it in place. I tossed the storage bird into the center of the altar. I could already feel the strain on the qi matrix holding the bird together. According to the waves of power it was emitting, this explosion was going to be a big one.

I sprinted as fast as my injured ankle could go, slowly picking up speed as I got the qi in my cores spinning up again. I reached the foot of the stairs when I heard the stone around the *nox* make an ominous cracking sound. It was almost free.

I took the stairs three at a time, flinging myself upwards as fast as I could go. I was bouncing off walls, using the momentum to help redirect me up the spiral. I was getting really tired of stairs. I think I might murder the first person that recommended I go anywhere with stairs after this.

The roar of anger behind me let me know that the *nox* was free and had found my traps. I didn't think I could go any faster, yet the door leading out came up sooner than I expected. I pulled the scepter out of storage and fumbled getting it into the lock. The sound of stone being shattered coming from below told me the giant cat was forcing its way up and through the narrow stairwell. I thought the *nox* might hate stairs as much as I did after this.

The door sprang open and I slammed it behind me as I headed for the opposite stairwell. I had just opened the door leading up when an explosion of stone blasted out behind me.

The *nox* slid across the storage room, slamming through empty weapon racks and crates of stuff I hadn't deemed valuable enough to take. I took off, pretty much flying up the final staircase to freedom. I reached the window with the rope zipline just as the *nox* busted through the door. I spun back around to face it, pulling out my final trap plate as I turned.

The big cat jumped to the center of the room, cutting off any chances I had of making it through the doors on either side of the room. I backed up until I felt the windowsill hit my lower back, ending my retreat. The *nox* paced back and forth, seeming to gloat at the final capture of its elusive prey. I looked it straight in the eyes, feeling the hatred for all things in its gaze.

"This has been fun, kitty, but I think it is time for me to go." It opened its mouth wide in a roar that shook my bones and rattled the loose stones on the ground. Lucky for me, it didn't throw off my aim as I tossed my final trap plate at its feet. Paws. Whatever.

The cat's eyes widened in surprise as it activated. Instead of casting out five whips in a flailing array of destruction, the fire strands wrapped around the *nox*, pulling its legs and tentacles tight against its torso. I turned and jumped out the window, trying to imitate my father and running down the rope leading to relative safety.

The sun had finally fallen behind the horizon, and it was dark enough that I had a chance to slip away from the monster. As I ran down the rope, I couldn't help but wonder, when was that stupid storage bird going to go off? Speak a demon's name, and he shall arrive…

The world was instantly transformed from night to day. I was lifted off of the rope and flung through the air. The heat wave that slammed into my back was hot enough to instantly redden any skin not covered by qi-reinforced clothing and armor.

I pushed out a bubble of air qi around my head from the meridian on the top of my skull, and tried to use the meridian between my eyes to force out a cushion of air to cover the front of my body. I saw a familiar-looking tower blur past, and a tree in the distance grew in size as I approached. I only had a moment to wonder at the sheer size of the giant oak before slamming through it at incredible speed.

The impact shattered the air qi cushion, and I spun down to the forest floor. As I was falling, I saw a giant cloud in the shape of a mushroom where the temple used to be. My last thought before hitting the ground was the sheer joy at teaching that stupid cat a lesson.

CHAPTER THIRTY-TWO

Plots Within Plots

I opened my eyes, and I was back in Roh City. I guessed I wasn't dead, because I knew I wouldn't be in Roh City if I had died. I was more than sure that Wrath would have blasted my soul to pieces if I passed into her domain again.

I looked around me, trying to figure out what the dream was trying to show me. Not seeing anything obvious, I started walking towards my family compound. I had 'come to' pretty close by, so it didn't take long for me to get there.

I saw candlelight flickering near the gate, and moved closer to see what was going on. Before I got close enough to see who was there, the candle was blown out and the gate was shut. A shadow detached itself from the wall and started down an alleyway headed deeper into the city. I decided to follow it.

It was close to the center of the city before it stopped, knocking three times, then two, on a small door that was hidden behind a bush. The door was pulled open from the inside, and I tried to slip in behind the mystery person. Instead, the door slammed shut in my face just as the light from inside showed me a glimpse of the person I had been following.

I couldn't be one hundred percent sure, but it looked like the guard captain Councilman Yisi had spoken to when getting all of his people released from prison. I pushed my ear against the door, trying to see if I could hear anything on the other side. I could faintly hear two people talking.

"…haven't heard anything either. The qi wave coming from the woods was in the direction of the ruins. I don't like this."

"I don't like it either. We should know something by morning. Our people in the ruins can't get a report to us faster than that."

"They might have found the secret hidden in the ruins. If we could find a way to freeze the qi around the city center, we would rule this city in a matter of days. The clan leader and chief elder would be powerless to stop us."

"Whether they found something or not, that qi wave has everyone on high alert. We will need to postpone our plans for a bit. First the dark stars falling in the middle of the day, then this! It is like the gods are trying to stop our plans."

"It doesn't matter what the gods want. Yisi will keep moving forward, regardless of the risks. The two of us need to make sure we position ourselves to end up on top, no matter the results."

"Yisi is a fanatic, but he is only days away from breaking through to Peak Sage. He is the only person strong enough to challenge the clan leader. He may be a Low Duke, but he is too old to be able to fight like he used to. Yisi is a match for the chief elder right now, but after his rise in power, even the chief elder working alongside the clan leader won't be enough to stop him."

"The majority of the Roh clan will stand with the elder. Most of them don't like the leader, but the elder is held in high esteem."

"It won't matter. Enough of the real fighters will stand with Yisi when they feel his power. A bunch of merchants and craftsmen have no chance against our men hiding in the woods. This will be the fastest coup in the history of the Southern Province."

"Either way, I think we should discuss a backup plan. I don't like not having a failsafe."

"I can't argue with that. If things turn against Yisi, we can…"

The two voices faded away as they moved deeper into the compound. I walked out to the nearest street, memorizing the location of the building with the hidden door. No matter how things ended up, the person who lived here wouldn't be skipping out on their punishment. I hated traitors. I couldn't leave the Roh clan with this pit of vipers hidden in their midst.

I didn't like what I was hearing. Even though the majority of the red robes had been killed, it sounded like Yisi was still going to move forward with his plan. Him being at Peak Sage meant that I was too weak to do anything to him, either. I would need to find a way to expose him before he could start his coup.

Otherwise, hundreds of Roh would die, weakening the entire region and making it easier for more *nox* to move into the area. Another thing I didn't like was how I had found these traitors. I had no doubt it was my uncle they were talking with, but I had no idea how involved he was in their plots.

Either way, it looked like my uncle needed to be taken off the board. His alchemy concoctions could give an edge to the people on Yisi's side, an edge that I didn't want them to have. I would have to come up with something soon.

I turned to walk back to my family compound, but a bright light brought me back to consciousness.

CHAPTER THIRTY-THREE

Oops

Ouch. That hurt. My whole body was in agony. I opened my eyes to look around, trying to diagnose my current situation.

The first thing I saw was the giant oak tree towering above me. It looked like a huge chunk had been taken out of the side near the middle of the trunk. That would help explain some of the pain I was going through right now.

It was difficult to figure out what was hurting the most, but I had it narrowed down to my front half. Crashing into a tree at ludicrous speeds could do that to a guy. If I hadn't gotten a cushion in place before impacting, I would be paste right now.

The sun was peeking through the treetops, letting me know it was still early morning. After a few minutes of straining, I was able to get back on my feet. A quick pat-down showed me that no bones were broken and I still had all my gear, even the pouch with the three remaining storage ravens. Except, interestingly enough, my boots. What in the stars was with me and boots!

At some point they had been blown off my feet. Or my feet had been blown off and the wooden medallion had already regrown them for me. Either option left me barefoot, but I couldn't help but hope for the former. I ran some qi through my body to diagnose any issues. My meridians were still showing signs of strain, although they were already looking better after only a few hours of rest.

The bones in my feet were still qi-reinforced, letting me know I had only lost my boots. I could see several fracture repair lines in most of my bones, letting me know just how injured I had been. The rest of my body was suffering from scrapes and bruises. That wooden medallion was turning out to be the best investment I had made since my reincarnation.

I knew that I had only survived by sheer luck and fortuitous timing. However, that didn't stop me from feeling a little pride at killing my first *nox*. Actually, I really needed to get back to the temple and find out if I actually *had* killed it.

I took a minute to dig around in my storage belt to find a replacement for my boots. Most of my stuff was meant for adults, so finding something that fit was pretty much impossible. I settled for cutting strips off a set of leather armor I had procured and wrapping them around my feet. It wasn't perfect, but beggars can't be choosers.

I spun out a thread of metal qi from a back meridian into my vest, powering up the qi matrix to build a replacement pair of throwing knives for the ones I had lost in the temple. I also reduced the armor back to a regular vest. It was already warm, so I didn't want to overheat pointlessly. I sent some qi into my clothes as well. A lot had been asked of them recently, making their qi stores pretty low. Finally, I carefully began drawing in all types of qi to cycle through my cores and refill the batteries in my belt. They were both nearly empty, making me vulnerable to higher-level cultivators. And *nox*.

I started heading back towards the ruins, thinking about my next steps as I navigated the thick undergrowth. I needed to find my friends, make sure my parents were okay, punish my uncle, find a way to stop Councilman Yisi, and figure out a way to get to the Southern Provincial Capital. It would take nearly two years of constant travel to reach it by foot, but I was hoping there was a faster way. If not, I would need to find or gather an expedition to travel with. A single person traveling alone was asking for trouble. Especially if that person was a child.

It was only a few minutes into my hike before I started finding signs of the explosion. Massive stones had been blown miles from the original site of the ruins, shredding trees and digging large furrows into the forest floor. The destruction was beyond any expectations I had formed. I had seen a storage device matrix fail in the past, but it was nothing like this. A candle beside a bonfire was too small a comparison.

I followed the trail of destruction back to its source, only to find a massive crater where the location of the ruins used to be. There was nothing left. It was like the heavens had used a meteor to smite the ruins, showing their displeasure of the deeds committed at this site, both past and present. For hundreds of yards in a perfect circle around the massive hole, the trees and foliage had been completely flattened.

On the far side of the crater, a stream of water trickled down the edge and was already forming a pool at the base. In a short time, this would be a small lake surrounded by a circular clearing with a ring of giant worked stones sticking out of the ground in the surrounding area. I couldn't help but wonder what future travelers would think happened here when they came across it.

After a thorough search of the area, I had no doubt the *nox* had been destroyed. It might have been tough, but it wasn't *that* tough.

I was searching farther afield, trying to find any large stones that might still have carvings from the cathedral, when I felt the wards I had left around the cave trigger. The group had finally made it to the rendezvous location. I decided that I had seen enough, so I started moving as quickly as my sore body would allow towards the cave.

The solo trip through the forest was thankfully uneventful,

allowing me to fully recharge the qi batteries in my belt and spend some time healing and reinforcing my body and meridians. The walls of my meridians were already starting to thicken from all of the abuse I had put them through. Soon, I would have to start making some alchemy pills to help the process along. I knew several formulas that would assist me in strengthening my body and cultivation system, obviously I just hadn't been able to take the time to make them.

My core walls were also showing signs of an increase in flexibility and robustness. The overuse of a channeling system was dangerous, yet the gains it could bring made many cultivators walk the knife-edge of disaster on their individual path to greatness. Rupturing a core or meridian wall was a hundred times worse than tearing a muscle, but you could eventually come back from it with advanced alchemy treatments and extensive meditation. Though it could prove disastrous to do so again.

I didn't have the time or inclination to go through that painful process, so I would have to be more careful moving forward. I couldn't afford a setback like that.

After my third round of layering reinforcing qi through my body, I decided to take a break. I was making good time, and I knew my body would need calories to keep up with all the abuse and tempering I was putting it through.

It was nearing midday, so some lunch was in order. I hadn't seen any animals or small game since starting off from the crater. I guess the massive explosion had sent all the wildlife into hiding. I could just eat some of the food in my storage belt, but I wanted something fresh.

I stopped next to a small creek and pulled out the heating stone from storage. I didn't want to take the time to make a fire. I then used strands of water qi to form a net to catch a few fish.

In just ten minutes, I had three trout the length of my arm. I quickly cleaned the fish and threw them directly on the stone. It took a short burst of fire qi to warm up the stone, and in just a few minutes I was scarfing down flaky fish as fast as I could pull it from the bone. Apparently, I was much hungrier than I thought. I washed off in the creek, packed the stone away, and got moving again.

It was nearing sundown when I crested a hill overlooking the region that hid the cave. The sunsets were beautiful in this place. I started to move down the hill when something told me to freeze. I took a moment to look around my immediate area, but I didn't find anything nearby. I cast out some qi threads underground to try to feel if anything was creeping up behind me. Nothing. Then I sent them down the hill into the places hidden by the trees around the area.

Found it. There was a group of five people creeping through the foliage at the base of the hill. From what I could detect of their motions, they had seen me when I silhouetted myself on the hilltop. What a rookie mistake! The easy trek through the forest had me believing there were no threats in the area. I knew better than to think things could ever be that easy.

The group had spread themselves out in a line before slowly moving up the hill. I couldn't see them yet, but I decided to take the initiative and push forward into contact. I crouch-walked until I could make out their shadows moving amongst the trees, then positioned my underground qi threads to snatch them all up at once. I didn't want anyone escaping to warn any potentially larger groups. I waited until the center person had stepped out from behind a tree, and launched my attack.

I wrapped three qi threads around each of them, making sure to cover their mouths and faces to limit any noise or counterattacks. I was squeezing them all a little tighter than what might have been required, but I didn't want anyone squirming free. I approached the central figure, figuring it would be the leader. The shadows cast from the light of the setting sun hitting the trees made it difficult to see who I was dealing with, so I moved until I was only a few yards away. I decided to use a similar tactic to what I had used with the men in the alleyway of Roh City. If it worked, why change it?

"Okay, here's the deal. You answer my questions, and I don't hurt you. You do anything *but* answer my questions, and you don't walk away from this. Got it?" I unwrapped the qi from around the leader's mouth, but what he said caused me to regret everything I had done.

"Son, is that you?"

Oops.

CHAPTER THIRTY-FOUR

Other People's Children

I gently set everyone down before dissipating the qi threads. In hindsight, it made sense that the group hiding in the cave would have people patrolling the area. Guess I should have thought of that before capturing all of them. Oh well, mistakes happen.

After getting everyone on their feet, I was bombarded with questions. Most about if I knew what had caused a massive wave of qi to pass through the area, but plenty more about if I had killed the monster. Surprisingly, no one asked about how I had easily subdued everyone. I guessed that Kory and the others had filled in a few gaps on what had been going on while they were all locked away. Eventually, I convinced everyone that we should get back to camp before I explained what had happened after they left. As we walked back to camp, my father moved closer to talk to me.

"Jim, your mother and I talked to Captain Kory about everything that has been going on. He told me that you were given a mission by the gods, and they gave you many gifts to help you on your path. Is this true?"

It was dark enough that he couldn't see me nodding yes, so I quietly answered him. "Basically, it is all true. I can't really explain everything that happened when I touched the testing stone, but the main points are all correct. After we get everything settled back in Roh City, I will have to move on. It may sound ridiculous, but the fate of our entire world depends on me completing my task."

He was quiet for a minute. "I don't like sending you out into the world like this. I take it that monster we saw had something to do with your mission?"

I sighed. "Yes, Father. The creatures are called *nox*, and it is my job to find them and kill them. I know you don't want me to leave home so young. Unfortunately, we have no choice."

It was his turn to sigh. "Then your mother and I will be joining you. Your Uncle Don or Uncle Hu will take over the family compound when your grandfather dies instead of me anyway. There is nothing holding us to Roh City."

"No," I quickly answered, "after I tell everyone what is going on back home, you will see that you can't leave the clan right now. Besides, no one knows these woods like you and Mom. I need you to stay here and make sure no more *nox* settle in the area. I can't clear a region just to have it infested again a short time later, otherwise I will be just like a dog chasing its tail. Killing the *nox* is only part of the mission. Making sure they stay gone is just as important. A large portion of what I will be doing is setting up strongholds throughout the empire where people are aware of the threat the monsters pose. Those strongholds will be vital to ensuring all of the *nox* are hunted down and killed."

It was several minutes before my father replied. "Your mother and I will discuss this. I understand what you are saying, but I still can't send you into the outside world alone. No matter what gifts the gods might have given you, an extra set of eyes wasn't one of them. Time will tell how this plays out."

I nodded my head in agreement. "I know, Father. I never thought I would be traveling alone. Once things in the Roh clan are settled, we will sit down together and come up with a plan."

He grunted in agreement, choosing to keep silent as we approached the campsite.

The space around the cave was completely different from the last time I had seen it. The indentation in the side of the hill wasn't nearly big enough to hold everyone inside, so they had stripped some large branches from the surrounding area and cut down enough small trees to make a miniature palisade in a semi-circle around the cave. Inside the enclosed area, there were six people laid out on homemade cots either asleep or nursing wounds. I saw my mother was among them. While rushing to her side, I saw Chu coming out of the cave entrance to intercept me.

"She is fine, Jim. Just resting. Between Valerie's healing medallion, your mother's herbs, and my own attempts at healing, everyone should be back on their feet by morning."

I let go of the breath I didn't realize I was holding in. "Thank the stars. It's good to see you, Chu. You and the others showed up just in time."

He looked down at his feet before answering. "We would have been there sooner, but a few patrols held us up. Kory wanted to make sure we took them all down before going into the ruins. He said it didn't make sense for us to leave someone to sneak up on us from behind."

I nodded to show I agreed. "That was the right call. Can you imagine what would have happened if an enemy patrol stumbled across you guys as you were transporting the wounded?"

Chu looked up. "It would have been bad. Some of the guys in those patrols were really hard to kill. Kory wouldn't have been able to fight them and protect everyone at the same time. Speaking of Kory, I know he wants to hear what happened. Come on, we already have a spot laid out for you."

I followed him into the cave, my father close behind.

Kory stood up from his place by the fire as soon as he saw me. The rest of my friends were sitting along the back wall to leave space for a few of the former prisoners to sit around the cookpot. They all looked tired and worn. I knew how they felt.

Kory indicated for me to take a place next to him as Chu shuffled over to my friends. Donny, Jamila, and Valerie all started to get up to greet me, but I waved them back down.

"We will catch up in a minute, I have something important to give to Kory first." I pulled out the items I had collected from the three scouts who had died during our escape. Well, all four had died, but only three of them died with honor. "I am sure you heard what happened to your people, but I thought their families would appreciate something to remember them by." I handed over the broken sword and bloodstained daggers first. "These two went down fighting. They were fearless." He took them from me slowly, showing the reverence the moment demanded. Next, I pulled out the necklace. "She died standing guard over us as we slept. Despite her own extreme exhaustion, she was willing to push herself to the limit to ensure our successful escape." I handed him the necklace before taking a step back. I felt bad because I had never learned their names. They had never introduced themselves, so I hadn't bothered to try to learn more about them. Now, I never would have the opportunity.

"Thank you," Kory said after clearing his throat. "Their families will be glad to hear that they all died honorably."

I couldn't meet his eyes as he talked. I felt too much shame at failing them. "I am sorry I didn't do more to save them. If we had more time, or if I had demonstrated more of my abilities, they might have pulled through."

Kory stood up and put his hand on my shoulder. "None of this was your fault. I heard about the traitor. I will need to conduct a thorough investigation when we return, to root out any other spies in our midst. When I get proof of who is behind this, I am going to make them pay for what they have done." I knew that their deaths weren't exactly my fault, but I still wished I could have kept them alive.

I was then nearly tackled off of my feet by my friends all

rushing over to me. There was a mad jumble of hugs and back-slaps while simultaneously being inspected for injuries. After a few minutes of that, they pulled back to talk. Donny was the first to speak.

"So, you already know what we are going to ask. We might as well all find a place around the fire so we can hear what happened. Make sure you start from when we split apart, and don't leave out anything!" I couldn't help but smile. Donny was just like an older brother. Well, younger from my overall perspective, but you know what I mean.

The people around the fire made room for us so we could all crowd around the cookpot. I was handed a bowl of food, and I recounted the events of the past few days between bites of stew. They were suitably impressed by my use of the Red Spring Wolves in setting up an ambush, and I think Jamila and Valerie were angry enough to get up and go kill the man who had kicked me in the head right this moment if I hadn't told them that he was dead already.

I told them about my escape from the torture room and discovery of the underground cathedral, but I left out my use of dark qi and the vision I had seen. Then I covered the jailbreak, with some people around the fire pitching in a few things I either hadn't noticed or had forgotten.

When I got to the fight with the *nox*, everyone became motionless, focusing all of their attention on my version of events. I took the time to explain more about the *nox*, what they were, their weakness to at least one element, and what they could do, to all of the people present. While I didn't know every person here, I was pretty sure that they would believe everything I had to say after seeing what the dark mana creature had done to the group of red robes. There could be no doubts after witnessing what it was capable of doing.

It was hard to repress the shudder that tried to pass through me when I thought of having to fight more of them. I could do this. I *would* do this.

After finishing up my story by explaining that the explosion was caused by the overload of a storage device trying to contain the cubes, one of the men across from me scoffed in disbelief.

"You expect us to believe all of that? A mere boy was able to defeat a creature that was massacring dozens of experienced warriors? And the simple destruction of a storage device is what caused that massive explosion? Child, I have seen a storage device explode, and it was nothing like what we felt. Who has ever heard of a statue used as a medium for creating extra dimensional storage in the first place? This is all a foolish child's fantasy." A few of the people around the fire nodded in agreement.

Thankfully, most of the adults present looked askance at the speaker. They knew enough to understand that what they had all seen couldn't be explained away as a child's imagination. I looked over to where Valerie and Jamila were seated.

"Speaking of storage devices, I haven't managed to give either of you one yet. Please take these. They were part of the set of four I found in the temple. It will surely help us in the trials ahead." I pulled out the ravens, letting them choose the design they preferred before returning the final bird to my pouch.

They were suitably impressed, thanking me before inspecting them. I was thankful that they just accepted the gifts without trying to refuse first. It really would help our group if they could carry more items and supplies. I would let them figure out a way to conveniently carry around the statues.

I also noted more than one set of eyes staring at my pouch with greed shining in their depths. Unsurprisingly, the man who had doubted me was one of them.

I looked right back at him, not afraid to let him know that I was aware of his avarice. He appeared to be in the best shape of all of the former prisoners gathered around the fire. His gray robes were only a little dirty, and his muscular frame showed no signs of wasting away in a prison cell. His blond hair and brown eyes marked him as a member of an inner branch family, making him minorly important in some circles. That explained his air of self-importance.

He had either told the red robes everything they had asked him after capture, or he hadn't been a prisoner for very long. I also didn't remember him being among the people willing to fight during our escape. He had spent the whole time helping the more injured people or sorting supplies when necessary.

"I am not imagining things," I said, "and I did not lie. Everything I have told you all is the truth. If you choose to be blind to what is right in front of you, I cannot force you to see."

His face reddened in anger. He opened his mouth to say something, but it was Kory who cut him off.

"I have seen what the boy can do, and I do not doubt a thing he has said. He has proven himself. You, on the other hand, I know nothing about. You look like a son of Elder Zarqua, but I don't remember seeing you in any of the tournaments recently. Or doing your clan service in the military, for that matter. You are a low-level Brain cultivator, so why don't I know you?" Kory had stood during his line of questioning, walking closer to the man as he talked.

The man stood as well, his face showing that he was only becoming angrier the longer Kory talked. "I spend my days helping my father in council meetings. I am too valuable to be wasted spending my time walking the walls or guarding a gate. I would never even be in this situation if I hadn't been sent to inspect the southern fields. Stupid farmers have let crop production drop by ten percent! I don't see how—"

Kory cut him off by picking him up by the throat. "No one is above service to the clan, no matter who their parents might be. And those stupid farmers do more for the clan in one month than you have your entire, worthless, *life*." He shook the man a little to drive the point home. "When we return to the city, you and your father will have to explain how someone of your power has avoided service to the clan for what I assume to be at least a decade! Have no doubt, the chief elder will be very interested in hearing your explanation." He let go, dropping the man to his knees.

Kory turned away to return to his spot by the fire. The man slowly rose to his feet, shooting a glare at Kory's back before storming out of the cave. As I watched him leave, his glare shifted to me as he disappeared into the darkness. Oh no, how will I ever deal with a man like him holding a grudge against me! How could I live with myself, knowing I had made such a powerful enemy! I snickered at my own sarcastic thoughts before turning back to the fire.

At some point, someone had refilled my bowl. I decided to finish the stew before moving to the second half of what I wanted to talk about.

Kory, my father, and another Brain cultivator were having a heated discussion about our next steps. Kory wanted to leave at first light and storm straight up to the chief elder, informing him of everything that had gone on. My father wanted to wait an extra day before leaving. The other cultivator wanted to split the difference and leave at midday, but keep quiet about everything until they could organize a full meeting of the council. I let it continue for a bit before I decided to cut in.

"Gentlemen. I have some information that you all need to hear before we decide anything." They stopped fighting and looked over at me. By this point, I was pretty sure we were the only four still awake. It had to be close to midnight by now, so everyone else had stumbled off to get some sleep. I pulled out some blank formation plates to carve while we talked. "I know who is behind the red robed attackers. This is just the first stage of their plan, and things are only going to get worse." That got their attention. "Councilman Yisi is about to reach the peak stage of Sage. Once he breaks through, he will attempt to kill the chief elder and clan leader. He has subverted a portion of the clan to follow his lead. I know for sure the guard captain that maintains the prison is on his side, as well as a few of the lower elders. The red robes who were hiding in the woods were supposed to be the core of his revolt. Without them, he won't have an easy opportunity to control the rest of the clan. That isn't going to stop him from trying."

I looked down at the formation plate I had been subconsciously working on. I was mildly surprised to see a variation of the trap I had used to capture the *nox* before the explosion. It was designed to trap a person using earth and air qi threads in a non-lethal cage framework. Now why would I carve that? Oh, that's right. I had almost forgotten. I set it down and picked up another blank plate to work on.

"My Uncle Hu has also joined their cause. I have no doubt that he has been working hard to supply Yisi's forces with alchemy pills and elixirs to help give them an edge in combat." I looked at my father as I finished speaking. His face had hardened into a grim visage. "I'm sorry you had to find out like this, but you needed to know," I said to him.

"No," he growled out, "I'm sorry I haven't put a stop to my brother and his foolishness before now. I know how him and his son treat you. I should have stepped in a long time ago, but I wanted you to have a rival to help push you through the first few steps of your cultivation. I see now that it was a mistake. I allowed his abilities in alchemy to blind me to the type of person my brother has become. We should sleep, and reconvene in the morning." With that, he stood and walked out of the cave. He was probably going to check on my mother, and most likely recount everything.

The other man, who I finally recognized as the family friend who had challenged me in the temple, followed close behind. After he left, Kory moved closer to me. He pulled a thick silver coin out of a pocket inside his vest, holding it in front of his face.

"This token allows me to send a single message to the chief elder. Once I use it, we won't be able to communicate with him again until we reach the city. Is there anything else I should know before sending him a warning about Yisi and the others?" It was a refreshing feeling for the adults to just believe me. They didn't even question the information I gave them.

I shook my head to answer Kory. "That is everything I know. If you can warn him about the coup now, he might have the chance to position some of the more trustworthy elders around the city. It could make a huge difference. I think you should send it now."

I looked down at what my hands had been doing again. This time, I had carved an especially nasty formation. It would shoot up a disk of ice at waist height before detonating, launching sharp shards of ice at a distinctly sensitive area into anyone nearby. I guess my subconscious was feeling vindictive.

Kory held the communication disk between his hands, concentrating as he pushed a good bit of qi into the silver token. He then held it close to his lips. Kory quickly and concisely communicated everything I had told him about Yisi and his plans before a burst of light shot straight out of the coin and into the night.

"He should get that in just a few minutes. I hope he can get in to see the clan leader before it is too late." He was bent over, as if the weight of the events over the past few days were crashing down on him.

"You should rest," I said after watching him. "I will emplace more wards so we can all get some sleep. We will need to move quickly tomorrow." He nodded and shuffled over to his bedroll mixed in amongst my friends. I couldn't help but grin. Kory was still making sure the boys were separated from the girls.

I carved three more traps before making six alarm plates. I was officially out of blank disks I could use. Getting some more as soon as I had time went towards the top of my to-do list. I walked out of the cave so I could position the alarms around camp.

Before leaving the palisade, I took the time to check on everyone to make sure there weren't any hidden issues that would slow us down in the morning. I saved my parents for last. It still made my heart feel lighter when I saw them. I finally moved outside the short wooden walls, grabbing my old warding system as I went.

Using the old plates allowed me to extend the perimeter out to nearly a hundred yards. I made sure to place them at equal intervals, that way there were no weak spots in the detection ward. As I turned to walk back towards camp, I could sense someone waiting for me in the shadow of the palisade wall. Thinking it was either Kory or one of my friends, I turned slightly so I could walk straight towards them. That meant I was completely unprepared for the fist that hit me in the side of the head.

"You may have these idiots fooled, but I can see right through you. If you give me that storage bird without a fuss, I won't kill you and hide your body in the woods." The unexpected punch had knocked me to the ground. Since my attacker hadn't been using qi, I didn't see the fist flying towards my face until the last second. I was able to turn my head enough that he didn't break my nose, but catching a blow with your temple didn't feel good either. It took me a bit to realize that the person looming out of the darkness was Elder Zarqua's son.

I guess he couldn't let the opportunity pass him by to steal a treasure from a child, especially when that child made him look bad. Why were there so many people like this in the world?

He moved to stand over me, positioning himself to kick me in the ribs while I was down. As a Brain cultivator, he would feel it if I used qi to stop him. Instead, I used the spirit wood ring I was wearing. I chose the stake form.

I activated it just as he tried to swing his leg into my side, using his own forward momentum to drive the stake deep into his leg. He opened his mouth to scream, so I spun up my cores and crammed a ball of air qi into his mouth to shut him up. No need to alert the camp to this.

I wrapped a qi thread tightly around his body and dragged him through the forest to a place where we could be alone. There was a spot less than half a mile from the camp where he and I could have a more private chat.

I healed the bruise on my head as we walked, making sure

to bury the blood trail he was leaving as we went. After reaching the small clearing, I took out his gag.

"Do you have any idea of how much trouble you are in?! Assaulting the son of an elder?! How dare you!" I was actually confused for a minute. Did this guy think he could attack a child, try to rob him, and just get away with it? If he thought that, what else had he been getting away with?

I took a deep breath to calm myself down, but it didn't work. This guy had really made me mad. Assaulting me after I had just saved his life? Not only that, I couldn't ignore his entitled attitude. There was no way this guy wasn't going around and terrorizing the people who he imagined were beneath him. I hated people like that.

"Listen up, you spoiled, worthless man-child. I am going to kill you and bury your body in the woods where no one will ever find it. As far as everyone else is concerned, you just disappeared after Kory called you out on dodging your clan responsibilities. They will all just assume that you didn't want to face punishment, so you ran away."

His eyes widened in surprise. "Kill me? You clearly don't understand the position you are in right now. My father is in charge of the clan treasury! He only answers to the clan leader, and if you think he will just let my disappearance be swept under the rug like some commoner, you are sadly mistaken!"

I let him finish his rant.

Then, I cut his head off.

There was just no getting through to some people.

It only took a few minutes to bury the body. I made sure to search him first, and I was surprised at how much coin he was carrying. He was walking around with almost fifty gold! Either the red robes had left his ridiculously large coin purse alone, or he had stumbled upon their treasury at some point during the escape. And then failed to mention it to anyone.

I moved the money to my treasury storage. I was also happy to see that the coin pouch he carried was larger on the inside than it was on the outside. It was a very cheap storage device, but I could see how it could come in handy. Since it wasn't formed using a complex qi matrix, I was able to safely store it in the buckle on my belt. While it wasn't big enough to hold all of the riches I had collected, it was more than enough to serve as a convenient place to store all of the chitin Kory had gotten from the scorpions we had killed.

That reminded me, I still needed to find the time to set up my traveling forge and make some better armor for my friends and I. While my leather vest was of very high quality, it was lacking in the qi defense category. If I were to wear it over a breastplate of the qi-resistant chitin, I would be much more protected in a fight.

After making sure the body was well-hidden, I quickly moved back to the cave. As it was, I would be lucky to get a few hours of sleep before everyone started waking up. Getting back into my bedroll, I made sure to spend a few minutes cultivating after storing my vest in my belt. I was still a long way from being able to compress the energy into my cores, but I was beginning to see signs of progress.

I was still circulating qi through my heart core to purify the energy when I finally fell asleep.

CHAPTER THIRTY-FIVE

Yisi Makes His Move

I was standing outside the central pagoda inside Roh City. Looking around, I saw a lot more commotion than was normal for this time of night. People were rushing through the area, everyone keeping their heads down and staying focused on whatever task they were about. I started walking towards the steps leading to the main entrance of the clan leader's home when the doors at the top were thrown open.

The chief elder and clan leader were leading a large group of people. I had only seen the clan leader once in my first life, but I had never forgotten the moment he had banished me from the Roh.

He was completely bald, and his back was bent from old age. If he could stand straight, he would most likely be close to six feet tall. You could tell that he used to be a formidable man, but time had worn him down. His white beard ran all the way past his belt, but even that was beginning to look thin. I could see why Yisi thought he could beat him. His wrinkled face was turned down in a scowl, and it was easy to see that he didn't like whatever it was the chief elder was saying.

From the quality of the robes each one was wearing, it looked like a meeting involving the council had just finished. Looking at everyone present, I noticed that almost forty of the hundred-odd elders were wearing some shade of red. Was it a fashion choice, or were they all in league with Yisi?

The group stopped just as they came within earshot. The clan leader turned to face everyone and raised his hands to silence them.

"You have all heard what was said. Send a group to bring Councilman Yisi to the central pavilion so that he may face his accusers. If this is true, he has much to answer for." He turned back around and started walking towards the pavilions on the far side of the city center. In a rather ominous display, all but a few of the elders in red left in the direction of what I assumed was Yisi's compound. The clan leader was oblivious to the division in his own clan.

Fortunately, the chief elder wasn't. He watched silently as almost half of the most powerful people in the Roh clan chose a side. They disappeared into the dark streets, leaving a much smaller number of elders to follow behind the clan leader.

We were running out of time. The clan leader had handled the situation poorly, allowing Yisi the time to organize his forces. I had a bad feeling about what we would find when we reached Roh City. Without the units Yisi had hidden in the forest, they would have to fight for every inch of ground, drawing out the fighting and putting more innocent lives at risk.

For a moment I wondered if it would have just been better to stand aside and allow Yisi to take over. No. While it would have saved lives in the short term, the type of leadership Yisi embodied would end with even more bloodshed.

I needed to wake up. We didn't have time to rest. If we couldn't return in time, we risked coming back to a smoking ruin. I would push for the more injured to stay behind while those capable of fighting rushed back to the city.

I knew I wasn't currently a match for Yisi, but a single pebble dropped at the right place, at the right time, could cause an avalanche. I intended to be that pebble. As far as I knew, Yisi had never seen my face. That meant he wouldn't be on the lookout for me.

I tried to concentrate on opening my eyes in the real world. I had always been pulled out of dream walking. I had never needed to bring myself out of the dream, so I wasn't sure where to start.

First, I tried using my cores, but nothing happened. Then I tried meditating, but after a few minutes I realized that wouldn't work either. Finally, I came up with a plan.

I started climbing the wall of the massive pagoda that was the clan leader's residence, using the intricate carvings as hand-holds. After making it up to the third level, I walked to the edge of the roof and looked down. I really hoped this worked, other-wise I was about to be in some serious pain. If I could even get hurt while dream walking.

I stepped back against the wall, trying to give myself enough room for a running start. I knelt down in a sprinter's pose, ready to take a leap off the edge and dive headfirst into the stone-cobbled courtyard below. Pushing off, I had just enough room to take three bounding steps before jumping off the ledge. I tried to position myself to hit with my head angled downwards, but three stories were not high enough to manage it. Instead, I performed a belly flop straight onto the stones below. Not my most graceful moment, I know.

Lucky for me, I felt no pain. Not so lucky for me, I was still stuck in the dream. How did I get out of this place?

I climbed to my feet just in time to see a group of seven people step into the lantern light of the courtyard in front of the pagoda. Yisi was in the lead, three other people wearing the ever-present red robes off to either side. The only person I recognized besides Yisi was the captain of the city jail to his right. The other five were all wearing fancy armor under their robes, the shiny parts gleaming in the flickering lights. They looked impressive. And powerful.

Their group was in no hurry, walking in a slow but purposeful gait towards the pavilions in the distance. Yisi himself was carrying a very impressive spear, its power coming off in waves. I was pretty sure it was at least a Master level artifact. The spear tip looked as if it was cast from bronze, while the shaft was some form of blood red stone. Maybe it was the reason for their choice in attire? The power it contained felt sinister, as if the shaft was actually formed from the blood of thousands of former opponents. Stars, maybe that was exactly what it was. Who knew?

As I moved to intercept him and his entourage, I was once again pulled backwards into a wall of light.

CHAPTER THIRTY-SIX

Time to Stop a Coup

I woke up to see my mother kneeling over me.

"Jim, you were thrashing around in your sleep. Are you okay?"

I shook my head, trying to wake myself up as quickly as possible. It was still dark outside the cave entrance. Maybe I still had time! I rolled to my feet, pulling out my armor and struggling to fit it over my head while simultaneously kicking my bedroll out of the way.

"Jim, answer me! What's wrong? And what in the world are you doing?"

I had inadvertently tangled my feet in my blanket, causing me to stumble around the camp while still trying to get my vest pulled down over my head. Stupid uncoordinated body!

Finally, I got the vest situated and plopped down to retie the leather straps around my feet and calves. I looked up at my mother as I was tying knots.

"We need to go. Yisi is making his move right now. Get everyone that can fight, and tell them to pack light. If we hurry, we might be able to reach the city before sunset. The fighting will most likely be dying down by that point, but the clan leader and chief elder might still be alive." I looked up after finishing the last knot on my foot wrappings to see my mother just staring at me, her mouth in a firm line.

"How do you know what is going on in the city? And what makes you think that there is any place for you in a fight like that? Those cultivators are powerful enough that a stray bit of qi from any one of them would kill you instantly. If you think I am just going to let you run off to your death, you have another thing coming!"

Our conversation—mostly her shouting—served to wake up the majority of the people in the camp.

I stood up and started to pack away my bedroll before answering. "It is too much to explain right now, but you could say that sometimes the gods show me things. I can't just ignore it, Mother. While it might seem impossible, I know I can make a difference. Somehow, Yisi has gotten his hands on at *least* a Master level artifact. It will give him enough of an edge in combat to make it close to impossible for the clan leader and chief elder to win. At best, they can only delay him. At worst, they are already dead. If that's the case, we will need to organize an escape for anyone who opposes them as quickly as we can. Time equals lives, and right now we are wasting them." With that, I turned and headed outside the cave.

When I got outside, I saw that the sky was already starting to lighten in the east. Looking around, I didn't see anyone else ready to go. Okay then, I guessed I was going to do this myself. I took a moment to feel what direction the wind was blowing. Success. I had another trick I had learned a long time ago, and I thought it was time to use it.

I spun in a quick circle, trying to find the tallest tree in the area. While they were pretty uniform in height, it looked like the tallest one was on top of the hill that contained our cave. It would work. I started up the hillside, trying to move as quickly as possible in the dark. Before reaching the top, I heard shouting from down below. It was my parents, and they were yelling at Kory. I didn't have time for this.

I spun out a thread of air qi and shaped it into a funnel before holding it up to my mouth. It should help my voice carry back down to the bottom of the hill without using all the qi of my voice amplification construct.

"Hey! Up here!" I shouted. "I know you don't want me to go, but I have no choice. Try to follow as fast as possible. I will try to save as many as I can!" With that, I started back up the hill and began climbing the tree. I hadn't used this technique in a few hundred years, but I was pretty sure I had enough qi stored up to make it work.

Upon reaching the top of the tree, I quickly stripped back out of my armored vest and put it back in my belt. I needed to be as light as possible to make this work. Then, I started spooling out an air qi thread from the meridian located in the middle of my back. It was important to make it as thin as possible while still being strong enough that it wouldn't break when it took my weight. I felt the early morning breeze pick up, lifting the thread higher into the air.

What I was trying to accomplish was something that occurred in nature all the time. When I was younger—well, younger the first time—I had seen spiders spooling out their webs in long strands that eventually lifted them off the ground. It allowed a nest of spiders to quickly spread out over vast distances, ensuring they didn't have to kill each other over territory. I just copied their idea.

Finally, the thread was long enough that it picked me off the tree and pulled me into the air. I kept extending the qi thread, trying to gain as much lift as possible. I also used my flight ring to help steer me clear of some of the taller trees in the forest. The higher I went, the faster the wind pulled me along.

I wasn't going directly towards Roh City, but I was going to be close. I should reach the city well before the sun reached its midpoint in the sky. I just prayed silently, hoping the good guys could hang on that long. I wouldn't be able to defeat Yisi on my own.

The sun started to peek over the horizon, causing the wind

to stir more violently and letting me gain even more speed. It felt as if the wind might even have shifted enough that I would pass directly over the city center. Maybe one of the gods had heard my prayer? I couldn't be sure, but I think I heard the tinkling laughter of Wrath on the wind. Huh. I thought she hated me? No matter, this wasn't the time to question a gift. No matter its source.

I squinted my eyes against the wind, trying to pull in more energy than I was expelling. I needed to stay at my peak, and more importantly, I needed to make a plan. It was time to stop a coup.

CHAPTER THIRTY-SEVEN

The Big Fight

After two hours of getting beaten about by the wind, I could finally make out Roh City in the distance. There were a few columns of smoke rising into the sky, especially near the middle of the city. I couldn't be sure, but it had probably been somewhere between four to six hours since the coup had started. That was a really long time for someone to be fighting. For high-level cultivators in the Sage to Duke range, it would mean their qi stores would be starting to run low. Not low enough to give me a shot at taking down Yisi, but low enough that they wouldn't be wiping out entire swathes of the city.

I was glad to see that they had been careful during the early stages of their fight to not destroy everything around them. I guess none of them wanted to win just to rule over a decimated clan. During some more serious fights I had seen in the past, entire sections of some cities had been left as nothing better than smoking ruins. When a high-level cultivator wanted to actually destroy a population center, it could be very difficult to stop them. I was proof of that.

I had been working through several strategies I could implement while flying. Seeing the city in relatively good condition meant I had to toss out a good percentage of them. That was fine, I still had several options I could choose from.

My favorite plan was to simply find a place to hide near the fighting and do my best to disrupt Yisi at a moment that would tilt the fight in the chief elder and clan leader's favor. If that didn't work, I would have to take more drastic measures.

The wind carried me closer while I was thinking. I started to look around for a place to land, but the smoke was making it difficult to see the ground. After passing the first few buildings, I saw a likely spot. The flat roof of Healer Hai's house made a nice, clear landing place. I spun out a few threads of air qi from each of my knees to help absorb the impact while shortening the thread keeping me aloft. I managed to touch down and stumble to a stop a few feet from the edge of the roof. I immediately crouched down to reduce my profile. I really didn't want someone to happen to look up and see me. I think I finally learned that lesson. Again.

Why that would become a problem was immediately apparent. A large contingent of people, close to a hundred, were kneeling in the street in front of the building with a ring of people in the uniform and armor of the city guard surrounding them. Unfortunately, those guards were all wearing a strip of red fabric tied around their right arm.

Yisi's forces were rounding up everyone they could find and making sure they couldn't fight back. I had to wonder, why weren't they wearing the regular red robes that all of Yisi's forces up to this point had worn? I pulled my vest out to get it back on, activating the sleeves and neck covering while I took a moment to think. It took a minute, but then I understood the genius of their plan.

If it looked like Yisi was going to lose, all they had to do was hide the strip of red and blend back in with the populace. The covered helms the Roh clan used meant that it would be difficult to recognize who was behind the masks. That made finding and rooting out all of Yisi's collaborators nearly impossible. I couldn't hold in the sigh that developed when I thought about how difficult this just became. Images of wrongful persecution and corrupt judges pardoning people for the right price flashed through my mind. If I couldn't find a way to stop this, the Roh clan would tear itself apart no matter who won the fight.

My train of thought was interrupted when a guard standing near the alleyway beside me backhanded a woman across the face. She fell awkwardly, trying to hold on to something in her arms. When she rolled to her side, I saw what had caused the problem. She was holding a baby.

"Shut that child up! I am sick and tired of hearing it! Either you make it be quiet, or I will!"

Nope. Not having that.

As he raised his arm to hit her again, I jumped off the roof. It was a quick fall, but it was more than enough time to activate the spear option for my spirit wood ring. I shoved the pointy end of the stick into the base of his neck where it met his shoulder. I landed on the ground behind him, my momentum providing more than enough power to shove the spear through the thin armor. And his entire body. I really didn't like people who hurt babies or mothers. Removing him from the breeding population was a good thing for everyone.

I deactivated the spear, allowing it to form back into the ring. The blood that sprayed out of the guard was honestly a little ridiculous. He stumbled around like a mobile red fountain, hosing down a good portion of the crowd. This, obviously, caused a reaction.

The remaining guards were trying to figure out what was going on while attempting to still control their prisoners. It was a perfect situation for someone who wanted to create a little chaos. Someone like, well, me.

I ran around the outside edge of the crowd, moving towards the next guard in line. I didn't want to use qi and alert the other guards, so I pulled a throwing knife from my vest. As soon as I had a clear shot to the next guard, I took it.

While the armor used by the Roh clan guards was of moderately good quality, it left a small gap in the front where the face covering didn't quite reach the breastplate. It was more than enough space for my throwing knife to find a new home in his throat. He dropped to his knees, gurgling blood sheeting down the front of his armor.

I pulled another knife free and tried to repeat the process. My plans for another quiet kill were dashed when the crowd saw what happened. Instead of pulling away from the bloody scene, they used the gap his death created to try to escape. I felt a few of the guards start to spin up their cores in preparation to bring their prisoners back under control. It was time to go loud.

I jumped as high as I could, using the flight ring to give me a boost. Then I spun up my cores, slowing time as I targeted the remaining guards. I still had plenty of throwing knives, so I used some threads of air qi I spun from my meridians to pull them loose and hurl them at Yisi's stooges. I used as much force as possible, not wanting to risk an innocent bystander drifting in front of the weapons. Or the knives failing to penetrate the guards' armor.

I slowly drifted back down to the street as I reduced the amount of qi spinning in my upper core. I still couldn't move my body, but I could see most of the guards go down as my knives impacted. I might have used an excessive amount of force, because they blasted straight through the guards and impacted with the ground behind them. The downward angle of the attack also caused the guards to be thrown down into the cobblestones and dirt of the street.

As soon as my feet touched the ground, I released my hold on time and ran to the edge of the crowd, dodging people as they scattered into the buildings and alleyways around us. I picked over the guards as quickly as possible, grabbing weapons and coin pouches while searching for my knives. I left the armor on the bodies, not wanting to take the time to collect all my spoils of war. They would all have to be repaired anyway.

Just as I was fitting my last knife back into its sheath, Healer Hai approached me from his house.

"Jim, is that you my boy?"

I looked up at him. He was looking a little rough, but someone of his strength and skills wouldn't be down for long. "Yes. Sorry it took me so long to get here. Can you tell me how bad it is?"

He took a minute to look around before answering. "I have a lot of questions, but I can wait until this is all over before I ask them. However it is that you can do this doesn't matter right now. What does matter is that you need to keep doing it. The city has been divided up into three parts." He bent down to draw a map in the dirt. He even used the blood from a nearby guard to help him draw. This dude was hardcore. "This area, the west, is mainly controlled by those guards wearing the red arm bands, while the south and east have been held and locked down by the army. Not many soldiers chose to wear the armbands, so they are fighting for the clan leader. I think it was mostly just the guards involved in the revolt. The northern part of the city is where all of the elders are fighting." We both looked up to see most of the devastation located in that direction. He looked back at me before continuing.

"I am not sure which side is winning, but I did see the clan leader and chief elder lead a small group to the fields north of here. When the elders tried to follow, that is when they turned on each other. As far as I can tell, it looks like anyone related to the former clan leader's family is fighting the people supporting the current clan leader. I just don't understand why. The old clan leader died over three hundred years ago! They have no reason to go after the current leadership. Most of them weren't even alive back then, and the clan leader we have now was chosen because he was the strongest elder at the time."

Well, that explained the lack of destruction inside the city. They had taken the fight north to help keep the collateral damage to a minimum. Before I could join them, I would need to at least clear out the west side. My friends and family would be coming in from the west. They would be walking straight into the hands of our enemies.

"Thank you, Healer Hai," I said, looking west. "I will do

what I can. While I finish clearing out the enemies here, I need you to send someone to the forces holding the south and east. Let them know they can start pushing into this part of the city." He nodded in agreement, so I used some qi threads I spun out from my knees to pull me back onto the rooftop.

I could get a much better vantage point from up here, not to mention how much easier it would be to get the drop on any enemy patrols. Literally.

I kept to the major thoroughfares as I leapt from rooftop to rooftop. It didn't make sense for them to set up strongholds in any of the alleyways, unimportant buildings, and compounds.

They would also want to keep their path of advancement and retreat to the jailhouse near the western road under control. Given what I already knew, it was the most probable location for their base of operations.

I saw signs of looting as I went, most of it around the nicer compounds or businesses. There were also a few bodies left in the streets, most of them people wearing simple robes with no armor.

After a few minutes of travel, I could see a row of wagons tipped over, forming an impromptu roadblock at an intersection up ahead. I felt my anger growing as I picked up speed.

I couldn't see into the buildings, but I was able to pick out eight people on the ground. There were a few archers positioned on the rooftops behind the wagons, so I targeted them first. I stopped a few rooftops away and pulled out my bow, lining up ten arrows in a row in front of me. Then I sent enough air qi into the bow that it started humming with power. My first arrow hit my target in the thigh, proving that my aim with a bow still wasn't where it needed to be.

It still had enough power behind it to nearly take his leg off. The next shot hit an archer in the side. He had turned to see what had happened to the first guy, making a shot that would have taken him in the chest into one that blasted his intestines all over the roof. That worked, I supposed.

The final archer was smart. He dove off the roof, landing on the opposite side of the building and taking him out of my line of sight. I changed targets to the men behind the barricade, picking them off one by one. I moved as fast as I could, trying to finish them off before the archer got away. The last two on the ground tried to hide behind the wagons. Instead of repositioning, I just shot through the wagons into the men on the other side. Their screams let me know it had worked.

After killing them, I took off towards where I had last seen the man who had escaped. I peeked my head over the side, nearly getting an arrow to the face for my trouble. I guess he had decided to stick around.

I activated the shield form on my spirit wood ring and pulled a throwing knife out with the other hand. I leaned out, taking his next arrow on the shield and throwing the blade at his face. Archers didn't wear the face covering on their helms since it would limit their vision. I was happy to take advantage. The knife struck true, dropping the man instantly. I used a thread of qi to retrieve my knife and moved on.

It kept going like that for a while, me bounding from roof to roof and taking down anyone I saw wearing Yisi's colors. I killed everyone without hesitation.

I didn't offer mercy because they didn't deserve any. These people turned on their own clan, killing indiscriminately and taking what wasn't theirs. I stopped counting how many I had killed when I hit seventy. Numbers didn't really matter, after all, only results. There weren't any signs of noncombatants anywhere. Either they had left the city, or Yisi's forces had gathered them up somewhere.

The position of the sun told me it was getting close to ten bells in the morning by the time I reached the jailhouse. I was pretty sure I had missed a few of the enemy patrols, but they had to be running low on people by now. I had faith that the troops coming in behind me could handle the stragglers.

I tried to refill my cores as much as possible while I spent a few minutes observing the enemy. They weren't very alert; most of them seemed to be just standing around. I guess they hadn't heard I was in the neighborhood yet.

There were six guards in full armor standing in a line outside the main gate. The thick door was wide open, but I couldn't see inside it from my angle. I was hoping to find all the missing people inside.

If the jailhouse was filled with innocent people, I needed to take down all the guards before they noticed I was killing them. Otherwise, they might try to use them as hostages.

I made my way over to the rooftop across from the jail, keeping low enough that they would have trouble seeing me. My change of angle let me see deeper into the entryway, but I still couldn't tell what was inside. I took a minute to try to come up with a plan. Nothing exciting came to me. I needed to take down the guards outside all at once, and I needed to do it without making any noise.

I was loath to use up the qi, but I didn't see any other option. I spun out six threads of earth qi down the side of the building and into the ground. I ran them deep enough that I hoped the guards wouldn't sense them as they went under their feet. They popped out of the ground near the base of the building, before sliding up the wall. They kept going until the tip of the threads were all at head height behind the guards. I formed a noose at the end of each before spinning up my brain core to slow down time. I didn't want to make a mistake. I shoved the threads off the wall and dropped the loops around each of their heads. In less than a second, I had them tightened around their necks.

I returned my perception of time to normal and jumped down. The qi threads tightened until their necks broke and I laid them gently on the ground. I didn't want their armor making a racket as they dropped.

I searched their bodies for anything useful, eventually finding a thick ring of keys on the guard who had been standing closest to the door. I moved towards the gate to get a better view of what was inside. I only saw a single guard sitting behind a desk. He was looking over a pile of personal effects, most likely trying to decide what it was he wanted to steal. Time to ruin his day.

I pulled a throwing knife free and side-armed it into his neck. Hey, if it isn't broken, don't fix it. After he fell out of his chair and started rolling around for a bit, I darted into the room.

It was some form of entry and processing area, with colored lines drawn on the floor leading to different doors. I ignored the colors and just opened the first one on the left in an attempt to move things along. It turned out it was the guards' break room. I interrupted a card game that had four players, along with half a dozen people laid out sleeping on some cots.

They all looked up to see who had kicked their door open. One of the men sitting closest to the door was the first to react.

"Hey, kid, how did you get out? We told you all to stay put or there would be consequences. Now that you broke the rules, we are going to have to make an example out of yo—ghck!" I cut him off rather abruptly by tossing a metal whip trap plate into the middle of the room and slamming the door shut. I heard some screaming and banging around for a few seconds, but by the time the thirty second timer had elapsed there was only silence.

I opened the door and used a thread of qi to retrieve my trap. No need to go in that room anymore. There *was* a need to clean off the formation plate though. It was covered in some nasty stuff. I recharged the trap using the energy from my own cores after wiping it down and moved to the next door.

This time I met with success. There were rows of cages holding people down both sides of a long hallway. I tossed the keys I had found into the first cell.

"Free yourselves. There aren't many of them left, and the army should be pushing into this location. You don't want Yisi's men to try to hold you as hostages. Arm yourselves and fight." With that, I dumped a pile of the weapons I had been hoarding in my belt onto the floor. That should be enough to tip the fight in their favor. Numbers and motivation counted for a lot in any fight. I heard some people shouting questions and asking me to wait, but I didn't have that kind of time.

For some reason, I had been getting the feeling that I needed to go north. Some hidden timer in my subconscious was almost up. I ran back towards the entrance gate and nearly ran into a group of people in armor. I nearly tossed my trap down in front of them before I realized their armor looked a lot more like Kory's than it did the guards. And there was no red.

"No time to talk, but there are people to save inside! I didn't have time to clear the whole jail, so be careful!" I jumped on the nearest roof, leaving a very confused group of soldiers to clean up the mess inside. Literally and figuratively, I supposed.

I used my flying ring for all it was worth, finally tapping into the qi batteries in my belt. I skipped from rooftop to rooftop in a straight line, heading for the northern edge of town. That feeling of danger was practically shouting at me now.

Something must have turned the tide to give Yisi the advantage. I pushed myself to my limits, my recent gains in strength from all the fighting allowing me to blur past groups of elders fighting in the streets of the northern quarter. I was lucky they were busy with their own battles, since most of them were strong enough to easily follow me if they wanted. I finally reached the edge of the city as the sun reached its zenith.

By this point, the clan leader and chief elder had been fighting with Yisi and his cronies for at least ten hours, maybe more. Unless they had been frugal with their qi, they had to be running close to empty by now.

I could see tiny figures battling in the distance before a large explosion kicked up enough dust to make it impossible to see what was going on. I took it a little slower now, wanting to get some idea of the situation before jumping in the fight. They had torn the earth apart for hundreds of yards in all directions. There were upraised stones and blocks of earth, craters, and the occasional crevasse splitting the fields apart. It slowed me down some more, but it let me conceal my approach.

The main fight was occurring in a freshly formed crater at the epicenter of destruction, making it hard to see what was going on.

When I was about two hundred yards away, I came across the first body. It was the captain of the guards, and he was missing a good portion of his head. I crouched next to the body and took everything I could find. He had two storage rings and a leather folder filled with papers. I hoped there was a list of names of everyone involved. Otherwise, we would never be able to find all of the members of Yisi's insurrection. After putting the rings in the same pouch as the raven, and the folder in my belt, I moved closer.

I eventually found all of the people I had seen following Yisi into the courtyard during my dream. All but one was dead, and the guy who was still alive wouldn't be for much longer. I made sure of that. I took all their stuff too.

I had to climb up a slight rise in the earth to look down in the crater, and what I saw wasn't good. Yisi was standing over the fallen body of the clan leader, while the chief elder was holding a dome qi shield in place around himself. Yisi was slamming the bronze and red spear into the shield over and over again, driving the chief elder into the ground. I could see the shield had started to crack, and Yisi was shouting some nonsense about how he was going to take his rightful place in the universe.

What a buffoon. Didn't he realize the Roh clan was only a minor power in the empire's power structure? Most people didn't even know it existed. If this was the pinnacle of his life's goals, I had to feel sorry for the guy.

The power levels Yisi was giving off were higher than they should have been at this point in the fight. He must have used his minions to take the brunt of the fighting before stepping in. His spear also had something to do with it.

Somehow, it was enhancing his qi and making simple blows more powerful than they should have been. I really wanted to take a look at its qi matrix, preferably not from the pointy end.

I moved around the rim of the crater until I was at a forty-five-degree angle from his back. I didn't want my attack to hit the chief elder if Yisi somehow dodged it. Once I was in position, I pictured the qi construct I wanted to form in my mind before draining all but a tiny portion of the energy from both qi batteries at once. There was only one chance to do this, so I wanted to bring as much power to bear as possible.

The qi construct snapped into place just as Yisi started to turn towards me. Since I hadn't been using my cores, he had almost no warning ahead of time.

I had chosen to use a wall of wind blades in front of a massive spike made up of all eight forms of qi that was intended to drill into the small of his back. My hope was that the blades would distract him long enough that he wouldn't see the spike coming. An old enemy had used the same attack on me a long time ago and it had landed me in a recovery ward for a week. I had still won that fight, but not by much.

Now all I had to do was give the chief elder a chance to strike while Yisi was down.

It turned out I completely underestimated Yisi's spear. He swung it at the wall of blades and deflected them all into the side of the crater. Then he raised the bronze spearhead to meet the tip of the spike coming behind the blades. The explosion upon impact blasted me up into the air, throwing me directly at one of the upraised stones along the edge of the field. The last thing I thought before impact was, 'How in the stars did he get a Grandmaster artifact?'

CHAPTER THIRTY-EIGHT

Wrath the Teacher

I opened my eyes to see my own body lying on the ground, with frozen flames surrounding the area. In the distance, the chief elder was hovering above the downed form of Yisi, the blast apparently knocking the Councilman into the wall of the crater. He was poised to strike with a fist aimed at Yisi's head, blue flames of qi frozen around his hand. If that punch landed, I was sure that Yisi would be dead.

I had done what I came here to do, but I didn't know why the world was frozen in time. I went to have a closer look at the two remaining combatants when a voice stopped me in my tracks.

"I wouldn't do that. You only have a few minutes until those flames eat through your little wooden disk and you die. I can't hold the world forever, you know."

I spun around to see Wrath standing next to my prone form. I was once again taken aback by her perfect beauty, while simultaneously terrified by the empty black holes where her eyes should have been.

"Wrath? What are you doing here? Why are you helping me? I thought you wanted to see me dead."

She raised her hand and an invisible power drove me to my knees. "Poor King of Fools. If I wanted you dead, you would be dead. Who do you think has been helping you all this time? Pride? He has only been using you to undo some of his old messes. I have been the one positioning you for victory. Who do you think brought that belt within reach of the Roh? Who has been showing you what you need to see when you dream? You would do well to remember that it took two to position you in this timeline."

I looked up at her from my new position on the ground. "You're right. Thank you, Wrath, for all that you have done for me." I meant it, too. If she really was behind all of my good fortune, she deserved every bit of my gratitude. After a few seconds the pressure let up, allowing me to stand.

"While reminding you of your place in the universe does bring me joy, we are running out of time. You need to expand your mind, and I cannot do that for you."

I hated not knowing what was going on. "What do you mean?" I asked. "I don't understand what you want me to do."

She sighed in a very non-god-like fashion before answering. "You need to stop the flames from destroying you. The only way to do that is to redirect them here in the dream world. It will cost you something, but the price is small compared to the alternative."

Okay, now I *really* hated not knowing what was going on. "What do you mean, it will cost me something? And how do I affect the real world from within the dream world?" She took a moment to look up at the sky. I couldn't be sure, but I thought I saw something flash to the surface inside the darkness of her eyes. Like some leviathan of the deep peeking out of the darkest parts of the ocean. I shivered as she looked back at me.

"I do not know what you will lose, but it will not matter if you are dead. The knowing of how to do this will push out the remnants of something else from your memories. Since the knowledge of how to affect the real world from the dream world is minor, so shall be your loss. If your luck is strong, you will regain those memories with time." She waved her hands as if dismissing the matter. "Now, as for how to do this, you will need to use mana instead of qi to redirect the flames. You already know how to manifest mana. Now you just need to control it. And hurry, you run short on time."

I nodded and immediately dropped into a lotus pose. I wasn't sure, but it kind of looked like she was straining against something. I decided not to waste time talking about it.

The first thing I did was try to cultivate by drawing in the qi around me into my cores. No matter how much I strained, I couldn't manipulate anything. Then Wrath gave me the hint I needed.

"No, King of Fools! You don't make mana by pulling qi into yourself! You manipulate the energy that already exists in the outside world!" It was like an explosion went off inside my head. Everything to do with the difficulties of combining the dark and light qi inside my cores made sense now. In the natural world, they touched each other all the time, while inside me they couldn't stand to be near each other. Somehow, the process of asserting my own dominion over the qi changed it. Mana needed to be pure and unchanged.

I reached out my willpower to the qi around me, and it reacted immediately. The six regular elements were combined into a wall of gray around my prone body within seconds. It took a lot more concentration to bring an equal amount of dark and light qi into the mix, but I managed it.

I finally got everything combined evenly. It was like building a brick wall, with the actual bricks being the common forms of qi and the dark and light qi as the mortar to hold it all together in the right place and pattern. As soon as the last 'brick' was in place, the energy combined into a smooth wall of opaque, bright white power.

Wrath took a moment to look it over before nodding her head and disappearing. Time instantly resumed, causing the wall of fire to smash into the mana construct I had in place. I also looked over in time to see the chief elder smash Yisi's head open like a watermelon. Ah, sweet justice. How disgusting you are sometimes.

The fire died down just before my mana construct ran out of energy. It was strange, but for some reason my perspective on the world changed as the mana dissipated. It was only right before I was once again pulled back into the light that I realized everything was taller, just like when I was awake. I had completely forgotten what I had looked like before I died, forcing me to appear as my current self even while in the dream world.

CHAPTER THIRTY-NINE

Working On It

I woke up coughing. I looked around to see that I was still on the edge of the destruction zone from the fighting. Oddly enough, nothing hurt as bad as it probably should. Either my body was getting tougher, or there was enough qi stirred up from the battle that my wooden medallion was getting a larger than normal influx of energy. I would have to think on the impact of forgetting what I used to look like later. I needed to move.

I stumbled my way over to the crater to see what was left of Yisi. I still wanted a look at that spear. When I tumbled down the slope, I saw the chief elder bent over the clan leader. He was deep into a trance, trying to draw in enough energy to bring the leader back from the edge of death. I wished him good luck and went to check on the bad guy's corpse.

There was a plethora of magical items festooned on his armor and body, so I took them all. I made sure to put what I could in a disk that could only be opened with dark qi. If I was searched, they would never find any of it. Good luck searching the fields for nothing, guys. There were three really nice storage items and I emptied their contents into my belt as well. I would look into everything I got later. Right now, I needed to hurry before the elder finished up.

I put a good portion of the most useless items I had collected in my belt back into Yisi's storage rings. Things like low quality weapons, the piles of red robes, and most of the cheap red leather armor went into his rings to free up space in my belt. I felt like there was enough in each that I might get away with taking the good stuff. Well, I hoped it was good stuff. Then, I went looking for the spear.

It took me a minute to find it, because it wasn't a spear anymore. There were pieces of the red material spread out all over the place. Upon closer inspection, I was convinced it was actually some form of stone. I picked up all of the biggest pieces I could find and stored those away as well.

The bronze spear tip was a mangled ruin. I broke off a finger-sized piece from the unrecognizable hunk of metal before dropping it back in the dirt. Apparently, a massive qi construct using all eight elements was a match for a Grandmaster artifact. Too bad. I could have done some interesting stuff with that enhancement power.

While I had a lot to look over, I didn't hold out much hope for being able to recreate the qi matrix it used. Maybe I could still salvage something from the mix though.

I finally made my way over to the elder and leader. They both looked to be in bad shape, so I spun out some wood qi threads to help patch them up.

It looked like the chief elder had brought the clan leader back from the brink of death. It would be impolite to not try to save him after all of his hard work, even though it was the leader's mismanagement of the clan that had allowed all this to happen. The chief elder would have been a much better clan leader, but it wasn't my place to make that decision.

The sun was low in the sky before the three of us were ready to stumble out of the crater. The clan leader was barely conscious, and I wasn't even sure if he knew I was there or not. The chief elder had the presence of mind to search Yisi before leaving, handing me one of the three storage rings after emptying it himself.

"This is for your help today, young Jim. Consider it a down payment on the rewards you have earned today."

I took it gratefully, not bothering to check if he had left anything inside. "Thank you, Chief Elder. I was only doing my best."

He simply nodded before hooking the leader's arm over his shoulder. I helped support the other side as best I could, and off we went.

The walk back to Roh City took far longer than it should have, even with all of us injured. I was pretty sure the chief elder was stalling. He didn't want to have to make it into the city just to start fighting again. I completely understood. Let those other elders earn their keep. I simply used the extra time to try to refill my qi batteries as much as possible.

We made it all the way to the northern road entrance into the city before anyone tried to stop us.

"Halt! Stand your ground and identify yourself!" I couldn't see the speaker due to the light in my eyes, but the chief elder apparently could.

"Dav, is that you? Get over here and give me a hand. The clan leader is injured. We need to get him to Healer Hai immediately. And send someone for Captain Kory. Have him meet us at the healing house." With that, we were whisked down the road on a wagon pulled by some form of lizard beast.

I used the time on the ride to try to cultivate, but once again my meridians were feeling the strain of the day. I needed longer than a few hours to let my body catch up, along with a few alchemy pills to help me recover. Speaking of alchemy, I realized that I wasn't quite done. I had an alchemist uncle who still needed a visit from the pain fairy.

After the fuss of getting inside the healing house, getting

checked, and eventually being shoved onto a cot in what I was pretty sure was normally a closet, I had a few minutes to myself to think. All of the excitement of the last week or so had been almost as crazy as my time guarding the northern border of the empire. I decided to look over what I had gotten from Yisi and his henchmen.

The folder from the former guard captain didn't contain any lists of names, but it did have more than a few plans about what they wanted to do after taking control of the clan. Let's just say I was very glad that I had helped stop them.

One of the more detestable plans was to force a marriage on any woman that was a part of a strong bloodline with a member of Yisi's group. There were notes about which young lady would end up with whomever had helped the most. Disgusting. A bunch of old men trying to force themselves on young women. It made me want to kill them all over again. Maybe I would get the chance to kill anyone I had missed some-time soon.

It also broke down how they would redistribute the wealth of the clan, starting with what was in the vault. It was inter-esting to see there was a third level of items, which of course made me wonder if there was anything I might find useful. Maybe I would get to see what was inside after my contributions to stopping the coup came to light...

I went to inspect what Yisi himself had dropped but, before I could, my door was thrown open and a whole group of people tried to pile into my room. I was nearly bowled over by my mother. She was very happy to see me alive while simultane-ously furious that I had run off and left everyone behind. I was going to try to explain, but Donny, Chu, Jamila, and Valerie cut me off with a flood of questions and shouting about the rumors that they had heard about me since reaching the clan. They were yelling all at once, so I genuinely had no idea what any of them actually said.

Last up was Kory. He was finally able to settle everyone

down long enough to let me know the coup had been put down and everyone they could find that took part had been rounded up.

I also found out that my father and Uncle Don were trying to track down my Uncle Hu and his son Xiao. They had escaped the city after emptying a good portion of the city's stores of medicinal herbs and one of the smaller treasury lockboxes. I guess I would need to track them down later. Or they would come after me. Either way, I had a feeling I would be seeing them again sometime down the road.

Kory finally finished up his retelling of events. They had come to the west entrance of the city in time to help stop several groups of Yisi's people trying to escape into the woods and were able to detain them. He then dropped the big one on me.

"When I reported to the chief elder, I told him everything. He knows about the monsters, your mission from the gods, your abilities they gave you, and your rescue of all the clansmen. If it weren't for you, Yisi would have won and the Roh clan would be no more. They are going to hold a meeting about you with what is left of the council when the clan leader wakes up."

Crap. So much for just receiving my rewards and getting out of this place. Now I would have to fight tooth and nail to escape the clan. My only hope was them being more worried about the *nox* than they were about keeping a powerful cultivator in the clan. Not likely.

I looked up at Kory. "That was probably a mistake. Now they are going to try and keep me here instead of letting me go. You know firsthand how important it is that I get out of here and kill the *nox*. If I don't, our world will be destroyed."

Kory shook his head. "No, I explained to them how important this all was. There is no way the clan elders would put the Roh above the good of the entire population of our world. Besides, they can't be dumb enough to doom us all to death in four hundred years over a single cultivator."

I raised my eyebrow. And Ming said I was the naïve one. "I hope you are right. Because if you are wrong, I need to get away from this town right now. Getting to the Southern Provincial Capital is vital to the next step in killing the *nox*. If we get separated, I will need your help gathering supplies for the journey. It is a long trip to the Capital, and I can't do it alone." My circle of friends nodded. I knew I could count on them.

They all backed out of the room while my mother went to see if Healer Hai was willing to release me into her custody. She wanted to take me home and I wasn't about to argue with her. Sleeping in my own room would be nice. So would hot food, and a warm bath. Thinking about it made me realize just how hungry and disgusting I was. Even though the enchanted clothing and armor had a self-cleaning function, my skin underneath did not. Neither did my foot wraps.

I was just about to reach into my belt for a snack and some replacement foot wrappings when the door to my little room was nearly torn off its hinges. There was an elder at the middle stage of Saint flanked by two men in the clan's military. I knew I should have let the clan leader die.

I twisted to look past him to see my friends and Kory being held against the far wall by spear point. There were over a dozen men in uniform inside the room, most of them focused on Captain Kory. The elder finally looked down at me.

"Boy. You are coming with us. We are going to hold you in a cell for your own wellbeing until the council can come to a decision on what to do with you. Your actions during Councilman Yisi's activities are still under investigation, so we don't want any harm to come to you until all the facts are brought to light."

I looked around the side of the elder at Kory. "I told you, Captain Kory. None of them saw the *nox*, so the threat isn't real to them. They would damn the world for their own personal gain." I could see the guilt in his eyes as he shrugged his shoulders in agreement. I met the eyes of the rest of my friends, each of them giving me a small nod to acknowledge the brief plan we had made. I looked back at the elder.

"The *activities* of Yisi are still under investigation? How about you just call it a failed takeover. I helped save this clan from certain destruction, and all the thanks I get are being thrown into a cell. Here, these documents will help prove *exactly* what his *activities* were going to be." I pulled out the folder from the guard captain and threw it at him. The papers scattered everywhere, helped along by a tiny gust of air qi provided by yours truly. Instead of keeping their eyes on me, the elder and soldiers were watching the folder and loose papers fly at them. Perfect.

I rolled backwards off of my cot towards the wall behind me. If my mental image of the building was correct, this should be an exterior wall. I used the qi from my batteries to slice an opening wide enough in the wall to squeeze through and I tumbled free into an alleyway running behind the house.

I immediately took off for the western road. I would have to find a place to hide in the woods while my friends gathered enough supplies for the two-year journey to the capital. I had faith they could manage. I just wished I could have said goodbye to my mother and father before leaving.

The explosion that rang out behind me from the elder making his own hole in the wall threw me farther down the alley. Instead of tumbling to the ground, I used the momentum in conjunction with my flight ring to launch me onto the nearest rooftop. I could hear the elder shouting behind me.

"Find him! You heard the clan leader! He has to be using qi, so track him down! He is only a Body cultivator, so there is no way he can get away!" Since I was still using my batteries and not my cores, it would be impossible for my pursuers to track me using their own qi senses.

I didn't have the energy or inclination to fight the soldiers anyway. They were just following orders. The elder I wouldn't mind teaching a lesson, but with my batteries at less than a quarter full, I wasn't sure if I could beat him without making a mess. Besides, I was tired. It had been a long day.

It was less than thirty minutes later when I had reached the western entrance to the city. I had only made one stop for more formation plates on my way out. I grabbed an entire bundle of fifty blank plates from the store I had purchased them from last time. I had left a handful of gold coins on the counter and bolted.

As I moved towards the city exit, I could only see a few guards looking out into the darkness. None of them were watching backwards. I needed to get them to all look inwards for a few minutes so I could disappear into the fields leading to the forest. I took a minute to make a few scratches on the ice trap I had carved while thinking of Yisi around the fire yesterday. Stars, was it really only yesterday?

Since I hadn't had a chance to use it yet, I decided this was the perfect opportunity. The adjustments were to change the angle of attack from horizontal to vertical. I didn't want to kill them just for doing their jobs. The angle would serve a dual purpose as well. I wouldn't be able to retrieve the disk, but I didn't want to leave it behind for someone to reverse engineer. The attack would flash out both into the sky and back to the ground, hopefully destroying the formation plate in the process. Two beasts with one qi attack.

I moved onto the roof directly beside the guards before throwing it back into the city. I waited for it to settle into place before detonating it. The spears of ice shot far into the sky before exploding. It reminded me of the light shows the alchemists in the Imperial City would put on during special celebrations. It also did a fantastic job of getting the guards to look away from the fields.

I once again engaged my flight ring, propelling me out of the city and into the countryside. I couldn't believe I almost hadn't taken this ring.

For the first several minutes of running, I was afraid to hear shouts coming from behind me. Instead, all I heard were crickets chirping away.

Now I just needed to find a campsite, figure out a way to communicate with my friends back in Roh City, plan a two-year excursion into hostile forest and swamps, get to the capital, talk my way into a meeting with the King of the Southern Province, and finally convince him to mobilize his forces in order to help me hunt down the *nox* all throughout the region.

It was going to take one hell of a plan, but I was working on it.

AUTHOR'S NOTE

Wow. What a journey this has been. My first book is finished. Hopefully the first in a long line of stories to come.

First off, I want to thank my wife Amanda for always supporting me these last 18 years. It has been one hell of a wild ride.

Next, I want to thank my three beautiful daughters. They are what has kept me going through all the bad stuff.

I can't forget to thank my brother, parents, and grandparents. I wouldn't be the man I am today without you.

I also want to thank everyone who has helped me proofread and edit this 400-plus page book. You know who you are. Especially Eric Peterson. You are very good at what you do. Without you, it wouldn't be this good.

I want to thank Dakota Krout and his team for picking up a guy who had absolutely no idea what he was doing and helping him make a pipe-dream come true.

Finally, I want to thank you, the reader. Without you, there would be no point to all of this hard work. From the bottom of my heart, thank you. Stick around for the next one. I have a lot of plans for Jim, and I didn't even get to touch on his awesome blacksmithing and alchemy skills. I promise, things are only going to get better from here.

-Michael Head

ABOUT MICHAEL HEAD

Michael Head is the author of the Threads of Fate series. He was severely injured while serving in the military, and used his time recovering to rediscover his love for books. After medically retiring, Michael went back to college to finish his degree and become a professor. When the coronavirus shut down his school, his wife encouraged him to finally take the leap and try writing his own books. He found his experience in combat allowed him to write detailed and realistic fight scenes. Those battles, combined with his attention to detail and ability to plan vast, elaborate, and comprehensive worlds, make for fast-paced and thrilling books. With, of course, the occasional touches of humor and sarcasm thrown in the mix.

He currently lives in Texas where his wife, who is still currently serving in the military, is stationed. His days are filled with hiding from their three daughters, two dogs, and three cats. He is also losing an ongoing war with the neighborhood squirrels, but he will continue to fight until the bitter end.

Connect with Michael:
Facebook.com/Author.Michael.Head
Patreon.com/Michael_Head
Sendfox.com/Author-Michael-Head